the
Revolutionary Alternative

the
Revolutionary Alternative

This is a work of fiction. All incidents and dialogue, and all characters with the exception of historical figures, are products of the author's imagination and are not to be constructed as real. When real life historical persons appear, the situations, incidents, and dialogues concerning those persons are entirely fictional and are not intended to depict actual events or to change the entirely fictional nature of the work. In all other respects, any resemblance to persons living or dead is entirely coincidental.

Cover and interior design by We Got You Covered Book Design
WWW.WEGOTYOUCOVEREDBOOKDESIGN.COM

the Revolutionary Alternative

Eliza Starkey

To my parents, grandparents,
great grandma, friends, and readers.

In memory of my characters...

Prologue

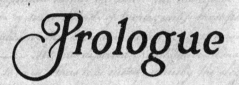

January 17, 1779

NEW YORK CITY, NEW YORK

The streets of New York pulsed with nervousness and fear. It had been six months since England had won the War of Colonial Rebellion, and the empire had quickly tightened its grip on the colonies, never wanting to release its hold. British redcoats marched up and down the streets in precision, ready to put an end to rebellious behavior and attitude. And it was working.

The redcoats, or as the colonists affectionately called them, the 'lobsterbacks' had quickly established that they meant business from the moment they stepped off their ship. The crime rate in the city had quickly plummeted, along with talk of the war itself. As soon as the redcoats noticed a person speaking of the rebellion – man, woman, or child – they received a warning look from the king's soldiers while they adjusted the muskets on their shoulders. This just made the colonists tenser, wishing that the war had ended differently, that General Washington had been able to defeat British, that the French had come to help…. Some of the more stubborn colonists picked fights with their new-found wardens, and the fights usually ended with the person either being bruised or being dragged away to prison. Sometimes both.

Today the colonists were even tenser than usual. It was execution day. None of the commoners knew who was going be killed, not the rich loyalists, not most of the soldiers. Only the governor, his herald, the executioners, and the jailer knew, and that made the patriotic colonists even more nervous.

The governor, his wife, and the governor of Pennsylvania were crowded into a booth. It had been constructed earlier that day and gave the three loyalists a fine view of the executioner's stand. The governor looked down at the crowd. Some squirmed anxiously, others stood like statues, frightened of attracting the soldiers' attention by moving. The colonists loyal to the crown, however, chattered excitedly, wondering who was going to die and catching up on the latest gossip. New York's rich sat in boxes much like the governor's, giving them shade, a good view, and a shield from the common peasants. They also pondered which criminals the king's men had captured, perhaps one of the rebels' generals! That would be exciting!

The herald cleared his throat, rolled his shoulders back, tilted his head, and then walked up to the executioner's stand. He looked at the three pairs of British soldiers, each duo holding the arms of an imprisoned man, one destined to die. The herald nodded his head slightly, indicating that the soldiers should also come up to the stand. The soldiers obliged but stood a considerable distance away from the herald. The herald nodded once more, and three executioners walked onto the platform. Each brandished a gleaming steel axe with a polished wooden handle.

A shiver ran down the spines of the colonists as the executioners walked just a few feet away. The governor, too, felt a chill run down his spine. Those axes were so familiar. The fate of the prisoners: almost his own. His wife looked at her husband's troubled face. She reached over and squeezed his hand. "It's for the best." She told him. He nodded reassuringly, but he couldn't help thinking that the axe was once meant for him. *I hope,* his wife added in her mind.

The herald locked eyes with the governor, who, after a moment of hesitation, nodded, allowing the herald to begin his speech. He could hear the man's throat clear from across the distance.

"Hear ye, hear ye! We have gathered here today to witness an execution, the execution of some of his Majesty's most despised enemies." The herald paused, allowing his words to sink in. He continued, "These three men have committed one of the worst crimes imaginable: treason!" The loyalists gasped appropriately, despite their prediction coming true. The patriots shifted uncomfortably and eyed the prisoners frantically. Their worst fears had been confirmed.

"Each of these men are known rebels." The herald explained, "and the killing of each will please his Majesty greatly. No, they are not the more infamous men, but infamous in their own right. The first prisoner shall now step forward."

Two of the redcoats dragged the first man towards the herald. The man stumbled and dragged his feet, hoping to slow his death. He wore a fine new grey coat with boots, but his shirt, blue, was frayed and worn.

"Remove the prisoner's head cover." The herald stated. The redcoats did so. They revealed a brown-haired man with a panicked gleam in his eyes. A gasp radiated through the crowd from those that recognized him. His hair was combed back nicely and tied in a ponytail, but his face was red from anger and, in some spots, blue from bruising. He turned his face to look down at the people, and he seemed to be taking it in, absorbing every last piece of life he could find. His eyes seemed pleading, frightening, and calm, all at the same time, like he knew his fate wouldn't change, but like death had come at the most inconvenient moment.

"Patrick Henry." The herald announced, "Traitor, guilty of treason to the crown and conspiring against the king. Have you nothing to say? Nothing?... Any final words?"

He didn't look at the herald. He looked straight at the governor. "I've said it before, and I'll say it again." He paused, waiting.

The herald looked at him sharply, "Well? Out with it!"

Patrick Henry cleared his throat and stared at the governor, who stared right back. "I know not what course others may take, but as for me, give me liberty..." He looked back at the herald, "Or give. Me. Death." Henry stared daggers at the herald, who gulped nervously. The prisoner looked back to the crowd.

"I have no desire to live in a country that is not independent, one that is under the shadow of a king's rule, one suffering under tyranny. I am a citizen of a free country, and I'm sure many of you are, as well.... I used to love England, the king, his laws; but that time is not now. I once gave a speech to a great number of persons, and those words I just uttered quickly embodied the American people. People recited my words all over the nation, here in New York, down in Virginia. I'm a Virginian man myself, and there was a time I viewed myself as nothing more than that. A colonial Englishman, loyal to the crown and his mother country. That changed. That man is not me. I am an Englishman no longer. I'm an American, a citizen of a free country, one without a king to pay taxes to or obey. I was born a Virginian, but I'll die an *American*."

"Traitorous last words, Henry." The herald sneered, "I don't think the king will like it one bit."

"It's only fitting. It's an execution for traitors, so it would be startling if no traitorous words were spoken." Patrick smiled, "You think I'm frightened to die? I am not. If it means dying for my country, good fellow, then I embrace death gladly."

The herald glared menacingly at the prisoner. "Then kneel."

Patrick Henry knelt and placed his head against the wooden block. He looked up at the executioner. "Sir, make sure it's quick, as to not frighten the women and children."

"Who cares if children are frightened? This is an execution! Not a war!" The herald sighed, "No more last words, none for either of those two men. Bring the second prisoner forward!"

"But sir!" one redcoat objected, "That's not-"

"Did I ask you to speak? Did I ask you to speak?" the herald roared, his voice low and dangerous, "Bring forward the prisoner."

Two redcoats helped move the second man, the sympathetic soldier watching on sadly. The prisoner squirmed anxiously, elbowing his two captors and dragging his feet as they pulled him along. When the sack was removed from his head, his auburn hair was affixed in all directions. His blue eyes darted everywhere,

looking for an escape route. He had outmaneuvered the British –
and sometimes his fellow countrymen – many times before, but
he knew that he could not now, not with so many people around.

"Thomas Paine." The herald paused, "Traitor, guilty of treason
and conspiring against the king. Wrote a rebel pamphlet entitled
Common Sense, a pamphlet that encouraged rebellious behavior
amongst the colonists. Make him kneel."

The two redcoats forced the man into position. Patrick Henry
turned to look at his neighbor, eyes filled with pity. "It's depressing
that they won't allow you to speak. It's undemocratic."

Mr. Paine just shook his head sadly, "I think that's why he won't
let us. He doesn't want any more stirring speeches like yours.
How long did it take you to write it? It was a fine little speech.
Admirable."

Patrick Henry smiled softly, "I made it up off the top of my
head."

"Will you two be quiet?" The herald said angrily, "You will not
whisper as if you were girls in my execution!"

"But we're not." Thomas Paine replied, grinning sarcastically,
"We're whispering like men." A redcoat kicked him in the side.

"Bring the third prisoner forward." The herald said. This man
walked with his captors, not dragging his feet or trying to escape,
but as though there was no place that he'd rather be. He looked
like a gentleman. Once the sack was removed, the crowd could see
his nicely brushed brown hair. His expression was calm, like his
was reading a favorite book in his beloved chair, instead of facing
certain death.

"John Adams." The herald announced, "Traitor, guilty of

treason and conspiring against the crown. The first to push for the rebel document entitled *The Declaration of Independence*, even one of the men considered rebellious enough to author it."

"I didn't!" John Adams snapped, his peaceful face suddenly contorting in rage.

The herald paused and looked at him, surprised. "Excuse me? Did I permit you to speak? Did I permit you to speak?" he yelled.

John Adams shook his head slowly, ignoring the rhetorical question. "You did not, but you spread the false-truth. It is true that I was one of the five selected to write the declaration, but I did not. It was my good friend, Thomas Jefferson, who writes ten times better than I, that penned the words. I merely helped with the phrasing."

"Trying to cast the blame on another!" The herald exclaimed. "John Adams was the loudest to nominate George Washington as the head of the rebel army. He spoke back to a king's official, he denied taking part in treason! Make him kneel."

John Adams shakily knelt beside Thomas Paine and Patrick Henry. "Well men, it was a good run. We've accomplished much in our short stay here."

"Aye." Thomas Paine agreed, nodding slowly, "That we did."

The governor looked away from the scene, his eyes closed. He looked away when the executioners raised their axes. He looked away when the axes fell, taking the lives of three men with them.

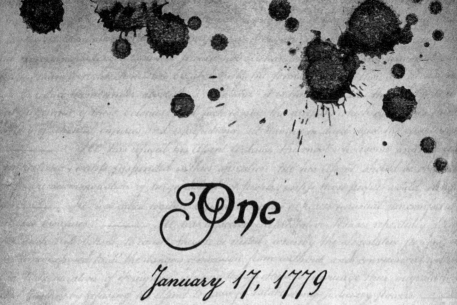

One

January 17, 1779

NEW YORK CITY, NEW YORK

BENEDICT

*H*e stood on the balcony, looking over the city, lost in thought. It had been five months since he had been appointed governor of New York, and he was still growing used to his title, his supposed power, his supposed respect. His people treated him with scorn. All of them. Even the loyalists.

You should have joined the British before you joined the war.

Traitor!

They should have a real Englishman be governor.

General Washington trusted you!

How can a patriot sympathizer, a former American general, a cripple, *be our governor?*

His leg was worse today, likely because he felt awful. Guilty. Traitorous. Defeated. He could have saved those men. He had enough authority, he could have done it. If he had saved them, they would've lived. But if he had done that, he would have thrown away his life. He would've been called a traitor by the Tories, been disrespected by all who met him. He'd lose everything – his job, his home, the little respect people had for him. He'd lose his wife....

"Benny? Benny! I was thinking that – Benedict?" He turned and saw her standing a few feet away.

He'd lose her. He'd lose this marvelous young woman who had agreed to spend her life with him, the one he cherished so. The one who he knew was a Torie, through and through. He couldn't bear the thought of being separated from any part of her, her serious yet playful demeanor, her intelligent mind, her fair face and figure.

"Benedict! What's the matter? You look awful!" She rushed to his side. At nineteen, she was less than half his age, but what she lacked in years, she made up for in beauty and knowledge. He hoped that his companionship could be enough to make her stay. He always feared she would leave him for someone richer and handsomer, more powerful and younger.

"It's nothing, kitten." He turned back to gaze at the city. He felt her head lean against his shoulder. Her wig tickled his chin. "How tall is that wig?" Benedict asked, looking down at her face awkwardly.

She giggled. It was such a sweet sound, "Only six inches. But Benny, please tell me what's the matter. I know something's on your mind."

"It was the execution." He said breathlessly.

"I thought so, you looked frightened there for a moment." Peggy said softly, remembering his paranoid face from earlier in the day. She gazed down at all the passing people and coaches in silence.

"Washington vowed to kill me after…after…." Benedict trailed off, not wanting to say the words.

"I know, sweetheart. Remember, Washington is in jail now. He's in your jail. You can go see him if you'd like. Just remember that he's in jail." Peggy told her husband, grasping his hands, turning to look up at his face, "You worry me sometimes, Benedict. I just wish that you'd open up more, tell me your thoughts, you know? I'm not going to judge you. I know that you don't tell me everything because of… my family's political standing, and that's understandable. You were a patriot for a long time, so I don't imagine that you dropped all of your beliefs as soon as you married me. Some beliefs are still with you, and they're quite strong…. I think that it's good that you are sympathetic to the patriots."

Benedict looked down at her in surprise, "You do?"

Peggy smiled at her confused husband's face, playing with a lock of hair, "Of course I do. That's what makes you a good governor, even if the people don't see it. You see from both sides of the story."

"I suppose I do…."

"You wanted to let them go." Peggy accused, the sweetness evaporating from her voice.

"Yes, I *did*." Benedict tried ignoring the icy bitterness in her tone and looked back to the streets below. He pulled away from her, leaning more heavily on his cane, wondering what to say. "How the herald was speaking…it just didn't seem fair. It didn't seem right, it didn't seem just!"

She stared at him for a minute. Had he offended her? He hoped that he hadn't. His mouth flubbed as he tried to find the right words to say.

"I agree with you." Peggy said calmly.

"You…what?" He looked at her in surprise. He knew her well, having spent nearly all of the past two years by her side; but in all of their time together, she had never expressed any patriotic tendencies.

She laughed at him, and her husband's eyes turned to the ground, his cheeks warm. She raised her hands in surrender, the coldness gone, love and playfulness having taken its place. "I'm sorry, Benny, I'm so sorry. I wasn't making fun of you! Your face was just so….it looked like this."

Peggy copied his previous expression, eyes frantic and darting, mouth pulled into a tight line. Benedict's own mouth turned upwards.

Her face changed from humorous to serious, "The herald wasn't right in how he performed the execution. It wasn't kind of him to taunt those prisoners, and I know he didn't tell the whole story, and it was just, just dishonorable, the way he wouldn't allow Paine and Adams to say any last words. If I remember correctly, Mr. Adams defended some of the soldiers during that massacre in Boston, and yet he didn't even mention it! You should've done something, but if you had done something- "

"Our reputation would slump even further." Benedict finished.

Peggy pouted and nodded sadly. She hugged her arms to her chest. "It was for the best."

"That's what you had said before, now I'm not quite so sure if you were right." Benedict sighed, staring off into the distance.

He knew it was hard for her. Peggy Shippen's reputation was nearly destroyed. She had come from a wealthy loyalist family, a beautiful girl, the belle of the ball. Then she had gone off and married some top-notch American general named Benedict Arnold – who was also deep in debt. With their marriage, Peggy's reputation plummeted, but not as drastically as it had when she began corresponding with her old sweetheart, John André, which raised a number of rumors in the Philadelphian social circles. When her husband's loyalties had begun to shift, Peggy began writing letters to André, a British major general at the time, to see if he could secure a spot in the king's army for him. Once Benedict was able to switch sides completely, the rumors about Peggy had evaporated and she had been praised by nearly all of the loyalists in both Philadelphia and New York, whereas Benedict was scorned and hated by the patriots. He had been one of Washington's most trusted generals, and if the patriots could lose him, who could they trust? It was excellent news for the loyalists, who quickly showered the Arnolds with praise about their treachery. The Arnolds were having the time of their lives, invited to every party, gala, ball, and social event. After a few months, however, all of the attention they were receiving stopped, invitations dwindled to nothing, and the rumors started up again. Peggy was accused of not being faithful to her husband, only marrying him for power, having an affair with André, *and* being a Whig. Benedict wasn't trusted by the Tories, people saying that if he flipped once, it was only a matter of time before he flipped again; some even said that he never really was with the British, that he was an American spy. It hadn't changed once Benedict had been appointed royal governor of New York. If anything, it had made the Arnolds even more unpopular.

Peggy hadn't taken her sudden unpopularity well. Once she had been asked to go everywhere with everyone, now nobody showed up at their door unless it was a king's messenger. They received few visitors, but they were always family members, and hardly anyone stayed over an hour. Benedict pitied her, knowing that if not for him, she would probably still be the belle of the ball.

"Dearest, you don't have to worry about all of my troubles." Benedict wrapped his arms around her, "It's clear that it's troubling you."

She sighed, "I know that you don't want me to think about such things, but I can't help it. Benny, you're my husband, your problems are my problems, and I can't help but worry." She smiled sadly for a moment before perking up, "That reminds me, Benny, I came to tell you that-"

"What's wrong?" A new voice asked. Benedict and Peggy turned to see the newcomer standing a few feet away.

Peggy ran out of Benedict's arms and threw her own around her friend. "André!" she squealed, excitedly. John André, governor of Pennsylvania, awkwardly gave her a hug, keeping a careful eye on Benedict while doing so. The two governors were good friends, but when it came to Peggy, Benedict was very territorial – something that made Peggy's over familiarity with young André occasionally unwanted. André, however, being the only person who seemed to enjoy their company, was often invited into their home.

Benedict glared at the younger, handsomer, more charming official in disgust. Peggy stepped away from André and brushed a speck of imaginary dust off his striking red uniform. She smiled up at him, André grinned awkwardly back. Benedict cleared his throat. Sometimes he didn't know why he invited the boy to stay with them.

"It's nothing." Benedict said, once both of them were looking at him. Peggy nodded enthusiastically. André looked between the two of them suspiciously, then nodded, knowing that there was something Benedict didn't want to share.

"Very well." André said, "I came to tell you that the servants are nearly done with dinner, so it is best if we head to the dining room."

Benedict nodded, "Very well. Peggy?" he offered her his arm, and she giggled as she curled her slender hand around his forearm.

"Oh, Benedict, you are so formal!"

"Governor Arnold!" the jailer exclaimed, "What on earth are you doing here?"

Benedict frowned. It was near midnight, and he was still full from his dinner. He didn't want to be interrupted by nosy redcoats. He wanted to be home before Peggy and André realized that he'd left.

"Does it matter? I'd like to meet with a prisoner." Benedict snapped.

"Can I see some clearance?" the jailer asked, then grimaced when he saw the angry expression upon Benedict's face. "I mean, you don't need clearance! You're the governor! Now who would you like to see?"

"A man that was once under my command, Aaron Burr."

"But sir? Are you sure that you want to see *him*? He's a rebel, you know." The jailer looked at his governor in astonishment.

"I *know* that he was a rebel. *I* was a rebel. He was under my command *while* I was a rebel." Benedict explained slowly and carefully, as though speaking to a small child, "Now, if it's not too much trouble, may I see Aaron Burr?"

"Why do you want to see him?" The jailer asked cautiously, not wanting to increase the man's grumpiness. He had heard stories of Benedict's temper, and it didn't often end well for those the temper was directed towards.

Benedict understood the man's suspicion. It was rather suspicious for a British governor to meet with a rebel soldier. Especially if the governor hadn't always been loyal to the crown. "I used to ask him advice when I was in the Continental, er, rebel army. I've been having some trouble on my mind lately, and I want to see what he thinks of it."

"I've been having trouble as well." The man nodded sympathetically, "I think that it's fine, but can you empty your pockets for me? It's just so I can see if you're giving him anything that might help him escape." he explained.

Benedict quickly took off his coat and shook it, allowing a pencil and a slip of paper to fall out. He picked them both up and handed them to the jailer. The jailer looked at the paper curiously, "A lovely drawing. Who is it of? Who drew it? You?"

"No." Benedict sighed, "I wish I did. It's my wife. The artist is the governor of Pennsylvania, John André."

"He's quite an accomplished young man." The jailer remarked, staring at the image. Benedict frowned.

"Can I please see Burr now?" Benedict impatiently asked, smoothing back his black hair, "I don't wish to be gone long."

"Yes, yes, of course, sir. Right this way." The jailer opened a door that he had been guarding carefully. "He's the only one left. You'll find him easily enough."

Benedict nodded thankfully, then turned to look at the man, "Is it possible for you to keep this visit off the record?"

The jailer's brow furrowed, "But I'm supposed to write down the names of everyone who-"

The governor huffed and fumbled with his purse, eventually handing the man a golden coin, "Well?" The jailer pocketed the coin and pointedly looked away.

Benedict ducked under the low-hanging doorframe, and the jailer closed the door behind him. "Burr?" He called, "Aaron Burr? Where are you, old friend?"

Benedict walked past the many cells, peering into each, before moving along to the next one. The air was thick and musty, and there was a foul smell that entered his nose. "Burr?" Benedict stopped once he reached the last chamber. He grasped the cold iron bars. He could hardly see a thing, let alone a man, "Are you in there?"

"General Arnold? Is that you?" A familiar voice asked.

"Burr?"

Two

March 1779

ALBANY, NEW YORK

ALEXANDER

Alexander walked briskly down the road. It was a well-traveled road, the kind used by everyone from craftsmen walking on foot, to fashionable ladies traveling by horse and buggy. It was wide, wide enough for two carriages to pass each other comfortably; and reliable, a road with very few pot-holes and bumps.

It was not unusual for him to see a farmer in a wagon or a few soldiers traveling down the road to the next town over. The farmers he waved at happily, sometimes spoke a word of greeting to. The crop-growers would always raise a hand in recognition and would occasionally stop and inquire about where he was headed. It was the soldiers that frightened him, they would watch him suspiciously as he walked past, never going by too fast, never too slow. Some would stop and ask him his business; others would warn that it wasn't safe for a person to travel alone on that particular road. The ones that gave him the willies were the ones that would look at him for a second and wonder where they had seen him before. To those Alexander just shrugged and would say something about being in the army during the war. He would always sigh in relief once the redcoats deemed that he was nothing more than a country bumpkin.

He wasn't. He was a soldier in the army, as he had said, but not one that the redcoats thought he was. Alexander spoke with a lingering British accent, as a result of growing up in the Caribbean, and every one of the king's men seemed to trust him a bit more than the native people. It was his one safeguard, but he didn't put much faith in it.

He was an American soldier, with high ranks. A former aid-de-camp to General George Washington, some would say he was the general's right arm. A man who had interacted with a great number of important figures during the war, from the fearless Marquis de Lafayette to the tactical General Henry Knox, all before he was the age of twenty-two. But he never told anyone that.

Ever since General Washington had been captured, Alexander had been on the run, wondering where to go, who to turn to, and why he hadn't pushed harder for Washington to make an escape. He didn't have many friends, and those few that he had were in prison, dead, or too closely connected with him. He had no one to look to for help.

So, he ran. He just went where his feet took him, sometimes begging for jobs and sleeping in the streets, sometimes foraging in the woods and taking catnaps in the trees. On occasion, he would even work for food and board, but he didn't do that often. He couldn't rest, couldn't let his guard down.

He sneezed and adjusted his hold on his suitcase.

As he approached a town, a particularly tall house caught his eye, it was nearly as tall as the church's steeple, built of redbrick and mortar. A charming house, with a grouping of stairs leading up into a curved entryway. Paving the way for the staircase was a place of mythical proportions: a garden filled with lush green grass, some vibrant flowers and herbs in pots, and a few flowering shade trees. The garden wrapped around the house, trees running along the sides of the home, hiding the ivy and other vines that clung elegantly to the manor.

Alexander stared at the home's majesty enviously, his hand resting on the white picket fence separating him from the property. He wished he had a home like that to return to. He shrugged it off and began walking past. First, he would visit the church, he told himself, then look for a job. It seemed a nice enough town, welcoming, though none of the homes were as welcoming and charming as that red brick-

"You there! Stop!" He jumped and turned around. To his immense relief, it was not one of the British redcoats, but a young lady from the red brick manor. She stood on the stoop, holding a watering can – one that appeared to be forgotten – as she watched Alexander curiously. She looked familiar. Maybe it was her light brown hair piled upon her head, adorned by rose-colored bows, that reminded him of the social butterflies from the cities. Perhaps it was her dark trusting eyes, kind eyes that reminded him of his mother's. Or it could simply be the fact that she appeared to be the same age as Alexander. He shook it off, it was probably just paranoia.

"Have I seen you before?" the lady asked, causing Alexander's heart to quicken its pace. She walked down the steps, never tearing her eyes from Alexander. She fingered the light pink fabric of her gown, one so full of ruffles that Alexander was surprised that she didn't trip when she walked. She glided over to the picket fence gracefully. She set the can down and leaned against the rails, trying to get a better look of his face. He didn't want to seem unsociable, especially in a new town, so he moved closer to her and rested his arm on the fence's post.

He smiled charmingly, "I'm sure I don't know what you mean, miss. Could you possibly tell me the name of this lovely town?" If he kept her talking, perhaps he could remember where he had seen her before.

She continued studying him, her forehead wrinkled in concentration. She blew aside a wisp of hair hanging in her eyes, "I do believe we've met. Your walk is very distinctive, and I know I've seen it before." Now he knew he must have met her. He knew he had a very recognizable gait, but he just couldn't recall who she was! "You're in Albany, it's in New York, a little north of the city." She explained, her pretty eyes flickering over him, a mixture of confusion and knowingness on her face, "What do you call yourself?"

"Lawrence... Johnathan Lawrence." He lied. He had started calling himself that ever since he escaped the British. It was a tribute to his late friend, John Laurens, who died in battle the year before.

"No, it's not." The girl said softly, turning her head in all directions. Seeing that they were alone, she lowered her voice to a hushed whisper, "You're a soldier, aren't you? One from the Continental army?"

"It'd be treasonous if I said that. Why would I say that?" Alexander said quickly, frightened by how much this girl knew about him. First, she had known his walk, seen through his name, and told him his occupation! ...How did she know him?

"It's not like it would matter if you told me or not. I wouldn't report you, and the only people I could tell are my family, and they probably know who you are, too." she whispered, smiling, dangling the sentence in the air.

He took the bait, "And who am I?" he whispered, unsure as to why he was smiling back at her.

She giggled and shrugged, the sunlight reflecting off her rosy gown, "I can't remember. I just know that I know you somehow. I remember your face... and your eyes."

Alexander blushed, but he silently wondered why he was blessed with beautiful blue eyes that caused him nothing but trouble. He felt silently relieved though; she couldn't remember him.

"Maybe if you tell me who you are, I'll know if we've met." Alexander suggested.

The young lady giggled, then quickly paled, having realized how improper she had been behaving, "Please forgive me, it seems that I have forgotten all of my manners!" She extended her hand out to him, warm and soft, which he kissed dutifully. "Elizabeth Schuyler, pleasure to meet you, whoever you are."

Alexander didn't chuckle at the girl's joke, as she expected, but instead he looked at her oddly. "'Schuyler' you said, as in General *Philip* Schuyler?"

"So you are a soldier," Eliza smiled, "That's what I thought. General Schuyler is my father."

Alexander laughed, then began speaking quite rapidly, so fast that Eliza could barely keep up with what he was saying. "I'm sorry for my poor manners as well! Oh, Miss Schuyler, I recognized you, I just couldn't tell from where! I've seen you at some social gatherings in New York City, and when you came to visit your father, and when you brought the soldiers those blankets you made! We've spoken before. I've met your father several times when I was working under General Washington, a fine man, your father. Oh, sorry, I forgot, my name is-"

"Alexander Hamilton!" She exclaimed and smiled happily, then quickly looked around in alarm, trying to see if anyone had overheard, and the two sighed in relief when they realized they were still alone. She leaned closer towards him, "Now you must tell me what you're doing here! It's just been awful since…since…. Ever since Daddy's returned from war, the British have kept a strict eye on him. Why, we're all practically on house-arrest, the way they treat us! I can only ever go into town with a lobsterback escorting me, and they always seem to be hanging about the place! One comes each night and inquires about the day's activities, if we've met anybody unusual, and to say that they're doing us a favor by letting Daddy live!

"They've practically taken over the running of the house, too! They don't live here or anything like that, but my sisters and I have to do all the work! One of the first things the soldiers did was dismiss all of our servants! Imagine that! They didn't even leave us one helping hand! I don't mind the work much, but my sisters hate it.

"I just wish that we were still at war! I know it sounds dreadful, Mr. Hamilton, but it's true! At least when we were at war we were sure that Daddy was happy, and that if he would die, he'd do it honorably, but now…. Oh, he's so angry about being forced into this. I know he's only obeying because he doesn't want the British to hurt any of us – my sisters, brothers, and Mother, I mean. It never seems like he's safe nowadays. Now the soldiers could decide that he's been corresponding with rebel spies and go…go…hang him or something!" Eliza stopped suddenly as she realized how unlady-like she had been. Luckily, Alexander hadn't noticed and was absorbed in her story.

"Why, that does sound awful! And I don't suppose you get much company." He said sympathetically, their rantings having broken the courteous ice of etiquette.

Eliza shook her head sadly, "Not a one. Nobody wants to be associated with the Schuyler family. A family that's both traitorous and cooperative with the British."

He frowned, "That does seem difficult."

"You're on the run, aren't you?" She asked him, not wishing to dwell on her problems. He smiled sheepishly, nodding.

"The British would pay a mighty price for the mere secretary of a general. I'm simply trying to make sure a certain secretary can't be found." Alexander explained, "I just want to stay in the same place, though. It's tiring, always moving. At least in the army I had companionship, now…I suppose you're the only person who knows my true identity."

"Not for long." Eliza smiled mysteriously.

Alexander looked down at her in alarm, his face pale, "Excuse me? You told me you wouldn't tell!"

"And I'm not," she laughed, "but I will if you give me permission, and I think you will soon enough." She explained.

"...What do you have in mind?" Alexander asked after a moment, both curious and cautious.

"You can board at our home for a while, I'm sure Daddy wouldn't mind, he'd encourage it probably. He's been longing for some company lately. We all have. But he wants to talk to somebody who understands war. You do, and you know him." Eliza explained, playing with her fingers, thrilled at the hope of having a guest.

"Not well." He admitted. He removed his tri-corner hat from his head, and ran his fingers through his hair, considering Eliza's proposal. He frowned when he remembered something Eliza had previously mentioned, "And that matter about the soldier that comes each night."

Eliza pursed her lips, considering the flaw in her plan. "You'll say that you're Johnathan Lawrence, as you told me. You can be a friend of the family, looking for a job, and Daddy said that you could board with us while you're in Albany. I'm sure the soldiers would be suspicious at first, but they'll probably fall for it eventually, hook, line, and sinker."

It wasn't a bad plan. Risky? Definitely, but not bad. If it failed, he would likely be dragged off to prison – or worse. If it succeeded, he'd have a roof over his head, food in his belly, and safety – more or less. There wouldn't be any more running, for at least a few days. But what if the soldier didn't fall for the trick? Then he'd not only put himself in danger, but Eliza and her whole family, and they were already being watched. If they were caught, they'd be dragged off to prison, too – and that was if they were lucky. He thought over the pros and cons of her suggestions until he finally came up with his decision.

Alexander looked the girl straight in the eye, "No."

Eliza's face dropped. It clearly wasn't the answer she had been hoping and expecting. "But Mr. Ham-!" She frowned when he held up his hand.

"It's Mr. Lawrence from now on." He shook his head, "There's no such person as 'Alexander Hamilton,' at least not anymore. I'll be on my way, go on to the next town." Alexander placed his hat back on his head, turned away from Eliza, and slowly started down the long, dusty road. He stopped in his tracks when he heard an unexpected voice.

"Wait." He turned around, surprised. There was Eliza, still leaning against the fence, looking at him with what seemed to be a mixture of pity, mischief, and hope.

"At least stay the night. Then you can go on to the next town, and you'll never see us again. Just, please, allow me a bit of company." She spoke so earnestly that Alexander couldn't help but look her in the eyes. He tried to tear himself away, to remember the dangers and costs of being found out, to say 'no', but he knew as soon as she spoke that he had to stay for a night. He couldn't explain why, but he knew he couldn't refuse her.

"Very well." He said, stepping closer, "But just the night, then

I'll be off at the crack of dawn. Agreed?"

Eliza nodded happily, letting him in through the gate, "Agreed. Now, let's go ask my father."

With that, the two walked into the Schuyler household.

He opened his eyes slowly. It was the clang of church bells that had awoken him. *Bong. Bong. Bong.* He blinked. He sat up in bed so fast that his head pounded. He rubbed it gently as he took in the unfamiliar room around him. It was nicely furnished, with a chandelier hanging from the ceiling. There was a nightstand beside him, empty, save for a candle and holder that had been set there, thoughtfully. His heartbeat slowly returned to normal as he registered that he wasn't in prison.

The sunlight that streamed through the window warmed him, making him smile faintly out of pleasure. The warmth of the bed added to his joy. It was the first good night's rest he'd had in a long time: an unguarded sleep. A sleep where he hadn't awoken on the hour, to make sure he wasn't being held captive by British regulars. He wondered how he had come by such a fine night's rest.

The memories flooded back to him.

Eliza. The red brick house that felt like a home. Seeing General Philip Schuyler. Meeting Eliza's mother, sisters, and brothers. The fear of being discovered when the British redcoat had come. Saying that he was a family friend. The expression on the soldier's face, skeptical then trusting.

I'll be off at the crack of dawn. It was past dawn.

Alexander leapt out of the bed in a flurry and quickly walked to the dresser. He thrust open drawer after drawer before seeing his freshly washed clothes folded neatly atop his suitcase. He quickly pulled on his clothes: stockings, shirt, breeches, and waistcoat. He hurried to brush back his auburn mane and frantically tied his hair together in a neat bow. He pulled on his shoes and briskly walked out the door, wondering what had happened to his hat and coat.

ELIZA

Eliza raced through the halls, searching for her older sister. She hadn't had time to put her hair in a coiffure today, so it curled around her shoulders, loose. Her blue everyday gown swished as she kept slamming to a halt, scanning each room, before moving onto the next. She nearly fell to the ground in relief when she found her sister absorbed in a racy French novel (all the rage) in the dining room, lazily eating a piece of buttered bread.

"Ann!" Eliza scrambled into the seat across from her; on a normal day, she would have scolded her older sister's reading selection, but not today. Angelica looked up, surprised, her foxy chignon bouncing when she did so.

"What is it?" she asked, leaning forward, intrigued by her typically calm sister's panicky expression and tone.

"I've been looking all over for you!" Eliza cried, "I need your help! There's a question I just have to ask you!"

"Well?" Angelica wondered, "What is it? I'm all ears."

Eliza's cheeks flushed, "It seems silly…." She looked away.

Angelica set down her book and wrapped her hand around her sister's, smiling, "Tell me, I won't make fun."

Eliza nodded slowly, believing her. The tips of her ears reddened and she leaned closer to her sister, "You know how at parties, all of the men and boys want to dance and speak to you?"

Her sister nodded slowly, slightly confused, "Yes?"

"How do you do it? Keep their attention? You'd be able to have a dozen suitors if you put your mind to it." Eliza asked desperately, "How do you attract them? You're such a flirt, but I was wondering how a person…less talented in that department might be able to…um… I have a friend who was wondering."

Angelica smiled secretively, seeing the reason for her sister's sudden interest, "Just be yourself, dear, and I'll make sure not to catch his eye."

Eliza frowned, not receiving the answer that she had been hoping. She looked up again, "But-"

"Why hello, Mr. Hamilton!" Angelica said loudly, kicking Eliza's ankles from under the table. Eliza whipped her head around in alarm, then having confirmed that Mr. Hamilton had, indeed, entered the room, looked back to Angelica. She quickly tucked loose hairs behind her ears, batting her eyelashes and licking her lips. Angelica grinned and let her eyes flicker to Eliza's, giving her younger sister a boost in confidence before both sisters looked back to the soldier.

"Hello?" Alexander popped his head into the dining room and took a seat beside Eliza's. "Hello, Miss Schuyler," he grinned at her and nodded politely to Angelica, "Miss Schuyler."

"...I wanted to thank you, Miss Schuyler," Alexander told Eliza, "for inviting me to stay here for the night. I'll be taking my leave now, go on to the next town. You didn't have to take me in, so I wanted to thank you proper."

He began to rise, but Eliza, panicked, pulled him back into the seat beside her, "Don't go quite yet! I made some breakfast, and I won't send you off without food! That wouldn't make me a very good hostess, now would it?"

Peg, the youngest of the Schuyler girls, wandered into the room, fingering her dark hair, lost in thought. "'Liza? Is breakfast done yet? I'm getting-" Angelica jumped to her feet and pushed Peg out of the room, much to the girl's protest.

"Go, get some breakfast in the kitchen if you're hungry! And get something for Mr. Hamilton!" Angelica hissed. Peg grumped and glared but moved onto the kitchen anyways.

Angelica quickly turned back around, intrigued by her two companion's conversation.

"Miss Schuyler!" Alexander shook his head, "That really isn't necessary! I'm fine, really!"

"No, I insist." Eliza began, standing, "Do you really think that I'd let you go on your way and not-" She began leaving the room, but Angelica turned her sister around and walked her back to the chair, sitting Eliza beside Alexander.

"Peg's getting him something," Angelica whispered into her ear, "No need to bother yourself, dear, just remember what I told you." She went back to her chair and watched the two intently, though trying not to make it seem too obvious.

Eliza tucked a curl behind her ear, wondering what to say, "...

How did you come to end up in Albany?"

Alexander turned to look at her, surprised and somewhat embarrassed, "It's a long story...complicated..." he quickly tried to change the topic, "Could you happen to tell me which of the nearby towns I'd be most likely to find a job? I don't want to stay here much longer, the redcoats might suspect if I stick around here too long."

Her face blanked. She suddenly couldn't remember the names of towns she had lived nearby and visited her entire life. Her cheeks grew hot and her heart began to pound, "I...uh, I...." Alexander's kind eyes watched her expectantly. Angelica's face landed in her hands, and she worked to repress a groan.

General Philip Schuyler entered the room, oblivious to the scene he was walking into. "Hello, everyone," he greeted the trio cheerfully.

"Hello, General." Alexander nodded respectfully at him, eyes torn away from Eliza.

"Hi, Daddy!" Eliza smiled, her cheeks as pink as posies, glad to be saved from further embarrassment. She frowned, however, when she realized something. "What are you down here so early for? You never come for breakfast earlier than noon."

"It's my door," Philip told her, "It's been creaking, and it's been irking me beyond belief. I came down to see Mr. Hamilton before he's off... and to see if I can find some oil. The only problem is, I don't know if the joints need to be oiled or if I need a new door altogether."

Angelica sighed dramatically, "I keep telling you, you have to-"

"I can take a look at it," Alexander volunteered, much to the pleasure of both girls, "It'd be the least I can do. Think of it as payment for my night here. If there's anything else you need help with, please, don't hesitate to ask."

"You'd do that?" Philip smiled, "Why thank you, my boy, that would be a help."

"Do you think that you could possibly look at my door?" Eliza asked, "It's been making some noises as well."

"Most certainly," Alexander nodded at her, smiling.

"*I* haven't heard anything," Peg stated, entering, balancing a platter full of breakfast.

"You haven't been paying attention," Angelica quickly lied, watching as Peg placed the tray in the center of the table, "I've heard it. It groans terribly." She nodded enthusiastically, Eliza giving her a small smile.

"I'll get right to it!" Alexander said, rising once more, but was this time pushed down by all the Schuyler sisters and their father.

"After you eat." Eliza told him. Alexander smirked sheepishly, but obeyed.

ALEXANDER

The next morning, Alexander decided to see if there was anything else the Schuyler family needed help with. It had taken him nearly all of the previous day to fix the door, (Eliza's door seemed perfectly normal) despite it being a minor fix. It partly contributed to the fact that Eliza had given him the wrong tool each time he asked her to fetch something. She once gave him an oilcan when he asked for a hammer, then a wrench, then a screwdriver. It was at least twenty minutes before she finally gave him the hammer (she kept getting distracted.) She had then convinced him to check every door in the house, twice, to be positive that there weren't any problems.

Another reason was because she kept cooking extravagant meals for everyone. The meals all lasted at least an hour, with the entire family: Philip Schuyler, Mrs. Kitty Schuyler, Angelica, Peg, John, Phil, and Rensselaer, along with Alexander, all sitting in the formal dining room while Eliza served them course after course. The general, his wife, and Peg all sat confusedly, apparently as bewildered as Alexander as to why the girl kept cooking.

Angelica didn't really take note of the meal, still reading her French novel, only ever looking up when her sister entered. He noticed that she kept sneaking looks at him when she thought he wasn't looking, but she didn't seem to want his attention – if anything she was trying to avoid it. She had pulled down her hair, turning it into a fiery shield, only a tiny bit of her face visible. She'd only speak to him occasionally, when Eliza was there, telling him about the different activities she and Eliza had participated in during the war; and as quickly as she spoke, she'd turn away, leaving Eliza to elaborate for Alexander's intrigued ears. Her introverted attitude confused him. She was so different from the girl he had met the night before: a talkative, flirtatious young woman who liked to be in the spotlight. As they were with Eliza, Philip, Kitty, and Peg were equally confused by Angelica's bizarre behavior.

The boys didn't pay any attention to their oddly behaving

elder sisters, but were instead fascinated by their plates, which were miraculously filling with all of their favorite treats. When Eliza was in the kitchen, Alexander asked the family why she was making so much food. They responded with shrugs (Philip and Angelica), the sound of forks scraping porcelain (John, Phil, and Rensselaer), guesses (Kitty and Peg), and, later, more food (Eliza).

Alexander had just finished fixing and inspecting the doors when the sun had begun to set. By then, Eliza had made dinner and insisted that he stay the night, and that he couldn't travel once it was dark. The general had agreed with his daughter, saying that it would be their pleasure to have him, especially after he had fixed the door.

He walked through the home's many halls, poking his head into different rooms, wondering how he couldn't find anyone in a house as small as this. He smiled when he peeked into the parlor, where Angelica was lounging on a chaise, reading her book. He entered and sat on the chair adjacent to her own, smiling good naturedly. Her chocolate eyes flickered towards him, and she filed her bookmark into the volume's pages. "Yes?"

"I was just wondering why you like that book so much." He said, "You're always reading it, it might strike one as being unsociable."

Angelica rolled her eyes, "Yes, I suppose how one could think that. If that's how I impress you, then I regret that I wasn't being entirely polite…but I have my reasons."

"Like?" Alexander asked, grinning.

She shook her head, "You're impossible."

"That's what most people seem to agree with…." He smiled in a joking manner, then his grin fell and his face turned serious, "But seriously, is there anything that your father would like me to tend to? Any chores that you know of?"

She shrugged, "You know how it is. Chores are chores, they're never-ending... nothing that I can think of in particular...." Her eyes brightened, "The fence! Eliza's been going on about how it's been in dire need of a whitewash. I believe she's out with Peg repainting it. I know she wouldn't protest your help. Peg is hardly helpful. She hates sitting on the grass, so she's always sitting on a stump and only able to reach a small portion with the paintbrush.... Yes, the fence would be helpful."

"Thank you, Miss Schuyler." Alexander stood and tipped his hat to her, "I'll see you...around lunchtime." He continued staring at her, expectantly before Angelica burst out laughing.

"Did it ever occur to you that I just might not be a people person?" She asked between breaths.

"Oh no," he said, "The first time I met you, you chattered up a storm and kept wanting my attention. Now you don't want anything to do with me. It doesn't take much of a genius to determine that something...changed."

She smiled sadly, "I suppose so. It's just...I remembered that you're Eliza's guest, and Eliza.... You see, she doesn't get that much attention from outsiders. She's Daddy's favorite, and probably Mama's, but she never gets too much attention from anyone else. I'm her best friend, and she never had that many to begin with. With me and Peg, it was different. We were the life of the party, everyone asking us to come to their home for a gala of some sort, and inviting us on outings. Eliza was always forgotten and left behind, though she was never really one of the girls. She's like a tomboy, but also incredibly domestic. She'd rather ride a horse or read a book than attend a party. Even at the parties, she seems to try to hide behind pillars or me and Peg. She'd rather be talking politics, or starting a fundraiser. So, you see, when I saw how much you fascinate her, I had to step away, give her the attention she wanted and not try to steal it away for myself."

Alexander looked down at her, his eyes unreadable, but clearly contemplating. A look of compassion and understanding settled on his face, flushing his cheeks, "I'll pay more attention to her, if that's what you're asking, but I won't do it just because you told me to. I enjoy her company, I truly do. She's an interesting young woman, I haven't met a girl like her before.... Do you think that's why she wanted me looking at all those doors and making me all those meals? Because of me?"

Angelica nodded, "Most certainly, cooking and sewing are her specialties. If she makes something for you, it's her way of showing she cares. She's not one to go buy something in a shop as a gift. She's sentimental that way."

"Thank you," Alexander smiled slightly before turning away, "That's helpful."

ALEXANDER & ELIZA

"Mr. Hamil-Lawrence!" Eliza waved to him with her paintbrush. She was in the front garden with Peg, painting the faded wooden fence. Just as Angelica had foretold, Peg sat on the stump a ways away from the white boards and leaned forward to paint, practically falling off her perch in her attempt to not stain her dress. She was frowning, evidently having been dragged unwillingly into the task. Eliza sat in the grass in a plain everyday gown, grinning, eyeing her guest with admiration. "Come paint with us!"

"Yes! Please do!" Peg jumped to her feet and shoved her paintbrush into Alexander's hands, "Pity there's only two brushes, if there were more, we could all paint together." Peg brushed past him and ran up the porch steps, triumphant in her victory, but cringed and turned back around when she heard the cheerfulness in her sister's voice.

"Don't leave, Peg! There is three!" Eliza held up another brush, and happily waved it in the air. Alexander watched as Peg's face fell and she slowly began trailing back, dragging her feet all the while.

"No, go on," Alexander told her, "I ought to be able to handle enough work for the two of us." Peg grinned widely, thanked him, and quickly retreated into the house before her sister could protest. Eliza smiled, humored by Peg's eagerness.

"I'd been hoping you'd come." Eliza told Alexander, patting the grass beside her, "This might take a while, though." She nodded to the multitude of fence posts that wrapped around the property. "I've only just begun."

"That's fine," Alexander remarked, plopping down beside her and dipping his brush into the paint pot, "I still don't believe that I've properly repaid my dept, and this can only benefit the both of us; you and your family with a fresh fence, and me with your company." Eliza tried to hide her smile.

The pair worked in companionable silence before Eliza set down her paintbrush, contenting herself by looking at her coworker, "What are you going to do once you leave here?"

Alexander shrugged, "I hope to get a job, permanently, but I don't believe that will happen. I suppose it will be the same as it has been for the past few months, get day jobs or work for room and board, forage and scavenge. It's not exactly the life I planned for when I came to America," he admitted, "but it's better than nothing."

"Where are you from?" she asked, admiring the stark contrast between his tanned skin and inquisitive blue eyes.

"Saint Kitts and Nevis," he replied, "in the Caribbean. I came to the colonies in '73 to get a college education."

She nodded, "That explains your accent."

His cheeks flushed, "It *is* a bit different than your typical British. Memorable in a way." He suddenly stuck his brush into the jar and turned to her, a serious expression on his face. She looked at him, curious of the sudden change in mood.

"Miss Schuyler, it appears that we'll be companions for a little longer than I had originally anticipated, so I'd like for you to call me Alexander." He smiled and extended his hand. She stared at it, hanging in the air, for longer than usual, and he wondered if he had acted out of line. As his smile began to shrink and he slowly withdrew his hand, she took hers in his.

"Eliza." She told him.

He looked at her, startled, "Pardon?"

Her big brown eyes sparkled as she gazed back at him, "Please, Alexander, call me Eliza."

The tension in the air dissolved and Alexander quickly relaxed and smiled at her while he adjusted his hat. "Pleasure to meet you, Betsey."

Betsey.

She liked that.

Eliza's mouth slowly began to curve upwards until her lips formed a wide smile.

Three

April 1779

PHILADELPHIA, PENNSYLVANIA

THOMAS

Thomas Jefferson stared at the cobblestone walkway, lost in thought. He was in the park, a place not far from the former Independence Hall. Only now it was called the Pennsylvania State House, a name heavily enforced by the British regulars that patrolled the streets of Philadelphia daily.

"State your name and business." He heard a voice say.

Thomas looked up slowly, "Hmm?" He saw one of the king's men looking down at him, his red coat gleaming – right down to the perfectly-polished buttons. Even his black boots were shining. Thomas looked at him expectantly, despite knowing what the man wanted. He liked keeping them on their toes, irking them, irritating them in all ways possible.

"State your name and business." The soldier repeated, adjusting the musket on his shoulder. Thomas noticed the gun's menacing glint in the sunlight, then he looked the man straight in the eye.

"It's Samuel Johnson, sir."

"Ah...yes," the soldier said, uninterested, "Your business?" The redcoat didn't really seem intrigued in who Thomas was, just in making the interrogated party nervous.

"Does a man need to have reason?" Thomas asked, touching his powdered hair thoughtfully. He looked down at his hand in disgust when he saw that some of the powder had made its way to his fingertips. He rubbed the powder off on his trousers and made a show of looking back at the redcoat. "I'm just sitting on a bench."

The soldier stared at him blankly for a second, then sighed. When he spoke, his words sounded rehearsed, as though they were drilled into the man's brain, "In this day and age, it is best if all colonists provide both a name and business when a soldier inquires. Even if the business of the person seems unimportant or usual. So, once again, I repeat my question: what is your business?"

Thomas groaned, "I don't really have one, all right? I just came here out of habit. I've had a great many things occupying my mind recently, and I just needed a quiet spot to ponder and reflect."

"You've been here before?" The soldier asked, startled, "...What sort of things?"

"Are you allowed to ask me those questions?" Thomas looked at the redcoat suspiciously. He leaned against the bench, using his arm as a cushion, while he waited for the man to answer.

"Any question one of the king's men asks of a colonist is required to be answered, no matter how unusual or uncommon." The man readjusted his musket once more, "And if questions aren't answered, the colonist in question might have to spend a night in…." The man trailed off, tisking unfortunately, but Thomas got the message.

"You're saying that if I refuse to answer, you'll throw me in prison?" He spoke in disbelief, but Thomas could hear a tinge of fear in his own voice.

The soldier nodded, confirming his theory, "For an undetermined amount of time."

For being a private person? Thomas chewed his lip before answering. "I live here, so I've been to the park multiple times. It's a fine place to wonder about life, which I do a quite a bit, so I find myself in need of a great many thinking spots. As to what is on my mind, I've lost a great many things in the past year, and I'm still recovering from it. Now, is that all, or must I tell you more?" He glared up at the redcoat and waited expectantly.

The soldier looked down at Thomas, insulted, "You will remember your manners when you speak to one of the king's officers. You're lucky that I won't report you for your disrespect, and that I'm only giving you a warning. Next time you won't be so lucky." The soldier scanned Thomas's face for any hint of cowardliness, but Thomas made sure to suck it into the depths of his soul, portraying nothing. The soldier grumbled when he couldn't find a sliver of fear. "Stand up." Thomas hesitated, "I said, stand up!" the soldier roared. Thomas scrambled to his feet, rising to his full height of six feet, two inches. The soldier gulped when he realized how much taller he was. Thomas towered over him by a good eight inches, and seven inches over most of his fellow colonists. Add that height with his flaming red hair, and it was no wonder that Thomas had started slouching and using hair powder. He was too recognizable.

The soldier now seemed scared instead of amused at Thomas's irritation, and he suddenly acted like a frightened puppy, while he was, in actuality, a respectable member of the British army. "I have now decided that your reasoning is…reasonable, sir, and that you can continue thinking. Good day, and g-g-goodbye, sir." The man quickly cowered away, in search of a much smaller colonist to annoy.

Thomas smiled softly to himself. His size nearly always intimidated people, nearly as much as his temper. He sat back down to continue exploring his thoughts.

The grass, he noticed, was a particularly more vibrant shade of green than normal. It provided a lovely backdrop for the willow tree's shadow. Thomas watched the peaceful sway of the willow's foliage and how it painted elegant green patterns against the blueness of the sky. The tree's rope-like leaves looked almost as if they were dancing in the wind, swaying first this way, then that. He could almost hear his violin accompanying the branches in their strange, beautiful dance.

His violin, one of such quality and sound, wasn't in his company any longer. Unlike some of his associates, when he heard that England had won the war, he had remained at his home for as long as possible, not wanting to run before it became absolutely necessary. Eventually, however, he had to escape, on the run, like so many others. If he stayed at his home, it would be like accepting an invitation to prison – or worse. He delayed his departure to gather essential supplies: all of his savings, and a proper amount of clothing, risking his safety in doing so. He was almost too late; he wanted to spend some last moments in his plantation's garden, running only when the British redcoats were practically at his doorstep. He had been so panicked while collecting his few bits of luggage, that he had forgotten one of his most favored companions: his Nicolò Amati violin. He heard later that he'd never be able to have it back. The British had burned his home, his beloved Monticello, to the ground.

He had fled to Philadelphia for safety, a city with so many residents – too many – it would be impossible for the king's men to search every Philadelphian, looking for just one man. It was easy to conceal his identity at first. Thomas had stayed at an inn that he'd never been to before, gone to shops where nobody knew him, and avoided his few allies in the city. He pretended to be a simple man named Samuel Johnson, who just happened to be noticeably taller than most, wore an excessive amount of hair powder, and had enough money to live modestly without working.

Thomas's fingers brushed each other, his elbows were on his knees. His eyes scanned his surroundings, absorbing the many different figures enjoying the park's fine views. He noticed the soldier questioning a lady around her mid-twenties. She seemed incredibly bored, while her companion, whom Thomas took to be her father, seemed insulted by the man's never-ceasing questions. He saw a young boy, with shiny golden hair, bent over a bush, examining something hidden inside. A squirrel, Thomas wondered, maybe a flower. He remembered when he was the boy's age, when everything was easy, when he didn't have to be inconspicuously scanning place after place for old friends, enemies – anyone who might recognize him and alert the authorities.

He sighed and closed his eyes, wondering if he would ever be able to again live with his guard down.

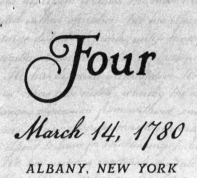

Four

March 14, 1780

ALBANY, NEW YORK

ELIZA

Elizabeth Schuyler fingered her intricately-arranged, coppery hair and sighed, admiring her reflection in the handheld mirror. It piled at least six inches above her head, and she was still growing used to the appearance. She could feel Angelica carefully add a bow to the back of her coiffure; Eliza smirked and rolled her eyes playfully at her sister's work.

"Perfect." Her sister stepped back to admire Eliza's hair, "Just lovely…. You excited?"

Eliza's face brightened and she nodded happily, then giggled when she noticed the way her hair bobbed unusually in the mirror. "And nervous, and excited, and nervous, and – and why do I need so many bows?"

Angelica blushed as she slowly removed the bow she had been

adding while her sister had been speaking. "You want to look your best, don't you? And you look amazing in bows, Mama always says so."

Eliza laughed dryly, "That's when I wear a dress with a sash, you know, the ones where I tie a bow in the back. She also says that when I put *four* bows in my hair, Ann. Not eight."

Whenever the Schuylers went to parties, Eliza always piled up her hair, and made sure a bow was facing in each direction. Eliza wasn't quite sure way she did it originally, but she did it out of habit now.

There were now four white bows in her hair, along with bows marking north-west, south-east, etc. "Please just take off the extras. You know that I want this to be simplistic." She gestured at them, thinking that she almost looked like a French pastry, in her fancy dress and multitude of bows.

Angelica sighed but cooperated.

The two girls were in Eliza's bedroom, with Eliza sitting at her vanity, and Angelica standing behind her, playing with her sister's hair.

Eliza could see Angelica's reflection in the mirror, and she studied her. Angelica's poppy-colored hair was done-up in a way similar to her own. Like Eliza, the eldest of the Schuyler girls was wearing a quartet of bows, each of them a pale purple, to match her dress.

Eliza fidgeted with the white lace ruffles of her gown. Her sister was finished attending to her hair and was now looking at the back of Eliza's dress, as though it demanded all of her attention. Eliza rose to her feet, allowing Angelica to examine it more closely. Satisfied with the back of the dress, Angelica pulled her sister towards the full-length mirror. Eliza stared at her reflection and turned to look at Angelica, a wide grin on her face. Angelica nodded, then moved her finger in a circle. Eliza obediently twirled around in her dress, showing it off.

"Well?" She asked expectantly. Her face was excited, eager for her sister's approval.

"It's certainly gorgeous." Angelica said slowly, "I just think that it needs more bows... and lace. Some more ruffles would be simply amazing, and-" Eliza sighed in exasperation. The two sisters never saw eye to eye when it came to dresses, which were often reflections of their personalities. Eliza liked simplicity where Angelica liked ornateness. Eliza was quieter and introverted, while Angelica was louder and liked to be the life of the party.

"I like it." Eliza looked at her reflection. She fingered the silky material that formed the skirt. It only had three layers of ruffles, all mostly hidden by the intricately designed lace. The plain white skirt reminded her of a lily of the valley flower, or a snowdrop. The sleeves ended at her wrists and were made of the same material of the skirt.

"Can you tie me?" She gestured to the sash. Angelica smiled and took the two ends of the sash in hand. She made the best bows. There was enough of the material left that it would drag behind Eliza when she walked, something she found particularly whimsical.

"I think it looks just like her." A new voice said. The two whirled around to see Peg closing the door behind her. "It looks wonderful."

Eliza smiled. Peg liked both simplicity and fanciness, so it was more likely that she would give a truthful opinion. Peg's dress was a light pink, with the sash in a slightly darker shade. Her brunette hair was in a coiffure, like her sisters, but she wasn't wearing any bows. Bribery couldn't even make Peg wear a bow in her hair.

"What a picture." Peg smiled dreamily, "You look simply stunning. I just can't wait!"

Eliza smiled thankfully, "Neither can I! I just hope this doesn't get ruined." She gestured to the dress's fluffy skirt – which was the result of wearing a hoop. Her sisters laughed.

"Just stay away from all the hustle and bustle and I'm sure that you'll be fine." said Peg, patting her on the shoulder, "And don't cook anything, you'd ruin it if you spilt anything on your dress."

"I just want to help." Eliza pouted, but nodded, understanding the consequences. "I don't know what I can do."

"Nothing!" Angelica said, plopping her sister onto her bed, "You get to do nothing and everything. Read a book, crochet, embroider. Anything really, anything that doesn't involve-"

"Me doing anything?" Eliza finished, looking at her sisters expectantly. Her face was bland, frowning.

Peg cocked her head and thought for a minute, "You're not wrong."

Angelica looked at the youngest, annoyed by her presence, "What did you come in for?"

"Oh, right." Peg turned away from Eliza, "I wanted to see the dress, of course, but I also wanted to tell you that I need some help." She turned back to Eliza, an exhausted, pleading look on her face, "It'd be so much easier if you were helping."

48

"So everybody keeps telling me." Eliza said quietly.

"Everybody *also* keeps telling you to do nothing." Angelica reminded her sternly, "Just don't lie down, I don't want you to spoil your hair. And…. do something to occupy your time."

With that, Angelica left the room. Peg lingered for a few moments before realizing that she was supposed to follow. And Eliza was left to wait.

ANGELICA

Angelica walked down the stairs, Peg on her tail, "Everything is all ready inside. Mother's nearly done with the cooking, the boys are staying out under foot, and Daddy's out in the garden doing something clever with the gazebo. The gazebo is just lovely this time of year! It will paint such a lovely picture, it will! Oh! I'm just so excited!"

Angelica continued walking, though she was grinning now in agreement, "It's not every day we'll see Eliza get married. It's funny, I always imagined we'd be married off before her."

Peg giggled, "Ironic, isn't it? I must say that she is pretty lucky, though."

Angelica smiled, "He's a dear, he's crazy about her, she's crazy about him, and he treats her like a princess. What more could she want…?" She stared fondly off into the distance before turning to her sister, "So what do you need me for? It sounds like you're all getting along fine."

"I need help with the flowers." Peg explained, "I went up and found some pink wildflowers in the nearby field for 'Liza's hair. You know the one I mean, it's only five minutes up the road? They're very pretty, little things and-"

"Peg!" Angelica snapped, looking at her sister harshly, "Why do you need my help?"

Peg nodded slowly in submission, her voice growing soft, "Right, I'm nearly finished with the bouquet. Those flowers are rather prickly." Peg raised her hands to show the thorn's stab wounds, but Angelica ignored her. She sighed after a moment, realizing that she was being unnecessarily unpleasant, and tried to be kinder.

"Why do you want flowers? Don't you think her bows are enough? She only ever wears her bows. I doubt she'll want flowers too, but I'm sure she'd wear them if we picked them. You know how she is, she doesn't like to hurt anyone's feelings." Angelica said, "Why don't I help you with your bouquet? Do you need me to pick anymore?"

"I picked them all!" Peg exclaimed, grabbing her sister and pulling her into the sitting room, "I'm just having trouble figuring out where to place them."

Angelica looked down at the coffee table's contents with surprise. "You said you were almost done with it." She picked up the bouquet, which consisted of three pale pink roses and a handful of white daisies. "This isn't almost done with it."

Peg shrugged and placed her hands on her hips. "I did the majority of the trouble; I picked all the flowers." She gestured to the multitude of blossoms on the table, ranging from sweet rose buds to erect lavenders, regal Queen Anne's lace to dainty primrose blooms, "I just don't know the proper way to arrange them. You're better at these things, you always know where things should go."

Angelica sat down on the stool near the table and began grouping the flowers into different arrangements. She rubbed her temples, considering the assortment, pondering potential bouquets she could create. "Do you think that you could possibly find some bluebells? And some ribbon?"

Peg nodded, "Why, of course. What color of ribbon?"

Angelica sighed, "What do you think I want? I want white." Peg nodded and quickly scurried out of the room in search of bluebells and ribbon.

Angelica arranged, then rearranged the flowers. What Peg had said was true, she was good at arrangements, but she just wanted these flowers to be perfectly situated, and they never seemed to be. How could it be that the blossoms never seemed good enough, that each grouping was worse than the last? Finally, after ten minutes of working, she realized that she wasn't going to be satisfied with any of the bouquets and just stopped working altogether. She held the final bouquet in her hand and waited anxiously for the arrival of both the bluebells and the ribbon.

She had been waiting for fifteen minutes when Peg arrived, clutching a handful of flowers and a scrap of white ribbon.

"What took you so long? I've been waiting for-" Angelica was cut off by Peg's non-stop chatter.

"I'm sorry, one of the guests stopped me to ask about the flowers, and we got to talking. Nice man, told him that-"

"Peg, you said you were talking to a *guest*?" Angelica leapt to her feet, surprised and concerned, "We don't have any guests. We don't have any friends to invite."

Peg looked at her sister strangely, "If we don't have any guests, then who is that collection of young men standing outside saying that they're our guests?"

Angelica thrust the flowers into Peg's already full arms, "Show me these guests."

Peg readjusted her grip on the hoard of flowers she was carrying with much exaggeration. Then she turned and began walking towards the house's side door. She paused while walking and looked to her sister, "Do you want to meet them or just see them?"

"Only see." Was her sister's reply.

Peg led Angelica to the side door, where she nodded to the obstacle. Angelica opened the door softly, and thanks to the well-oiled and cared-for doors, it opened easily and without sound. Peg walked down the steps and onto the grass first, the skirt of her dress matching the grass blades smashingly. She guided Angelica towards the front of the house and nodded to the crowd of men standing near their gate.

"The guest I was talking to said that he was a friend of Alexander's. Well... actually, he said that they had met." Peg explained as Angelica sized them up.

"He actually said that?" Angelica whispered.

Peg nodded and sighed, "Why are you so worried? We haven't had guests in forever!"

"Peg," Angelica turned to her sister, "The reason I'm worried is because Alexander doesn't have any friends."

Peg looked shocked, "But I thought we were his friends."

Angelica sighed, amazed by the shallowness of her sister, "We *are* his friends. He doesn't have any friends beside you, me, Daddy, Mama, John, Little Phil, and Rensselaer."

"And 'Liza." Peg added.

"And Eliza." Angelica echoed, "Now to the point, I'm also worried because I recognize those men, and it's certainly not because they're his friends."

"Where do you recognize them from?"

ELIZA

"Eliza! Eliza, open up!" Angelica's fist pounded against the door and made quite a sound, but her voice was muffled as a result of the closed door.

Eliza discarded her book and jumped off her bed. She had obediently not laid down and had taken care not to let her hair touch anything, but now her neck hurt from looking down so much. She pulled open the door and quickly stepped to the side when Angelica marched in with an anxious expression on her face. Peg stumbled in a few seconds later, panting.

She wasn't used to so much exercise. Angelica had briskly begun walking to the house after Peg asked about the guests; and, Peg, who was shorter and had normally-sized legs, found it very difficult to chase after her fast-moving, long-legged, taller sister. Peg sat on the bed in relief as her older sisters spoke. When she sat, the ribbon and the many flowers she had been carrying tumbled onto Eliza's bed. Peg quickly began collecting the flowers and adding bluebells to Angelica's bouquet.

"Angelica! Ann, what on earth is going on?" Eliza asked, playfully, "Do you need my help decorating the staircase?" Her playfulness left when she noticed the look on Angelica's face. "Angelica, what is it? What's happened?" Eliza moved to her vanity's chair to sit when Angelica closed the door.

"We have a problem." Angelica began, "There is a group of men outside claiming to be Alexander's friends and guests."

"But that's impossible." Eliza said, "Alexander hasn't told anyone but us his real name, and he isn't in contact with any of his old friends."

"Exactly." Angelica clasped her hands together, "Well, they introduced themselves as friends of Johnathan, but you know what I mean. The point is that they're not his friends, I know this because I recognized them. They're the British regulars."

Eliza's face turned white. Peg gasped, "Oh, Ann, why didn't you say so? How did you recognize them?"

"Simple, they carried themselves like soldiers, and after all the times they've escorted us into town, I've gotten to know a few of them, though I've tried not to grow attached. I saw some of them in the crowd. There's about a dozen or so of them out there. If anything, I'd say that they're on to Alexander and that they want to arrest him." Angelica stated. There was a worried look on her face, an expression that was reflected back to her by her two sisters.

"We have to tell him." Eliza recovered the first. "All of them. Mother and Daddy, and the boys as well."

"I'll go tell Mama and Daddy and John and Phil; hopefully one of you or one of the boys can convince Rensselaer. He never listens to me!" Angelica complained, she began lifting her finger to point at Eliza, who shook her head. "Not you either?"

"None of us." Peg said.

"He'll probably listen to Alexander." Eliza suggested, "You know how much they idolize him."

Within three days of him staying, Little Phil and Rensselaer had tried (and failed) to make toast and oatmeal – all by themselves – for Alexander. Whenever Alexander was off to fix something, John was there, waiting with a hammer or a nail or exactly what Alexander needed whenever he needed it (despite Alexander's fondness for Eliza, he privately considered John a better assistant.) He peppered him with questions, wanting to know what it was like to work for the great General Washington, and fight in different battles. The two younger boys listened to Alexander's frequent stories with just as much pleasure.

The three sisters contemplated the suggestion, "Yes, that would probably be most effective." Angelica admitted, "But who will tell Alexander?"

"I will, of course." Eliza stated, "I've been wanting to see what he's been up to, I haven't seen him all day. I miss him."

"Good, you go tell Alexander," Angelica nodded, "I'll go find Mama and Daddy and John. Hopefully he'll be able to manage his brothers."

"Can I find Daddy?" asked Peg, "Then we all have somebody to tell!"

"NO!" Angelica and Eliza shouted, Peg shrank back in surprise.

"Why don't you...continue playing with your flowers?" Eliza said kindly, "You know that I need somebody to make my bouquet, and I'd love it to be you. Why, look at how well you've done so far! This is, by far, the best bouquet you've ever made."

Peg frowned, "That was Angelica. I'm just adding bluebells."

Eliza frowned back, unsure of how to respond, "...Well, keep up the good work!"

Angelica hoped that Peg wouldn't worm her way into telling somebody. She wasn't the smartest thing in the world, and it was more likely that she'd mess up the message and Daddy would end up thinking that some old war buddies had come for a visit.

Before Eliza could say anymore kind words, Angelica grabbed the girl by the wrist and began pulling her to the door.

"Where on earth do you think they would be?" Eliza asked, her hand lightly grasping the staircase's banister as they walked down.

Angelica thought for a moment. "Mama might be in the kitchen, and the boys are probably playing out in the garden, and knowing Alexander-"

"He's probably making last-minute checks." Eliza finished, "That's likely where Daddy would be as well."

Philip Schuyler had also become fascinated by the young man boarding in his home. Like Eliza had predicted, they became fast friends, talking about war, politics, and literature. Alexander, realizing that he had a growing fondness for the Schuyler family, had found himself a job as a clerk in Albany, and the family had let the soldier board in their home ever since. Despite his job, he and John had taken over nearly all of the general's chores, which had been a relief to the rest of the Schuylers, but was a disappointment to the general himself. As a result, he was often at Alexander's side, trying to help with anything and everything.

"I'll go to the garden and look for them, you go tell Mother." Eliza instructed her older sister. Angelica nodded. The sisters parted ways, Angelica heading deeper into the home, Eliza racing towards the back door.

As suspected, Eliza found both her father and Alexander in the garden. Alexander was staring at the gazebo, hands on his hips, with a determined look on his face. Philip clearly had no clue what the younger man was doing, but was trying to mimic his stance and expression. Eliza scanned the gazebo to see what the matter was. It took her a minute, but she giggled when she noticed.

The land where the gazebo had been built wasn't flat; as a result, the gazebo was tilted. Alexander had taken to calling it "the leaning gazebo of Albany;" he and Philip always laughed about it, as it apparently was a reference to some structure in the Old World, but Eliza didn't see what was humorous about a falling building.

"My dear Hamilton, I don't think you need to move the gazebo." Eliza teased him. "It looks fine where it is." The two men turned in surprise, both with smiles on their faces.

"I know, I know." Alexander grumbled as she scooted up beside him, "I just want everything to be perfect for our wedding." He kissed her hands, and smiled down at her, she fell into his arms, happy.

"That's impossible, but it's sweet of you to try." Eliza giggled, standing on her toes to kiss him. Philip averted his eyes as Alexander eagerly bent his head down for another. She laughed but put her fingers on his lips, shaking her head, "I came out her for more than a kiss, you know." He frowned dramatically, causing her to laugh, and grinned in response.

"There's a group of redcoats out by the gate dressed as civilians saying that their your guests for the wedding." Eliza looked up at her fiancé as he put his arm around her, his face pale. "Ann's positive that they're here to arrest you, and I'm worried that she's right." She could watch his mind turn from curious, to concerned, to planning, all by the intensity of his eyes.

"Let me think about this." Alexander pulled away from his bride and his father-in-law-to-be and sat on the gazebo steps. He closed his eyes and processed the information Eliza had told him. His mind reeled through every possible scenario until he finally found one that he liked.

Alexander looked up at the two Schuylers, both watching him expectantly, "I'm rather certain that I'll be on the run again before the day is through, but I think that we ought to enjoy it. First, the wedding is still on."

"Alexander!" Eliza scolded, "Do you honestly think that-"

"Hear me out!" he held up his hands to quiet her, "Hear me out!" He continued once she stopped, but she still watched him skeptically, "Two, the wedding doesn't go quite as planned."

Philip's forehead crinkled in confusion, "What do you mean?"

"You're still marrying us, Angelica's still the maid of honor, Peg is still the bridesmaid, John is still my best man, and Kitty and the boys are still the audience. I'm still groom, Eliza's still bride. All that is the same. We do the vows and the rings, but we make a change in that. The rest of it's essentially completely different." Alexander finished.

"What's your plan?" Eliza asked curiously.

"That, my Betsey, is what I will tell you next."

ANGELICA, ELIZA, & PHILIP

After the first few weeks of Alexander's stay, the Schuylers could tell that there was something between their guest and Eliza. When surrounded by the family, they stumbled through conversation, trying to be gentlemanly and ladylike, trying not to be too familiar. Though they tried to keep it hidden, it was plain to see the growing fondness between the two young people, and Alexander soon announced his intention to call on Eliza and it was not rebuffed by Eliza nor her father. Not two weeks had passed before the couple found themselves in a sweet, passionate courtship. Soon the pair became inseparable, Alexander helping Eliza with her cooking, and him reading poetry to her in the library. They'd take long walks through the property's garden, and lounge around in the study speaking about history, politics, and literature, or they would bend their heads towards one another and whisper sweet nothings into the other's ear. The pair had quickly discarded formalities not long after the start of their courtship, and the Schuylers would often walk through the sitting room and find Eliza's head on Alexander's lap, discussing everything under the sun. Whenever they were apart, their sweetheart was all either one of them could speak of. Eliza chattered happily with her sisters and mother, a vibrant, excited look in her eye whenever she spoke about her 'dear Hamilton.' Alexander was just the same, a smile constantly on his face, always wanting to tell anyone present about how wonderful his 'Betsey' was, his nickname for her becoming a term of endearment. It couldn't have been more than two weeks of this that the family had to admit it: Eliza and Alexander were head-over-heels in love. And it wasn't long after when Alexander found himself in the garden, on one knee, holding his hands out to Eliza, asking for her hand.

Eliza had wiped away her tears and widened her grin and nodded breathlessly. Alexander's smile grew so wide that there didn't appear to be room for it on his face. He scooped her into his arms and twirled her in the air, her laughing all the way. When he set her down, Eliza curled herself into his arms and placed her mouth next to his ear. In a hushed whisper that only Alexander could hear: "Yes."

And now it was time.

The "guests" were all standing in the garden. Angelica watched curiously as some of them walked over to the left side, where, traditionally, the bride's family would be standing...sitting. Since only six people were expected to attend the wedding, Kitty had made sure that the family wasn't all crowded on one half of the walkway. Instead, John and his brothers stood on the right side, for Alexander. They, along with Kitty, Angelica, and Peg, watched curiously as some of the guests walked behind the ladies and stood with the bride's female family members. Kitty, having been alerted by her oldest daughter about the possible danger as a result of the "guests," did her best to ignore them, as did her daughters and her two eldest sons. Rensselaer, who had lived for a grand total of six years, however, found these new people very interesting to look at, no matter how much his brothers badgered him to look away.

As maid of honor, Angelica stood near her father, who would perform the ceremony. To her father's right stood her younger brother John, Alexander's best man. The ceremony was scheduled to take place in the gazebo, so Angelica and John were standing outside, near where they expected Eliza and Alexander to stand. Peg stood by Angelica, fidgeting excitedly. She kept whispering things to Angelica, but Angelica stood silently, impatiently waiting for her sister's marriage.

Angelica watched as Alexander stood in the gazebo, his bright blue eyes filled with happiness. She didn't know all of his plan, she didn't expect anyone but Alexander knew it in full, but she hoped it would succeed. His auburn hair was brushed back in style and tied with a nice black bow. He wasn't wearing his uniform, with its brilliant blue fabric and golden accents, but a nice suit. Black. She knew he wished he was in his uniform. The suit was just part of the disguise, though one had to admit he looked rather handsome in it. His eyes looked down the aisle excitedly, waiting for his bride.

Waiting, waiting. Until finally she came.

There wasn't any music, just the soft footfalls of Eliza's shoes, which was exactly the way she wanted it.

She was magnificent. Her caramel-colored hair, which Angelica had worked so hard to arrange, was piled perfectly, with each of her four white bows shining proudly. Her dark black eyes, ones that Alexander admired so, were filled with such excitement and wonder, never flickering away from the groom's. Her smile was lovely, she was grinning from ear to ear. She carried one the bouquets that her sisters had worked so hard on (the bluebells, unsurprisingly, had been bunched together on one side, but Angelica had had time to move some.) Her dress hid her feet, and Angelica could see the ruffles bouncing with each step she took. The sash, as expected, dragged behind her as she walked, but she didn't trip. Eliza subconsciously touched the base of her neck, then her hand fell away, back to the flowers.

She gracefully climbed the steps of the gazebo and took Alexander's hands in hers. They looked at each other like there was no one else in the world.

The general cleared his throat, ready to speak. Eliza glanced at her father for a second before turning back to Alexander.

"One year ago," Philip began, "This young man came to board at our home. And since then, he's become like family. Today, he will be. My daughter, the bride, took to him the quickest. I remember that first day," he chuckled at the memory, "she made countless of pastries and meals for all of us. We were all bewildered, trying to figure out what on earth had gotten into her. That day, Al-er-Johnathan helped fix some doors in the house, and Eliza helped, in a way, she made sure that he stayed. She kept giving him the wrong tool after tool, kept interrupting him to give him more food. He did stay for the next day, and the next, and the next, as Eliza kept finding activities to keep him occupied. I believe that he eventually gave up trying to leave, because, unsurprisingly, the pair fell in love. And now, they are ready to join, to go out on their own as husband and wife. Before I begin, however, would either of you like to say something?"

Angelica's face felt wet. She could hear Peg crying, but she couldn't see her. Her eyes were fixated on the two, her baby sister, her soon-to-be-brother.

Eliza's own eyes were watery, Alexander couldn't believe his luck. He swallowed, feeling his own cheeks wet, "Eliza, my Betsey, dear Betsey, would you soberly relish the pleasure of being a poor man's wife?"

She smiled back up at him, "I'll relish the pleasure of being your wife." Alexander smiled, enveloping her hands in his own. The couple smiled dumbly and dreamily at each other for a few seconds before the general began to speak.

"Do you, Al-er-Johnathan – what's your last name again?" Philip asked, confused, racking his brain for the answer.

"Lawrence." Eliza whispered, Alexander smiled. Philip nodded and continued, "Do you, Johnathan Lawrence, take Elizabeth Schuyler as your lawfully wedded wife, to have and to hold, from this day forward, for better or for worse, for richer or for poorer, in sickness and in health, to love and to cherish until death do you part?"

Alexander looked down at Eliza, "I do."

"And do you Elizabeth Schuyler, take Johnathan Lawrence as your lawfully wedded husband, to have and to hold, from this day forward, for better or for worse, for richer or for poorer, in sickness and in health, to love and to cherish until death do you-"

"I do, I do, I do!" Eliza said giddily, she was beaming, and her almost-husband was beaming right back at her.

"Now for the rings." Eliza heard her father say. She watched Peg present the couch cushion that held two rings. Eliza wondered which was hers, Alexander hadn't shown them to her yet (the rings had just finished being crafted.) Peg handed the cushion to the general, then quickly retreated back to Angelica. Alexander selected a thin ring, picking up both rings in the process. Eliza cocked her head, surprised. The rings were conjoined. He presented it to her, but she looked at him confusedly. Wasn't he supposed to slip it onto her hand?

"Read it." He whispered. Eliza picked it up and held it to her eyes. *Alexander 1780*, read one ring, and the other, *Elizabeth*. "Oh, Alexander!" She cried softly, looking back up at him, tears streaming down her cheeks.

He took it from her and slowly pulled the two apart, creating two different rings. "They can be worn together, as one ring, or separately, as two." He told her, sliding the *Alexander* onto her finger. She then grabbed the remaining ring, the thin golden band meant for her own, and slid it onto his finger.

"I now pronounce you husband and wife! You may kiss the bride!" Philip announced, but the newlyweds were already in a kiss, long and tender and loving. The family and "guests" cheered, waving hats and bouquets in the air.

Alexander pulled an inch away, eyes concentrated on Eliza with fierce determination, as though he would never look away. He put his hand up to her cheek and just let it hover, barely brushing her skin, shaking uneasily. She covered his with her own and cupped his hand to her cheek. Sniffing back tears, she whispered, "Go."

He hesitated. "I don't want to leave you."

"Go." She repeated, "I'll be all right, I just need you to be safe."

"I love you, my Betsey." He choked.

"I know," She sobbed, "and you know I love you."

Alexander, tears in his eyes, pulled himself from Eliza's grasp and began running down the aisle as fast as his legs could carry him. Eliza watched him run away, a shocked, confused expression clearly displayed on her face. She whispered, for only herself to hear, "I love you, my dear Hamilton, my husband."

The "guests" all turned to watch as Alexander ran down the pathway by the side of the house and disappeared. Peg stopped sniffling and just looked around her. Just moments before everybody had been so happy, cheering for two joined persons, now only the birds were chirping. Angelica walked up to the gazebo and wrapped her little sister into a hug. Eliza fell into the embrace, and leaned her head against Angelica's shoulder. She began to cry, sad tears now, not ones of joy. She shook erratically, and her sister struggled to hold her still. Her mother walked up beside her and put an arm around her. The three of them began walking to the house, Eliza crying loudly and sobbing all the way, Angelica's and Kitty's heads simply bowed in shame, crying silently to themselves. Phil and Rensselaer ran after them, unsure of what to they should do, but knowing that they didn't want to be left behind. The general glared at the redcoats, who were looking at themselves as though the appearance of a uniformed soldier would answer everything.

"I think it's best if the lot of you left." The general said to the men, "But thank you for being here."

Most of the group began shuffling out, but one walked up to Philip and his two remaining children. He introduced himself as Robert.

"I just don't understand it." Robert stated, "Johnathan never seemed the type to run away, he was a gone man when it came to her. Miss Schuyler was the center of his world."

"I don't understand it fully either." Philip admitted, absentmindedly, but he looked straight at the soldier when a thought occurred to him, "...How did the two of you meet?"

"I was escorting Miss Schuyler to a store to do some shopping, and Johnathan tagged along, I don't think either one of them really realized that I was there." Robert reported.

"Oh, you're one of those soldiers." John said, pretending to have been unaware, "I thought you looked familiar."

Robert's cheeks flushed, "Yeah. A group of us heard that Johnathan and Eliza were getting hitched, and we figured that since you didn't have any friends that came to call on you anymore that we'd come to support you. We didn't wear our uniforms because we thought it might frighten you, think that we were going to arrest Mr. Schuyler here or something of that nature."

"That was very kind of you, son. You didn't really have to do that." Philip told him, tears beginning to run down his cheeks when he shook the soldier's hand.

Robert smiled kindly, sympathetic about the sudden turn of events, "Well, see you around, mister. See you soon, Miss Schuyler?" he asked hopefully, turning to the girl.

Peg shrugged, "I'm not sure, I believe that I'll be tending to 'Liza for a while. She'll be wonky for days."

Robert nodded, "Months, I'd say, the way she loved him." With that, he shook their hands and left.

"What do you think, Daddy?" Peg asked once all of the soldiers had left. John looked at his father, equally interested by his reply.

"I think, Peg, that we just made a terrible mistake." Philip told her, nodding his head sorrowfully.

"We were being unnecessarily impolite," Peg scolded, "I mean, they didn't have to come here to support 'Liza and Alexander."

Philip's jaw tightened, wondering how his daughter could be this dim-witted, "How could I have known that they were here to support them if none of us knew that?"

Peg cocked her head, her lips pursed, as though the thought had just occurred to her, "I knew."

ELIZA & ANGELICA

Eliza stared daggers at her. They were sitting in the parlor, the six of them. Angelica and Eliza were sitting on the loveseat, though they sat on opposite ends, at least a foot between the two of them. Angelica was draped causally on the chair, very comfortable, but one wouldn't have been able to tell by looking at the slightly pained expression on her face. Eliza was sitting at the edge, erect, her brows narrowed as she glared menacingly at Peg. Philip and John gulped nervously and slowly began moving to the edge of the sofa furthest from the girl. Kitty sat in a chair near her youngest daughter, but she slowly scooted away, towards her daughter who didn't look as though she would be the target of Eliza's outbursts (Phil and Rensselaer had been sent into the nursery after Eliza began looking murderous.) Peg shifted in her seat and bit her lip, fidgeted with her hands, and sweated profusely. She kept stealing quick glances at her older sister, then quickly averted her eyes back to her shoes, nervous at what the fury of a woman of twenty-two years would do.

Eliza nodded slowly and sighed, breathing in and out for a few moments. She closed her eyes, digesting the information her sister had brought to light, trying to control her emotions. She smiled ironically at her sister, chuckling dryly, "You're saying that Alexander ran away for nothing, then?"

Peg nodded slowly, looking at the oriental rug on the floor, "Yes," she mumbled.

"I see." She nodded slowly, then turned her attention to the window, trying to focus on something more pleasant, but soon tears began rolling silently down her face. The dam broke and all her emotions came pouring out, her eyes wild and angry and crying, her face tight with rage. She stood and began to pace, unable to sit still any longer. She shook her head from side to side, clenching and unclenching her fists. "He had that all worked out, when we turned to the soldiers he would run away, he'd run off to Philadelphia. You should have seen the look on his face! The words he said to me! He didn't want to go, but I told him he had to! But the soldiers were actually guests, and there was no reason for him to run at all!" She laughed crazily at this point, "and to think that none of you dared to ask the soldiers what they were doing! Peg!" Eliza turned to her younger sister, "You! You talked to them for fifteen minutes! You knew that they were those lobsterbacks! And you didn't even think to tell us, even after Ann went on about having to warn him! Now Alexander is halfway to the next state when he should be home, with me! We couldn't even get properly married! I don't even know what to call myself now! Am I still Miss Eliza Schuyler? Or am I Mrs. Eliza Hamilton? What about Eliza Lawrence? I really don't know anymore!" Eliza shrieked and began pounding up the stairs to her room.

Mrs. Schuyler looked at her daughter with disappointment, "Really, look what you've done! I've never seen her in a fit like this before! In fact, I don't ever remember her having a temper!" Kitty walked away, distraught.

"I don't suppose that you're going to scold me, too?" Peg looked at Angelica.

Angelica looked lazily back at her, "Not really, but you could've at least tried telling us before we started the ceremony."

"Why would I have told you, if I thought that you knew? I thought it was just one your games-" Angelica held up her hand and Peg shut her mouth.

Angelica walked away, muttering, "I'll go talk to her," under her breath. Philip looked solemnly at Peg and stood to leave, John following, looking sympathetically back at his sister.

Angelica walked into the kitchen and grabbed a cookie, leftover from the spoiled wedding. She smiled sadly at the memory of the day before, where she, Eliza, and Alexander had baked cookies, laughing and teasing one another, waiting eagerly for today, never anticipating how wrongly the day would unfold. She then went to the staircase and began climbing. When she came to Eliza's closed door, she leaned against it for a moment, listening to the muffled sobs coming from within. Angelica sighed and knocked on the door gingerly. "Eliza? I brought you something."

She could make out a faint "Go away," from the room, but she opened the door anyways. Eliza was on her bed, sobbing into one of the pillows, no longer caring if her hair was a mess or a beauty. Angelica sat beside her and listened to her erratic breathing. After waiting a few minutes, Angelica watched Eliza's crying begin to subside and her breathing returning to normal.

"It's been quite a day, hasn't it?" Angelica said softly. Eliza's face turned away from the pillow and to her sister. Her eyes were red and swollen from crying. They were watery and glassy.

"You're still here." Eliza stated, eyes bleary and dazed.

Angelica pushed the cookie towards Eliza's mouth, "Eat. It will make you feel better."

Eliza took a timid bite, causing crumbs to fall to her pillow. She lazily moved her hand to scoop them into her palm and tossed them into her mouth, though most crumbs ended up on her cheeks. "Thank you." She said quietly.

"Feeling better?" Angelica asked, smiling motherly at her sister. Once Eliza had finished her cookie, she sank back into her pillow and closed her eyes.

"Yes."

"I thought so."

The sisters sat in silence for a long while, Angelica stroking her sibling's hair comfortingly, Eliza breathing in-and-out, and crying softly. Angelica waited until Eliza began sitting up to speak.

"What do you think you're going to do?" Angelica asked.

Eliza shrugged and sniffed back a few tears, leaning her head against her sister's shoulder. "Honestly? No idea. I have no way of writing to him, I only know that he's headed to Philadelphia.

He said that he'd write as soon as he arrived, so it'll be weeks… if I'm lucky, but I'm afraid that he won't be able to come back here."

Angelica nodded understandingly, "I don't believe he will. He did make quite a scene out there, and there is bound to be talk amongst the soldiers. I wouldn't be surprised if they start coming and questioning us today. Asking about why he was running, questioning his identity, and-"

"Oh stop! Stop!" Eliza cried, pulling away and slapping her sister's wrist, "Ann! Please, don't talk like that. You're making me feel even worse! We were so stupid! We just hastily jumped to an irrational conclusion without even considering any logical ones, or asking Peg's opinion." She groaned and leaned against the wall.

"That's where you're wrong, dear." Angelica said after a minute. Eliza looked at her, confused. "Think of it this way: say that I was right, and the soldiers were out to arrest Alexander. Say that we didn't suspect them, then Alexander would be in prison, probably on his way to gallows, and we'd all be in jail. And, honestly, when do we ever ask Peg's opinion and it works out?"

Eliza snorted, nodding playfully, "True."

Angelica placed her hand on her sister's shoulder, "Look, I'm glad things worked out the way it did. It proves that the lot of us are quick on our feet. But at least you know if you can overthink having a few friends over, you can think yourself out of everything."

Eliza's smile grew wider as her sister spoke, but it suddenly became a frown, "But I didn't think of anything. You were the one that suspected the soldiers, and Alexander was the one who came up with the plan."

"True." Angelica stated, "But I'm not the one who's about to do something very very brave." She smiled at Eliza's confused face, and poked her nose, "You're going to get Alexander back."

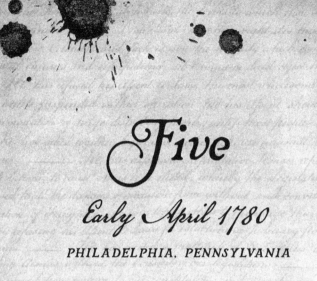

Five

Early April 1780

PHILADELPHIA, PENNSYLVANIA

THOMAS

Thomas looked up from his book, startled.

Rap! Rap! Rap! The knocking at the door sounded urgent and was increasing in volume.

"What is it? I'm coming, I'm coming!" He set the book on the end table beside him and slowly pushed himself out of his fluffy armchair. Thomas quickly walked to the door and unlocked it. He thrust it open and looked out into the inn's hallway. Nothing but the door across from him.

"Really?" He said to himself as he began turning around to retreat back to his novel.

He stopped when he heard an impatient "humph!"

He looked down. There, looking up at him, was a short man tapping his foot impatiently. He was dressed in black, and his usually serene expression was, instead, irritated. Even his powdered hair seemed agitated.

"Tom!" The small man hissed.

Thomas blinked in surprise, he looked up and down the hall, making sure nobody had heard him, "Jemmy?" He couldn't believe what he was seeing.

The little man put a finger to his lips and stormed into Thomas's apartment. Thomas quickly closed the door to deal with his unexpected visitor. The man sat in Thomas's chair, glanced at his discarded novel, nodded approvingly at Thomas's reading selection, then gestured for Thomas to sit in the chair opposite of him.

Thomas stared at him in amazement, "Jemmy, Little Jemmy, how I've missed you." He sat down next to him, "Jemmy, how on earth did you find me? I've been keeping myself so well hidden! Where have you been? I haven't seen you in years!" Thomas let loose a long breath as he sank into his chair. A thought occurred to him. "Why are you here?"

James Madison's eyes, bluer than the clearest sky in May, studied him contentedly. His two hands lay clasped upon one knee. "Easy enough. You've never been to this…inn before, and you've been to most in the city. It was just a matter of time before I found you."

"I'm living under a false name." Thomas pointed out.

"I didn't ask for a 'Thomas Jefferson,'" James looked surprised and insulted by the remark, "It took some courage, but eventually I simply asked if there was a tall man with carefully powdered-hair that has been living in this establishment for at least four months." With the exception of Thomas, James had a difficult

74

time approaching people and starting a conversation.

"How did you know I had my hair powdered?" Thomas inquired, impressed by James's powers of deduction.

"You're six foot two and your hair is about as fiery as it gets. And so…" James trailed off. "I'm sorry for barging in on you like this, unexpected-like, but as soon I heard you were here, I simply had to see you."

"It's fine." Thomas said briskly, "What are you doing here?" he asked his old friend.

"Right." James causally pulled a piece of parchment from his coat pocket, "I'm here about this." He waved the paper before Thomas's eyes.

He looked at the paper, waiting for James to elaborate, but the little man just stared at him, waiting. Thomas rolled his eyes and smiled, "What is it?"

"That," James smiled mysteriously, "is my idea…. Prepare to be amazed, good friend, at the genius this piece of paper has to offer! The idea came to me months ago, and it's taken some planning, but I do believe that it could work." James rubbed his hands together excitedly, "Tom, do you still want America?"

Thomas looked at his friend, surprised that he would even ask, "With all of my heart. Why do you ask such a thing, Jemmy? You've known that for years."

"It sounds exciting and inspiring…. Imagine if we could do that, though!" James paused for dramatic affect. Thomas looked at him, one eyebrow raised.

"Really, Jemmy? Really? That's your brilliant idea? If you can recall, we tried that already. It failed."

James sighed, "What I'm trying to say is that we can try again. I hope to do so, and I have a plan to make it succeed!"

"Not bad." Thomas replied coolly, "I'm listening. Do remember though, that you're committing treason."

James shrugged, "If I remember correctly, you wrote a document freeing the colonies. You also signed it. Compared to that, what's so treasonous about hearing me out?"

Thomas chuckled, "Touché. What's your plan?"

The smile on James's face grew wider, "Picture this, a group of leaders that will free the colonies. All sorts of leaders, all people who believe in our cause."

Thomas blinked, "Isn't that the same as congress?"

"Not exactly, more of... a new and improved congress, except... not." James replied, then waved the sheet of paper, "This is a list of names whom I think would be perfectly suited for leading the second War of Colonial Rebellion! Jemmy Madison, Tom Jefferson, Samuel Adams, Alexander Hamilton, Dr. Benjamin Franklin, Aaron Burr, the Marquis de Lafayette, and to finish it off, his Excellency, General George Washington."

James watched as Thomas slowly nodded his head, "Right, right. I see where this could work, but the problem is, I don't know who a good many of those people are! Who's Hamilton and Burr?" Thomas asked curiously.

"Alexander Hamilton was General Washington's most trusted aide-de-camp, and the general looked to him for advice. I figured that if the general trusts him, then we can trust him to help us." James explained, "Aaron Burr was a patriot soldier under General Benedict Arnold, a man who was a good friend of his. I believe that if we were able to recruit him, then we would learn valuable intel about how the governor operates."

Thomas thought about the idea, "It's a lovely plan, but how will you pull it off? Dr. Franklin is in France, along with the marquis, and the general's probably the most guarded prisoner in the colonies! How do you figure we get them to join?"

"First, we write a letter to the doctor and to the marquis, then we wait. I'm rather certain that the marquis will come as soon as we call. I heard that he bought a boat just so he could sail here the first time, as nobody would let him on their ship. As with Washington and Burr, we'll have to be rather clever to break them out...."

"Wait, Burr is imprisoned as well?" Thomas asked, "Only me, you, Adams, and Hamilton are free?"

"Currently appears to be. The only people that I know for certain are out of jail are the two of us and Dr. Franklin and the marquis. I just assume that Adams is free, since there haven't been any executions lately. As for Hamilton, I have no idea." James admitted.

Thomas sighed, "The plan itself – if it worked – that is, would be miraculous; but I don't see any possible way in which we could do it."

"Could you at least help me try?" James looked at him with hopeful and pleading eyes. Thomas sighed.

"The only people I know on the list are Adams, Dr. Franklin, Washington, Lafayette, and, of course, yourself. So, if we are to ever start, the best course to choose would be finding Adams." Thomas explained, "But first, we have to think like Adams."

James watched him curiously, "How does Adams think? I don't remember ever meeting him."

Thomas wiped his forehead with the sleeve of his shirt, and laughed half-heartedly, "If only it was that simple! I don't know how Adams thinks. He's...unpredictable."

"Marvelous." James's leg began to twitch. If there was anything that got on his nerves, it was unpredictability. "Are you sure you have no idea where he might be?"

"Your guess is as good as mine." Thomas told him.

"In that case...."

Thomas stumbled over James, accidently pulling both of them, headfirst, into a mud puddle the size of the Atlantic. Thomas stared down at his mud-splattered, mahogany waistcoat – imported from Paris. He bit his lip and clenched his fists when he realized that the stain wasn't going to come out.

"-and I don't want you bothering my customers or even hanging about this place again!" The red-faced, angry tavernkeeper slammed the door behind him, leaving James and Thomas lying in the alleyway.

"Oh, this is wonderful!" Thomas snapped, inspecting his soiled overcoat and trousers.

"It's not as though we were being that rude," James muttered, getting to his feet and dusting himself off. Thomas snorted, not seeing how him asking every person in the bar if they had seen Sam Adams lately didn't qualify as rude (James was too frightened.)

James had avoided landing in the main portion of the puddle, managing to keep his clothing from getting too terribly dirty.

Thomas grunted when he realized that it wouldn't have mattered if his small friend had landed in the middle of the mud, he never wore anything that would noticeably be stained, only black. James smoothed back his hair and extended his hand to Thomas, helping him up. "You're right, Tom, this is far from wonderful. We're no further along with finding Adams than we were two weeks ago! Didn't you say that this was his favorite Philadelphian tavern? If the regulars haven't seen him, how will we ever find him?"

"I was actually talking about the state of my person, but that's wretched as well." Thomas took off his coat and shook it, pieces of sludge flying off into the street. He grumbled, putting his coat back on, "It's so difficult to find fabric in this color these days."

James, used to his companion's love of finery, though confused as to why this was the topic he was most concerned with, sighed and fished through his pockets. "Here." He held out a small white handkerchief and began to dab lightly at Thomas's soiled lapels.

Slightly embarrassed by James's mothering, Thomas snatched the handkerchief and began wiping the dirt from his waistcoat, mustering a "Thank you, Jemmy."

James, knowing not to embarrass Thomas any further by acknowledging his thanks, turned and began walking out of the alleyway, becoming lost in thought. At first his steps were cheerful and lilting, almost as though he were skipping, but then they grew slow and somber as his mood darkened. Thomas hurried to catch up with him, deciding to return the handkerchief after he had properly washed it. The small man looked to his towering friend, his voice small and saddened, "Well, where should we go now?"

Thomas considered the question, "I'm not sure, we've gone

everywhere...." He opened and closed his mouth, tapping his fingers against his thigh as he tried to think of some examples.

"The docks." James reminded him helpfully.

"We've searched the docks," Thomas snapped his fingers.

"And the markets," He added.

"We've also searched the bookshops and other stores," Thomas remembered.

"And the high-end neighborhoods," James remarked.

"The lower end ones as well," Thomas shivered at the memory of the dirty streets.

"The taverns four times over," now James was the one shivering.

"And the park." Thomas concluded, placing his muddy hand on his companion's shoulder. James eyed it warily, then looked into to Thomas's face, "Don't worry, Jemmy. We'll find him. I know we will."

James stared at him for a moment, then his lips curved into a smile.

Six

Mid-April 1780

PHILADELPHIA, PENNSYLVANIA

ELIZA

Eliza hoisted her travel bag onto her hip. She hadn't been to Philadelphia in years, but the city seemed unchanged.... With the exception of British soldiers constantly a stone's throw away.

She walked through the streets, keeping her eyes out for Alexander. When Angelica had first insisted on her running away to him, Eliza had immediately dismissed the thought. It was wild and impossible, she had said; but now, here she was, walking down Broad street, looking for her husband. After days of planning, Angelica and Eliza had gathered enough supplies for her trip. As predicted, the redcoats had begun questioning the Schuylers about Alexander's sudden disappearance almost immediately. Eliza had been the one interrogated the most, but she pretended that her fiancé must have been too scared to marry, and her family quickly supported her story.

Knowing that she would've been forbidden to leave otherwise, Eliza had snuck out of her home and stolen a horse from a neighboring farm (she left behind some coins as payment), riding to Philadelphia as fast as she could, riding fifteen miles a day at times. Unlike most girls she knew, Eliza didn't mind riding a canter astride rather than a walk on side-saddle, she preferred it actually. She also didn't mind getting her feet dirty. When she was younger, one of her favorite activities had been horseback-riding, but as she had grown older, it had grown less acceptable for her to ride like a boy, to ride at all, so she had given up her riding in exchange for her embroidery and cooking. She still sometimes missed the exhilaration of feeling a horse beneath her legs, though.

She had packed few clothes, only a few everyday dresses, a fine gown, and a pair of John's clothes to ride in, along with her multitudes of bows. Currently, her hair was brushing against her back, braided instead of in a coiffure, as it was easier to blend in when her hair wasn't in a fashionable state. Her simple blue dress dragged as she walked, causing her to trip when she moved quickly. It was really quite annoying.

She quickly spun around when she saw a tall man wearing a tri-corner hat brush past her. She frowned when she realized it wasn't Alexander, her heart plummeting to her stomach. In the past few weeks, she had learned just how much she had relied on him, how used she had grown to his constant companionship. She missed waking up in the mornings and finding a love letter on her nightstand that had not been there the day before. When she had first started receiving them, she thought them silly, but sweet, the way he described her as his "angel," sometimes writing in the margins because he didn't want to use two sheets of paper. Now she'd give anything just to have a short note from him. Before their wedding, she had never really been apart from him more than twenty minutes; and even in that short amount of time, she always looked forward to seeing him again, looking forward to the hugs and kisses of greeting. Now, her heart ached. It had begun the first day of him leaving. At times it felt that he was just in the other room, until she remembered that he couldn't be. All day long she had found herself wanting to tell him different things that had happened, escapades he would laugh at, scenarios he would frown at, but she couldn't tell him any of those things. He wasn't there. Most of all, she just missed hearing his voice, those hours they had spent under the shade tree with his arm around her, telling her stories. She missed sitting in the study, embroidering while he read to her poetry. She missed playing the piano and him singing the words in the wrong places. She missed hearing him call her "Betsey." She missed him.

She continued walking and saw an inn with a few guests hiking up the stairs to enter. There were two men that she noticed in particular, though they were not in motion. One was short, no taller than her bosom, his expression sweet and boyish, though Eliza couldn't place his age. There seemed to be an ageless quality to him. His clothes were entirely black, save for his white shirt and silk scarf, and his hands were on his hips, occasionally glancing at the man sitting beside him. The other man, who appeared a decade older than she, had fiery red hair and a look of intense concentration. His form of dress was much more sophisticated than that of the shorter man's. With his hunter green waistcoat and grey-blue overcoat, Eliza could tell that he was a follower of fashion and the life of the party. Both men were deep in thought and didn't notice when a person would bump into them or glare at them for being in the middle of the stairwell. Eliza drifted towards the inn, wondering if Alexander was staying there.

"Excuse me." She said to the men as she approached the steps, "Gentleman?" she stopped and watched them. Their expressions reminded her of Alexander when he was deep in concentration.

The redhead looked up, then smiled, "I'm sorry, miss, I'm afraid you caught me while I was lost in thought. What can I do for you?"

Eliza smiled happily, glad for the man's polite and eager assistance. "Would you happen to be staying at this inn?"

The man nodded, "Yes, miss. It's a fine inn, if you're thinking of renting a room. I've been living here for about a year now, and I have to admit that I've been rather satisfied by its service."

"Oh, I'm not staying here, but I may need to later... I'm looking for my...a friend of mine. Have you happened to have seen a man lately? One with the most brilliant blue eyes you ever saw? He has auburn hair, and he talks rather fancily when he's in the company of educated men, but he usually talks more plainly. A little taller than myself, talks often. Explosive personality. His name is... Johnathan Lawrence." Eliza explained hopefully, "He usually wears a tri-corner hat."

She had now caught the attention of the shorter man, who seemed annoyed by the interruption initially, but a sweet look settled on his face as he grew intrigued by her missing person.

The sitting man shook his head, "Can't say that I have, but this is a big city, it's likely that I saw him, and just forgot. I'm sure you'll find him sooner or later."

The short man mumbled something, something Eliza couldn't understand. He rocked back and forth on his feet. The sitting man cocked his head, "Speak up Jemmy, I can barely understand a word that you're saying." He turned back to Eliza, "He's awfully shy, doesn't like talking much to people. Gets too flustered."

James's face grew pink, and he rocked more on his feet, "I...err, you don't seem exactly certain about what his name is."

"I'm sure I don't know what you mean!" Eliza said quickly and defensively, "I know his name very well, thank you!"

Thomas frowned, "Jemmy, that was not polite at all!" James turned away, cheeks red, irritated by even having to speak in the first place. Thomas sighed and rose to his feet, surprising Eliza by his immense height. He was a full head taller than Alexander, and two over Eliza. He bowed slightly, "Samuel Johnson, at your service. This is my friend, James...Howe, he's not very sociable, though typically much kinder. Shy. Pleasure to meet you."

"Elizabeth Hamilton." Eliza extended her hand for Thomas to kiss, "Nice to meet you as well. Thank you anyways." She began turning to go when Thomas stood up and touched her shoulder. She looked back, startled.

"Would you like for us to help you look for him?" Thomas asked. Eliza smiled softly, surprised and encouraged by his offer. James, on the other hand, looked as though his best friend had just betrayed his trust.

"What?" he hissed. "Why?"

Thomas sighed and looked back at him, "It's not like we have anything better to do. I'd like to help her, and besides, you never know, we might find Adams while we're at it."

James grumbled grudgingly in agreement. After weeks of searching, they had still come up short, despite spending nearly all of their time looking for Adams (they had not yet branched out of Philadelphia.) The situation had not helped James's temper. The three began walking in the direction of the park.

"If you don't mind, could you help us look for a man as well?" Thomas asked, "He has greying hair and a large nose and blue eyes. The bushiest eyebrows. They look as though furry caterpillars climbed onto his face and never left." Eliza covered her mouth as she giggled at the description.

"If you don't mind," she began, "Why are you looking for him?"

"Not at all." Thomas replied. James looked up in alarm, "We have a plan that we'd like to propose to him, as we're certain he can help, but we just haven't the faintest idea of where he is. And if you don't mind, why are you looking for your Mr. Lawrence?"

Eliza smiled sadly, "I've come to Philadelphia and I know that he's been here for at least a few weeks. He's a great confidant, and I hope to see him again." She looked away, a saddened expression on her face. Thomas watched her sympathetically as she looked around for her Alexander.

They walked in silence.

By the time they reached town square, hours later, all three were deflated. Eliza was unlucky at finding her husband, and Thomas and James still had yet to find Adams. They all collapsed on a bench to rest, with James resting his head on his hand and Eliza resting her bag on her lap.

"Sir!" she looked up when she heard a voice cry out unexpectedly, "That is most untrue! Untrue in all manner of speaking!"

She tuned out the speaker as an argument began to erupt. Her companions seemed equally uninterested by the sudden commotion, that was, until violence began to break out.

Across the square was a group of men, who both seemed to be arguing and agreeing with each other at the same time. Most were dressed in long overcoats and donned tri-corner hats. Eliza couldn't quite tell what they were agreeing on, but they were all quite passionate about whatever it was. A small squad of soldiers marched over and barked at the group.

"Please, lower your volume. You're disturbing the peace." One of the soldiers said. The group of men watched him and his comrades angrily, glaring at the redcoats.

"Why?" One burly man asked, "Aren't we allowed to speak? Or are we too lowly for his Majesty to even hear our voices?" his companions whistled, clapped, and cheered in agreement.

"Quiet!" The soldier said warningly, then realizing he wasn't being complimentary to his king, added, "You're allowed to speak quietly."

This seemed to rile the crowd. The civilians began shouting at the soldiers, which quickly caught the attention of Thomas, James, and Eliza, along with the rest of the people in the square. The shouting increased, and the soldiers began to shout as well, crying out warnings, some reaching for their muskets. Some of the colonists began kicking at the redcoats, others began throwing a few punches.

"You have been warned!" a soldier yelled when one of the civilians pushed him to the ground, "Men, fire!"

Eliza watched in horror as the redcoats dropped to their knees and pointed their muskets at the crowd of men. She put her hand on her mouth to keep from screaming as she heard the crack of the muskets releasing their bullets. There was a puff of smoke, the sounds of screams, and then the *thump* of dropping bodies.

She could faintly see the other colonists in the square, watching the scene with shocked expressions on their faces. James was trembling beside her in fear, and Thomas in rage.

"End to King George!" she heard a voice cry out from somewhere in the battle, "Freedom for all! For America! For freedom and liberty! For General Washington!" She could hear some claps and cheers from within the fighting, supporting the voice, but they were quickly silenced by the next round of the soldiers' volley. Clouds of smoke. *Thump. Thump. Thump.*

Her heart fell to her stomach when she realized she recognized the voice. She jumped to her feet, causing the bag to fall to the ground, and began running over into black smoke and the screams of the fighting.

"Alexander!" she called, "Alexander? Alexander!"

Thomas, along with James, jumped in alarm and began chasing after the hysterical girl. "Come back!" Thomas cried, under his breath he muttered, "Please don't get killed."

"Alexander!" Eliza called, making her way through the crowd of civilians and soldiers. She heard the *pop* of the muskets and screamed, feeling one whiz past her waist, "Alexander! Answer me! Alexander!" The gunpowder hurt her eyes, she stumbled through the crowd yelling his name.

Thomas and James were standing a good distance away from the fighting, they scanned the crowd nervously, getting glimpses of the girl shuffling through the mob. "Elizabeth!" Thomas shouted, "Get out of there!"

"What do we do?" James asked quietly, tugging on Thomas's sleeve, his voice even fainter than usual, "We can't just leave her in there!"

"I know." Thomas said, "I'm thinking."

Eliza tripped and fell to ground, her hands breaking her fall. The cobblestones were dirty and covered in a thin layer of gunpowder. She felt somebody step onto her hand, causing the man to trip and fall onto his back. She yelped as she lost traction and her arms gave out beneath her, sending her sprawling out on the ground. She screamed when she saw a man lying beside her – dead. His eyes stared glassily at her. She felt the sudden urge to vomit. She heard a voice call out her name. She felt a hand grab her arm and pull her to her feet. She felt herself being enveloped and being dragged out of the fighting. "Alexander? Where are you, Alexander? Oh, please be alive. Please be alive."

ELIZA & COMPANY

She was shaking, both from cold and fright. She couldn't see anything. It was black – black as night, black as charcoals left behind from yesterday's fire. She moaned from the pain of her throbbing headache.

"Shhh...." She heard someone say softly, stroking her hair affectionately, "It's all better now. It's stopped, Betsey. You're safe." She groaned. Her eyelids fluttered nervously before she slowly opened them. She saw something... brown? Her eyes took their time to adjust, but they did eventually. It was the brown fabric of a very familiar overcoat. It felt soft and warm.

"Alexander...?" She whispered, partially asleep.

"It's all right. I'm safe. I'm here." He said comfortingly, resting his head on her own. They were sitting on the bench, his arms wrapped around her protectively. She could make out the fuzzy figures of Thomas and James. Thomas stood a couple feet away, looking at her with pitying eyes. James looked down at her, shaking himself out of fright and worry.

"Are you better now?" Alexander asked. She managed to nod. She slowly began to sit up straight to get a better look at her surroundings.

"What happened?" She rubbed her eyes drowsily. Slightly dazed, she looked across the square and saw a half dozen corpses, the argumentative men lying on the ground. The squad of soldiers, acting as though they hadn't killed anyone, were looking around for somebody to take away the bodies before they alarmed any more people. The few colonists she had seen before, the fellow witnesses to the fighting, were long gone, having abandoned the place out of panic and fear.

"Massacre." Thomas stated, voice tight and bitter, frame rigid.

"You were in the thick of it." Alexander explained, "I can't believe you weren't killed! By the time I got to you, you were in shock, surrounded by all that smoke and death. Oh, I, augh! You never should've gone in there. What the devil were you thinking, Betsey?"

She pulled away from him, arms crossed, eyebrows narrowed. "Well, what was I supposed to do? I just heard you shouting, and I knew you were in there, I just wanted to get to you, to make sure you were *safe*." She thrust her arms around him again, kissing him on the cheek, "I'm just so relieved that you're all right, that you're alive." He clutched her head, fingers entwined with her tresses, and pulled it towards his chest. He sighed slowly, and the two remained silent, simply enjoying each others company once more.

"I suppose this is where the lecture comes about not getting into any political arguments?" Alexander asked her, playfully.

She shook her head, "Oh, I know that it's pointless to even try telling you. It'll never happen. You have too strong of opinions."

The pair smiled happily at each other.

"You're arguing like a married couple." Thomas remarked.

Alexander and Eliza looked at one another, flushed, then Thomas, then each other again. "…We are." Alexander explained.

"Are you sure?" Eliza asked him, "The ceremony seemed rather hasty."

He grabbed her hand and waved it at her, "You've got a ring, don't you?" he asked, the golden band catching the sun's fading light.

"True." She grinned, then remembered her manners, "Oh, Alexander, this is Mr. Johnson and Mr. Howe. They were helping me look for you."

"Thank you." Alexander said, nodding to the men, "Thank you for trying to look after her. I know she's a handful."

"I thought we were looking for a Johnathan." James said frankly. Thomas looked at his friend, surprised by how comfortably he had spoken.

"Er…" Both Eliza and Alexander made unintelligible sounds. "It's Alexander… and also… Johnathan?" Eliza suggested.

"You're Alexander Hamilton." James concluded.

The couple stared the man for a few seconds before reacting. Eliza reached for her husband in fright, whereas Alexander looked as though he was about to punch James.

"How did you figure it out?" Eliza asked after a moment.

"Simple." James smiled slightly, "You introduced yourself as Elizabeth Hamilton, kept calling out for an 'Alexander' hysterically, and just said that we were looking for him," he pointed at Alexander, "when you told us we were looking for a Johnathan. And you also said that you were married."

Eliza blinked, looking at Alexander, "I'm sorry."

Alexander, reaching for her hand, opened his mouth to say something, but Thomas cut him off. "Don't apologize, in fact, we couldn't be happier to see you!"

Alexander looked at him skeptically, "Why?"

Thomas cleared his throat, "Jemmy, would you like the honors?" James quickly shook his head, having said too much already.

"As I suspected." Thomas said flatly, then lowered his voice until it was nothing more than a hushed whisper, "I must confess that we haven't been entirely honest with you as well. My name isn't Samuel Johnson. It's Thomas Jefferson, and this is my friend and colleague, James Madison." He waved his hand gesturing at James, who nodded quickly in acknowledgement.

"Thomas Jefferson?" Alexander repeated, "As in author of the-"

"Yespleasedon'tsaythataloudinpublic." Thomas said quickly, "Jemmy had the idea to start a new- why don't we go somewhere more private?"

COMPANY

"Thank you," The Hamiltons nodded as Thomas held open the door to his apartment. Alexander and Eliza ducked through the door, their arms still wrapped around each other protectively. James quickly scampered into the room and began placing books on their proper shelves, putting empty drinking glasses and plates on the table, hastily trying to clean up the place for the lady.

"Sorry it's such a mess," James apologized, sitting on his cot in the corner, "Ever since I moved in with Tom, it's been rather cluttered, and... we didn't have the chance clean up today!"

Eliza laughed as she daintily alighted on a cushioned chaise by the fire and placed a discarded candle stub on the end table. "It's fine, James. I have brothers, I know how two bachelors live." She watched as Thomas sat on the chair across from her.

"We spend most of our time out in the city looking for Adams," he explained, "We don't typically find ourselves in much company, thus...."

"You don't find reason to keep the apartment in perfect order?" Alexander finished distastefully, making himself comfortable on the chaise. Thomas glared at him, then stopped suddenly, when he remembered he had to be welcoming.

James blushed as he joined the trio in the living area. While they had been speaking, he had quickly and poorly made his and Thomas's beds, adjusted the pillows and hid books that had wound up in peculiar locations.

"Right...." Thomas said tightly, still irritated by Alexander's comment.

"So?" Eliza leaned forward, "What was so important that we couldn't speak of in the square?" Alexander also leaned forward, even more interested than his wife.

Thomas grinned, happy to move to a topic with which he was less testy. "I heard that you were an aid to General Washington, Mr. Hamilton."

Alexander nodded slowly, unsure of why that mattered, "...Yes, I was one of his closest and most trusted companions during the war. What of it?"

"Then I assume that you are very much a supporter of an independent America?" Thomas questioned.

He nodded enthusiastically, "Of course, I'd do anything for it."

"And you?" Thomas wondered, looking to Eliza.

Her head bobbed slowly, then more excitedly, "Yes, yes. My father was one of best generals in the war, Philip Schuyler, and he raised my siblings and I in a very patriotic fashion. I'm no more of a loyalist than any of you."

Thomas's lips twitched, but he looked at James, who nodded slightly, giving permission. "To put it plainly, Jemmy and I wish to start a new War of Colonial Rebellion."

Alexander and Eliza stared at them, unblinking. Thomas and

James stared back, shifting uncomfortably as they waited for a reaction.

Eliza burst into giggles and leaned back into the chair. The gears in Alexander's brain quickly began to turn and his face grew hopeful. Thomas's and James's faces turned the color of a British uniform, embarrassed by the girl's reaction. Eliza's face quieted and she quickly collected herself once she saw the fuming faces of the Virginians. "Oh," She realized, "you're serious."

The pair were still crimson but were lightening to pink. Alexander cleared his throat, "How, exactly, do you propose that we do this?"

"We plan to recruit significant and valuable assets to our cause and try to promote rebellion and sow seedlings of war in the colonies." Thomas explained. He frowned, suddenly seeing how hopeless it sounded. James blinked, his sweet face looking even more childlike than usual.

Alexander's hopeful face grew disappointed, as he evidently agreed with the plan's lack of substance, "Any specifics?" he sighed.

James quickly shuffled about in his seat as he searched his coat for his slip of paper, "Me, Tom, Adams, you, Aaron Burr, Dr. Franklin, the Marquis de Lafayette, and General Washington." He sheepishly looked to Alexander, mumbling, "I compiled this a few months ago, at the time it seemed...achievable." Despite his slight fame as a wordsmith, James often had trouble speaking the words that floated so easily from his pen to the page.

Eliza sighed and leaned against her husband, who seemed deflated. He slowly shook his head, "How long have you been at this?"

"Only a few weeks." Thomas said, "We've been predominately searching the city for Adams, but I believe that he may be in Boston. It's been a stroke of luck that we've come upon you, Mr. Hamilton, we doubted that we'd ever be able to find you."

Alexander frowned, his voice bitter, "The general's in jail, and Lafayette's overseas with Dr. Franklin. I've never even heard of Burr, but I suppose that he will be equally unreachable." He quickly stood to leave, pulling Eliza up with him. She looked stunned by his quick change in temper.

Thomas's eyes widened and he quickly grabbed Alexander by the arm, who turned to him, a flash of anger in his eyes. Thomas let go and stepped back, "Please, Mr. Hamilton, don't go. We'd just like to try, what's the harm in listening?"

Alexander looked at Eliza, his face softened, and they sat once more. James sighed in relief.

"Thank you," Thomas smiled, "My plan was that I'd write to Dr. Franklin to see if he would aid us."

"Lafayette was one of my closest companions," Alexander revealed, "It would be easy to convince him to come. He's quite an adventurous fellow, always to take a challenge. If I wrote, all I'd have to do is invite him and he'd come running."

"You haven't seen him in years," Eliza reminded him, "He might not be so eager to throw away his life. He could have a wife now, and children."

Alexander smirked, "He had a wife and child then, too."

Eliza considered this, "You still haven't seen him in a long while. Maybe he's grown used to France and wouldn't like to leave."

Alexander nodded at her, then turned to Thomas, "She has a

point. It won't be as easy as you think, Mr. Jefferson, not everyone will come just because you ask. Take Dr. Franklin for instance, the man's seventy-three, he won't be as willing to come as a younger man. And this Adams, he's just a ruffian who convinces drunks to toss tea into saltwater. He's no mastermind, he's just a crackpot criminal. There are few people who know my general better than I, and I know that he would not come just because an old acquaintance of his had some silly idea! He'd want sound logic and reasoning behind a plan. Whenever a battle is on the horizon, he always chooses the best possible course of action: whichever fight will be short, effective, and will not lose many lives. With your plan here, it's simply a surefire way to get everyone involved killed!"

Thomas's grip tightened on his chair, his face enraged, "It is not a silly idea! It is not! And who cares if nobody listens to me? At least I'll still have a plan and try to enact it, unlike you, you coward!"

Alexander shot to his feet, fists clenched, causing Thomas to rise on the defensive, "I am not a coward. I've seen more than you could ever imagine."

"Alexander...." Eliza's voice warned. James suddenly grew much less comfortable and began shifting in his chair.

"I've starved in the trenches," He continued, his eyes not wavering from Thomas's, "I've fought against everyone from plantation owners to Brits to even my own soldiers. Washington himself considered me one of his best, and he never gives compliments. Never. I am *not* a coward. Call me a coward one more time, I dare you."

Thomas opened his mouth to make a smart remark, but then

saw the nervous expressions on the little man and the lady. He blinked and tried to contain his anger, looking back at Alexander, "I apologize for speaking rashly and calling you a coward, will you forgive me?" he asked, though his voice was considerably calmer, it was still tinged with bitterness.

"I will not for-" Alexander began, but looked down when Eliza touched his knee. Her eyes were wary and commanding, silently reprimanding him. He sighed, nodded, and raised his eyes to Thomas, "I accept your apology. I hope that you will accept mine. I also spoke out of line, your idea isn't silly, it just seems impossible."

"It is *not* im-" Thomas thought better of his words and extended his hand, "I accept your apology." Alexander shook, and the two seated, though the looks thrown towards each other were less than pleasant.

"I understand that you would say it sounds impossible," James mumbled, "It does. I just hope that it's impossible enough to succeed."

The glares being thrown across the room halted on Alexander's part, and he turned his head to James, "What did you say?"

He shrank into his chair, shy, "I just hope it's impossible enough to succeed."

Alexander's frown slowly turned into a grin and he laughed, "Mr. Madison, I do believe that is a possibility."

"Huh?" Thomas and Eliza were confused.

He turned to his wife, "The plan *is* so ridiculous that it might actually have a shot at success!" She smiled slowly as she realized what he implied.

Thomas grinned, "So, you'll help us?"

Alexander nodded, "I'll certainly try. Come, Betsey!" He grabbed Eliza by the hand and picked up her bag, walking in a skipping gait.

"Wait, where are you going?" Thomas wondered, but Alexander was already out the door.

It was Eliza who answered, "We're going home. He wants to start writing." With that, James and Thomas turned to each other, faces beaming, hardly believing their luck.

ALEXANDER & ELIZA

"Alexander!" She laughed once she closed the door behind her. "What's the rush?"

He was halfway down the inn's steps when he answered her. "Two reasons. Reason one: I want to write my letter to Lafayette as soon as possible; and two: I don't think much of Jefferson. He seems awfully quick to judge and seemed to think less of me the moment I dragged you out of that massacre! He seems to think I'm just a mere puppet, ready to do his bidding."

"You barely know the man. Don't form such harsh opinions," Eliza told him, "When we were looking for you, he was very determined to help me find you, which I think is sweet, as he didn't have to do it. I think that you just have two personalities that clash, but I'm proud of you for choosing to help him and Mr. Madison."

Alexander smiled slightly, cheeks red, staring off into the night. He suddenly swirled around, and he smiled at her warmly, taking her hands in his. "I rented a flat a few blocks away. I was thinking that we could make a home in New York later on, near your parents. I thought that you'd like that."

"I would." Eliza said smiling sweetly, leaning against his shoulder as they walked. She just watched him, letting him guide her down the road.

Alexander looked at her, eyes sorrowful, "What is it?"

"It's nothing…" She whispered, "I just missed you."

He smiled, "I missed you, too."

They continued walking in silence, Alexander keeping his eyes on the road while sneaking glances at Eliza, who just watched him as he steered her. He sighed, "Tell me, something is bothering you. What is it?"

She frowned, sighing, "It's just that you worry me sometimes. Nothing's going to work out like those fantasies in your head, and that scares me because you're so impulsive, and that you talk yourself into the stickiest of situations. Just now with Mr. Jefferson, earlier today, the massacre. I barely paid attention to it 'til I heard you. It frightened the wits out of me, dear Hamilton. I was terrified in there, in all that death and blood, just wondering if you were alive." She sniffed and leaned her head against his chest, and he wrapped his arms around her.

"It didn't start out violent. Far from it, actually." Alexander whispered into her hair, "It was just an argument on politics. It was nothing serious, it was amusing, actually… but I want to make clear to you that I didn't set out to cause harm."

"I know you didn't." Eliza replied, looking up into his eyes, "It just was so frightening. Hearing your voice, but not seeing where you were. All that smoke – it made my eyes burn!"

Alexander nodded, and stroked her hair before they began walking again, "I know, I know. Imagine my surprise though, Eliza! Here I was, still stunned by all the sudden turn of events when I saw you, whom I thought was safe and sound in Albany, all petrified and screaming in the midst of all the smoke and bodies. It was awful, I tell you! Just plain awful, my Betsey!... Why did you even come here in the first place?"

Eliza laughed, "What was I supposed do to? Stay at home while you were here? Of course not. You're my husband, Alexander, and I love you with all of my heart. I'd follow you anywhere. If you had taken a ship to France, I'd be there right along with you. You're going to have to get used to the idea of having a companion. Somebody has to keep you out of trouble."

Alexander smiled, "Well, I'm flattered. But I would have preferred you being in Albany. This new war that Jefferson and Madison were speaking of…it seems like it will get messy."

Eliza shrugged, "Then I guess I better get used to getting my hands dirty."

He smiled at her. Eliza stopped for a moment, wondering, "How were you able to get out? Didn't the British know you were part of the massacre?"

Alexander shook his head, "No. I only went into the thick of it all when I saw you. I had been hanging on the outskirts, knowing that nothing good would come of it. I didn't have any blood or powder on me, so when I brought you to the bench, I just claimed that you thought I was in the fighting. Soldiers didn't even doubt it."

It wasn't long before they arrived at the inn and Alexander inserted the key into the door. He turned the knob and kicked the door open. He smiled and held Eliza's luggage out to her. She looked at him quizzically, but accepted it. "What do you need me to hold it-"

In a sudden flurry of laughter, auburn hair, and white and blue fabrics, Eliza found herself swept off her feet and cradled in her husband's arms. "Welcome home, Mrs. Hamilton." Laughing, arms wrapped around his neck, she kissed him on the cheek as his strong arms carried her into their apartment.

He sat her on the small bed in the corner and sat in the chair across from her. Elbows resting on his knees, he watched her, smiling. "I've missed you."

"And I you." Eliza, setting the bag aside, jumped to her feet and enveloped his head in her hands. She kissed his nose and lips, and he leaned forward, then hesitated, seeming to remember something, and pulled away.

Eliza frowned, but Alexander took her hands in his. His warm blue eyes locked her chocolate own, "As much as I'd love to continue, my Betsey, I have to write to the marquis." With that, he kissed her hands and turned to the desk behind him. He pulled out the inkwell, quill, and paper, ready to begin writing.

She wrapped her arms around his neck and leaned her chin on his shoulder, watching his pen flicker over the page. His head leaned against hers, and Eliza couldn't help but feel a sense of disappointment. She had come all this way for him, and yet their moments of intimacy had been so short. Was this how it was to be? Was the magic of courtship gone? Or was this just the result of Mr. Madison and Mr. Jefferson, pulling his thoughts from wife to work?

But she knew in her heart that it was only temporary, that Alexander would be entirely hers, as soon as his letter was done.

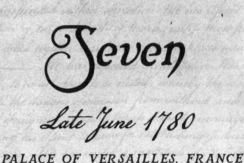

Seven

Late June 1780

PALACE OF VERSAILLES, FRANCE

BEN, LAFAYETTE, & ADRIENNE

Dr. Benjamin Franklin fingered the two letters curiously. One, addressed to him, was covered in a simple childish scrawl, handwriting he recognized, but couldn't quite place. The other was in fancy calligraphy, the writer proudly displaying his swirling penmanship. They were both from the same place, Franklin could tell that by just looking at the stamps, which were matching. They were from Philadelphia, his hometown. The wax on his letter had been stamped with haste, whereas the other had been stamped carefully, like the writer had been trying to make a good impression.

As he walked, he could hear a chorus of greetings as he passed the many French men and women in the halls, to each he nodded politely, distracted by the letters. The letters, for reasons he could not explain, filled him with the sudden urge to read them, to reply to them as soon as he was able. Ben moved swiftly, as swiftly as his old legs could carry him. At age seventy-four, he was still fit as a fiddle (albeit a very frail fiddle, but still), and was one of the most respected and famous men in the world.

He wasn't welcomed everywhere in the world, though. When he had been younger, the English had showered him with affection whenever he stepped foot into their country. Now, he knew, that entering England meant death. America was the same. If it was its own country, not ruled and dominated by England's tyrannical shadow, it would be a different story. He'd be one of America's greatest heroes; he'd be awarded high honors, and children would follow him through the streets, gazing at him in wonder. But going to America also meant death.

It was in France that he could find a place he called safety. Friendly with America during the War of Colonial Rebellion, Ben had been the one who had tried the hardest to convince the French to join the fight. France, though she sent weapons and supplies into the hands of the patriots, had been reluctant to join them in battle. They were still recovering from the Seven Years War, the French officials had told Ben, and as much as they wanted to aid America in their pursuit of justice, it just wasn't possible.

It was possible, France could have easily sent troops and attacked the British, helping win America their freedom. But that was the reason they weren't helping. France was in a state of poverty, the aristocrats living in luxury, the poor barely making it by. If France had joined in the fight, it would be like handing over the kingdom. Ben knew that the poor would rebel eventually, that if France had joined the fight, they'd only be encouraging behavior that they wished to avoid in their own country, behavior that would be inevitable.

Still, he was grateful for their hospitality. King Louis XVI had allowed him to stay on, even after Britain had won the war. The French people adored him, the king had told him when Ben had approached him about his departure, so, why leave safety for almost certain death? Besides, it didn't hurt that the king had the world's most famous scientist living within his borders.

As Ben walked through the corridors, he found himself in a nearly abandoned wing. It was the wing in which he spent most of his time, where his own and the apartments of his closest companions were. He stopped when he reached a chamber, his destination. As he raised his hand to knock on his friends' door, he heard a frightening cry, causing him to step back in surprise.

"Gilbert! You moved!" a woman shrieked.

"I'm sorry, *mon amour!*" a man's voice called back. Ben sighed and pulled at the door, which opened with ease. He strolled in, holding the letters behind his back, and observed the bizarre scene before him.

Gilbert was sitting in the center of the room, kneeling. His knee rested on a pillow, and he was pointing his sword towards the sky, like he was slicing the air while in battle. His wife, Adrienne, was seated in a well-cushioned chair, a paintbrush in her hand. She dabbed a bit of color onto the canvas in front of her and stared at it for a moment in dismay.

"I didn't get your sword quite right." She stated, disappointed.

Gilbert lowered his sword and walked behind her, gazing at the portrait. He rested his hand on her shoulder as he studied her work, "It looks fine to me." He admitted, not seeing the problem.

She shook her head, "That's just it. It's fine. It's not great, it's just *fine*." Adrienne scowled, grabbed a palette knife, and began chipping off the wet paint. Gilbert returned to his previous position, sighing. This had evidently happened many times before, and from what Dr. Franklin could tell, Gilbert was tiring of it. He looked up when he saw a flicker of movement coming from the corner of the room.

"*Bonjour, Monsieur* Franklin!" He exclaimed, jumping up to greet his friend. He sheathed his sword and embraced the doctor, kissing his two cheeks. Gilbert pulled Ben to a chair near Adrienne's, which Ben eased into gratefully. Gilbert sat on the floor looking up at the man in gleeful fascination, the way a child would when listening to a particularly intriguing story.

"*Monsieur* Lafayette." Ben nodded to the young man, then to his wife, "*Madame* Adrienne."

Adrienne wasn't paying attention to Ben, her focus was on Gilbert, still on the floor. She pointed angrily to a chair, which Gilbert sheepishly took, though he continued looking at the floor longingly.

"Letters? From America!" Lafayette looked at the papers in Ben's hand after tearing his eyes from the comfortable marble. Ben nodded slowly, and the young marquis snatched the one for him.

Lafayette quickly opened his note and scanned the handwriting. "Hamilton." He stated, looking back to his companions, "It's from my good friend, Alexander Hamilton, one of my closest friends during the war. He was *mon* general's aide-de-camp." He returned to the letter and began reading it aloud. His thick accent was hard to understand, as Lafayette still had trouble reading English and he often stumbled through words.

"*Mon* dear friend, Lafayette," He read, translating some of the words into his native tongue, "I haven't written in months. It's been ages since I've felt safe enough to do so, and even now *mon* hand shakes as I pen these words. I cannot make small talk, for the reason for me writing is imperative. I just wish that this letter was one simply inquiring about your wellbeing! But, alas, it is not. I assume that you know the dreadful state in which my country is in? The red gleam of uniforms is all that I ever see anymore! Whenever I walk the streets of the city, I'm constantly looking over *mon* shoulder, looking to see if I am being followed by undesirable men of the crown wanting to make my acquaintance. Recently, however, I have been approached by your friend Mr. Jefferson, along with one his colleagues. The two of them have concocted a plot to start a new revolution; one, I believe, could be possible, if only you would help us! You were one of the best generals in the entire war, one of the few people the soldiers treated with respect – one of the few people *I* respect. If anyone could inspire courage in the hearts of the American people, it is you. Before you shake your head and mutter to yourself, *non* it is *mon* general, remember that the general is imprisoned. Currently, you, along with Dr. Franklin, are the most famous – free – patriots. You, with your strategy, inspiration, bravery, and, quite frankly, stupidity on the battlefield, and Dr. Franklin with his own charm and negotiation abilities on the political and social side of fighting for our freedom. That is why, I beg of you, Lafayette, please come and fight once more for our cause! Besides, we may or may not be planning to relieve the general from his prison sentence. Your humble servant, A. Hamilton."

Both Ben and Adrienne looked at Lafayette, wondering what his reaction would be. Lafayette slowly lowered the letter away from his face and smiled eagerly at his two companions.

"I'll go at once! Doctor, you shall come, too! For freedom and liberty! To save *mon* general! *Au revoir*, my Adrienne! Kiss little Patsy and Georgie on their cheeks for me! *Au revoir*! To save America! Goodbye, my country! Goodbye! And *bonjour* to my old friends! We shall soon reunite and fight for America!" Lafayette, by the time he had finished speaking, had made his way into his bedchambers, found his luggage, and was quickly cramming different odds and ends into it: his war uniform, his hat, some stockings, shirts, a waistcoat, his trousers and undergarments, shoes, and more stockings. He looked around for his sword before realizing he was wearing it. He shoved his spyglass into the bag, along with money. Bags of golden francs, silver and copper coins, rolls of paper dollars. Money, heaps and heaps of it.

Back in the parlor, Ben sighed and turned his attention to his own letter, knowing what was to come next. Adrienne stood and made her way to the bedroom

"Gilbert!" Adrienne marched over to her husband and slapped him, he looked at her, stunned and dazed.

"I'll write." He mumbled, rubbing his stinging cheek.

"You're not going." She told him.

This caught his attention. He frowned and grabbed the handle of his handbag, "And why is that?"

"Because I barely see you anymore!" She exclaimed, her anger melting away into an upset, sniffling rant, "Your children hardly even know you! Georgie doesn't even know to call you 'dada'! You're always off on some...adventure! You're either with the Freemasons or reminiscing about the war, looking through your old maps and your letters and your uniforms! You've only known Patsy for about a year! I've known you for nine, but it feels like we haven't talked in seven! I just want to get to know you, Gilbert, is that too much to ask?" Lafayette lowered his travel bag and looked at his teary-eyed wife, a startled, troubled expression on his face.

He hadn't ever thought of it that way before, but the more he thought about it, the more he realized that Adrienne was correct. He *was* always away, either talking politics with friends, or talking war with the Freemasons. Whenever he was home, he liked to shift through letters from his general and his war friends, thinking about how he'd rather be fighting in the dirt than living lavishly in a palace. His children, Lafayette saw through new eyes, didn't ignore him, as he had originally thought, but he ignored and avoided them. He hadn't spent time with Adrienne in ages, the portrait being the first activity they had done together since, since...when? He couldn't remember. Sure, he remembered playing chess and talking literature with her when they were children, but he couldn't recall anything recently.

Lafayette had been avoiding his own family.

"*Mon Dieu, mon Dieu.*" Lafayette sank onto the bed slowly and covered his head with his hands, blinking and shaking his head in shock and regret. "I can't believe what I've done, oh Adrienne, I can't believe what I've done." Adrienne sat beside her husband and put her arm around him. She rocked him back and forth slowly.

"It's all right." She repeated softly, wiping away her tears, trying to ignore Lafayette's own, "It's all right."

"But it's not." Lafayette told her, "You're right. I don't even know you anymore. I just know the fourteen-year-old you. I don't even know my own children. I don't know Georgie's favorite toy, or Patsy's favorite animal. Nothing. Their names, that I know. Nothing. Nothing. Nothing!" He moaned in frustration and turned away from her.

"I don't blame you, Gilbert, *mon amour*." Adrienne whispered, scooting closer to him, resting her head on his shoulder, "not in the slightest. You're overwhelmed, that's all."

"Overwhelmed?" he laughed crazily, looking back at her, "How am I overwhelmed? I've just been doing the same things over and over again. I hardly pay any proper attention to you. Not the attention that I should. I've been so selfish, just wrapped up in my past."

Adrienne sighed, though she didn't deny his words, "You're a country boy, not a city boy. You've been a soldier for years. As soon as you came home, you were invited everywhere, Gilbert. It's been two years, and you're still the talk of Versailles. It's too much for you. You're trying to focus on your happiest moments, when you were away from all the hustle and bustle of Paris, and just doing what you do best. Fighting. Gilbert, I want to be part of your happiest times, I want to make *new* happiest times. I just don't want you to be killed before I get a chance to have time with you. To get to know the Marquis de Lafayette, my husband."

Lafayette gazed at the parchment in his hands. His eyes

flickered over his friend's words, looking at them differently. He rested his head on Adrienne's for a moment, then kissed her on the forehead. They smiled sadly at each other for a second. He nodded and got to his feet, leaving her in their room.

He began walking back into the sitting area, where Dr. Franklin had finished reading his own letter, one from Thomas. "I agree with Adrienne." Ben said flatly. Lafayette nodded, miserable. Adrienne made her way into the sitting room and sat back in her chair. She sighed and smiled, gladdened by the turn of events, though slightly saddened by her husband's disappointment. She studied her painting and began making adjustments to it. Lafayette sat on the chair facing Ben, waiting to hear what he had to say.

"You do need to spend time with your family, Gilbert, I would know. I had a son." Ben said.

Lafayette frowned, realizing what Ben was implying, "*Je suis désolé*," he apologized.

Ben shook his head, "He's still alive. We just don't like to acknowledge each other's existence. He was one of the best things that ever did happen to me, though. I would've done anything for him. I just didn't spend much time with him. Eventually, when he was all grown-up, I began spending more time with him. I used my position to benefit him. I even made him a governor in America, but in doing so, I made him a loyalist. We don't speak to each other now." Ben paused and stared a hole into the ground, "I'd give anything to rewind time, to tell myself to spend more time with him. You have time now, Lafayette. Use it. Spend it with your family."

Lafayette smiled, it was a sad smile, but appreciative of the old man's words. "*Merci*, sir. I plan to do so as soon as I can."

Ben smiled back at him, "Good. Now, the other reason I agree with Adrienne is far more political. The letter I received was from Jefferson. He laid out the basics of his plan, and I think that it's impossible. It's more likely to get him, and all those involved killed than to start a war. It would be a British victory, and if the two of us were there as well, we'd only be the most talked of prisoners. It'd be a death wish to go."

"I think it sounds exciting." Lafayette admitted, "but I see your point, *mon amie*. I will not go. In fact, I'll try to convince *mon* friends to halt their plan, that way they stay safe. I only fear...." He trailed off, unsure of how express himself in English.

"What is it?" Ben asked, then read the concerned look on the marquis's face, "Oh, I see. Jefferson likely won't pay you any heed. He has nothing to lose. He's pigheaded at times. Stubborn. Is it he whom you worry over, or is it your friend?... What was his name again?"

"Hamilton." Lafayette explained, "He is even more stubborn and impulsive than Jefferson. I don't know if he's married, but if he is.... I fear that she may soon become a widow, if what he says is true. If they really plan on releasing *mon* general, then they're in for quite a battle. I just hope I can help, in whichever way I can."

Lafayette quickly left in search of pen and paper. If he could convince Alexander to stop rebelling, then he could – wait. Was it right to send his friend a note asking him to stop, when he didn't truly believe that his friend should stop? *Non*, Lafayette decided, it was not. He would encourage Alexander in every way he could, sending everything that the new rebellion required. What did they need? Money, he could send money. He had plenty of that. Weapons. He could buy weapons, along with ammunition, uniforms, anything he could think of. He may not be able to go in person, but he hoped that his colleagues would sense his spirit.

Ben smiled, happy that the young man wasn't sending himself and others to their doom. Maybe he was becoming soft in his old age, but he didn't want anybody to die.

Adrienne smiled; she was happy as well. Gilbert would be staying, he'd try to spend more time with her and their children. She couldn't wait to get to know him again…. She began thinking about the different activities they could do. There was this upcoming ball, and they could stroll in the palace gardens in the starlight, and – oh! She just couldn't wait!

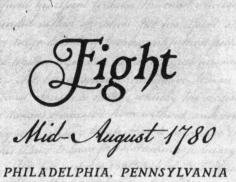

Fight

Mid-August 1780

PHILADELPHIA, PENNSYLVANIA

ELIZA

My Dearest Angelica, Eliza dipped her quill into the inkpot, considering her first sentence. There was so much to say! There was so little to say. She wished she could tell her sister all that was happening, but she knew she couldn't. It would risk everything. Receiving letters from her sister was now one of the few bits of stability in her life, even if all of her replies were filtered.

Ever since she and Alexander had partnered with Thomas and James, Eliza's life had almost tipped completely upside down. She had grown accustomed to answering to the name "Mrs. Lawrence" and calling Alexander "Johnathan" in public. She knew not to speak to anyone outside of their circle confidentially, as they might be a spy for the British. She was used to keeping her eyes peeled for any men that looked even the slightest like Mr.

Adams. She had also become exceedingly well-versed in politics and military-strategy (and she was the daughter of a general!) It had become second-nature for her, all of the strangeness; it had become a new sense of normalcy.

But only the letters were the true normalcy. She had forgiven her sister Peg, and was now corresponding with her regularly, though she didn't write as freely as she did to Angelica. Of course, none of her mail was sent, or addressed, to her. It was sent to a Mrs. Lawrence and was delivered to Thomas's flat, who would then give the letters to Eliza when she would visit. Angelica, her sister with whom she was closest, was her favorite pen-pal. With a completely different outlook on life, Angelica often helped Eliza see things in a different light, something she found particularly comforting now. Her letters were often full of wit and bits of wisdom that Eliza treasured with all of her might. Even if nothing applied to her situation.

She sighed, ever since the massacre, tensions had changed in the city. The colonists had been and still were outraged by the deaths, though their fervor had simmered in the months past. Ten men had died, but the British barely acknowledged the massacre beyond a hasty public apology for their image. Rumors about the massacre and anti-British stories began to circle. The colonists seemed to be stronger than they had been before, though still weak and feeble. It imbittered her, knowing the British had tried to cover up the story as easily as they could. Although she felt awful about those ten men, she was gladdened that their deaths had brought her, along with other colonists, closer to revolution – though they didn't know it yet.

Eliza moved her mind from the dark thoughts and back to her sister. She was about to dab her quill to the page when she heard an irritated groan. She quickly set her pen aside, knowing that Alexander was now upset about something and, whenever he was irked, wanted a good listener.

He was leaning against the closed door of their apartment, holding a letter in his hands. It was wrinkled, like he had crumpled and uncrumpled the parchment many times over. His eyes were closed, his face calm. His tri-corner hat was slumped, almost deflated looking.

"What is it?" She asked. Alexander looked up at her and sighed in frustration, slapping his cap onto the coatrack. He waved the letter in the air as he tossed his waistcoat onto their bed.

"This. Just came today off the ship. It's from Lafayette." He explained, his voice was slightly lower than usual, a sign that Eliza knew well. He was angry and trying to control his temper.

"Well, that's wonderful." She said casually and began folding his waistcoat once she sat on their bed, "What did he say?"

"He said nothing good." Alexander exclaimed and began pacing in front of her, "'*Monsieur* Hamilton,'" he began to read, "'I greet you happily! I'm happy you are safe, and away from harm, *mon amie*. Sadly, I bring you sad news. I am unable to come and attack the British redcoats with you. I wish I could come, but it recently came to *mon* mind that I haven't been spending the proper amount of time with *mon* family. In fact, I haven't spent any time with them since I've arrived in *mon* homeland. In *mon* place, I shall send money, along with supplies, such as clothing, weapons, and ammunition. If you desire anything else, write and you shall receive.'" Alexander's voice became increasingly aggravated with each sentence he read.

"He's not coming!" He exclaimed, "How is he not coming? The Lafayette I know would be on the fastest ship here, carrying his sword up in the air and flashing a smile to all the colonists as he arrives. How can he not be coming?" Alexander raised his fist and punched the air, "He's the most charming man I know, the one who could make everyone get along, and he's not coming! What am I to do? Oh, what am I to do?" He ran his fingers through his chestnut locks in despair.

"I, for one, think that he has noble reasons for not coming." Eliza said, "Family is very important, and he shouldn't neglect his to come at your beck and call."

"But I *want* him to come at my-" Alexander paused, considering what she had to say, "I see your point. When you say it like that, I do support him staying. But when it comes to the rebellion-"

"He's your best smooth-talker, best free general, best fighter, best everything?" She set aside the coat and laid down on her back, so she was looking at the ceiling, with her feet dangling off the edge of the bed, hovering inches above the floor. She fiddled with the necklace around her neck as she waited for an answer.

He sighed, "Regrettably so. The plan suddenly just seems so hopeless." He laid down beside his wife, propping his head up with his arm, "I mean, what are we to do? He says that he'll send money and supplies, but we have no use for them at this time, or even a place to properly store them. By the time word gets to him that we've no need for such things, we'll be up to our heads in muskets and canons!" He grasped her hand and stared at their entwined fingers.

"Don't you think that you're overreacting just a bit?" Eliza asked, curling into the crook of his arm, "I doubt that he'll send a shipload of supplies." She grinned playfully up at him, but he frowned sadly down at her, closing his eyes.

Alexander shook his head slowly, opening his eyes to look back at her, "This is Lafayette we're talking about, he once bought an entire regiment guns, clothing, and ammunition. His pockets are practically endless, and he's passionate about the rebellion. He'll send shiploads! I just wish that he was here instead of this-this-this letter!" he tossed it aside, causing it to roll to the edge of the bed. Eliza's eyes lingered on it before turning back to her husband.

"I best go off to find Jefferson and Madison, and explain what has come up." Alexander eased himself into a sitting position, and looked back at his Betsey, who was still lying quite comfortably on the bed. "Would you like to come along?"

She smiled but shook her head, sitting up beside him, "I'll stay. I'd like to finish writing a letter to Ann, and I have to go shopping. You go." She kissed him on the cheek before he stood.

Alexander nodded, short and quick and understanding. "I'll see you in an hour or so, then. Tell Ann I say hello." He turned to go, then looked back at her, "Love you."

"And I you." She smiled back at him.

Eliza watched as the door closed. She hoped that he wouldn't get into too much trouble. Alexander could be a handful at times, as there were very few people that truly paid him any mind. He had a strong personality, one that had been drowned out by many other strong personalities in the war, one that often clashed with most of his colleagues. Jefferson was a person that he disliked with passion. It was a pity, Eliza thought, as he and Thomas were so similar. Lafayette, she knew, was one of the few people that he liked, she supposed that was why he had taken the Frenchman's refusal so hard.

She picked up the crumbled letter and slowly unwrapped it, searching for where Alexander had left off. It was such pretty calligraphy, she thought. Eliza wished she could write as prettily as the marquis, but she knew that even if she could, her phrasing would be just as awkward and clumsy as the Frenchman's. She supposed her longing was a side-effect of living with and being the wife of a brilliant wordsmith, one with penmanship just as stunning as the words he penned. It didn't help that her two other companions were just as gifted in the department of word-craft, all three of the men always seeming to know exactly how to say something elegantly, while also cutting straight to the point. She wished she had that ability. She shook her head, dragging her thoughts away from wistful thinking and towards the task at hand.

If you desire anything else, write and you shall receive. I do hope, with all of mon *might that you will be able to start a new war, one that you win. This plan I hear to free* mon general, *I hope it succeeds as well. I wish you the best of luck. But, Alexander, please do not do anything rash!!*

Signed, the Marquis de Lafayette, Eliza noted. She smiled when she read the man's last line. He apparently knew her husband well, but not well enough, she knew, to know that he was probably doing something rash the very moment those words were penned.

Late September

THOMAS

Thomas sighed as he leaned back in his chair. James was sitting beside him, gazing into the hearth, a disappointed look on his face. They had been searching for Adams every day for months, to no avail. The man seemed to have vanished from the face of the Earth.

Thomas glanced at his companion, whose brow was furrowed, whose arms were crossed. Thomas could tell James was thinking of all the places that they had searched. He couldn't think of a place that they hadn't.

It had been months since they had begun looking, and now, even they were beginning to admit defeat. Alexander and Eliza had both searched endlessly for Adams, but after the first few months of looking, the young Hamiltons had begun to give up. Eliza had turned to housekeeping, and to making sure her three male companions were taking care of themselves (they often forgot to eat and would work themselves to death before being reminded of sleep.) Alexander had found himself a somewhat stable job as a lawyer's assistant, and the couple had begun to turn their minds to more domestic activities, trying to find a larger home and getting their daily routine in order. Alexander had continued searching during the rare times when he was not working or with his wife, still hopeful, but had slowly dwindled away from the daily searches as his temper clashed more and more with Thomas's. When Lafayette had written to Alexander, that had been the final straw. He had nearly given up on searching for Adams, on the new rebellion altogether, just appearing to search once a week, if that.

Now, Thomas and James were beginning to feel the hopelessness of the situation as well.

"It's useless, searching." James said, to himself or his companion, Thomas couldn't tell.

"It appears to be." Thomas had taken a blow as well. About the time Alexander received a letter from Lafayette, Thomas had received one from Dr. Franklin. Much to his disappointment, Thomas's old mentor encouraged him to give up the resistance, to instead try to give into his talents. Become a music teacher, or a professor at a university, Ben had suggested, just don't try to get yourself killed. He had very nearly gotten himself killed when he wrote the former declaration. How would searching for Adams affect that?

Still, the letter had brought subjects to light that Thomas had been trying to avoid: the longer they search, Adams only seemed to be further and further away. He also tried to not think about his depleting funds: Thomas's and James's fortunes, their only form of income, were shrinking, and he knew the two of them couldn't go on much longer without finding jobs of some sort.

Alexander's and Eliza's near abandonment had also smacked Thomas's usual self-confidence, but it was the letter that had begun to eat away at it. He thought of the letter's suggestions constantly, the temptation of running away to some country town, creating a new identity for himself, and becoming a teacher. He also knew that he couldn't leave behind his best and closest friend. So, he stayed, even if his enthusiasm was being drained.

James, Thomas could tell, was feeling his own confidence turn to dust. James still searched persistently for Adams, but the little man's personality had taken a turn for the worst. He rarely spoke, even to Thomas, and never on his own accord. He only ever spoke when he was posed with a question; and when he did speak, his answers were short, few word sentences with a tint of anger and despair in his tone. Thomas often saw his friend rocking on his feet, his nervous habit, and wrinkling his list of names, which he always kept in his pocket. Even Little Jemmy was losing hope.

Thomas wondered if they would ever start a new war, or if America would just become a footnote in the world's history.

Nine

ADRIENNE & LAFAYETTE

"Daddy! Daddy!" Lafayette bent down and scooped up his daughter as she wobbled towards him. She grabbed his hat and poked his ear. Lafayette grimaced for a moment, but smiled widely when she giggled; his heart was warmed.

They were in the sitting room, Lafayette and Adrienne; Georgie and Patsy. Adrienne was sipping tea with Georgie on her lap, and she was smiling. She smiled as she watched her husband ruffle Patsy's hair, stick out his tongue, and make crazy eyes.

Ever since she had reprimanded him, nearly six months before, Lafayette had tried to be an active part of his children's lives. She knew that he was falling in love with them: the way his eyes lit up when Georgie had finally called him 'Daddy'; the way he played endless games of 'tea party' with Little Patsy. If anything,

Adrienne believed, he had begun spoiling them. He only searched for the best of toys, even taking his old playthings out of retirement (though Patsy didn't share his fondness of the beautifully crafted toy soldiers, and Georgie thought that they were teethers). They followed him everywhere that he went, Patsy skipping behind him as he walked and conversed with Dr. Franklin, and Georgie stumbling to him whenever Lafayette was seated.

Sometimes Adrienne thought that they preferred him to her.

Despite all his attention to his children (and his Adrienne, the two of them often took nightly walks through the palace halls, and Lafayette had been posing for many more portraits by his wife. He and Adrienne had also become formidable at chess,) Adrienne could tell there was something on his mind. He always seemed distracted. Even when he was discussing one of his favorite topics he would stare off into the distance longingly, sometimes minutes at a time before continuing the conversation. Ben had noticed it too. Adrienne had had many long conversations with him, trying to figure out what the problem was. Adrienne knew it was obvious, and so did the doctor, they just kept trying to walk around the answer.

When Lafayette had gone through his different toys in search of games for their children, he had immediately repainted some of the little French and British soldiers, coloring them a dark navy blue: the color of the Continental army. Though Patsy would always push them aside to make room for her dolls, Lafayette paid special attention to the little army, separating them into different battalions, always giving his mismatch of French and American soldiers the upper hand over the toy Britons.

Whenever Adrienne was painting, Lafayette, sword in hand, would regale her with stories about his adventures in America. He would describe them vividly, sometimes even stabbing the air with his sword, dramatically reenacting past battles, and impersonate different officers, then realize he was supposed to stay still.

Adrienne also knew of the large amount of money that had mysteriously disappeared from Lafayette's account no more than a day after he had received that Hamilton letter. And how all of the books he had been reading were either on war strategy and/or history. And that he wrote to his colonial friends nearly every week.

Lafayette was still filled with nostalgia, even if he was paying his family attention. Nearly all of his thoughts, though, were about this new war that wasn't even started. Adrienne doubted about it would ever start, his friends were just trying to hopeful.

She missed when they were children, and how Gilbert's thoughts were only about his studies and how to amuse her and her four sisters. She expected things to be the same even after they married; but as soon as it happened, he had been sent off to the army. He had rarely ever been home, and when he was, it was only for brief visits. Then he had gone off and joined the Freemasons, and all he would ever talk about was independence and how he was in the same club as those American rebel leaders. Only months later, without warning, did he decide to leave for the colonies, not thinking to tell Adrienne about his decision in advance. He had fought for ages it had seemed, and returned only when it was too dangerous to stay. Then he was showered as a hero in France. He finally started getting to know his wife again, along with his children. And still all he thought about was his glory days back when he was third-in-command of the Continental army.

Adrienne knew that she wasn't being entirely fair. She could understand that her husband missed something that never even existed; but she also knew that she wasn't being unreasonable in wanting his complete attention at times. She just wished he could understand that.

She set the teacup on a coaster and began bouncing Georgie on her knee. Patsy hugged her father's neck, then began sliding off the lounge chair. Her little legs shook as she ran over to Adrienne, who patted her curls lovingly. Almost immediately after she left, Lafayette grabbed hold of a thick volume that was sitting on the nearby table. He opened it to its bookmarked page and began to read. It was a book on strategy, and he had been studying it intensely in the past few weeks, hoping to find any bit of information that he didn't already know. Any information that might be of use to his friends in America.

After searching through the pages for a few moments, he slammed the book down in frustration. He stood up and began to walk back and forth in a march-like pattern. Adrienne looked on in pity and was happily distracted by Patsy demonstrating her skipping abilities.

Lafayette sighed. His pace became more hurried, his face more irritated and wild-looking. He longed to be away from the palace, to be doing something more productive than just reading his textbooks. His fists clenched and unclenched, so hard that it looked as though his bones might shoot out of his skin. He closed his eyes, knowing that there was nothing else that he could do for his far-off friends. He couldn't send supplies, as Alexander had written to him saying that the weapons would just add suspicion. He couldn't convince the king to send troops, as there was officially no war for them to fight, just a group of revolutionaries with a plan. He'd go there himself, but he had agreed to spend time with his family.

Lafayette turned to look at them. It was a perfect little family, the three of them: Adrienne, Patsy, and Georgie. He just didn't understand how he couldn't focus on them. He loved them with all of his heart, but he could never stop thinking about war. Not for long periods of time. Even when he tried to avoid thinking about it, it always somehow wormed its way into his thoughts, igniting his passion for the subject with a new fire each time. He wished he could switch the rebellious part of his brain off, but he never could.

He sighed, longingly looking at his family, feeling the invisible barrier that kept him from fully coming into their lives, but not knowing how to overcome it.

He didn't see how he could nurture his passion for America's freedom *and* focus on spending time with his family. He wished he knew how.

LAFAYETTE

Lafayette laughed as he brandished his sword, riding through the field on his snowy white Arabian mare. The redcoats leaped out of his path as he led his squadron against the Britons. He spied

Alexander in the distance, blocking a sword's slice with his rifle, then kicking the man to the ground. Ahead of him was General Washington, urging the men forward. He shouted to his men, remaining steadfast, stoic, and surprisingly calm under fire.

"*Attaque!*" Lafayette shouted to his men, "Force them to the river!" he pointed with his sword. He swerved in his saddle and watched as Washington gave him a nod of approval. Lafayette smiled.

He heard a pop of gunfire.

The great general put a hand over his chest, a surprised look on his face. The blood began to soak his shirt and spill onto his hand. He locked eyes with Lafayette, opening his mouth and closing it, but no words came out.

"Noooo!" Lafayette screamed, hand outstretched like he could save his general as Washington fell over in his saddle, eyes closed.

The world around him stood still. The noise of the battle seemed to disappear, and the scene seemed to slip away entirely. He couldn't tear his eyes from Washington, dead in his saddle. He felt his eyes beginning to water, and felt a great pang in his chest. He lifted his hand to his heart and bowed his head in respect, but was surprised when his hand felt wet. His uniform was growing stained. Red puddles surrounding the lapel of his uniform. He gasped, choking for air.

He was falling, falling. Screaming, screaming.

"Noooo!" Lafayette screamed, sitting up right.

"Hey, hey," Adrienne sat beside him, holding him. Her eyes were worried and frightened, but relieved that he was awake, "it's alright, it was just a bad dream."

He looked to her, his heart pounding hard, as though it would fly out of his body if it had enough momentum. He looked down and touched his chest, trying to convince himself that it truly was a bad dream. There was no hole, just smooth, pasty skin. He breathed slowly, and closed his eyes, then quickly opened them, still seeing the frightening image of the general, *his* general staring at him with his hand over his heart. He ran his fingers through his long chestnut hair, shaking his head.

Adrienne curled up beside him, sitting cross-legged, holding onto his shoulders, rubbing his back. "It's alright, *mon amour,* I'm here. Gilbert, what was it? What happened?"

He looked at her, her face nearly hidden in the shadows, and shuddered. He pulled the blankets closer around himself. "The general," he rubbed his nose and wiped a tear from his eye, "the general," his voice quivered. "We were in battle, we were winning…. He looked at me, really looked at me, Adrienne," he looked at her, and grabbed her chin, turning her face towards him. "He looked at me like he admired me, like he was about to say he was proud of me…."

"And?" Adrienne asked, leaning against him, eyes wide.

"He was shot." Lafayette stated. "He put his hand over his heart," he copied the motion, "and he was trying to tell me something, but-but-but no words came out." He cried. "Everything seemed to stop, and then my uniform became blood-soaked and I was falling off my saddle, I think I was shot-" he couldn't speak anymore. He just began to sob, shaking, covering his face with his hands, and sobbed.

Adrienne held him, trying to keep herself from crying. She tried to steady him, but he just kept shaking. He trembled erratically and laid back down, his head in her lap, crying.

She hugged him, whispering that it was just a dream, unable to keep herself from crying. They sat there, huddling in the darkness together, crying themselves to sleep.

ADRIENNE

"I'm worried, Ben." Adrienne said when he answered the door. She was standing out in the corridor, wringing her hands, shifting from foot to foot, her dress hanging limply on her thin frame. Dark puddles hung under her eyes from lack of sleep and crying.

The old man quickly stepped aside so she could enter. She practically stumbled into the room until she made it to the lounge chair in the sitting room.

"Whatever for?" Ben asked, although he could tell from the tone of her voice that it was nothing good.

"It's Gilbert. He's getting worse." Adrienne's voice was higher than normal and tinted with both fear and worry. Her face was sorrowful and pained. She looked at Ben with a tinge of hope in her eyes. She suddenly looked much older than her twenty-one years.

Ben sat across from her and looked at her pityingly, "Tell me. What's happened?"

Adrienne, her eyes still swollen from crying, began to speak. "Something's wrong."

"What has? Is it bad?" his voice was calm but urgent, pressing the lady to continue.

She nodded with such intensity that Ben felt himself grow cold. Her face grew pained and she ran a finger by her eye, like she was trying to wipe away non-existent tears, "Last night," her voice was unsteady, her face pale and haunted, "I woke up to the most frightful noise. It scared me, so I turned to wake Gilbert up to see if he heard it…but it was him, Ben! He was shaking and moaning and shouting. It just frightened me so that I just sat there, watching him kick and scream!" she shuddered, "Then he shot up like a bolt! Like somebody had tied a rope about him and yanked him up screaming. He was awake then, but he looked so frightened!" she closed her eyes, remembering the moment. "He was still shaking, I don't remember what I said to him, something about it just being a bad dream, then he just kept touching his chest, almost like he was trying to convince himself that it was still there. I just held onto him, and he tried to explain what happened. He was fighting in this field with the general, and the general was shot, then Gilbert was! Then he just started crying and trembling, and crying and trembling! He just kept shaking!" She cried, looking at her friend, "I'll never forget it, Ben, he just kept crying, then he fell. Ben, his head was in my lap," she sniffed, "And he just couldn't stop sobbing! Sobbing – he was crying like a baby! It was like he was little Georgie and he just couldn't stop! He just sat like that, his head in my lap, crying like a babe, for hours until he fell back asleep. It was hours before I could doze! I just couldn't go back to sleep Ben, I just kept rocking him and telling him it was alright. It was just so…horrible to see him like that!" She cried, putting her head in her hands, "I've never seen him so frightened, Ben! I don't think anyone has! Oh, Ben! What can I do? Tell me, what can I do?" She looked at him with such fear and hope, that he was speechless.

Ben looked at his young friend in shock and sorrow upon hearing her story. He handed Adrienne a handkerchief, which she dabbed her eyes gratefully with.

"Thank you." She whispered.

"Anytime." Ben replied, "Adrienne, I need to tell you something, but I don't know what you'll think of it."

She cried, "What? Tell me, Ben! What's wrong?"

"There's nothing exactly wrong," Dr. Franklin explained, "Gilbert just needs some help, and I think I know what he needs."

Adrienne nodded profusely, "Tell me. I'll do anything to make him better."

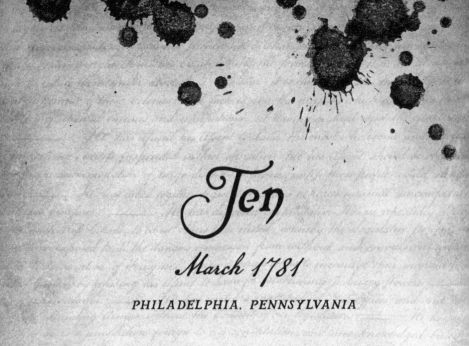

Ten

March 1781

PHILADELPHIA, PENNSYLVANIA

ALEXANDER, ELIZA, THOMAS, & JAMES

Eliza held Alexander's hand, his thumb caressing her fingers, stopping to smile when he touched her ring. It had been a year since they were wed, and each was happier than usual. Thomas and James walked behind the joyful couple. Their pace was significantly slower, their heads bent to the ground, confidence gone. Thomas took long slow strides, James quick short ones, just enough so that they would stay in pace with one another.

They were there for Eliza, who had become a close friend of the pair since her arrival the year before. Although they, particularly Thomas, didn't always get along with her husband (sometimes the fights grew violent,) the two did care about their sweet, even-tempered companion. They were always happy to see Eliza, especially when she came with Alexander, as she was the only one who could break up their quarrels peacefully.

Though Eliza had been worried that Alexander's work would pull them away from each other, it had only made their moments together sweeter. At times it was still as though they were in courtship. Alexander would sometimes surprise her with poems and love letters on the pillow beside her when he went to work before she awoke, and they still made time for enjoyment, sometimes going to the park or just staying at home, enjoying each other's company.

To celebrate their anniversary, Alexander had Eliza pick whatever she wanted to do, and promised that they would do it. Much to his surprise, she had insisted on bringing Thomas and James along for one final hunt to look for Adams, the first all of them had gone on in many months.

"It's not too late," Alexander said wistfully as she pulled him through the loading dock, "We could go out to a restaurant or a café, have dinner or-"

"What use would that be?" she asked him, "We're at least doing something productive. It's not like we can find him by sitting in a café."

"It could be a special café." He muttered. It appeared to be impossible to convince her to leave Thomas and James.

The four of them were clustered around the loading dock, looking at the different sailors and merchants and civilians gathered round to watch the ships. Alexander grimaced when he caught a whiff of the salty sea air. A group of civilians were all gaping at a large ship docked nearby, and Eliza turned to see what the commotion was.

It was massive, one of the largest ships any of them had ever seen. Its sails were lowered, and one of them caught the sun's glow, allowing the soft warm light to trickle down onto the deck, like a waterfall hitting the rocks. The bow was decorated in the shape of a mermaid. Her hands were folded, and she appeared to be rising up from the waves. The sailors busily rolled barrels down the ship via the boat ladder. The lettering, scrawled in a mesmerizing night-blue cursive, read *La Attaque*.

Alexander looked at the name confusedly, "Who would name a boat, 'the attack?'"

They watched as a young man dressed in a light blue French military uniform began walking down the gangplank. His hair was perfectly powdered, his hat perfectly perched. His gloved hand was resting on the hilt of his sword. He carried himself with such self-confidence, such poise, and had such a lovely posture, that Eliza had to fight the urge to curtsy. He waved happily at the crowd of civilians by the dock. His small, trim figure and tall, graceful height seemed to draw the eyes of all the nearby civilians. Despite his impressive appearance, they just stared at him like he was a dull attraction at a carnival, bored and emotionless. He smiled weakly. Then fell on his face.

He was just a few feet away from the dock when his foot caught on his leg, causing him to trip. He landed on the dock, his hands breaking his fall. His hat flew off, and his wig was askew, but he appeared unharmed. The Frenchman blinked in alarm as he realized what had happened. One of the sailors, a man of roughly forty years, helped the young officer to his feet.

"Are you all right, Mr. Motier?" The sailor asked. The soldier nodded, righted his wig and replaced his hat.

"I thank you for your help, *Monsieur*. Now, do you know where the – how you say?" The Frenchman's brow furrowed as he realized he didn't know the proper phrasing.

Alexander looked at Thomas, who was looking at him. They both looked at the Frenchman, then back at each other.

Alexander rushed forward, and, having his arm curled around Eliza's waist, (who was tending to James's tie, who had Thomas's hand on his shoulder) began dragging the three along, as well. He maneuvered his way over to the sailor and the foreigner, his hand held up in the air, "Excuse me, cousin?"

The Frenchman and the sailor looked up in alarm as Alexander approached. The sailor sized up the young man and seemed to think him an annoyance; the Frenchman, on the other hand, looked very gleeful about Alexander's joining of the conversation. The Frenchman hugged Alexander tightly and kissed both of his cheeks. He pulled away, grinning. Alexander chuckled lightly.

Eliza and James curiously looked at the Frenchman while Alexander conversed with the sailor. "This is my cousin, he doesn't know much English." He then looked to the Frenchman, "*Monsieur*, what have I told you about tripping?"

The Frenchman smiled happily at Alexander, and rushed to give him another hug and a kiss on the cheek, "I haven't been so excited in ages! May I bring *Monsieur* Adams? I found him on the ship!"

Alexander looked at the man dumbly and gave him the quick, dazed nod of his head.

"So you're Lafayette?" Eliza asked, sitting in a chair. She watched the marquis in fascination, who seemed delighted by her attention.

"*Enchanté.* Officially, it's Marie-Joseph Paul Yves Roch Gilbert du Motier, the Marquis de Lafayette." He clarified, sipping a cup of tea. "But *oui*, you can call me Lafayette, *mademoiselle.*"

They were in Thomas's apartment, a place where they could speak freely and not be crowded. Everyone was scattered about the place, Thomas and Alexander putting chairs around a table, James sitting *at* the table, Adams pacing the floor, and Eliza and Lafayette in the sitting area.

"It'd be *madame*, actually." Eliza told him, "I'm married."

"To whom?" Lafayette inquired, turning to look at the rest of the men, who now seemed angry at the seating arrangements.

"Me." Alexander grinned proudly, pushing a chair between James and Adams. It bumped James's elbow, causing the little man to glare up at the soldier.

"Well, congratulations!" Lafayette quickly set his cup on the table and ran over to his friend, whom he happily embraced. Alexander patted him awkwardly on the shoulder, looking down at the man affectionately, while also waiting impatiently for the Frenchman to finish. He had forgotten the marquis's love of hugs. Lafayette stepped back and shook Alexander's hand, "I don't recall you being married while you were in the army. When did this happen?" He looked at Eliza, then at Alexander, waiting for the answer.

Eliza blushed and fidgeted with a curl that had come loose from her pile of hair, "About a year ago."

Lafayette clapped his hands and grinned from ear to ear, "This is splendid and also incredibly disappointing!"

The entire group looked at him in confusion, wondering if they had heard him right. Alexander wondered if his friend had used the correct wording. The Frenchman wasn't as fluent in English as he believed. "...Why would it be disappointing?" he asked.

"Because, *mon amie*," Lafayette explained, "I figure that you'll get yourself killed sometime soon. You are too reckless." He smiled again and thumped Alexander on the back before sitting at the table.

"Thank you?" Alexander pulled out a chair for Eliza, who padded over to sit. He pushed her in and took the seat beside her. By now the rest of their companions were also seated, all ready to begin explaining the plan.

Alexander felt a new wind in his sails, the arrival of Lafayette and Adams revived their cause, and he felt just as patriotic as he had at the dawn of the first war. Thomas stood from his seat and thanked the group for gathering.

"Please, enough with the chit-chat." Adams snapped, "You all dragged me over here, and I'd like to know why."

Adams had been a sailor for the past few years, which was the reason nobody had been able to find him. He had, by chance, been hired by a Frenchman with the name of Motier to sail to Philadelphia. While sailing, he had recognized his young passenger and asked why he was returning to the colonies. Lafayette didn't say until Adams revealed his identity, and then he invited the man to join him in search of his friends.

"It's simple." Thomas said briskly, glaring at the man from Massachusetts.

"In a way." Alexander spoke under his breath, but his words were still audible. "I'd like to know," he said louder and more pleasantly, "why you're here, Lafayette. I thought that you couldn't come."

Lafayette shrugged, "So did I. Ever since I had returned from the war, you see, I had neglected *mon* family. I thought mostly about the war, and I got excited when you wrote to me, telling of your idea. Adrienne, *mon* wife, confronted me about it – not spending enough time – and I began spending more time with her and *mon* children. I still thought of America constantly, though, but it began to affect *mon* health in November. I had this horrible dream where *mon* general was killed and I was shaking and screaming all over. It frightened the wits out of Adrienne, and she told me to come here for a holiday. She told me to take as long as I'd like, so I assume that she gave me permission to fight. I'm not sure. Then, I bought a big boat and sailed, and here I am!"

"And Dr. Franklin?" Eliza asked, "Will he come as well?"

"*Non*." Lafayette shook his head sadly, "He thinks me coming here is a bad idea, though he's the one that told Adrienne to take me here. I think that he thinks that if I have enough of war that I'll get better. I have felt better lately, ever since I left, so maybe he's right."

"Wonderful." Alexander said bitterly.

"I know!" Lafayette grinned, not detecting the sarcasm.

"So, the most famous man in the world won't come here. Now what are we supposed to do?" Thomas thought aloud. Everyone turned to James, who shrank into his chair. He looked at his feet as he pulled out the slip of paper and handed it to Thomas.

Thomas looked at the list in dismay and back at James, clearly unsure of how to respond. James sighed and cleared his throat, face pink. He opened his mouth and nervously began to speak, haltingly and slowly, "Dr. Franklin isn't exactly... vital to my plan. He was just, um, there for a publicity and social standpoint. So, um, we will continue the plan exactly as...planned." He sighed deeply and looked immensely relieved at finishing his great speech.

"In case some of you have forgotten," Adams intervened, "not all of us know about your plan. Please, elaborate." He brushed back his greying hairs and scratched his nose, his eyes not leaving James for a second. James looked at Thomas and shook his head, he was not going to speak anymore.

"Sorry, we forgot," Thomas muttered, "Jemmy and I – well, Jemmy actually – planned that once we found and recruited you, Lafayette, and Hamilton, that we would first break General Washington out of jail, so he can lead an army, and then break out Aaron Burr. Burr is, we believe, a confident of Governor Arnold, who, as you know, was a former general in the War of Colonial Rebellion. Burr was placed under his command several times, so we have reason to believe that the two knew each other. Also, Burr has been imprisoned much longer than the average soldier, which might be the result of Arnold wanting to continue their relationship without meeting Burr on the streets. All evidence further confirms our theory."

"That is just what it is." Adams stated angrily, "A theory. You don't have any proof that this 'Aaron Burr' is still imprisoned because the governor wishes him to be. For all you know, he could be imprisoned for misbehavior!"

"Have you ever even *had* a plan?" Alexander retorted, "Because if you ask me, all you've ever done is make people mad and get them to dump tea into the ocean. Don't reprimand people about something that you've never even done yourself!"

Adams's face grew enraged, "You listen to me, mister. If you think for one minute that-"

"*Excusez moi! Mon* general is still in jail?" Lafayette asked, eyes wide, finally translating Thomas's words. "This is an outrage!" Lafayette stood up and pushed his finger onto the table, "He ought to be released as soon as possible! I thought you had freed him!" he looked at Alexander in disapproval, "I thought that you had freed him." He repeated.

Alexander frowned and grabbed the marquis's arm, trying to ease him down. "I said that we were trying, and that we had a plan. I'm sorry if you interpreted the words differently."

Lafayette sat back down, folded his arms across his chest, and grinned, his good humor having returned, "No, no, I understand. What is your plan?"

Eliza groaned, "Not very good."

"In my defense," Alexander began, now looking at his wife, "I'm not in New York, so I have no idea on how to infiltrate a jail *in* New York, and we haven't even discussed this in months."

"So, you have no plan." Thomas intervened.

Alexander glared at him, "This is a private conversation. Go and argue with Mr. Adams."

"We're all at the same table, so I, for one, would say that all conversations taking place here, are the same, *singular* conversation. And as far as Mr. Adams is concerned, I prefer arguing with you, as you don't have as good of points as he does." Thomas smirked and sank back in his chair, feeling triumphant.

Lafayette grabbed hold of Alexander's arm and tried to ease him into his chair. Eliza grabbed his other, trying to help. Alexander resisted but eventually gave in, glaring at Thomas all the while. Thomas adjusted his collar and continued smirking tauntingly.

"You were saying?" Lafayette asked, his eyes flickering between the two combatants, still holding tightly onto Alexander's arm. He could remember when they were in the army, when Alexander, due to his explosive, impulsive nature and aptitude for insulting fellow officers, would, at times, get into multiple fights per day. He would never back down, seeing no honor in refusing a challenge, no matter how many times Lafayette would try to dissuade him. At times there was more peace on the battlefield than in camp. He was better now, taking care not to call anyone names or insult them in any manner, though he still was easy to offend. Lafayette, looking at the heated glares thrown across the table by Thomas and Alexander, remembered that it would take more than one man to restrain Washington's most trusted aide-de-camp.

"Right." Alexander reluctantly turned back to his friend, Lafayette nearly falling to the floor in relief, "I have the basics of an idea. The basics. Essentially, we sneak in and we render the jailers unconscious, grab the keys, and free the general."

"That doesn't sound very plausible." Lafayette pointed out, "There could be soldiers, many of them. We can't all fight easily. We can," he pointed to himself and to Alexander, "But I doubt the others can or will. And also, won't his cell be much more guarded than the average bread thief's?"

"That's exactly what I said." Eliza stated, "He's just too stubborn to see fault in it."

"I'm not too stubborn to admit that it's awful." Alexander explained, "I just don't like mentioning it. Besides, it's better than nothing."

"He's got a point." Lafayette replied, "Now, why don't we go save *mon* general? Now!"

"I don't think we should." Adams said.

Alexander, Eliza, James, and Thomas looked at him in surprise. Lafayette looked ready to put a sword through Adams's gut.

"Why – you – how –" Lafayette threw his hands up in the air in frustration. His mouth opened and closed but no sound emerged. He moved his hands around, pointing to the door, then Adams, making swirling and stabbing motions, then gave up on speaking altogether and slumped into his chair.

"It's not that I don't think we should free Washington first," Adams began, but was soon cut off.

"Oh, good." Lafayette said, his optimism spiking, "I was worried that we'd have to duel."

"I'd rather not." Adams said flatly, "What I'm saying is that I think that we should free Burr first."

"What? Whatever for?" Thomas asked, "Then the grip on Washington will tighten."

Adams brushed his fingers against the table, "Not necessarily," he said mysteriously.

"What are you thinking?" Thomas took the bait.

"Say that we break Burr out first, but it doesn't appear to be done purposefully, what if it looks as though the jailer…slipped up; thus causing his prisoner to…" Adams twirled his finger in the air, "Disappear."

"I like it." Alexander said, "But how does that prevent them from keeping an even closer eye on the general?"

"If it looks like an accident, there would be no need to guard the general from something that doesn't exist." Adams replied.

The group contemplated the proposition for a moment.

"If we do break Washington out first," Adams continued, "it's likely that they would increase the security over any prisoners that are significant. And by significant, I mean any of those rebels that are secluded or somewhat important."

James considered the idea. He hadn't thought of helping Burr escape first, he had just assumed that Washington would be the top priority. Adams's suggestion did make sense. James hated to admit it, as it betrayed ever fiber in his being, but releasing Burr first was the best option. He didn't think much of Adams. He was grouchy and unthankful and seemed to think that everything should be perfectly planned and executed. James wasn't used to having such distasteful feelings inside of him, and felt incredibly let-down after meeting the man.

Thomas had forgotten how irritating Adams could be. He couldn't believe he had spent over six months searching for the man. Part of him wanted to be annoyed at Jemmy for dragging him into this; but, in all fairness, Jemmy had never met the man before and only knew him by reputation. Thomas was slightly stunned by how quickly Adams had taken control of the situation, being snappish and somewhat off-putting, not even attempting to be polite and sociable, quickly getting on his nerves and those of his companions. Sadly, the man did have a point. It'd be best to save Washington for last, after the rebellion was more stable and defined.

Alexander didn't care for Adams either, not one bit. He wasn't sure who was worse, him or Jefferson. He wondered why Jefferson had spent forever looking for the nuisance, why *he* had spent forever looking for the nuisance. To the task at hand, he told himself. He had to focus on the task at hand. Burr or Washington. Burr or Washington. He tried not to be biased. He knew the general so well that he could respond to petty letters from congress under the general's name, without even asking Washington how he would react. Washington would just read the letter over, marvel at how much it sounded like himself, then sign his name. He was one of the most important figures in Alexander's life. Although Alexander had never met Burr, from what he had heard, it was clear that he could be a potential spy, at the very least, a stew of intel. What Adams said made sense. The increase of guard would make it very difficult to save his general. Burr would be the first.

Eliza knew that the general was important. She didn't believe she knew how vital he would be, but she knew that Washington was a natural born leader – and one of Alexander's closest allies, one of the few people that could stand his temper. She thought over what Adams had set to the table. He flustered her, and she didn't like him much, yet she knew that his presence and opinions were inevitable. Burr did seem like he'd be useful, and she understood that if he was guarded, it would be horrible trying to get to him. She was decided. She just hoped that she wasn't choosing unwisely. Eliza wasn't a soldier, she knew that, but all the strategy was very exciting!

Lafayette was conflicted. His general was like the father he never had. He was one of the first people to notice something about him – something that wasn't his money. He was amongst Washington's most trusted generals. How could he leave him? How could he desert him? Then again, what would Washington want him to do? He thought of himself as a general. He had a small brigade of troops, one a nice pretty lady, and one a cranky old man. He had the choice between rescuing two valuable troops. Who should he choose? A higher-ranking general? Or the man who knows important information?

"I vote," Lafayette exclaimed, "That we help *Monsieur* Burr first! As much as it pains me to abandon *mon* general, I think that this is what he'd want me to do…. When do we start?"

"I agree with Lafayette," Eliza said, "I'm not entirely sure how all of this will work out, but Burr seems to be the both safer and more beneficial option."

"As do I." Thomas stated, "Though it may be difficult, I'm willing to attempt the feat."

"I, too, am willing to take the risk." Alexander admitted, "We'll have to delay saving the general, but I'm nearly certain that this is the right choice."

"I agree." James said quietly. The group stared at him, waiting for him to elaborate. He shrank into his chair, pink.

Adams smirked, looking smug, proud of his triumph, "Well, what are we waiting for? Let's get going!"

LAFAYETTE

My dearest Adrienne,

I hope you are not too surprised to learn that I am, once again, at the center of the rebellion! It is great fun, I assure you. Maybe, when I come home, I can teach you how to shoot a redcoat! Would you like that? I'm leaving Philadelphia, now I am off to New York City. I'm feeling wonderful. I haven't a bad dream in weeks! I hope this letter receives you in good health.

Kiss the children on their heads a thousand times for me. Tell them that their daddy is a great hero. Keep some of the kisses for yourself. Love you all. Greet Dr. Franklin for me. Why does he not come? You should come to America sometime...just not in war. Please don't come during war. Very bloody. I could show you where I have been, and you can see where I have fought and lived.

Forever yours,

Gilbert

Eleven

April 1781

SOMEWHERE IN NEW YORK

COMPANY

Thomas yelped when he hit his head against the bow of the wagon. He rubbed it gingerly, biting his lip to keep from showing the pain. He fingered the reins, which was a string of rough leather. He wrapped a portion of the rope around his hand. The horses took no notice, they just kept on walking. They were brown beauties, dutifully pulling a heavy 2000-pound wagon, along with the many different odds and ends it carried.

Lafayette, happily paying for all their traveling needs, had insisted on purchasing a wagon and two horses to help move their belongings from Philadelphia to New York. They had protested first, but the protests dwindled once they remembered that Lafayette was the bearer of an almost endless fortune. All of their goods – Thomas's books, Alexander's and Eliza's few meager belongings, Lafayette's weapons and supplies, along with practically everything the six of them owned – was crammed into the tiny vehicle, and it still had a bit of room for seating.

Alexander, Lafayette, and James, who was only thirty, all walked alongside the slow-moving coach. The others had been surprised to learn their companion's young age, but Thomas had explained that he was assumed to be older as a result of being so small and sickly, being quiet, and having, at times, a sweet n' sour personality. He received a glare from the man in question.

Eliza sat on the bench, beside Thomas, who took turns driving the wagon with Alexander. Adams sat in the wagon bed, sometimes walking when James grew too weak. Much to the relief of all his companions, Adams kept quiet, keeping most of his opinions to himself. He read and napped throughout the journey, only talking when he thought they were moving too slowly, too quickly, or too-much-of-anything-he-could-think-of.

Eliza fingered one of her locks. She hadn't been piling it lately, as it seemed pointless to do so when all she did was sit in a wagon, instead it hung in a limp braid, though some of her curls were left hanging down the side of her neck. She winced whenever the cart creaked, both from fear that the coach would give out, and from the fact that it sounded awful whenever it did so.

"Alexander?" she called lazily. Her husband jogged up beside her. He was sweating profusely, his hat providing his only bit shade; it was before noon and all the shade was on Lafayette's side of the wagon.

"Yes?" he asked, his breathing heavy.

"Have you ever traveled on this road?" She asked him, "Is it much further to the city?" she hoped that it wouldn't be too much longer, she was growing weary from spending all her time sitting on a bench embroidering, or walking alongside the horses. They had been traveling for weeks and it felt as though they hadn't covered any ground.

He looked around at the scenery, his forehead wrinkled while he sorted through his memories. Eventually he looked back up at her, "I'm not sure. I might have. It seems familiar, but then again, almost all roads look familiar to me, even if I've never traveled them."

"That happens an awful lot." Lafayette ran up to the front of the wagon, so he was beside Thomas, "You'll never believe how often I thought I knew where I was, even when it turned out I was just walking in circles."

"That often?" Thomas asked, "Seems like you'd second-guess your navigational skills after a time."

Alexander nodded, "Sometimes. It's the price of being a soldier. You're rarely in the same place for long…. Some areas you get to know well, even if they aren't your home. I could guide you around Valley Forge with my hands tied behind my back, with a blindfold shielding my eyes-"

"I could do that as well!" Lafayette put in.

"-But some places I'd just be guessing my location." Alexander continued, mopping up the sweat on his forehead with his shirt sleeve, "We had it much better off, though. The British had no clue where they were."

"*Oui!*"

"…We had people from all over, so there was nearly always at least one person who knew where they were. We'd have

Virginians camped beside Pennsylvanians beside New Jersians, along with some foreigners." He explained to Thomas, who kept his gaze steadily on the road, but sneaking quick curious glances at Alexander.

Lafayette pouted, "Not as many Frenchmen as I hoped."

"Yes, there were foreigners." Alexander said woodenly. He smiled up at Eliza, tipped his hat, and he, along with Lafayette, began to fall back.

Eliza was still smiling when she heard Thomas gasp. She looked up quickly to see the commotion, and her hand flew up to her mouth in fear. The two looked at each other, both wide-eyed. Eliza turned to Adams, who was reading.

"Adams!" She hissed; he looked up. "Regulars!"

He looked about to complain about her interrupting his reading when he registered her words. She could see his hair inch up his forehead as his eyes grew to the size of saucers. He crawled to end of the wagon and said quietly, but urgently, "The regulars!"

The whispers of Lafayette, Alexander, and James spreading the news to each other filled her ears, making her even more frightened.

She gulped and wished this wasn't happening. She could feel the tension in the air grow more potent as the trio of red-coated soldiers approached. Thomas brought the wagon to a halt, ready for the routine questioning.

"Good day," The tallest soldier said, his cheerful British accent making James cringe. "Sorry to bother you, but protocol.... Where are you all headed? Your business and names, please."

Thomas's hands began to sweat.

"A good day to you as well," Thomas replied, forcing the smile on his face. Eliza was impressed by how sincere it looked, "We're all relocating to New York, and we figured that we might as well all travel together. We don't have that many belongings, so my companions and I were happily surprised by how perfectly everything fit into our little contraption here."

"Yes…" The soldier said, peeking into the cart, seeming to believe his story, "It is rather small…. Your names, now."

"I'm Samuel Johnson." Thomas fibbed, "There in the back is James Howe." James waved shyly. "In the wagon is Michael Adams, and-"

"I'm sure that some of us would like to introduce ourselves, Mr. Johnson." Alexander cut in, stepping forward, exaggerating his accent. "Johnathan Lawrence," he shook hands with the soldiers, grinning easily. He turned to look at Eliza, but seeing as she was pale, figured he would continue.

"This is my lovely wife, Elizabeth." He smiled, gesturing up at her. She managed to return his grin, if somewhat shaky.

"Why does she look so frightened?" one of them asked, suspicious. Eliza felt insulted that he had asked Alexander and not her, but then realized that she would've been too frightened to muster a word anyways.

"She's got a horror of soldiers." Alexander lied, "Some French ones killed off her daddy back in the French and Indian war."

Lafayette raised his arm in protest and was about to say something when Alexander hastily cut him off.

"And that's my good buddy, Gilbert. He's mute." Alexander could've fallen to the ground out of relief when Lafayette kept his mouth shut. The soldier nodded at him, believingly.

"Very well, then. You seem like honest enough folks," the soldier said, "You can move along." The trio began moving away from the coach, and the entire group stared after, wondering when their heart rates would return to normal.

"Why am I mute?" asked Lafayette once the soldiers were out of sight and they were once again on the move.

"I couldn't risk you saying anything." Alexander explained, speaking with his natural light Caribbean, "It's so obvious that you're French, and you know Englishmen are always suspicious of your country's inhabitants."

Lafayette nodded understandingly, "I'm happy that we're not going to jail."

"We all are." Adams groaned from inside the wagon. And that was the first time that everyone was glad he opened his mouth.

"You... bought a house?" Thomas repeated, shocked, unsure he was glad to hear the news or not.

They were all crowded in the middle of the inn's lobby. The hustle and bustle of the place was now drowned out over the new information. Eliza collapsed into a chair, equally uncertain of how to feel. Everyone's focus was on Lafayette, who seemed confused by the mixed looks he was receiving.

"The inn is too crowded. I like privacy. So, I bought a house." He explained. "Why are you so confused?"

"We're not." Alexander replied, "We're just...stunned? ...

Surprised? …Unsure!"

"Oh, *oui*." Lafayette nodded, thinking his companions were confused as to how and when he had made his purchase, "I slipped out yesterday while you were booking some rooms, I knew I wasn't going to like it here. Too crowded. I found a house I liked, a few blocks from here, and the people said they were moving out. So, I bought it. Pretty house." He smiled pleasantly, but his expression faltered when his look was not reciprocated.

He shrugged and turned around and began picking up different bags, ready to begin reloading them onto the wagon.

"What are you doing?" Adams asked him.

Lafayette bent under the weight of so much baggage and stumbled into a wall. "Moving into *mon* house." He grunted, pushing back his hat to help improve his vision.

"With *our* suitcases?" James asked.

Lafayette looked at them, surprised by their many questions, "You're coming, too."

The group looked at each other, then at Lafayette. They rushed to help him with his luggage.

"Why did you decide to buy this?" Eliza asked as they pulled up beside the home. It was painted white, with a picket fence surrounding the property. The front of the house was nearly hidden by the amount of rose bushes in the front garden. She smiled at all the windows, two of them were on either side of the front door, painted dark hunter green, which was in the middle of the home. There were two miniature dormers sticking out from the roof, where Eliza assumed the attic was.

"How much was this?" she breathed.

"Only one hundred pounds." Lafayette told her.

"What?" Alexander exclaimed, not knowing that one could carry that quantity of money on his person, "You paid that much... for a *house*?"

"Of course," He replied, looking at his companion as though he had been insulted, "That wasn't that much money."

Thomas stopped the coach and slowly lowered himself to the ground. The property was lovely. Sure, the home was a bit small, but it was much larger than his apartment – and it was beautiful to boot. It wasn't his Monticello, but it did ease the homesickness that had been plaguing him for years.

"Not bad." Adams said after he climbed out.

Alexander helped Eliza down, and she pulled him towards the garden. "Oh!" she said, pointing to a pale pink rose, "Isn't that gorgeous?" He nodded, grinning, delighted by the joyful expression on her face. She smiled at him, then quickly became sidetracked by another flower.

Lafayette stood back and observed the scene: Eliza inhaling each flower's scent, Alexander being pulled along in her escapade; Thomas looking at the roses happily, sometimes fondly stroking their petals and leaves; James walking peacefully through the garden, smiling blissfully, and being stunned after almost being run over by Eliza. Lafayette laughed as Alexander mouthed "sorry" to his comrade, and the corners of James's mouth curved upwards. Adams walked to the middle of the gardens and looked the house up and down.

"It'll have to do." He declared.

Lafayette frowned… then quickly smiled once more at seeing his friends all so happy. He bounded up the short hill which led up to the fence and let himself in through the gate. The aroma of flowers was strong, it reminded him of all the fancy ladies in France, the ones Adrienne found annoying and dull, with all of their overwhelming perfume. He didn't like perfume, but he liked the flowers. He began walking through the garden and to the house's door, which opened only after he kicked it.

Adams brushed past him, jolting him in the process, and stood in the center of the entryway. Lafayette, rubbing his arm, squeezed beside in him and began taking in the scenery. To the left lay a dining room, complete with table, chairs, and a fine china cabinet. To the right was a small study with many different seating arrangements and bookshelves. Attached to the dining room wall was a small staircase leading up to the attic.

The entryway suddenly became much more crowded as everyone filed in.

"You're sure nobody is living here?" Eliza asked him, looking around at all the furniture skeptically.

"*Oui*. It came with the house. Actually, I bought the furniture as well and left it in the house, but I think that qualifies as came with the house." Lafayette explained. He turned to face all of his companions, "The layout is quite simple. Study right. Dining left. Kitchen past dining. Everywhere else is bedrooms."

"How many bedrooms?" Thomas asked once the Frenchman was finished, hoping and praying that he wouldn't need to share a room with some of his companions.

"Seven. Enough for all of us, plus *Monsieur* Burr and *mon* general." Lafayette turned in a full circle, examining the house. He nodded, "I hereby dub thee, *Nouvelle Maison!*"

"What?" Thomas, James, and Alexander cried in unison. Alexander tried to stifle a laugh.

Eliza, confused, tugged on his arm and whispered into his ear, "What does 'no bell maize on' mean?"

"*Nouvelle Maison*," Alexander corrected, "He just named the house...New House."

Lafayette, grinning, clasped his hands together. "Now, let us unpack!"

For Adams, unpacking meant discovering which chair in the study was the most comfortable. James volunteered to help move the packages into the dining room, where everyone could shift through and find their belongings.

Thomas, Alexander, Eliza, and Lafayette walked back to their wagon, staring ahead at their daunting task. They quickly formed an assembly line: Eliza in the coach handing luggage to Alexander, who would then pass it on to Thomas, who would run it to the garden, where Lafayette was waiting to take the package into the house.

"I just can't believe he went and bought a...house." Eliza said, tossing her luggage down to Alexander.

He chuckled, "You're telling me. I've never met anybody with his kind of money. Sure, I've met rich – well, you're rich-"

"Daddy is." She corrected, "I'm just as rich as you."

"So, you're saying that we're almost broke." Alexander

had abandoned his job after the group decided to move their headquarters to New York. He had brought his and Eliza's savings with him, but he knew it wouldn't be long before he'd have to begin job hunting. He hoped that Lafayette wouldn't catch wind of his financial troubles, as he knew the marquis would give him a small fortune as charity, and Alexander did not want to hurt the man's feelings by refusing. He did know, however, that if he and Eliza did begin to starve and grow short of money, that he'd ignore the blow to his pride and accept any help Lafayette was willing to give. He just hoped that it wouldn't come to that. He shook his head, trying to rid the bad thoughts from his mind.

He thrust the bag into Thomas's waiting arms, who quickly retreated up into the garden, "Before the army," he told his wife, "I had no idea that kind of wealth was even possible. I've seen him buy the best supplies for one hundred starving soldiers, all without batting an eye."

"It's kind of peculiar how much he doesn't care about it." Eliza mentioned, "Money, I mean. He's so selfless about it."

"He doesn't really. He was born a country boy. He once told me one of the main attractions of joining the army was that he didn't have to attend parties each week." He responded.

Eliza laughed, "I can understand why he'd think that. They get terribly boring, and you always have to watch what you say, as the wrong person might be listening."

Alexander nodded in an exaggerating manner, "I've been to some. Even more vicious than the battlefield."

"Aaron Burr is being housed in a place called the 'King George Jailhouse.'" Alexander pointed to its location on a map.

Ever since they had moved into *Nouvelle Maison*, Lafayette had begun purchasing different odds and ends he thought would be useful. Some, like maps of New York City and food, were helpful. Others, like an English-French dictionary, were not so helpful (he fell asleep the first time he attempted to read it, though the amount of time he was able to keep consciousness was admirable.)

Everyone was crowded around the table, Alexander at the head, as he was the one presenting the plan. James, Thomas, and Adams watched him from one side, while Lafayette nodded slowly on the other. Eliza came in, balancing a platterful of freshly-baked muffins in one hand and her knitting bag in the other. She set the tray down, and the revolutionaries temporarily forgot about their plan and focused instead on devouring her pastries. She sat beside the marquis, who was holding two muffins in his hand and was trying to fight for a third.

Eliza took out her knitting needles and continued knitting a green scarf for her husband. Alexander tried to focus his colleagues on his map, which was now sprinkled with crumbs. He tried to dust them off, huffing whenever a new, smaller particle appeared. Eventually he gave up. The group watched him, chewing and swallowing, waiting as though nothing had happened.

Alexander sighed and pointed back to the map, "As I was saying, Burr is being kept in the 'King George Jailhouse.'"

"Do you have any idea of how to infiltrate it?" Adams inquired, his tone cross, as though he believed Alexander was no further along than he had been before.

"I do, actually. In the past few days, I've been walking past the prison, and have noticed something of interest. It is, I believe, our key." Alexander kept quiet now, loving the eager looks in their eyes – for both muffin and knowledge.

"The key is to have one of us visit Burr." He said, "I noticed a great many different people, poor colonists mostly, coming to the jail carrying baskets. One of the guards would permit the said people into the prison, and they would later file out, their baskets emptied. I stopped one of the ladies on the street, one who came out with an empty basket, and inquired what she had been doing. She kindly informed me that she had gone to give her husband some home-baked bread and some warmer blankets, as the ones at the jail were rotten and moth-eaten. I interviewed a few others, and their answers were along the same lines. My plan is simple. One of us, preferably one of the most kind-hearted, will go to the prison under the guise of a visitor and familiarize themselves with the area, while also building a friendship with Burr, and becoming just a piece in the background as far as the jailers are concerned. After a month or so of visits, our spy will come as usual, render the guards unconscious, find the keys, help Burr escape, and return here. All the while, the rest of us will be out on the other side of the jail making a disturbance. Any questions?" Alexander asked.

The group thought over his idea, nodding to themselves and each other, considering the different outcomes of such an event. Adams raised his hand; the rest turned to him, wondering what he was about to say. Alexander nodded at him, allowing him to proceed.

"Do you," Adams began, "have anyone in mind to perform this task?"

Alexander shrugged, "At the time the idea occurred to me, I just assumed the least suspicious and gentlest person would do so. Who do you think should do it?"

Thomas, James, and Adams looked across from them. Eliza's eyes widened in surprise and she dropped the scarf into her lap; Lafayette chewed his muffin more slowly. He swallowed and cocked his head, pointing at himself and Eliza, "Us?"

"It makes the most sense for one of you to do it." Thomas said, "Jemmy is sweet-tempered and polite, but likely wouldn't be able to get the message across. He'll get frightened, and when he gets nervous, he doesn't like to speak. If that happens, the whole operation would be doomed. He's also too short, *memorably* short." James glared at him, but did not deny the accusations.

"Adams has too strong of opinions and is snappish, and he's not the type to go anywhere unnoticed." Adams nodded despite being insulted. Thomas gestured to himself, "I am simply too tall, and I'm quick to disagree and bicker, which makes me memorable. Hamilton, you're charming, but you're also easy to annoy and aggravate. And you like to argue, something that would be disastrous, since we're trying to stay unnoticed. You're nearly impossible to miss." Thomas said bluntly, causing Alexander's face to grow pink, though he remained silent, understanding Thomas's point. Thomas looked back at the marquis and Mrs. Hamilton, "so that leaves you two."

Lafayette shook his head in refusal, "*Non*! I can't do it! I won't!"

"And why is that?" asked Alexander, seeing no reason in the world why Lafayette wasn't perfectly suited for the job.

"The same reason you said I was mute!" Lafayette exclaimed,

"The British don't trust foreigners. Especially aristocrats, for the matter. And besides, I can't even pass as a colonist. *Mon* accent is too thick, and I can't speak like an American."

"He's got a point." Thomas stated, "His accent *is* quite thick."

"But he has to go!" Alexander exclaimed, "He has to!"

"For what reason?" Adams asked, wanting the decision to be done and over with.

"So Eliza doesn't go!" Alexander cried, "I don't want her to get hurt!"

Lafayette snorted, "Oh, so it's perfectly fine if *I* go."

"He doesn't mean it like that." Eliza said, patting her friend's shoulder, "He just constantly wants me to be safe, which is incredibly sweet, but also annoying. At times, in his over-protectiveness, he tends to forget that I can do more than just keep house... I've done many things to help our cause."

"Like what?" Lafayette asked.

"During the first war, I made blankets, repaired clothes, collected food, raised funds to help the soldiers, things like that." Eliza explained, "I've never done any infiltration work before, or anything remotely like that, but I think that I am up to the task."

"I think that what you've done is very admirable," Lafayette complimented, "*Merci* from the soldiers. I agree with you. It doesn't sound too complicated; I think that you'll do well at it."

By now, Alexander, Thomas, James, and Adams, were deep into the argument about whether or not Eliza should go. Alexander spoke mostly about her protection and safety, while Thomas and Adams listed reasons why she was best suited for the job. James, arguing quietly, was adamant that Eliza was the best and only option, but didn't think that she should go as it might be dangerous; as a result, none of the other combatants paid him any heed. The others were standing and pointing fingers in all directions, their voices sharp and commanding, trying to be as loud as possible. James, still trying to make his point, shrank deeply into his chair, frightened by the commotion that he was in the middle of.

Eliza stood up and began lightly tapping her water glass with a silvery spoon. The men continued arguing, either not hearing, or not caring. She continued tapping; eventually, Eliza feared that she might break the glass from hitting it too hard. Then she tried to get their attention by speaking.

"Speak up." Lafayette encouraged, "I can barely hear you, and I'm paying attention to you."

Eliza sighed, but nodded, she wasn't used to speaking loudly. She raised her voice slightly. "Gentlemen! ...Alexander? ... Thomas? ...Adams? ...Alexander!"

They continued arguing, though she caught James's attention, who quieted and watched her, obedient. She bit her lip and shifted awkwardly on her feet, unsure of what to do. She timidly watched them, opening her mouth, then deciding on keeping it closed. She raised her hand, then lowered it, nervous by their incessant shouting. Eventually, however, she couldn't take it anymore.

"Oh, will you be quiet?" she nearly screamed.

The men jumped, startled by the sudden noise. They slowly sank into their respective chairs, ready to listen, slightly embarrassed by their quarrel. Alexander stared at her in wonder, never before hearing her speak so loudly.

"I have something to say." Eliza smoothed her rosy dress and straightened her bows. "I'd like to go."

Alexander shot out of his chair, "You will not!"

Eliza put her hands on her hips, her eyebrows narrowed at her husband. "I don't see why I shouldn't go! Sure, it may be dangerous, but what of it? In fact, if I remember correctly, all of you have been in much more dangerous situations than befriending a prisoner! I think that it will be fun, and if you'd listen to them," she pointed at Thomas and Adams, "for once, you might see that they have some good points. I'm not agreeing with you on this one. You've risked your life for your country, Alexander, why won't you let me risk mine?"

He opened his mouth to speak, but she held up her hand, "No. I know what you're going to say. I may be your only family left, but that doesn't give you the right to swaddle me with blankets so nothing ever harms me. I'm going!"

Alexander slowly nodded, not wanting to accept her decision, but knowing that she wouldn't be swayed otherwise, "If that's what you'd like, Betsey, I won't stand in your way."

Eliza grinned, proud of her victory, "Now, when do I start?" her smile faltered, "…How do I start?"

Thomas looked down at the map, breathing slowly, considerably calmer, "I'd say that you should start within the week. How you should act, perhaps a little dumb and slightly irritating, so the soldiers don't suspect you and want to see the least amount of you as possible. With Burr, act mysterious, but friendly enough that he won't have the urge to tell on you."

Alexander groaned, "For once, I actually agree with him."

Eliza laughed, "Well, that's progress!"

ELIZA

Eliza tucked a loose curl behind her ear, and looked around, anxiously. Tugging her cloak closer around herself, she walked towards the jail. Her braid hit against her back as she walked. She ignored her want to pull it nervously. To help fool the guards, she carried a basket filled with rolls, which was covered by a blanket.

Now, one day later, Eliza wondered if she could do what she had been so insistent on the night before. She shook it off, knowing that the more she thought about it, the more skittish she'd become. She straightened her posture and walked determinedly to the door, where a prison guard was standing, bored by his assignment.

"Good day." Eliza said cheerfully, holding out her hand and grinning happily.

The red-coated guard eyed both her and her hand skeptically. Her smile faltered as she put her hand to her side. She knew that the soldiers could be very stone-like and distant, but she had never met one who wasn't friendly and polite.

"Who would you like to see?" The guard droned, clearly uninterested in her attempt to be courteous.

"A Mr. Aaron Burr, if that's possible." Eliza told him, slipping into her role, "I'm a friend of his. I haven't seen him in a good while though, but as soon as I heard he was in jail, I simply just had to come and visit! I made this blanket for him, see here?"

she jiggled the basket, making the blanket stir, "and some bread. I make such good bread! Everybody says so. Why just last night, a friend of mine said that he'd pay me to make him bread every day! Imagine that! I just shook my head, I'm not sure if he was teasing-like, but I couldn't honestly take him seriously- "

"You're free to go." The guard quickly opened the door and shoved her inside the jail, not wanting to hear anymore of her chatter.

Eliza stopped talking. She sensed the gloominess that was radiating from the room, and shivered, a chill having run up her spine. It was a dark, dank place, not fit for anyone. It smelled…she couldn't quite place the scent…it seemed familiar, but at the same time, foreign and unlike anything she had ever smelled before. She brought the cloak to her face, clogging her nose. Everything in the room seemed grey and depressed, even the wooden doors. Wooden doors. They were all around her, surrounding her, they seemed like they were closing in on her. She shook her head, telling herself to not think so foolishly. It was just the disheartening atmosphere affecting her. She felt as though she were in the face of a clock, with one door to mark each hour. She closed her eyes and shook her head, reminding herself to stay focused and not act like a frightened kitten.

There was a man sitting in a chair in the center of the room, his eyes closed. His breathing was slow and peaceful. He was asleep. Eliza silently congratulated herself on her 'too talkative' act and wished that her luck would continue. She slowly moved over to the sleeping man and nudged his foot.

"Hello?" she whispered, "Sir? Are you awake?"

The man leapt to his feet, "Get right back into your cell, you filthy-" He looked down at the young lady holding a basket. She was shivering from both surprise and the chill.

"Sorry to frighten you, miss." He stammered, "You see, many prisoners happen to slip out ever once in a while, and it's a gut reaction-"

"That's perfectly understandable." Eliza said, "Sorry to wake you, but-"

"You're a visitor." The man finished, "Who'd you like to see?" He pulled a clipboard out from under his chair. He walked to a small desk in the corner of the room, where there was a quill and inkpot.

"You're the jailer, aren't you?" she asked him, thinking that his bulking stature would be difficult for her to knock unconscious on her own. She'd have to ask Alexander and the others about adjusting their plan.

"Yep." He replied, "That's me. Not much I do though. Just sit around and wait for visitors, soldiers bringing more prisoners, or prisoners trying their luck at escaping."

"Sounds awfully dull." Eliza said softly, "Well, I hope that you'll be plenty busy soon. Now, I'll be on my way. If you'll just tell me which way to go...." She turned around, keeping her eyes wide, pretending that each door looked more daunting than the last. She tried telling herself that they didn't look scary in the least, but she couldn't deny that she felt just like the frightened girl that she was portraying.

"You'll have to tell me who you're looking for." The jailer said, waiting impatiently.

"Oh, right, how silly of me." Eliza giggled, "I'm here to see Aaron Burr. I'm a friend of his, I've brought him some bread and this blanket. I made both! It doesn't seem like he gets very much of company, now does he?" she leaned over the jailer's shoulder, looking at his list. Next to all the names were checkmarks, showing how many times that prisoner had been visited. Besides Aaron Burr's, there was none.

"Not a one." Said the man, "It appears you're the only person that knows him. He's been here coming on three years now, and not a friend ever came."

"The poor man." Eliza said, clucking her tongue, shaking her head in pity, "I just moved here to the city, and I just heard that he was in jail. We haven't seen each other in ages, I suppose I know why now. Which door is he?"

The jailer pointed to one off to the side, "That one. Now, I'll need your name. I have to know who's visiting in case it's a person who might be dangerous or an escapee prisoner who's trying to release one of his buddies." He said the words slowly and carefully, not believing his company to be very competent.

"Oh, how frightening!" Eliza exclaimed, "It's Elizabeth. Elizabeth…Campbell?"

The jailer nodded as he scratched that onto a piece of paper. He penned a checkmark beside Aaron's name, then he marched over to a nail on the wall, where there was a string of keys hanging. The jailer fingered through them until he came to the desired one. He walked over to the door and unlocked it. It swung it open, creaking eerily, sending a chill up Eliza's spine. She coughed as some dust went up her nose.

"There used to be a whole bunch of soldiers in here." The jailer explained, "Now it's only him. You'll find him easily enough." Eliza nodded, though she was trembling.

"Hey, Burr!" the jailer yelled into the hall, "You've got yourself a visitor! Name's 'Lizabeth!"

"Elizabeth?" Eliza heard a dry, parched voice call back. She knew he must be pondering who was coming, but she hastily pushed herself through the doorway and began walking down the path. The jailer closed the door behind her, she sighed, glad that he wouldn't be listening in on their conversation.

It was dusty in every cell. Cobwebs were everywhere. She didn't like spiders. Or rats. She yelped when one ran over her foot. Their whiskers twitched and they squeaked miserably as they encircled her feet. She hopped around them, keeping her eyes on the ground, trying to avoid touching any. That's when she noticed them.

Footprints. They were bigger than hers but smaller than the jailer's, and they looked recent. Beside nearly all of the left footprints was a small circle, like the mark of a cane. There were many of them, some leading from the end of the passage, others to. Whomever they belonged to had come here often. Whose were they? Eliza didn't know. She figured that she'd ask Burr once he grew accustomed to her. Her breathing stopped when a question entered her mind. If nobody had ever visited Burr, then how come there were so many footprints?

She finally made it to the last cell, where a small stool had been set. Unlike everything else in the room, the stool seemed to be the only object that didn't have an inch of dust covering it. Or any dust at all, really. She wondered who had been coming here.

Eliza peered into the darkness, unable to see past a few feet, despite it being the middle of the day; but she could sense that there was something moving towards her. She nearly jumped when a man appeared, coming out of the shadowy darkness, carrying his own stool. He sat on it, watching her intently.

His hair, black, fell to his shoulders, and was loose. His dark eyes seemed haunted but curious about his visitor. He was lean, very lean. She wondered when the last time he had eaten a proper meal was. He shivered. His complexion was unusually pale, but dirt-smudged. His cheeks were sunken in. She could tell that beneath the dirt and grime, that he was quite handsome, and that he would clean up well. Unlike her husband, he seemed to have an aristocratic look to him, she realized, he had seen much better days, while one could tell from Alexander's calloused hands and shiftiness that his had been poor.

She watched him for a moment, then looked away, trying to focus on something more pleasant than his sickly frame, but there was hardly anything more cheerful in the room.

"I've brought you some things." She forced her voice to be loud and commanding, like her older sister's, "A blanket and some bread loaves." She lifted the blanket from the basket and maneuvered it through the gaps in the iron rails. He watched it for a moment, and looked to her, suspicious, then he gently took hold of it. He draped it around his shoulders to stop his shivering. Eliza passed him a bread roll, which he accepted more quickly and bit into heartily. Once he finished chewing, he looked up at her, intrigued.

"Who are you?" he took another bite.

"A friend." She replied, "I heard that you were here, so I took it upon myself to make you more comfortable."

"I don't remember you." He stated, inhaling the mouth-watering aroma of the loaf before shoving the last remaining bite into his mouth.

"I wouldn't expect you to." She handed him another roll, which he looked at in surprise and delight. "We've never met."

He accepted it, but paused before bringing it to his lips, "Then why are you here? Why are you doing this?"

"To bring you a blanket and some food.... Do I have to have a reason?" Eliza asked him mysteriously. She gazed at the grey brick wall beside her, pretending to be uninterested in her companion.

"No, I suppose not," He said after a moment, "...Do you do this with all of the prisoners?"

"No. Why would I do that?" Eliza asked him.

"I don't know." He muttered, then looked at her, a thoughtful expression on his face, "What makes me so special?" he asked, biting into the bread.

"Who said you were special?" she handed him another roll.

The man smiled at her for a moment. "I'm Aaron Burr, though I suppose you already knew that."

Eliza nodded, "I'm Eliza Campbell. Now, Burr, how did you come to be in this cell?"

"Please," he said, "Call me Aaron. All anyone calls me anymore is 'Burr.'"

"Aaron then."

"I came here the same way many others do nowadays. By fighting on the 'wrong' side." He used air-quotes. He took another bite and slowly chewed before continuing. "I fought for the rebels and I got caught. Simple as that. I've been here ever since. This whole hall used to be filled with us. Soldiers" He gestured to the empty cells. "Now, I'm the only one left."

"Do you know why?" Eliza asked him.

"Not at all." Aaron replied, shaking his head like he asked himself that every day, "I haven't been outstandingly good during my stay, but I can't say that I was one of the bad ones. Sure, I acted up at times, but only because the lobsterbacks were asking for it. I don't know why I'm here. I expected to be gone after only a year. But here I am, rotting away."

Eliza snorted, "You're hardly rotting…. Do you get any visitors?" she asked, trying to sound like she wasn't very interested.

Aaron hesitated, biting his lip, "No. Only you."

She knew that he was lying, but she pretended to believe him. She leaned forward and lowered her voice. "Now, since I brought you some bread," she handed him another roll. "Can you do something for me?"

Aaron shrugged, "That depends. If it has anything to do with being outside of this cell, I don't think it'll happen anytime soon."

"I'd like for you to pretend that you knew me when we were children." Eliza said, "If anybody asks, like the jailer, or the redcoats. Pretend that you knew me, and that I always chat up a storm."

Aaron chewed, watching her suspiciously, "Why?"

"Let's just say that it will benefit you eventually if I continue coming here." Eliza said carefully, "and I can't let people know that I don't know you."

Aaron watched her, thinking about what she said, "You're going to break me out." He concluded, "Why?"

"I never said that." Eliza said, "I'd just do what I told you."

Aaron nodded slowly, "Fine, I'll do it. Anything in particular I should mention?"

"You haven't seen me in years and that you forgot how much of a talker I was." Eliza held out her hand, "Is it a deal?"

Aaron's dirt-encrusted hand slowly moved out of the cell to shake, "It's a deal."

"Very well." Eliza stood up and handed him the last two loaves, "That's all I have for now. I'll see you next week."

Aaron grabbed them and nodded, "See you next week then." He mumbled, disappointed that the visit would end so soon. He watched as the girl walked off, wondering why she was so interested in him.

Eliza hoped the man would uphold his end of the deal. He was a nice enough man, but she wasn't sure if he would follow through.

She was just about to pull open the door when it unfurled. A tall man, leaning on a cane began walking in. She quickly jumped back to make way for him and snuck a quick glance at his feet. They were roughly the same size as the footprints. He had long, dark hair and grey eyes. He stood to the side and held open the door for her. His uniform, she noticed, was bright scarlet. He was a British officer, something of that nature.

"Sorry, miss." He said, "I didn't know anyone was here." Eliza was stunned by his lack of accent. She smiled sweetly, trying to seem like a simple-minded girl who wasn't taking much notice in the man.

"It's all right." She replied, sensing that he was somehow important. Maybe it was the multitude of medals on his uniform, or maybe it was the fact that he seemed to radiate power. Whatever it was, Eliza didn't want to upset him.

She quickly ducked through the door, feeling triumphant at knowing who the other visitor was, but feeling nervous as well. Aaron had pretended that he didn't have any visitors, so had the jailer. There weren't any marks on the jailer's clipboard that indicated a visitor; and yet, there were many footprints, and also a visitor. Eliza wondered if it was Governor Arnold. She wasn't sure if she wanted it to be him or not.

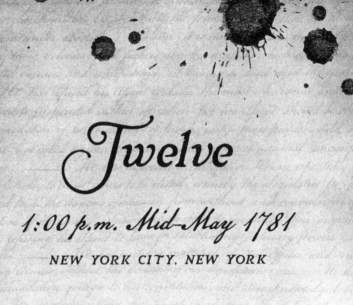

Twelve

1:00 p.m. Mid-May 1781

NEW YORK CITY, NEW YORK

THOMAS

Thomas rubbed his hands together, looking at the crowd anxiously. He glanced down at Adams, "Are you sure that this is a good idea?"

Adams groaned, "Do you really want me to answer that?"

He considered the question, "No, I guess not." He fingered the silky fabric of his waistcoat anxiously.

Lafayette put his arm around Thomas's back, patting his shoulder, "It's fine, *mon amie*, we've run this through our heads countless of times. It can't go too terribly wrong."

"What is your definition of 'terribly wrong?'" Thomas inquired, shaking off Lafayette's comforting arm.

Lafayette blinked and pursed his lips. After a moment of deep concentration, he shrugged. "I don't know. But please, let us get on with it before you grow too paranoid!"

Thomas turned towards the crowd, sighing, "Fine."

They were on the backside of the jail, leaning against the brick wall, eyeing the passing crowd. Some of the colonists spoke quietly amongst themselves, collected in different circles. They laughed occasionally, polite titters from the women, loud guffaws from the men. A few civilians set up stands and appeared to be peddling goods. Others walked in search of uptown. Overall, it was a rather bustling square.

"Ready?" Lafayette inquired, glancing around eagerly, bouncing in excitement.

"As ready as I'll ever be." Thomas mumbled.

The two men stepped forward, trying to edge their way into the middle of the crowd, with Adams standing a few feet to the side. They were ready to enact their plan.

Thomas clenched his fists, breathing heavily, and tried to look angry. Lafayette did likewise. The two companions stared bitterly at each other, both trying to look as enraged as possible. Adams gasped dramatically and put his hand to his mouth. "Ohh!"

Lafayette stamped his foot, looking surprised and riled, "*Monsieur!* That is most untrue! Take it back!"

Thomas snorted, crossing his arms, "Why should I? It's only true!" He felt slightly guilty having a false argument with his friend, but was relieved when the colonists began to gather around them in a curious ring, interested in the dispute. Thomas sniffed the air, "And you smell like horse manure."

The crowd, along with Adams and Lafayette, gasped appropriately. Lafayette's face turned red, though Thomas and Adams knew that this was a sign that Lafayette was trying to contain his laughter, most would assume that he was very insulted. Lafayette bit his lip, "That is too far! It is not I who is horse manure, but it is you!"

Thomas tried to look taken aback, and, judging from the growing crowd's lively reaction, he did a fine job of it. He laughed, "Well then, if I'm horse manure, then you are -"

They continued trading insults, getting louder and showier, drawing a larger and larger crowd, one that was itching for a fight.

ELIZA

Eliza adjusted her grip on her bread basket as she walked.

Over the past few weeks, the revolutionaries had been trying to make sense of the mysterious visitor with a cane, but they were puzzled and perplexed. Thomas speculated if releasing Aaron was the right thing to do, wondering if he would just bring trouble, but his theory was quickly dismissed.

Each week she had returned, bringing bread. The second time she had visited, she asked Aaron who the visitor was; he answered hesitantly, claiming that there had been no visitor. She had given up on asking after that. Aaron, she thought, was beginning to trust her, and she didn't want to throw away that bond by asking too many questions. Her visits had been getting increasingly longer, and she had been coming more frequently, listening to Aaron tell her stories about his life in the army and in prison. She never told him any stories about her life, though he seemed to sense that she wouldn't, as he never asked. She had begun growing fond of him, looking forward to his company and stories. He didn't seem to anger easily, and she was glad to have a person with even-temperament in her life separate, even if it was just for the time being, from her new life. His stories, as much as she enjoyed them, saddened her.

Aaron was orphaned at a young age, and was sent to live with his grandparents, both of whom died within the same year as his mother and father. Then he went to live with his uncle, whom he tried to run away from multiple times. He graduated from the College of New Jersey when he was only seventeen, trading ministry, which he originally intended to study, for law. Soon after he graduated, he enlisted in the army, where he fought in Canada and also New York. While fighting, he told her, he had fallen in love. Of this, he didn't say much, and Eliza, seeing that it was a sensitive topic, didn't press him for details. She assumed that it had ended badly and that he wished to forget it. After the war had ended, Aaron began marching back to New York City with some of his companions, where he hoped to live peacefully as a lawyer. His hopes were dashed, however, when redcoats, upon seeing the enemy uniform, had seized him and thrown him into prison. He had been there ever since.

Eliza tucked a loose curl behind her ear. Their plan was simple, and she hoped that it wouldn't fail. While freeing Aaron, some of her co-conspirators: Thomas, Lafayette, and Adams, would engage in a false argument, which would (hopefully) catch the attention of the jailer and guard. She prayed that their plan would succeed.

Her eyes flickered to a shop nearby the jail, and she smiled.

James was looking intently through the shop's window, curiously eyeing its contents. Beside him, leaning against the wall, was a man wearing a tri-corner hat, his face hidden by the newspaper he was reading. He lowered the paper an inch, allowing her to see his eyes. Though slightly concerned, Alexander watched her, encouraging. He lowered the paper more, offering her a small smile, mouthing "Good luck." She smiled back, knowing that she would need it.

As Alexander showed James an interesting article in his paper, Eliza approached the jail, smiling at the guard. He was sitting in his chair, as usual, and seemed very unhappy to see her. In the past few weeks, Eliza had learned that the man wasn't a fan of conversationalists, or of people in general. "Hello," she greeted him; he rolled his eyes, uninterested.

Eliza looked up when she heard shouting, she cringed. It must be Thomas and Lafayette. The guard was reaching for the door, wanting to avoid saying anything more to the girl, but was surprised when the door was opened by the jailer. He looked drowsy and irritated. "Can't a man get some sleep around here without a racket?" he grumbled. He looked at Eliza, surprised, "Good day, Miss Campbell."

"Good day, sir," Eliza nodded to him.

"What on earth is that sound?" The jailer grumbled, looking at the guard, "Do you know?" The guard shrugged.

"I saw some sort of fighting on the backside of the jail," Eliza lied, "It must be that…. Should you investigate, that way it doesn't get out of hand? Surely some soldiers would get them in line."

The jailer and guard looked at each other. Before the guard

could protest, the jailer nodded, "Of course, we'll go look right now." He pulled the guard to his feet, practically dragging him towards the noise.

"Wait!" Eliza cried, the jailer turned to her, "May I still go see Aaron? Mr. Burr? They seemed awfully rowdy, and it might take you some time to get them in order."

The jailer considered her request for a moment, looking at Eliza. She did her best to look like nothing more than the simple-minded girl that they had come to know as Miss Elizabeth Campbell. "I don't see why not," the jailer remarked, "You know where my keys are, don't you?"

Eliza nodded, grinning, "Yes, sir. Thank you, sir!"

The jailer turned away, and he and the guard continued in the direction of the fighting.

Eliza wasted no time in hurrying into the jailhouse. Setting her basket on the chair, she quickly retrieved the key ring from the nail on the wall. She selected one and inserted it into the lock, jiggling the key, and frowning when it didn't turn. She leafed through the ring, selecting one she took a liking to, and tried again, failing. She sighed as each one failed to unlock the door. She grumbled and groaned, trying to find the correct key.

"This must be it." She breathed, holding up the last one. She felt her heart pound, despite having a perfectly honest reason for being there. Eliza scolded herself for being so jittery and inserted the key into the lock, fiddling with it until it opened. The door swung free, creaking all the while. She slowly made her way into the hall.

"Aaron?" Eliza called. Her voice echoed against the corridor's walls and bounded back to her.

"Eliza?" He asked. His voice sounded refreshed, "How are you?"

"I'm well." She said, "Do you know where the key to your cell is?"

"Yes!" Aaron said, rushing to his cell's door and pressing himself against the iron bars, straining to see what was happening, "Right beside the door, the one you came in from." Eliza whirled around. "Do you see it?"

"Yes!" She called back, "I do." She reached up, pulled it off the hook, and hurried to the cell.

Aaron was leaning against the door, smiling at her charmingly, "Finally freeing me, eh?"

Eliza laughed, nodding, "You've waited long enough, haven't you?"

He shrugged comically, "I guess so." Aaron watched as she inserted the keys into the lock, both of them cheering when the third one turned. She opened the door and grinned, happy by how quickly she had discovered the correct key. Aaron stood in the cell, now looking hesitantly at Eliza, unsure of what to do.

"Aren't you coming?" Eliza asked, "We don't have much time."

"Why are you doing this?" Aaron wondered, stepping out of the cell, an honest expression on his face, wanting to know why he was being saved.

"I'll explain later." She said, pulling Aaron out of his cell. The pair quickly began moving out, Eliza retrieving her basket, while also returning the keys to their proper places, and closing the doors behind them.

Once out of the jail, Aaron laughed, the sun streaming down on his ghostly pale complexion. "I haven't seen the outside in…I don't know how long!" He stared up at the blue sky with a childlike look of wonder, "It's so lovely. The colors are so vibrant and crisp and cheerful! ... What is that noise?" he asked in alarm, his delight replaced with concern and fright. Eliza looked at him in surprise, hearing the angry shouts as well. It sounded like a large crowd was near them.

"Quickly!" She began walking towards the street, "Follow me!" She turned to look back at Aaron, who quickly fell in step beside her. The two briskly walked down the street, Eliza stopping at the shop where she had seen Alexander and James.

"Eliza!" Alexander smiled, looking up from his seat, setting down his paper. He and James had been waiting on a bench. She sighed in relief as he rose to stand by her side.

"Who are you?" inquired Aaron, slightly confused by the new people. James looked at him shyly and curiously.

"This is my husband, Alexander, and my friend, Jemmy," Eliza introduced them, Alexander tipping his hat and shaking Aaron's hand, James grinning at the escaped convict. "They'll be taking you home," Eliza explained.

Aaron looked at her, surprised, "But I thought -"

"I have to pretend that you were already gone," Eliza told him, "I need to find the jailer. You can trust them. You'll see me soon enough, it won't take me that long." Aaron nodded dumbly. Eliza quickly turned around, walking in the direction of the shouting, leaving the trio behind.

By the time the jailer and guard had arrived, Lafayette and Thomas's false argument had escalated. The crowd watched eagerly, shouting encouraging words to their chosen team, cheering each time when Thomas or Lafayette, who were engaged in a shoving contest, would push their opponent.

Adams, noticing the newcomers, coughed loudly, "Well look at that! It's the redcoats!"

Lafayette let go of Thomas's collar, and Thomas placed the marquis's hat back on his head. The two quickly disappeared into the crowd as the colonists' attention was drawn away from the fighting and towards the authority figures.

"They're probably going to arrest those men that were fighting!" Thomas shouted in a deeper voice.

"Yeah!" Adams agreed.

"But it was just getting good!" somebody protested. "I hope it's something else!"

"Um...." The jailer's face was blank.

"I'll bet it's a wildcat!" screamed Lafayette, happily playing the part of a confused and excited citizen, "Oh, a wildcat! How dastardly! It'll be – how you say? A disaster!"

"There are wildcats in the city?" exclaimed a woman, placing her hand over her mouth. A lady beside her shrugged, unknowing.

A man behind the pair shook his head, looking at the marquis, "No, Frenchie, I'll bet that there's a prisoner who has a wildcat friend."

"Prisoners have wildcat friends?" a woman with a baby shrieked.

She looked at the guard and jailer, "Why don't authorities control prisoners with wildcat friends? I don't want my baby to be cat food!"

Thomas had to keep from smiling as the crowd continued spreading absurd rumors and asking questions. This was working perfectly.

The jailer, after a moment of pondering, spoke, "I assure you, as frightening as it is, there have been no prisoners at this prison with wildcat friends.... I think."

"Wolves!" an elderly lady cried, "Some wolves ate my husband! Back in the French and Indian War, it was. He was there, fighting like a lion, when he was shot!"

"Did the wolves eat him, while he was lying suffering from that wound?" another person asked.

The old woman shook her head, "No. The bullet was to the heart. Died that very instant. No, it was a while later that his best friend was out looking for him, when he found him all covered in bite marks. Wolves for certain!"

"The prisoner has pet wolves!" the man with the horse declared, "How could you keep this from us, jailer?"

The jailer, confused, looked at the guard, "The soldier would like to answer that question."

"Who cares what that dolt thinks!" the man cried, "I hate those British redcoats!" The patriotic citizens shouted in agreement, angry.

"Foreigners killed my husband!" the old woman shrieked.

The colonists began to move closer to the jailer and the guard, who both were looking uncomfortable. The crowd was beginning to look more like a mob, and the pair of red-coated men began backing away slowly. Lafayette, feeling sympathetic, looked at Thomas. "Do you think that Eliza would've had enough time by now?"

Thomas thought for a moment, "I'd give her another minute. What are you thinking?"

"Let's tar and feather those redcoats!" The man with the horse and cart declared. The colonists shouted their agreement. The jailer and guard were looking very, very nervous.

Thomas looked at Lafayette in alarm; Lafayette decided to take matters into his own hands. He spun around and pointed into the opposite direction, "Look everyone! It's a prisoner and his three wildcats! *Mon Dieu!* Is that a wolf!"

The crowd suddenly turned and looked in the direction Lafayette was pointing, "Get him!" someone called. The colonists quickly ran off in search of one fictional prisoner, three fictional wildcats, and one fictional wolf.

A moment later, only Thomas, Adams, Lafayette, the jailer, and the guard remained in the square. The jailer looked at them for a moment, "I wasn't expecting that." The guard shook his head, agreeing.

Lafayette walked up to them, "They wanted to tar and feather the both of you." The jailer and guard shivered, not liking the image in their minds.

Thomas looked up as Eliza turned the corner, running as fast as she could in her dress. Eliza quickly scurried up to the jailer and guard, breathing heavily and looking panicked. Thomas, Adams, and Lafayette tried not to meet her gaze, trying to make the impression that they didn't know each other.

Adams, grabbing Thomas's arm, began pulling him away. Thomas, seeing that they should make their escape, nudged Lafayette, and the trio slowly turned in the opposite direction once the jailer's attention was entirely focused on Eliza.

"He's gone!" she cried after regaining her breath, "Aaron's gone! What happened to him?"

"What!" cried the jailer, "How? He was there just this morning when I gave him his breakfast!"

Eliza tried her best to look frantic, "What do you think happened to him?"

The jailer stroked his beard, worried, "He must've escaped somehow." He looked at the guard, "Did you notice anything out of sorts?"

The guard shook his head. The jailer groaned and kicked at the dirt, grumbling.

"Is there anything I can do?" Eliza's face was wrinkled and stressed, she tucked a wisp of hair behind her ear.

The jailer shook his head slowly, "No, nothing. I'll have to start looking for him."

"I hope you find him," Eliza readjusted her hold on her basket, trying her best to look disappointed and worried. Her eyes flickered towards the jailer as a thought occurred to her. She held out her basket, "Here, you'll probably get hungry while you look for him." The guard took the basket and grinned when he saw the numerous loaves of bread inside.

The jailer smiled at her, "Why thank you, Miss Campbell." Eliza curtsied, knowing that giving them the bread increased her innocence in the man's eyes.

"Well, I better get going," She told them, "Good luck finding him." With that, she turned in the direction of home, excited to see Aaron.

COMPANY

Thomas, Lafayette, and Adams were practically falling atop one another when they returned. It was late, a half hour after their distraction's finale – they had learned that they didn't know New York as well as they had believed. Lafayette shambled up the steps and dramatically slumped, eyes closed and tired, onto the door. Thomas reached above the Frenchman's head and knocked politely.

Lafayette fell into Alexander's arms when he opened the door. Alexander nearly lost his footing when the marquis lurched onto him, but somehow managed to stay upright and help Lafayette to his feet. He brushed himself off, and shrugged, panting. Alexander chuckled at his friend's absent-minded appearance.

"We're exhausted." Thomas reported, "We've been running about the city for nearly a half hour. Practically as soon as we finished our diversion, we got lost!"

"Do I want to know what happened? The diversion, I mean. It sounded rather loud." Alexander asked, walking into the dining room, nodding politely at Adams before sitting in a chair. There were books, maps, and some crumbled balls of paper strewn about the table, all waiting to be studied. Thomas noticed the inkwell and quill and figured that Alexander had been trying to form some sort of plan.

Thomas followed him in, "Not particularly. But I'll give you the moral, don't ever try to make a crowd angry, it doesn't always end well."

"I assume you created a mob." Alexander smiled good-naturedly and leaned back in his chair.

"Yes, well, we didn't, we just riled them and encouraged their behavior…." Thomas, licked his lips, annoyed by straying off-topic, "The mob wanted to tar and feather the redcoats, and believed a prisoner had pet wildcats and wolves! People can be so incompetent!" Thomas explained, agitated. Alexander chuckled at the humor of the situation.

"Alexander, I was thinking that perhaps you and Eliza could find a place in- Oh!" James and Eliza walked in, carrying a bowl full of fresh bread, a pitcher of milk, and a jar of jam.

"You're back." She said, sounding slightly disappointed.

"Yes, we are, thank you for alerting us." Adams grumbled.

Alexander sighed and started stacking his books and rolling up his maps, setting them and his writing materials near the edge of the table so he could take them back to his room. Eliza and James set their provisions on the table, where Thomas quickly grabbed a slice of bread and began slathering it with the strawberry jam. Eliza quickly left, and returned with a few plates, napkins, and drinking glasses. She poured the trio some milk. Adams smiled as he sipped it.

"Jemmy was helping Alexander and me choose between different places to make a home," Eliza explained, blushing and nodding to the stack of maps, "I'd like someplace in New York, not too far from Albany, where my family lives." She took a seat beside Alexander, leaning her head against his chest.

"That's...nice." Thomas stated.

"I like New York," Lafayette grinned, "...What about Harlem?" The couple shared an excited look.

"Where's Burr?" Adams asked, annoyed by the couple's house-making plans.

"Did you learn any valuable information?" Thomas pressed.

"No, we didn't try." Alexander said, "We figured that we'd wait until all of you were here before doing so. We simply told him that we were patriots who had wanted to free him. Then Eliza went and made him a banquet-"

Eliza laughed. "He was practically starving to death." She input teasingly, "And it wasn't a banquet. Must you exaggerate everything?"

"The diversion didn't sound too terribly pleasant," James remarked, "What happened?"

Thomas bit into the bread, "When should we start questioning him? I'd like to do it sooner rather than later."

"New Jersey is nice, that's where I'm from, though it can be a bit rough around the edges." Aaron entered balancing a pile of books stacked so high that it obscured the view of his face.

"My goodness, Aaron!" Eliza watched as he blindly stumbled around the room, searching for the table.

"Let me help you with that!" Alexander jumped to his feet and relieved Aaron of half the books.

Aaron grinned and readjusted his grip on the volumes, "Thank you, Alexander," His eyes widened in surprise when he noticed the amount of people in the room. "New people! Hello!" He smiled energetically, "Thank you for rescuing me!"

"You're welcome!" Lafayette smiled.

Thomas's eyes flickered over the man, he wasn't overly impressed by him, but then again, none of the people at the table were quite what he had originally he expected.

Adams said nothing.

"Why don't we…" Lafayette suggested, but was silenced by the talk of the others.

"Later, let him adjust-"

"I'd like to be sharp mentally when I ask him my-"

"You do realize that he's-"

"I think a good night's rest will do us all a bit of-"

It was Aaron's voice that drowned out the others. They turned to look at him, the scrawny, observant, clever man that they would get to know so well. "I know that none of you are entirely comfortable around me quite yet," he began, "and I expect it will be long before you will be. As much as I'd like to know why you released me, I know that you need to be cooperative and not so full of adrenaline. I shall take my leave of absence now and retreat to my quarters." They awkwardly watched as Aaron slowly walked away, muttering about how he couldn't remember the last time he slept in a real bed.

"Hello?" Aaron said timidly the next morning, leaning against the dining room doorframe. The group was gathered about the table, Alexander, Eliza, and Lafayette on one side, Thomas, James, and Adams on the other. Lafayette leaned against his arm as he lazily spooned oatmeal into his mouth.

"Isn't that a little unmannerly for an aristocrat?" Eliza teased, eating a jam covered roll.

"This aristocrat is very tired and didn't sleep well and doesn't care much about manners at the moment." Lafayette mumbled.

The table was filled with breakfast: pancakes and waffles on one plate, a bowl filled with freshly baked rolls, a group of hard-boiled eggs, a large bowl of sugared oatmeal, and a smaller one beside it filled with berries. There was a small jar of strawberry jam, and next to it lay a pitcher of milk, and beside that, coffee and tea. There was also a stack of plates, bowls, glasses, silverware, and napkins at the end of the table, ready to be used.

"Hello?" Aaron said a bit louder, he quickly stepped back, thinking his volume too bold. The group turned and looked at the scrawny man standing in the doorway. He was clean, having taken a bath, and seemed to have had a good night's rest. He watched them all shyly, smiling slightly, then frowning, unsure of what to make of their staring expressions. He seemed so different than the man they had interacted with the night before.

"Come." Thomas gestured to the head of the table, "Sit. Eat your fill."

Aaron's grin returned, and he walked into the room quickly. He happily grabbed a plate and began filling it with all that was in sight. He paused as Eliza giggled.

"What?" he asked, eyes wide, thinking that he had taken too

much. He began to put an egg back onto its proper plate.

"Oh, nothing," she said, shaking her head, "continue." Aaron placed the egg back onto his dish, glad that he wasn't being rude. He set down the plate and began filling a glass with coffee. "You just reminded me of my father when he'd return from war. He'd eat everything we would put in front of him!" Eliza explained, sensing his apprehensiveness. He looked up at her as he ladled some oatmeal into a bowl, then began sprinkling some berries into it.

"Really?" Aaron asked politely, his voice low.

"Yes." Eliza nodded, "Please, eat all you'd like. I figured that you'd be hungry, so I made a bit extra."

"You cooked all of this?" Aaron asked in amazement, looking at the table in a new light. He gawked at it for a moment before she began speaking.

"Nearly, really all these ones know how to do is fight, talk politics, and argue." Eliza said, smiling amiably.

"Is that a compliment?" asked Thomas.

"I cooked eggs." James stated.

"I laid out the bowls and plates and other dinnerware," Alexander said, "I also made the oatmeal."

"It's a little sugary." complained Adams.

"Nobody asked you." Alexander snapped, licking his lips and taking a drink of water, "I'm used to making it this way."

Aaron spooned a bit of the oatmeal into his mouth, "I think that it's delicious."

"Thank you."

"If you don't mind," Aaron began, after a moment of silence, sitting, "Who are you all exactly?" He looked around the table curiously, wondering who these friendly people were.

"Thomas Jefferson," Thomas replied, then introduced the others, each nodding courteously, but they all frowned at the newcomer's reaction. Aaron looked as though he was going to faint.

"This… is quite the collection of people." Aaron stated once he had collected himself. He sipped his coffee, and closed his eyes for a moment, as though digesting the information. When he opened them, he appeared calm, as though he had come to peace with his jailbreak and the identities of his helpers. "Why did you release me?" he asked.

"We're trying to start a new rebellion," Thomas explained, "And we're recruiting different people to aid our cause."

"But I'm just a soldier." Aaron insisted, "I'm not very important. I haven't done anything as splendid as most of you."

"We think otherwise." Alexander said, smiling.

Adams cleared his throat, bored with the niceties, "It's time to drop the act, Burr. Who was that visiting you all of those times? Was it the governor?"

"Adams!" Eliza hissed, giving him a reprimanding look, "I told you to let him get used to us!" Adams shrugged, not seeing the difference in whether he had waited or not.

Aaron's eyes widened in fear. He glanced at his companions before slowly nodding. "Yes, it was Benedict." He admitted.

"Ha!" Alexander exclaimed, grinning, "I knew it."

"Technically *I* knew it before you." Eliza corrected him, laughing, "I was the one that ran into him."

"Yes, but you told us, so I knew it, too."

"Quit bickering, you two." Thomas said, "Stay on topic." The couple quieted, content with glaring playfully at each other. "So, care to explain why he was visiting you?"

"He was having trouble." Aaron explained, placing his hands in his lap, "and I was helping him with it."

"What kind of trouble?" Thomas asked, wondering what could possibly be so worrisome to the governor.

"Well, Benedict was never what one would call 'secure'. He's been worried about his wife, Peggy." Aaron said, "I'm his confident. I served under him in the army back when he was still a patriot, and he took a liking to me. He heard that I was in prison a few years ago and began coming weekly, sometimes daily, whenever something was troubling him."

"What's wrong with his wife?" asked Alexander, curious.

"There's nothing wrong with Peggy, but then again, I don't know her very well." continued Aaron, "It's Benedict. He's practically convinced himself that she's going to leave him for somebody else."

"Who?" Eliza asked, leaning forward, eyes wide.

Adams looked at her in disgust, "Is that relevant?"

She shook her head, "No, but I'd like to know."

"Sorry to disappoint." Aaron continued, "Benedict thinks she'll abandon him for anybody with more money, power, handsomer – the usual. Sometimes he thinks that she'll run off with Governor André, as they were sweethearts when they were younger. I just think that he's being paranoid. That's why he spoils her so. Whenever she asks for something, he gives it to her. And Benedict's in debt…deep in debt. And he keeps spending money, keeping up his extravagant lifestyle and making sure Peggy's living the way she wants to."

"I don't remember him being very insecure when I met him." Alexander stated.

"He wasn't." Aaron groaned, "He always did have trouble with his money, but then he met *her* and he's been the most insecure husband in the world."

"So did you learn any information that may be useful for our cause?" asked Thomas, hoping that they didn't release the man for nothing but gossip, "The governor's wavering in his loyalties? Anything?"

Aaron snorted, "There's no way he will ever be a patriot again. Peggy's the one who made him a loyalist in the first place."

"What's her maiden name?" Eliza asked, thinking.

"Shippen. Peggy Shippen." Aaron replied.

"Oh no." Eliza moaned, then turned to her companions, "Peggy's family remained neutral throughout the war, but everyone knew she was loyalist, and if Benedict would do anything for Peggy-"

"Exactly." Aaron finished, "And so he's been coming to me nearly every week to tell me about his problems. Marriage, debt, things like that."

"Is any of this important?" asked Thomas, "Have you learned *anything* of interest?"

"...No." Aaron sighed and shook his head, "I've been more like a doctor in the past few years than a soldier or spy. If you're asking for military secrets or his whereabouts, all I can say is that Benedict is only trusted enough to be the governor. All those medals he has are for show, so the colonists can see what 'rewards' they get if they abandon the rebel cause. As for whereabouts, he spends most of his time at home. He doesn't have many friends."

"Do you know who his friends are?" Alexander asked.

"Yes. Me, Peggy, and André." Aaron said dryly. "That's it."

"What?" Eliza stated.

"After he turned traitor, he lost all of his friends on the American side, and none of the Britons really trusted him, with the exception of André. So, now, neither he nor Peggy has friends."

"I feel sort of bad for her." Eliza muttered.

"Why?" Adams looked at her in confusion, "There's no reason to be."

"She was a social butterfly, the kind of girl everyone wanted to know. It must be hard on her, not having anyone to talk to besides her servants." Eliza explained, frowning sympathetically, "I know that I was going stir-crazy before he showed up." She nodded her head to Alexander, "I only had my parents and siblings for company for a long while, with the exception of some soldiers, and I didn't really try to get to know them, and as much as I love my family, it got boring very quickly."

James groaned. Thomas looked down at the chair beside him, as James was almost slumped to the floor, feeling deflated.

"What is it?" Thomas asked.

"Him." James pointed at Aaron, who was drinking some coffee.

Thomas nodded softly, "You're thinking that helping him escape was a waste of time?"

James nodded, "Exactly."

Aaron looked down at his pancakes, "I'm sorry that I'm of no use."

Lafayette looked up from his oatmeal, which he had been

stirring lethargically. "Don't say that. The more the merrier. I'm happy to have a new ally."

Aaron nodded uncertainly and slurped his oatmeal off his spoon.

Thomas and Alexander frowned, not so sure if they agreed with the marquis's statement.

Thirteen

May 1781

NEW YORK CITY, NEW YORK

BENEDICT

*P*eggy stared out of the carriage window and sighed, resting her chin in the palm of her hand.

Benedict cleared his throat, running his fingers through his hair, looking awkwardly at his wife, "It's a beautiful day, dearest; the park will be lovely for a stroll."

Her eyes flickered over to him, "Yes, I suppose it will be."

He frowned, a look of concern washing over him. He leaned forward, touching his hand to her knee, "What is it? You've been much quieter these past days, what's the matter?"

She slowly raised her eyes to meet his gaze, "It's nothing important, Benedict. I guess I have been quieter lately... I've been thinking."

"About what?" He asked curiously.

She tugged at a blonde curl, "It'd surprise you...but I've been doing an awful lot of thinking about – Benny, is it true that there are spies? In the city? That they're there simply to find true loyalists and those who still resist our king?"

He looked away, face solemn, "As much as I'd hate to admit it... yes. There are spies, there are always spies, there have always been spies! I can't imagine this whole big world without them."

Peggy frowned, forehead wrinkled and strained, "Why do you keep them out there, can't we leave the people with a bit of freedom? I know it would just be awful if I couldn't trust anyone, not even my own friends and neighbors." Benedict stared at her for a moment, stunned.

"What is it?" she wondered.

He shook his head, absentmindedly touching his hair, "...Are you beginning to be sympathetic to the rebels?"

Peggy smirked and adjusted in her seat. She pulled the coach's curtain back a hair, allowing her to get a better view of the outdoors. She stole a glance at Benedict, "I confess that I do indeed, at times, have beliefs that fall in line with those of the rebels.... You should hardly be making such remarks though, I know you disagree with what the king and parliament believe just as much as I disagree with those patriots."

"That may be so, Mrs. Arnold," he smiled, "and yet I still hold my position, despite it being known to the government my sympathies."

"Benny," she shook her head, "You know that that 'important government position' is nothing but hogwash. They don't trust you for a minute. It's only a show."

"I know that," he nodded, cheeks flushed, the remark stinging slightly. He looked out of the window, watching the busy city streets while his temper cooled. Peggy, knowing that she had upset him, remained silent, waiting for him to turn back to her.

The streets were bustling, as usual. Some people glanced up at the coach, but they didn't bother to look inside or tip their hats. Most were just walking on the cobblestone streets, heading to their homes or their shops. Some people, Benedict could tell, were shoppers. The shoppers were mainly rich aristocrats, as the carriage had entered a higher-end neighborhood, and the poor and common folk had no business there. Some wigged ladies carried parasols as they peeked into boutique windows, their husbands or suiters stood nearby, swinging golden-chained watches in their hands as they discussed everything under the sun. There were some girls he could see who didn't wear wigs, but instead arranged their hair in elaborate poufs. Some of those young women wore multiple bows in their hair, some none; the richest wore strands of pearls, encircling their hair like garland on a fir tree.

Benedict smoothed back his dark hair and rubbed his cane's wooden handle, deep in thought. He missed Burr. Aaron had escaped from prison weeks before, which had come to Benedict as a shock. Still, he believed that he had had it coming. He had kept the man imprisoned much longer than the time of his sentence, frightened that his companion would abandon him with his troubles as soon as he was permitted. He didn't wish to think about where he had gone. He just wished that he'd be able to cope with his worries on his own.

A flash of powdery blue caught Benedict's eye. He focused

on the color, which he immediately recognized. It was a man dressed in a glistening baby blue uniform. He watched the man, who was moving in a hurry, as he moved through the streets. He was instantly recognizable, with his fancily curled tresses, and his cheerful gait. He waved at some of the people happily, though they ignored him, causing his grin to falter.

"Stop the coach!" Benedict called. The driver tugged on the reins, causing the horse to stop.

Peggy looked at him in alarm, "Benedict! What has gotten into you, Benny? This is nowhere near the-"

He looked back at her, "Pardon, but do you mind if I go do… something for a bit?"

Peggy crossed her arms and shook her head, "Benedict-"

"Please, Peggy, sweetheart?" He pleaded, frantically looking between her and the man in the blue suit.

She looked at the frantic expression on his face and slowly nodded, "All right then."

"Thank you!" He quickly opened the door and began climbing out, Peggy handed him his cane. He waved the coach on and turned around, walking after the blue-coated man as fast as he could.

The man was well ahead of him, walking briskly, as though he was in a hurry. Benedict tried to rush after him, but his leg dragged, causing him to lag behind. The man continued down the street until he came to a corner; he looked around for a few seconds, as if he were lost, then he nodded to himself and began skipping down the next street. Benedict grumbled at the man's unnatural joyfulness, but the man's dallying had bought him some time. He continued after him.

LAFAYETTE

The Marquis de Lafayette hummed to himself as he skipped through the busy streets of the New York. He was to meet Alexander at a small eatery, and he was certain now that he was on the right track. He was certain because he saw Alexander waving to him at the street corner. The Frenchman jogged up to his friend, who was standing by the door of the shop.

"Marquis," Alexander clasped Lafayette's shoulder, "this is a place I would come to often back in my college days."

"Is it good?" asked Lafayette, hugging his companion and kissing his cheeks.

"Most excellent!" he exclaimed, grinning as he held the marquis at an arm's length.

"Better than Eliza's?" Lafayette was nearly drooling at the smell of buttery bread that wafted out the door, but he eyed the place suspiciously, not believing anything could be better than Mrs. Hamilton's pastries.

Alexander hesitated, "Eliza is a rare species. Nothing can compare to her culinary concoctions. This, however, is a close second." He held the door open for his friend, who walked through cheerfully, gladdened by the praise Alexander gave the establishment, and sat at a small table. Alexander tossed a coin to a girl behind the counter, and spoke softly to her while she wrote on a notepad. He lingered at the counter until she handed him two slabs of bread on a plate, heavily laden with peach jam. Alexander walked them over to the table and sat down in an empty chair. Lafayette reached for a slice hungerly.

He looked up as a vaguely familiar, red-coated man leaning on a cane entered. He was in his early forties, Lafayette guessed, and he watched as the man glanced at him, then quickly looked away. The man walked up to the counter and asked the girl for a strip of note paper. She watched him in surprise before tearing a sheet out of her book and handing it to him. The man sat in a nearby chair and pulled out a pencil from his pocket. The man began writing and Lafayette turned his gaze back to Alexander.

"So, what's so important that couldn't be discussed at home?" he asked, turning his thoughts to the reason why he had been invited on such an excursion.

Alexander swallowed his bite of bread, nodding, "Right. I don't trust Burr."

Lafayette blinked, "You always have been rather frank. Whatever for? He seems like a nice enough man."

Alexander shrugged, "I don't really know, it's hard to explain."

"Is it because you don't like him?" Lafayette asked, "If that is the case, I don't see how you trust more than ten people."

Alexander glared at him, "It's not that, I do like Aaron, I like him just fine.... I trust Jefferson, I don't *like* him one bit, but I do trust him. With Burr...." He stared at the window, as though the words he was searching for would appear on the glass, "...It just seems like there's something he's not telling us."

Lafayette laughed, "Of course he's not. I wouldn't expect him to divulge all of his secrets minutes upon knowing us. We're not exactly... ah..." Lafayette frowned.

"Welcoming?" Alexander suggested.

"*Oui.*" Lafayette nodded, "*Oui,* that's the word. Eliza is, certainly, the rest of us? We're not exactly very charming."

"You're nice." Alexander said.

"And you're too prickly." Lafayette shoved a piece of bread into his mouth and nodded. "Right. Good bread, but Eliza's much better."

"I used to think that it was the best." Alexander chuckled to himself, "I didn't know her then."

Lafayette nodded, smiling in good humor before turning back to the darker subject, "I don't see why you shouldn't trust him for the matter, he seems like an honorable fellow."

"There's just something about him that seems... off to me." Alexander explained, "Do you know what I mean?"

"*Non,* not really. I find English people off, but I've always considered it cultural." Lafayette stated. After thinking for a moment, he added, "Though I have met an Englishman that I thought was very odd. Snake-like and sneaky."

"Who?" asked Alexander.

Lafayette frowned, "I met a relative of King George's once. He seemed – he was nice enough to talk to, but he seemed very slippery as well. So, I suppose I understand what you mean when it comes to Burr, but I don't see it in him at all.... The snake was the one that told me about the war."

"I assume he was on the king's side, considering you didn't get along?" Alexander licked a layer of jam off his fingertips.

"You assume correctly, still I feel indebted to him, even though we disagreed." Lafayette said dramatically.

"Is he the *only* Englishman?" Alexander asked, smiling in a joking manner, knowing the answer.

Lafayette thought for a moment before nodding, "Essentially. I don't know many English people."

The man stood up from his chair and walked briskly past Alexander and bumped into Lafayette's chair. Lafayette looked up in alarm, "*Excusez moi, monsieur!*" but the man was already out the door. He frowned and turned back to his companion, who was busy looking at a piece of paper.

"Interesting?" teased Lafayette.

"Hmm?" Alexander looked up, "Oh, that man dropped this when he bumped into you. It's a note of sorts. Do you think it would be best to return it?"

Lafayette considered his proposition, "Personally, I do not like that he bumped into me; but morally, it could have been an accident, so I say we go." Lafayette stood up and quickly opened the eatery's door and looked out into the street.

Alexander quickly caught up and stood beside him. "Do you see him?"

The marquis looked in all directions, but he could not see the man with the cane, "For a man with a limp, he sure moves fast. He's gone." He turned back to his friend, who was looking at the note curiously.

"What is it?" Lafayette asked.

"The writing on here," Alexander explained, "It appears to be a letter of sorts."

Lafayette swatted his hand, "You should not read somebody's private papers. There could be important information in them!"

"Once upon a time, I was *paid* to read papers with important information in them." Alexander said, "What makes this any different?"

"They aren't addressed to *mon* general!" Lafayette crossed his arms, "You're not one for respecting privacy, are you?"

"Not unless I'm ordered to." Alexander admitted.

Lafayette stomped his foot, "Then, as your higher-ranking officer, I order you to stop reading!"

"But it's addressed to me." Alexander smiled and chuckled at the Frenchman's angry then dumbfounded face.

"What?" asked Lafayette, looking over Alexander's shoulder, "Is it a secret message?"

"I don't think so…" Alexander stated, "It's written in English." He gasped as he looked at the bottom of the page.

"What is it? What is it?" Lafayette tugged on his arm, "Who's it from? Who's it from?"

Alexander looked at him, his eyes wide with fear and excitement, "It's from Benedict Arnold."

COMPANY

"'A. H. Please come to the Governor Arnold home tomorrow at noon. Use the name of Alexander Smith. I have information that may be of use to both you and your cause. Your obedient servant, Governor Benedict Arnold.'" Alexander lowered the paper from his face, "What do you all think?"

The group was crowded around the table, everyone sitting in their designated spots, considering what he had to say.

"That man," Eliza dropped her sampler and thread in excitement, "Did he have dark hair and use a wooden cane?"

Lafayette nodded, "And a bright crimson uniform with many medals!"

She leaned her head against Alexander's shoulder, "What do you think that you should do?" She picked up the sampler and fiddled with the embroidery she had stitched while waiting for an answer.

He stroked her hair as he contemplated her question, "Honestly... I think I should take him up on his offer."

"What!" Thomas jumped to his feet, "You're going to step willingly into a trap? I thought you were smarter than this, Hamilton!"

Alexander looked up at him, letter in hand, "I think that it's worth the risk. Why not take the chance?"

"I agree with Jefferson." Aaron said, nodding adamantly, determined, "It sounds just like a trap to me. It could just be a bunch of soldiers waiting to arrest you."

"How did he even find you?" demanded Adams, "We haven't given anyone our true names, with the exception of Burr..." Adams turned to look at him, "YOU! Who did you tell? Who did you tell?"

Aaron held up his hands in surrender and backed away from both Adams and the table, "I haven't spoken to or seen anyone except all of you since my escape! How could I have tattled?" he asked in defense.

"You could have snuck out and told a friend waiting down the road!" Adams accused.

"I can testify that he did no such thing!" Eliza said, standing up, "He's been either helping me cook or reading in the study all day for the past few weeks! He couldn't have done anything! And besides, he doesn't know anyone but us!"

"You *were* a close friend of Arnold's," James mentioned quietly; Thomas nodded, realizing that this was a good point.

"That's behind me!" Aaron exclaimed, amazed by how quickly his allies could tear themselves from his side, "And how could I have told him when I didn't even know you all?"

"He confesses!" Adams shouted, smiling, hands in the air, shaking victoriously.

"You knew Eliza." Thomas stated, "You could have figured out who she was."

"In my defense, I'd never even heard of her, or her husband, before the jailbreak." Aaron said, "I couldn't have done it." Alexander frowned, disappointed by his lack of fame, but saw Aaron's point.

"Surely you've heard of her father?" Thomas said coolly, "A certain General Philip Schuyler of the Continental army?"

Alexander stood up, "I won't go! If this is how you're all behaving, I won't go."

Thomas opened his mouth to argue against the decision, but then closed it, realizing that was what he wanted, and nodded. He took his seat and the rest of the group followed suit. Adams glared at Aaron from across the table, who pointedly looked away from him.

"So, you're not going?" Lafayette asked, disappointed.

"Not if it will risk destroying our little revolution here." Alexander said, "I'd go if we were all getting along and on the same page, but obviously, we're not. As a result, I'm not going."

Thomas chuckled, "I doubt that will ever happen."

"What?" asked Lafayette.

"That we'll ever get along." James explained, "We *never* do."

"I get along with all of you, and we get along well enough as a whole." Lafayette said, "I don't see what the problem is."

"You – and Eliza – are the only people who truly seem to get along with everyone." Thomas told the Frenchman, "The rest of us would go around in circles for hours if the two of you weren't here."

"Or until somebody realizes that the argument is *pointless* and will just make everyone grouchier and decides to *stop* said argument." Alexander put in. Thomas glared at him, then turned back to Lafayette.

"Right. Still we need not burden ourselves with this…" Thomas waved his hand in the air for emphasis, "…This, this trick! The conversation is over. Hamilton, you're staying here, you are not to leave for the Arnold home." Thomas abruptly began walking away, seeing no need in continuing the conversation.

"Why do you tell me not to go when I already said that I'm not going?" Alexander asked, "You treat me like a child at times."

"And I have good reason to." Thomas turned to look back at him, "You act like one at times." He continued on his way, heading to his room.

Lafayette and Eliza instinctively grabbed hold of Alexander's arm. "Calm yourself, *Monsieur*. He means well." Lafayette comforted as Alexander thrust himself into his chair.

"I know he does." Alexander stated, "I just don't like admitting that he does."

Eliza sat and put her arm around him, "I know, but I'm glad that you're not going. Thomas is correct, it may be dangerous."

"It *will* be dangerous." Adams corrected, standing, "So it will be awful to our cause if he goes."

"I don't think that it will be awful for our cause." Lafayette exclaimed, "I *want* him to go. I think he will learn valuable information."

"…That comes with the price of being captured!" Adams finished, "The risk is greater than the reward."

"It just adds to the adventure!" Lafayette argued, rising to his full height, towering over his opponent.

"An adventure that may very well get him killed." Aaron suddenly snapped, jumping to his feet, unable to contain himself any longer in his chair, "I've started to care a great deal about all of you, and I don't want to see any of you throw your lives away, just because of some chance!" Eliza's head whipped around to face him, surprised that he would even suggest such a thing. Lafayette opened his mouth and closed it, finding nothing to say. Alexander nodded softly and fingered the brim of his tri-corner hat. Aaron frowned, seeing the surprise in all of his companion's faces.

"I won't go." Alexander stood and walked away, leaving Eliza, Aaron, Lafayette, Adams, and James to wonder what to do.

ALEXANDER

Alexander stood awkwardly at the door, unsure if what he was doing was the right thing. He closed his eyes, reached out his hand, and knocked three times on the imposing navy blue door. He waited, rocking on his feet, swaying from side to side. Why was it that he was so nervous?

He both sighed in relief and jumped in surprise when the door opened. Peggy stood there, holding a broom, an apron tied around her slender waist. He smiled shyly, her piled, flaxen-blonde hair reminding him of Eliza. The fact that she was wearing a pink bow made him even more comfortable.

"Hello?" She said, apparently confused as to why there was somebody at her door. Then her expression brightened, then dimmed, like she was trying to hide a grin. Alexander could see that she was trying to act calm and collected, but he knew she must be very excited. He remembered Aaron mentioning that the Arnolds never had any visitors, so the girl must have been on the verge of fainting.

Her stormy grey eyes quickly scanned him, and she smiled, a bright smile that lit up her face. It didn't look like she had smiled in a very long time.

"Hello." He replied, bowing slightly, trying to be friendly while retaining a businesslike personality. Peggy curtsied politely and smiled sweetly. "I'm here to see Governor Arnold." Alexander explained, "My name is Alexander Smith, I was told to meet him here at noon."

He studied her face, searching for signs of distrust. She looked surprised at first, which Alexander took as disbelief that somebody had come to pay a visit. She nodded slowly, then more vigorously. She turned her head around and yelled into the house, "Benedict!

You have a guest!" She hopped up and down in glee and began skipping lightly away, then turned back to Alexander, seemingly have temporarily forgotten him in her joy. Her cheeks flushed, embarrassed at being caught in her act of happiness. She righted her posture, remembered her manners, and hid the broom behind her back, "You may come in."

Peggy stepped aside, giving room for Alexander. She led him to the parlor, where he sat on a small lounge chair. She then instructed her guest to wait while she went in search of the governor. She turned away and began to leave, beaming at the pleasure of having a guest.

"Wait!" Alexander called, hand outstretched, Peggy whirled around, happy to be delayed.

"Yes?" she asked, eyes wide, smile soft and welcoming.

"You were sweeping," he stated, "Why would a person of your standing do so? Don't you have servants?" he frowned, seeing how rude and spoiled he sounded. He quickly scrambled to make amends, "I'm sorry, that was terribly impolite of me – Sometimes I speak before I think and – I-I-I'm sorry-" he flubbed.

"No, no." Peggy shook her head, her smile faltering, "It's fine. We had to dismiss the last of them a few months ago. We didn't have enough money to… pay them." She stood there for a moment before walking off, silent.

Alexander sighed, knowing very well that his question had disheartened the cheerful girl's mood. He frowned, regretting his quick mouth that he was so grateful to have when dealing with Jefferson. He tried to take his mind off of it by examining the scenery.

At first glance, the room was impressive, with vibrant colors and wide array of materials. The closer Alexander looked, however, the less impressed he became. The glittering objects were few and far between: a silvery candlestick here, a small white statue on the fireplace mantel there. Some of the furniture seemed cheap, some of it lavishly expensive. What Aaron had said was true. The Arnolds were trying to make it appear that they lived lavishly, even when they couldn't.

He was surprised by Peggy confessing so frankly their lack of money.

Alexander was staring into the fireplace, unlit, when he heard somebody clear her throat. He looked up; there was Peggy, apron and broom gone, smoothing her rosy gown. She seemed desperate for attention, her peppiness having returned, the awkwardness of before having evaporated.

"Governor Arnold will see you now, Mr. Smith." She nodded at him to follow her. Peggy turned to leave, Alexander jumping to his feet to follow. After walking through a series of rooms before making it to the stairs, Alexander wondered if he had ever seen a house with that many unused rooms. Every other room seemed to be a sitting room or a dining room, and yet there were so many other rooms that seemed to have no purpose at all. Peggy began to hike up the stairs, one hand on the railing, the other raising her gown an inch, making it easier to climb. Once at the top, she scurried down the hall and knocked on a large dark wooden door. Alexander heard a muffled voice coming from within before Peggy opened the door, indicating that it was time for him to enter.

He did. The room was the most practically decorated he had

seen in the home: a desk, three chairs, a rug on the floor, and a fireplace. The man sitting behind the desk shifted through some papers before looking up at his newfound companion. He nodded at Alexander as he sat, and smiled brightly as Peggy walked a few steps into the room.

"Will he be staying for lunch, Benny?" she asked, hands clasped behind her, a hopeful and curious expression around her eyes.

"I expect so." Benedict replied, mildly intrigued by the question, then turned to Alexander, "Do you think you will?"

Alexander shrugged, "I'm unsure. Should I be expecting to?"

"Yes!" Peggy exclaimed, answering for her guest. She then hurried out of the room, shutting the door behind her, joyous at how long the visitor would be staying.

"So you've met Peggy." Benedict said, grinning tiredly as he pushed aside the papers. Alexander nodded slowly, becoming more business-like. He was annoyed at how familiarly the governor was speaking to him, like there was no ice between them.

"I suppose I have. And you called me here for a reason?" he spoke irritably, staring off into the distance, looking out the window, avoiding eye contact. "I wouldn't have wanted to come here if I had known we were only going to make small talk."

Benedict rubbed his head, beads of sweat rolling down his neck, wetting his crimson uniform. He seemed distressed by the visit, "Yes, quite right."

"Then get on with it, please. What's your reason?" Alexander spoke harshly, looking into the man's face, knowing that he was going to get more answers from him acting gruffly than kind.

"I don't want to be with the British anymore." Benedict said flatly, "I would like to help in your rebellion."

"Who said that we were planning a rebellion?" Alexander asked, surprised and frightened. He reminded himself to look casual, showing no expression, "How did you find me?" he tried to shift the topic into a safer direction.

"It was by luck, actually." Benedict told him, "Yesterday, I was riding in a carriage with Peggy when I saw Lafayette walking down the street. I stopped the coach and chased after him, well, as fast as I was able." He gestured to the cane leaning against the desk. Alexander vaguely remembered the accident at Saratoga; he hardened his heart, allowing no pity for the cripple. "And I saw him meet with a fellow that I recognized, though I couldn't tell from where until I came closer. That was you. When you walked into the café, I hurried in after you, knowing that if you were meeting with Lafayette then the two of you were planning something. I figured you were the brains of the operation, as I remember you being a very intelligent young lad – and Lafayette isn't one that I'd trust to plan anything other than an invasion or siege. So, I wrote to you, and here you are."

"And where does a rebellion come into play?" asked Alexander, annoyed by the man's simple explanation, "That sounds like hogwash."

"I said to myself, Benedict, what do you think two important, rebel leaders would be doing after a failed rebellion? Starting a new one, I thought. Was I right?" Benedict inquired.

Alexander frowned, seeing logic in Benedict's thinking. "Why do you want to quit being a British puppet?"

"I don't like that term, but it's not inaccurate." Benedict

grumbled, "My reasoning is because... I don't feel right anymore. Two years ago, I could have stopped the execution of Patrick Henry, Thomas Paine, and John Adams, but I was too much of a coward to put a stop to it, worried about what might happen if I did intervene. Nobody trusted me, not the loyalists, not the patriots. The patriots despised me for betraying their trust. The loyalists, sure they adored me at first, inviting both me and Peggy to these lavish parties and galas, to show how much they wanted to thank Peggy for making me switch sides. It was also to show how much a rebel traitor would be rewarded. After a few months or so, it all stopped, the party invitations dwindled to nothing. We were shunned. The loyalists and the British suspected me of flipping. After all, if I'd flipped once, why not do it again? Peggy, she was associated with me, she married a top-notch rebel general, why not shun her too? Sure, she made her husband a fine British soldier, but maybe he was just pretending and he had actually made her an American sympathizer. Our lives have become a wreck, simply because I switched sides!... Now I want to right that wrong." Benedict looked at his guest, eyes wide, searching for even a flicker of sympathy. He saw none, so he continued.

"I was given the position of governor simply because they wanted to keep me occupied. None of the British, with the exception of my friend, André, trust me. The job is just to keep me busy, unable to cause trouble. My deepest of sympathies lie with the patriots, Peggy knows that. She says that's why I'm such a good governor, that I can see from both sides. I don't think I'm a good governor. How can I be, when everyone hates me? I regret choosing the British. It was a matter of money and keeping Peggy happy. I was never good with money, and she's used to having an endless stream of it." He sighed, and looked at Alexander, "I'm just rambling on, aren't I?"

Alexander nodded, "Yes, but I'm not complaining. My one question: what honor is there in betraying those who had your trust?"

Benedict chuckled dryly, shaking his head, "None. Funny, honor was what I valued most. I believed that I'd gain honor by squashing the rebellion and aiding the king. I was wrong. There is no honor in betraying those who have your trust, my boy. Honor is important, something you should always keep clean and tend to. I should know. I've lost my honor. I've lost the trust of everyone but my wife."

Alexander said nothing, the wisdom of the man's words sinking in. Benedict rubbed his hands together, "Now, I told you I had information that you might find valuable, did I not?"

Alexander nodded vigorously, abandoning his annoyed act, happy to return to a subject he was interested in. Benedict smiled, "I have an idea as to how General Washington can escape."

His guest nearly fell out of his chair. Benedict laughed softly. Alexander blinked a few times, his guise falling to pieces, his boyish excitement emerging, "Please, do tell. How can we free him? I've been trying to plan that for *months*, and have had no luck."

Benedict rolled his shoulders back, "As governor, I can request to see a prisoner without much of a reason. If I want him to come here, for, say, dinner, he'd be allowed to come here for dinner. And the security around my building isn't what one would call 'watertight', he could vanish mysteriously while here."

Alexander nodded slowly, thinking the idea through, "How would that end for you? The governor helping the most heavily-guarded prisoner in the colonies escape. I don't anticipate that would go over well with King George."

Benedict shook his head, chuckling lightly, "No, I don't suppose it would. Say an accident happened, causing me to lose consciousness or be locked in a closet as the prisoner escapes, I don't think that anyone will blame me. After all, it would hardly be my fault." He said, his eyes wide and gleaming with rebelliousness.

Alexander laughed, "I like your plan. But why would you help us?"

"You said 'us', so there's more to it than just you and Lafayette?" Benedict asked.

"I will reveal nothing." Alexander said, reminding himself to be more cautious, his cold demeanor returning, "And you didn't answer my question."

"You didn't answer mine, but I don't suppose you ever will. I told you that I wanted to right my wrong, and freeing him from jail would be a chance to prove that, would it not?" Benedict looked at him pleadingly, his eyes begging for a chance.

Alexander studied him, "How do I know that I can trust you?" he asked. Benedict contemplated the question and was beginning to open his mouth when the door flew open. Both of the men looked up in surprise and fright, their talk making them paranoid.

"I brought tea!" Peggy announced, bursting into the room, holding a platter. "And biscuits!" She set the platter onto Benedict's desk and began pouring some tea into a teacup. "Do you take sugar, Mr. Smith?"

Alexander gulped, his heart slowly returning to a normal pace, he took a deep breath and nodded, "Yes. Two."

Peggy ladled two sugar lumps into the tea and stirred. She handed it to him and watched him expectantly. He brought the tea to his lips and took a sip.

It was awful. So awful that Alexander wondered if Peggy had bothered to put more than a teaspoon of water in it. The flavor was much too strong, so much so that not even five sugar lumps would alter the flavor. He somehow managed to force it down. He smiled gratefully at Peggy, who beamed at his approval. She began adding half the sugar bowl, a good portion of the milk, and a tablespoon of honey to Benedict's tea. As she stirred, Benedict mouthed 'sorry' to Alexander. He shuddered, figuring he deserved it. Having had over two years of Eliza's cooking, Alexander was used to eating only delicious foods. This tea did not fit Alexander's definition of delicious.

He vowed that, even twenty years later, he would never take Eliza's cooking for granted.

He reached over to grab a biscuit, hoping the bread would absorb the awful flavor, but he discovered that it tasted more like brick than bread. Peggy seemed to be the only one enjoying the meal, having a bit of tea (one sugar) and a biscuit which she routinely dunked into her drink.

They ate mostly in silence, Benedict and Alexander looking away from each other, pretending to be preoccupied with the meal. Peggy kept stealing glances at their guest when she thought he wasn't looking. Then she burst, a flood of questions and stories tumbled out of her mouth, getting the attention of both the governor and the soldier. Peggy asked Alexander about himself and his life, with which he provided the vaguest answers he could muster, and she told him about hers. Fifteen minutes had passed before Peggy finished and began gathering the plates and the empty teacups – formerly filled with tea which Alexander was surprised at his ability to keep down. Once completed, she left, allowing the two men to continue their conversation in private.

"Sorry that I didn't forewarn you." Benedict said, "Ever since we had to dismiss the cook, it's fallen to Peggy and me to manage the meals. I've tried teaching her, but she's still learning."

"That was the worst tea I've ever drunk." Alexander muttered, not caring if Benedict took offense, "but the biscuit was tolerable."

"The first time she made tea, I spit it on her dress. In the end, I purchased her a new dress and explained that the spitting was the result of a hiccup." Benedict said blandly, shaking his head, marveling at his luck, "I still can't believe she believed me."

"Please, I must depart soon," Alexander stood to leave, nodding courteously to his host, "but please answer this one question, how do I know that I can trust you?"

Benedict smiled mysteriously and rose to his feet, shrugging. "That's the thing, you don't."

★ ★ ★

COMPANY

"My Alexander!"

"That Hamilton!"

"Alexander?"

"Hamilton!"

"*Monsieur?*"

"What has happened?" Aaron asked, rushing into the dining room, law book in hand, their shouting having interrupted his reading.

Eliza, Thomas, James, Adams, and Lafayette were scattered about the room. Eliza had a laundry basket on her hip, looking worried, Lafayette toted another basket behind her, wearing the same face as she. Thomas entered and slammed a book onto the table, his face red and enraged. Adams's hat fell to the floor and he was taking off his coat, having just come back from town. James quietly spooned soup into his mouth, cheeks flushed, huffing and trying to deal with his emotions.

"He's gone off and gotten himself killed, that's what!" Thomas snapped, "And now he's dragged us down with him."

"He's gone to visit the governor?" Aaron's face turned white, his hand flew up to his head, clutching his hair, "Why, that's awful! When did he go?"

"It's near one, is it not?" Adams asked, looking at the grandfather clock in the corner.

"*Oui.*" Lafayette said, setting down the laundry, "It is. Thomas and *Monsieur* Adams went into town near eleven and have only recently returned. We thought Alexander was with them, but he wasn't. It only makes sense that he went off to see *Monsieur* Arnold." Lafayette tried to suppress his grin, but found it difficult.

Aaron cocked his head, "I've been studying my books in my

room all day, so I didn't see anything. Eliza, don't you think he would've told you?"

Eliza nodded, slowing sinking into a chair. The basket, forgotten, fell away as her hand flew to her pale face, "Yes, he did, in a way.... I saw him leave."

"Why did you not follow him?" Aaron sat in a chair beside her, frowning, his voice panicked and worried.

"I didn't think that there was need to." She explained, tucking a lock of hair behind her ear, "He told me he was going into town, and I didn't ask where."

Thomas moaned in anguish, running his fingers through his red hair, "You didn't think to ask?"

She shook her head, her eyebrows furrowed, "Of course not. He said he wasn't going there last night, and I didn't think he was lying, it would be out of character for him do so. But come to think of it, it is unusual for him to do something...truly reasonable." She slumped into her chair, her arms folded across her bosom, pouting.

"We're doomed." Thomas held his head in his hands, falling into a chair beside James, "The redcoats are probably on their way here already. Hamilton's in jail, soon we'll all be in jail! I don't want to go to jail! I'll die if I go to jail!"

James patted his friend on the shoulder absentmindedly, unfazed by his dramatics, "You're not going to jail, Tom, and stop acting like you are. Alexander, if he is in jail, which I doubt he is, would never confess to having allies. For now, we just have to worry about his well-being. We don't need to worry about our own."

James frowned sympathetically at Eliza before giving Thomas a slap on the back, "Enough with the theatrics! Act rational!"

"Do you think we ought to go searching for him?" asked Aaron, "To make sure he's safe? Good God, I hope he's well."

"I doubt he's safe. He's probably in jail." Thomas stated, tugging at his ponytail.

"Yes, we've heard of your fear of jails." Adams snapped, as though speaking of prisons caused him physical pain.

"I don't see a point in searching." Eliza said, pulling at her skirts anxiously, "I know he'll come home eventually."

"Then what do we do?" asked Aaron, rising to his feet, breathing heavily.

"We wait." Lafayette said, "I've become very good at waiting for the last few minutes."

Aaron sighed, "Wonderful."

The group jumped when they heard the doorknob twist and the front door spring open. They nearly trampled over each other as they raced to the room's entrance, trying to see who it was, while also remaining hidden in the small room.

Alexander wondered why everybody was watching him and sighing in relief from the dining room.

"He lives!" Lafayette exclaimed.

"I can't believe it!" Thomas shouted, "He's alive!"

"Why didn't you tell me where you were going?" Eliza shrieked, running over to hug him. He smiled as she kissed him on the cheek and nose.

"What's the commotion?" he asked when she pulled away.

"We thought you were dead, or on your way to being dead." Adams stated.

"That's it in a nutshell." Aaron replied, frowning.

"Why did you think I died?" Alexander inquired, placing his hat and coat on the rack.

"You went to see the governor." Thomas said angrily, "You directly disobeyed my orders."

Alexander shrugged, "Technically, I'm higher-ranking in the military, so I don't have to listen to you; and, also, you're not my mother or the general."

"Or your wife." Eliza added.

"Or my wife." Alexander corrected himself.

"I was a governor once, and – what does rank have to do with this?" Thomas asked, his nose crinkling, his cheeks flushing.

"Nothing really, I just wanted to annoy you." Alexander said, "As for the governor, I just decided that it was worth the risk. So, I took the risk, and we now have a new ally."

"What?" questioned James.

"Benedict?" Thomas's voice suddenly grew higher pitched.

"Yes." Alexander said, "He's offered to help us, and I, for one, happen to think that he was worth listening to."

"You told him that?" Thomas exclaimed, growing even angrier.

"No. I hardly showed that I agreed with him." Alexander explained, "He just told me a plan of his, and I listened to it. I told him that he could proceed and that I'd help him."

"What is this plan?" asked Adams.

"Freeing Washington."

"*Mon* general!" Lafayette began hopping and clapping, happy.

"How is that even possible?" James asked.

"Simple. As governor, he has certain privileges, such as inviting prisoners to his house without reason. One such prisoner may vanish under mysterious circumstances, and, if he plans it right, will make it look like it was an accident." Alexander concluded.

"How magnificent!" Lafayette finished expressing his joy.

"I don't believe he'll go through with it." Adams said adamantly. Thomas nodded in agreement.

"Did he want any sort of payment?" Thomas asked, "… Does he know about us?"

Alexander shook his head, "He didn't mention any sort of payment. He only knows about Lafayette. He saw Lafayette yesterday when we went to a store, and he tailed him. He asked if there were more, and if there is indeed a rebellion, but I wouldn't answer one way or another. He is suspicious, though." He frowned when he saw the disapproving look on Thomas's face.

Thomas shook his head, "I can't believe you did that, Hamilton." He turned away and began to leave. Adams nodded curtly at Alexander and began walking after the redhead. James followed his friends back into the study, though he smiled softly at Alexander, proud of his triumph.

"I thought that they'd be happy." Alexander said disappointedly, leaning against the wall.

"I am!" Lafayette exclaimed, hugging his friend tightly, "I'm very happy."

"You're always happy." Alexander stated, patting the marquis awkwardly on the back.

"Not always," Lafayette corrected, pulling away, "I was sad in France."

"You shouldn't have done that." Aaron said coldly, "Who knows what will happen now that the Arnolds are involved?" His expression brightened, he grinned and shook Alexander's hand, "Though I must say I approve heartily!"

Eliza put her hand on his shoulder, looking up into his eyes, her own filled with sympathy, "I'm happy for you…. They'll come around, they're just blinded by what might have happened instead."

Alexander nodded, "I know. But still. It's not helping my opinion of them!"

"Yes, the fact that you only like me, Lafayette, and Aaron is not new," Eliza laughed.

"Madison's nice enough," he admitted.

She rolled her eyes and shook her head, "Come," Eliza began to pull him into the dining room, "Tell us what happened."

Alexander laughed, walking into the room, his arms around her and Lafayette; Aaron tagging along behind them, "I will, I'll tell you everything. But first, could you make me some pancakes? I just had the worst meal imaginable."

Fourteen

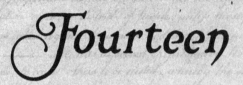

June 6, 1781

NEW YORK CITY, NEW YORK

WASHINGTON

Former General George Washington of the Continental army pondered about where he was headed. The shades were drawn in the carriage, obscuring his view of the outside world. A scarlet-coated soldier sat across from him, ready to slap the prisoner's hand if he tried to adjust the curtain, or to contain him if he did anything more reckless.

Luckily, Washington was an obedient (some would even say charming) prisoner, sitting still and erect, hands clasped and in his lap. He did not speak, knowing that his traveling companion would not say anything in return.

Washington licked his lips and rubbed his hands together, recalling the day's sudden turn of events. He'd awakened in his cell, as always. He was kept in solitary confinement, which would be dreary for some, but not for a man who didn't have many true friends and confidants. He missed his closest friend: his dear wife Martha, with all of his heart. He longed to be in their parlor, sitting beside her, spending time with her grandchildren, Nelly and Washy. He knew that she, all three of them, were home safe in Mt. Vernon, but he couldn't help but worry. He had been in jail for three years now, never released to visit his family – though he wrote them every day, and eagerly awaited the Sabbath, when letters from Martha, Nelly, and Washy would arrive. He also anticipated the daily, although brief trips to the outside of his cell when a soldier was brought to speak to him. The soldiers always tried to be as friendly, if a little gruff, as possible. Washington knew their visits were only to keep him sane. One couldn't go too long without speaking to another human being and not experience mental decay, he knew.

The day had been as he expected, which consisted of walking the length of his cell, reading through his collection of letters, writing some to his many friends and family members (though he had regrettably lost contact with some of his closest aids and generals after being captured,) and reminding himself of the proper forms of etiquette in… any scenario really. It was lunch that had held the unexpected surprise: a visit from a soldier, a captain. Nearly all the other soldiers he knew were mere jail guards or privates on patrol, all having been one of the king's men for less than two years. The captain informed him that he would be meeting with somebody for dinner, and that he should prepare himself. Washington had shrugged, believing his dinner companion to be an important officer coming for a visit, but the theory quickly washed away with the water when he was brought out of his cell to bathe, and was given fresh new clothes that made him look like the general he was, and hair powder. His coat, he regretted, was scarlet; he much preferred the patriotic navy of the Continental army, but he saw no use in complaining. And now he was off to have dinner. Somewhere.

Washington craned his neck, stretching. The redcoat watched him, wondering if the man was trying to look out the window, but quickly realized it was just an older man making himself more comfortable.

Washington flew forward as the carriage slammed to a stop, the redcoat rubbed his head, having bumped it against his headrest. The sound of a coachman walking up to the door filled Washington's ears, so it was no surprise when the door opened within seconds, revealing a short, chubby-faced man in a bright crimson uniform. The coachman nodded at Washington, indicating that he should begin to move down the steps. Washington hesitated, receiving a quick kick in the ankle by his traveling companion. The former general stared warningly at him before slowly, much to the annoyance of the redcoat, making his way to the ground.

He stretched, causing his back to crack, along with the coachman to chuckle. Washington quickly took in his surroundings as he adjusted his black tri-corner hat. He was in the front of a fine house, one without much of a garden, but still nice. It was a towering two stories, the white paint and navy blue shutters and door only adding to its dominating presence. Columns held the front of the house aloft, giving it the regal feel of Greek architecture. It looked almost like a Georgia plantation.

The redcoat began to push him forward, clearly bored by the amount of time his prisoner was taking to admire the scenery. Washington soon outpaced him, walking briskly yet elegantly to the porch. The redcoat stood behind him, hands clasped respectively, though he seemed bored. The coachman stood at his side, looking at the tall man in awe.

"Mr. Washington, sir?" the man said softly, "I saw you a few years ago; I fought against you in the battle of Brandywine."

Washington looked down at the man out of the corner of his eye. When he nodded, it was barely detectable, "How very fortunate for you." He spoke kindly, though he was confused, unsure of why that was an accomplishment. He brushed the imaginary dust off his cuffs and adjusted his jacket and collar, anxious to be rid of the unsoldierly privates.

The coachman beamed, happy to have spoken to the famous man. The redcoat cleared his throat, "You are not to speak to the prisoner." The coachman ignored him by asking if he should knock on the door.

The redcoat brushed past his companions, hitting Washington on the shoulder and nearly tripping over the coachman, "Obviously," he said, "you have not been an officer very long. Every British gentleman knows that he must knock on the door! I'd even expect the prisoner to know that he should knock on the door."

Washington said nothing for a moment, but when he did, the redcoat looked appalled. "Obviously, you must not be a proper gentleman. As a proper Virginian gentleman, I know the guest always has the servants knock on the door, if some are present at the time of his or her arrival."

The redcoat huffed and stamped his foot, "We are not your servants!"

Washington smiled ironically, "I never said you were. You did."

The redcoat opened his mouth to say something, then realized that he could find no suitable response. He grudgingly knocked on the door, which was opened seconds after his hands pulled away, as though a person had been standing just on the other side, waiting for the knock to come.

Peggy, dressed in her finest gown, curtsied prettily. "Welcome General Washington!" she said dutifully, fluttering her eyelashes in the way one would expect from a girl of high society. She then nodded politely at the lobsterbacks, as though she was surprised by them being there, "Soldiers."

"You are not to address him as general, miss." The redcoat said briskly, "He is but a mere prisoner."

Peggy frowned, then smiled smartly, "The last time I saw him, he was the general, so that is what I think of him as. Is that a crime?"

"You've met?" the redcoat dodged her question by asking another.

Washington bowed deeply and kissed Peggy's hand, "Miss Shippen, a pleasure to see you again."

She smiled when he returned to his full height, "Always the gentleman, aren't you, General? It's Mrs. Arnold now. I married Benedict *years* ago." She gestured for the men to enter, "Do come in, I've been a horrible hostess, leaving you out in the cold." The former general's face had clouded at the mention of the man's name. He tried to stop his mind and face from becoming stony and unwelcoming, wanting to retain his social charms and graces, but remembering Benedict brought unwelcome memories. Washington also wondered how it could be cold in the month of June.

Peggy stepped aside, making room for the three newcomers. The redcoat snaked his way in first, and was followed by Washington, who moved slowly and methodically. The coachman shook his head, "As much as I'd love to, ma'am, I must remain with my carriage." He tipped his hat at the lady and Washington, then spun around and began strolling lazily back to his waiting vehicle. The redcoat huffed, disappointed that his prisoner was treated with more respect than he.

Peggy closed the door and led the two men into the parlor, where Benedict was standing, waiting, a slightly embarrassed look cowering behind the wintery gaze in his eyes.

Washington stared at him in open disgust, no longer trying to bury his feelings. He remembered the deep stabs of anger and hurt and betrayal he had felt when the man had abandoned him for the British, he remembered it as clearly as yesterday. He was puzzled by the man that was standing before him, wondering how he ever could have respected him, praised him, even admired him. Washington wondered how it felt, to be standing so elegantly and causally in a scarlet uniform, when Benedict had once stood so proudly in Continental blue.

Benedict sheepishly avoided his former commander's eyes, looking instead at the soldier. All of the shame in his eyes evaporated, anger's harsh glare replacing it, causing him to lean on his cane more heavily, "Who's that?" he demanded.

The redcoat bowed showily and lowly, wanting to impress, "I, Governor Arnold, am Private Albert Eldridge, assigned to escort and watch prisoner Washington during his dinner." The redcoat rose only when he had finished speaking.

Benedict looked down at the man, unimpressed. "Why are you here?"

The redcoat seemed puzzled, but answered, "To watch prisoner Washington, as I have told you."

The governor flinched, "Did I not say that I was to dine with Washington *alone*?" his face was contorted with rage.

Private Eldridge trembled under Benedict's gaze, "Yessir. My commander said, however, that given your and Washington's history, that it would be best if I- "

"Do I not outrank your commanding officer? A simple jail guard, I presume?" Benedict spoke harshly.

"Yessir." Private Eldridge managed to nod, apparently not as tough as he acted when questioned by an authority figure, "You do."

"Then I dismiss you. Go, wait out in your carriage until I, or Peggy, escorts the general back to his coach." Benedict waved him away, then turned his back on the man, uninterested in further conversation. Private Eldridge turned away, glaring heartily at Washington as he shamefully and slowly made his way to the exit. "Why are you *still* here?" Benedict's voice echoed in the halls of his home. The soldier, no longer wanting to dawdle, quickened his pace, nearly running out of the house, and somehow managed to shut the door quietly.

Benedict turned back to face Washington, his face trying

234

to maintain his pretense of authority, but bits of shame and cowardliness were creeping back into his eyes. Washington took note of it, and looked away from the man with the stoniness all of his former soldiers could recognize and name. It was a tactic he had employed often, never mentioning what the soldier had done to displease him, but treating him coldly and courteously, causing the man's guilt to swell. "I would applaud you, had I not seen such a display from you before."

Benedict chewed his lip in silence, not wanting to sit, knowing that it would be admitting that Washington was more powerful than he.

It was true, what Washington said. Benedict had once been famous for his temper and rude behavior towards lower-ranking officers, and also ones with higher-rank, only ever obeying orders when he felt like it.

He turned to Peggy, who was standing a few feet away, hands clasped, observing the peculiar scene while trying her best to look pretty. "Is the dinner nearly done?" he asked her, his voice quieter and mellow.

She nodded, "Yes, but I don't know why you hired a cook to prepare your meal. Is my food not delicious?"

Benedict quickly shook his head, then, confused, rapidly nodded, then, upon seeing the blank look on Peggy's face, settled on speaking. "Your food is delectable, cupcake, but Washington hasn't had proper food in months, and I wanted to present him with his favorites. I don't believe you know how to make his most favored of meals. So, you can see how I didn't think that he was ready for your culinary delights."

Peggy nodded, seeing the logic in this, "Would you like for me to join you, or would you like your meal to be private?"

"Private, but tomorrow, pick whichever eatery you would like to go, and go there we shall." Benedict smoothly said. Peggy bounded away, happy with the turn of events, and looking forward to the next day's outing. Benedict turned back to Washington.

"Forgive me if it seems unusual, but I prefer dining in my office." Benedict said, beginning to leave the room. He waved his head, wanting Washington to follow. Washington hastily caught up with him, but slowed his pace considerably once Benedict took the lead.

"You're limping." Washington stated, no sympathy, no cruelty, just a statement of fact.

"A combination of an old war injury coming back to haunt me, and old age. Mostly being a cripple." Benedict explained, arriving at the stairs. He slowed, having a slight difficulty maneuvering his good leg, his cane, and his bad leg up the steps. Washington dutifully stayed a few feet behind, his arm waiting to catch the governor if he fell.

Benedict safely beat the obstacle that was his staircase and began limping to his study, the room with which he had seen Alexander. Benedict held open the door for Washington, who ducked in the room briskly.

The chairs had been rearranged. Benedict's remained behind his desk, but one of them was stranded on the other side of the room, and the other had been moved closer, giving it the appearance of an odd table. Benedict's papers had been cleared and placed on the bookshelf.

The host moved to his seat and clumsily lowered himself into it.

Washington sat in the opposing chair, sinking into it while also maintaining his natural regal air and incomparable posture.

"Why did you bring me here?" asked Washington, his voice calm, even though it had been a question he'd been dying to ask the moment he laid eyes on his host.

"Must a man have a reason to dine with an old friend?" Benedict wondered innocently. Washington stared at him and cocked his head, watching Benedict expectantly. The governor flinched under his gaze, "I mean, ally."

Washington nodded, pleased at the man's correction. "Yes.... We are not friends, we never have been, so I'd appreciate it if you didn't act like we were." Washington replied.

Benedict looked away, "I know that you're still hurting about what I did, and am sorry you are. I just did what I needed to."

"You didn't have to betray our country. But you did. For nothing more than money and a happy wife." Washington sighed, leaning his head against the back of his chair.

"I find it preferable when she is happy." Benedict shakily grinned, but turned away from Washington's icy stare. "...I said I was sorry, didn't I?" Benedict suddenly snapped, rising slightly, then fell back into his chair, unable to stand long without the aid of his cane, "to be honest, I'd rather not talk about it." He said more softly.

Washington was studying him when Peggy entered, pushing a cart filled with their dinner. She set a plate laden with pork, bread, cheese, and pickles before him, setting a near identical one in front of her husband. She handed the two of them their utensils and napkins, which they quickly set in their appropriate locations. Washington happily sipped the water from the cup she handed him, water he could tell was sweetened with lime. She made small talk while she served, asking Washington questions that he politely answered. After what seemed much too long to be delivering food, she left.

They ate in silence for a time before Washington spoke, "I have a question, Arnold." His statement seemed hinted with respect, but the adding of his last name, Benedict knew, meant that Washington still thought that he had a bit of power over the governor. Benedict frowned when he realized that his old commander was right.

"I expect I know what it is." Benedict stated, trying to be unintrigued by his guest, "'Why am I here...' am I correct in my assumption?"

"Yes." He said, his voice just as formal and cold, "You did not answer my question before. You were dodging around its boundaries." Washington accused.

Benedict nodded, "I confess that I did. I invited you here for two reasons. One, to admit to you that I am sorry for betraying you. My life has been most miserable ever since."

"You didn't expect it would be awful?" Washington asked, feigning surprise.

"Of course not!" Benedict exclaimed, slamming his fork down, "I was promised power, money, and adoration! I was given a good command in a professional army! Then I became governor, but I received practically no power because nobody ever listens to me! Sure, I was given money, but I've always been horrible at keeping track of it. Adoration comes and goes. The patriots immediately despised me, as I expected, and the loyalists showered me with praise. After a few months, however, they practically abandoned me and Peggy. They suspected me of flipping once more, or never having flipped in the first place. They avoided Peggy because she was connected to me, and it's been hard on her, having no company. Not even a lady's maid! I'm trying to save all the money we can, but it's hard to do that and make her happy."

Washington ignored the plea for sympathy, "So, you're sorry that it didn't work out the way you hoped?"

Benedict frowned, "Not exactly, I do wish things could've worked out better, but I've been plagued with guilt the past few years. I was at this execution years ago, the execution of-"

Washington raised his hand, knowingly, "Please, don't speak their names, they were good men who believed in creating a better world. They died unjustly."

"As you wish." Benedict replied, "I knew that I could've saved them, but I was too frightened to do so. I have nightmares of that day often.... I suppose you wonder why you're still amongst the living?"

"Yes, that is a question I ponder daily." Washington admitted, confused by the sudden change of topic. He did wonder it often, there was no point for the British to keep him alive, he had been the rebel's most famous general, it seems that they would delight in his death, but now all he did was rot away in prison. He believed he was kept alive as a result of Providence, the divine force he believed had protected him from injury throughout the war. "What of it?"

"At first, once you were captured, you were put in prison while awaiting execution. Some officials got it in their heads that it'd be best if you lived, for you to think constantly of what you'd done. I won't say how the seedling got planted in their heads, but I believe that we can both agree that it worked out for the better." Benedict munched on a pickle, "Eventually they started wanting to kill you off again, but I made sure that you lived. After all, you'd have to live with leading a failed rebellion against the king, and doesn't that sound awful? Putting a person through that? That's what the officials thought. I knew it wouldn't bother you too much, it wouldn't eat you alive as it would with other men. I thought that you'd prefer to live, so you lived. I never told anyone that it was I who helped you stay alive. Not even Peggy. Sometimes it makes me worried, after all, you swore that you'd kill me someday. But I think I did the right thing."

Washington frowned, unsure of what to do with the newly revealed information, "I suppose I should thank you?"

Benedict shrugged and continued eating, "That was what I was hoping for, but I understand if you'd rather not. I wouldn't expect you to."

His words caught Washington by surprise. It was unlike Benedict to not require an answer. This whole dinner had been very un-Benedict. The general he had known would've thrust his fork on the table, stared him directly in the eye, and said 'yes' as soon as the question was out of Washington's mouth. He seemed ashamed, honest, and less intense than the man Washington once knew and trusted; he was casual and humble, not stiff and arrogant. He seemed wiser.

"What is the second reason?" he asked, wondering if the new Benedict would continue, or if the answer would be something he expected from his old general.

Benedict looked at his plate, then at Washington, "Please, eat your fill before I answer that question."

Washington swallowed his bite of pork, confused by the statement. He was hungry. Hungry for both food and information. He ate a few more bites, leaving very little of his meal on his plate. Once he finished, he returned his gaze to his companion. "I have completed my meal. What is it?"

Benedict breathed in deeply, then exhaled. He met Washington's gaze, "The point of this dinner wasn't exactly to confess my regret."

"Then what was it?" Washington leaned forward, intrigued.

"It was to release America's best general from his confinement." Benedict said quickly, then winced, "You're not returning to jail, I'm helping you escape."

Washington sat as straight as a lightning rod in his chair, shocked by the revelation, "What? What do you mean?"

Benedict quickly walked to the shelf where he was keeping his inkpot and quill. He grabbed a piece of paper and returned to the desk. Pushing aside his plate, Benedict sat down. He dipped his feather-pen into the inkpot and began to write. "This is the address of a man I know you can trust, he's been trying to find a means to release you for quite some time now. I learned his whereabouts recently, and we discussed the best way to release you. You can trust him with your life." He thrust the paper into Washington's hands, who quickly began to scan it.

"Who is this man?" he inquired, looking up. Benedict was busy rearranging the plates, upturning his own and setting Washington's askew. The general's brow furrowed, trying to understand what his host was doing.

"I don't wish to alarm you, so I'll keep his name private." Benedict said, placing the inkpot and quill back on their shelf, "But you know him well, very well. There may be others in on the plot, but I only know of two. The man didn't say much, he still didn't know if he could trust me or not."

Washington watched him cautiously, "How *do* I know if I can trust you?"

Benedict smiled up at him, "I'll say the same thing that I told him, 'you don't.'"

Washington frowned, "How do I know if I can trust *him*?"

He laughed, shaking his head slightly, "Because, sir, he's one of the people who admires you the most. A person you admire as well, who's been an invaluable help to you during the war. I believe that he'd travel the world to fight by your side; they both would." He handed him a candlestick, "For this to work now, I'll need to be unconscious."

"What." Washington stated, staring at the candlestick in his hand, wondering how he couldn't accept this with ease. He used to be able to deal with the unexpected much more easily, he figured all the time in prison was making him rusty. "Now?"

"No, of course not, that would be silly." Benedict used his cane to help him across the room. He moved the curtain to the side, revealing a small pile of clothes. "Those are for you. Change into them. They're servant's garments. There is a horse out in the back. Steal him and ride to that address as fast as you're able. Peggy is usually getting ready for bed by this hour, so it's highly unlikely that she'll find you."

Washington set the candlestick on the desk and picked up the clothes. Benedict turned around to face the wall as his companion changed.

"Why are you helping me?" Washington asked as he buttoned his shirt.

"I want to do a bit of good...." Benedict replied, "Are you finished yet?"

"Yes." Washington shook the white powder out of his hair, revealing his auburn curls. He donned his new tri-corner hat, "How do I look?"

Benedict turned around and inspected him, "More like a commoner than a servant.... It'll do."

Benedict briskly sat in his chair and handed Washington his cane. "Please, put that a few feet away, out of my reach. I need it to look like I couldn't defend myself." Washington did as he wished. "Do you understand your instructions?" Benedict asked, holding his hand up before Washington could strike. He nodded.

"Yes. Leave house, steal horse, and ride to safety." Washington recited, "Though, I'm afraid that I have one problem."

"Do tell."

"What if this is just a setup to throw me into prison once more? Or to kill me? Or is this a stunt to make you more popular?" Washington asked.

Benedict laughed, "Do you honestly think that I would arrange this entire thing to send you back into prison? You came from prison in the first place! I've been keeping you alive for years, good general. If I wanted it, you would've been dead ages ago. But you're not. I doubt that I'll ever be popular, and if I was trying a stunt like that, I'd try to make it so I don't look like a weakling."

"What do you mean?" Washington cocked his head.

"The plan is for you to knock me unconscious, so it looks like you tried to use this as a chance of escape. That rids attention from me, making people think that I'm a loyal Englishman, but in actuality, it lets people's guard down when they're in my presence. That allows me to learn information that may be valuable to our friend." Benedict explained, "Now if you don't have any more questions, I'd like to be unconscious before the night is through."

Washington grabbed hold of the candlestick and raised it above his head. He began to bring the stick down, then stopped. "Are you sure about this?"

"Do you honestly want me to answer that?" Benedict asked, "Just get on with it!" Washington swung the candlestick and Benedict slumped into his chair, asleep.

WASHINGTON & COMPANY

Washington's horse slowly turned onto the dark street. There was one house, he could see, with a candle in the window. There were other houses on the street, but no light shined from within their walls. After coming to a stop, Washington slid off his horse, uncomfortable from riding bareback, his back pains returning as a result. He tied the horse's reins to a fence post and slowly made his way towards the candlelight.

He had made it to the street Benedict had instructed him to

go to, but he couldn't help but squirm with fright. What if it was just a trick and there were soldiers in the home instead of helpers? What if the contact had been taken off to prison, and he had no place to go? What if the people in this home didn't know of whom he was speaking? He shivered and bumped into a fence. He patted it, searching for the latch. Finding the switch, he opened it and began walking on a path of grass. He could tell that he was surrounded by bushes. Their eerie shapes seemed to twist in the darkness, though Washington knew that he was only imagining it. He scolded himself silently about letting childish fears entertain his thoughts. He made it to the front door, darkly painted, staring imposingly at him. He gulped and slowly raised his hand, ready to knock.

He quickly pulled it back when he heard shouts coming from the inside of the house. He shook his head, reprimanding himself. How could he, Commander in Chief of the Continental army, be skittish when it came to knocking on a door? He summoned up his courage and pounded on the door, wondering if he would be heard over the bickering. Once he was sure he would be heard, he straightened his posture and stepped back, trying to look important, and waited.

The door flew open, answered by a young woman. She seemed exhausted, barely seeming to notice the shouting, as though it were a daily occurrence. Her piled hair, decorated with bright yellow bows, seemed deflated, as if it, too, was tired. Her angular cheeks and curving eyebrows had a familiar quality to them, though he was certain he had never met the woman before. She would be very pretty, he guessed, when she smiled. She was frowning

245

now, like his appearance seemed to be very unwanted. She rolled back her shoulders and smiled, dark eyes sparkling, trying to be welcoming. She *was* quite pretty when she smiled.

"Can I help you?" she asked him.

"I'm not entirely sure." Washington informed her, "I was sent to this street to see a-"

She held up her hand, "Stop right there. Wait here." She turned away, closing the door slightly but still allowing Washington to spy through the crack. The young lady then went into the next room, where the shouting seemed to be coming from. He caught brief snippets of multiple conversations, though they confused him: "You told him where we live?" "We have to leave!" "How is it that you can be such an idiot?" The voices quieted when she entered, but quickly picked back up again when she left, this time pulling with her a young man; all the voices seemed to protest her dragging him away. He seemed to be coming unwillingly, as he was still facing the room where the argument was, and was voicing his opinion quite loudly. The girl stopped pulling after a while and waited until he was finished speaking, then she began dragging him to the front door, which he went to slightly more willingly than before. Washington turned his head away, giving them privacy.

"What is it?" Washington could hear him ask, the voice somewhat familiar.

"You tell me." The girl crossed her arms once they were both at the front door, nudging it open. The young man looked up at Washington, eyes widening. Washington's own eyes grew in size when he recognized the man's face.

"Hamilton?" He gaped at his old aide in surprise.

"Your Excellency!" Alexander smiled up at his general, then looked down at his wife, "He was telling the truth!"

"Arnold?" Washington inquired.

"Yes, I was unsure whether to trust him or not." Alexander explained, pulling Washington inside the home. Eliza closed the door behind him.

"That's understandable." Washington said, "I, too, was hesitant."

"I won the argument." Alexander muttered under his breath, pulling his two companions into the next room. Eliza sighed, exasperated.

"I was right!" Alexander announced to the table. Washington's eyes widened at the number of familiar faces turning to look at him.

"*Mon* general! *Mon pére!*" Lafayette nearly jumped over the table to his commander. He embraced him happily, kissing his cheeks many times, and held him close, grinning. Washington looked down at the excited Frenchman, hugging him back.

"I have waited so long to see you again!" Lafayette exclaimed when he finally released Washington from his grasp. He stood at arm's length away, happily looking up at the man whom he had waited so long to see.

Washington nodded approvingly at the excited Frenchman, "My boy, it's good to see you again." Lafayette smiled as though he were a son being praised by his father, but glared at Thomas when he was pushed aside.

"I can't believe he actually did it." Thomas said, speaking to both Alexander and Washington. He shook Washington's hand in respect, pumping it enthusiastically, and nodded politely to Alexander before stepping away.

"Nice to finally see you again." Adams bowed slightly from where he stood, "We've been working to set you free for some time now. It's wonderful to have you back."

"That's the first thing that he's said that I agree with." Lafayette announced to nobody in particular.

Washington's mouth twitched as he scanned the room. His gaze landed on Aaron. "You," he pointed, "You look familiar."

"I was under you a few times during the war, sir. My name's Aaron Burr, I was a lieutenant colonel." He explained.

"I've heard your name before." Washington said, nodding slightly, "Yes, you were among those praised highly for their work. You were to be promoted, be one of my aids, but...."

"We lost." Alexander finished.

"Precisely." Washington stated, "And you are?" he nodded to James, who was smiling at the tall man from his chair.

James blushed sheepishly, "I'm Jemmy Madi– uh – I mean, uh, James Madison, I helped with....um.... I...." he looked away, face as red as a cherry.

Thomas explained, "Jemmy doesn't like to talk much. It was his idea to release you, and Aaron, from jail, and to start a new revolution."

"In that case, I thank you for your work." Washington said, nodding politely at the little man, who turned even brighter at the compliment, "But why did you release me?"

"We needed you to lead a new army." Thomas said, "There was nobody else to fit the bill. It had to be you." Even though the general had been in the room for no more than two minutes, everyone could feel his importance and commanding presence;

the urge to please the man seized the group as they watched the great General Washington.

Washington, cheeks slightly pink, didn't know what to say. He eased himself into the chair at the head of the table, then looked back at the awed looks of his companions, "I am taking somebody's seat, aren't I?"

"No, that chair is for you. Aaron sits at the other end." Eliza explained, "The rest of us sit in between the two."

"What is your name?" he asked, interested by the lone woman in the crowd of men, "I don't believe that we've met."

She shook her head, curtseying politely, "We haven't. It's Elizabeth. I'm General Philip Schuyler's daughter, Alexander's wife. I used to make blankets and sew and mend clothes for the soldiers during the war." She collected her sunflower skirts and sat in her seat, causing the others to follow suit. Washington nodded, seeing the resemblance, and complimented her on her war efforts.

"Please," Washington said to the team, "Tell me of your war. When can I begin working with the new army?"

The revolutionaries looked at each other and squirmed in their seats, some staring at the table, ashamed.

Washington frowned, sensing the unease, "Well?"

They continued looking at each other and at the table, none wanting to deliver the unwanted news. Finally, Thomas spoke up. "Um, we – err, you see…we don't have one."

Everyone looked to Washington, to see how he reacted. They quickly looked back at the table, apparently fascinated by the wood's knots and lines.

"You don't have one." He repeated, his face tight and rigid with disapproval, "Then why did you break me out of jail?"

"You're best at making people want to listen to you." Lafayette whispered, staring a hole into the wood. "The rest of us are no good. They argue too much." He nodded to the others.

"Thanks." Alexander muttered under his breath.

"So, you don't have a plan?" Washington asked, "You just have a bunch of people sitting around a table wanting to start a war?"

Thomas nodded, cowering under the general's harsh gaze.

"Wonderful." said Washington, leaning against the back of his chair, rubbing his temples, "I can't make *any* group of people follow me at the moment. So, you broke me out of there for nothing. We have nothing. No revolution. Nothing at all."

"Why can't you help us?" asked Eliza, looking up at him.

"I escaped from jail, knocked out the governor, and am currently hiding from redcoats. I don't expect that tomorrow I'll be considered a free man. It's more likely for me to be declared 'most wanted man in the colonies.'" Washington said bitterly, he sighed and looked at the group. "So, do you have any ideas? I'm good at fighting battles, not starting rebellions."

The group looked at each other, confused and thoughtful.

"Oh dear." James said the words that were on all of his companion's minds.

PEGGY

Peggy knocked on the door of Benedict's study. "Benny?" she

called. No response. She slowly creaked the door open. She could spot his cane lying on the floor, "Benny, would you like me to get that for you? You can't bend over and pick it up." She waited to hear a reply. "Benedict?" her voice grew worried when there was none.

She quickly walked into the room. She gasped when she saw her husband. He was slumped in his chair, unconscious. She rushed to his side. There was dried blood on his head, not much, but some splattered on his forehead and some had wet his hair. She examined it, not surprised that it was a head blow. She put her ear to his chest, not caring if her hair or nightdress would soil. *Ba-bump. Ba-bump.* She nearly laughed in relief when she heard his heart. He was alive. She looked at his face, cupping it with her hands.

"Benedict." She stated, picturing what had happened in her head. "Oh, Benedict."

BENEDICT

Peggy dabbed at his forehead, happy that the wound was closed. He rubbed his head gingerly. "It hurts."

"It's likely to." Peggy said, "Not many people get blows to the head from George Washington."

Benedict smiled cockily, "Does this make me a war hero?"

She looked down at him, "You were already a war hero." She adjusted his pillow.

He pushed himself into a sitting position, "Does it make me a better war hero?"

"You're my war hero." She said, kissing his head in the spot furthest from the wound, "How are you feeling?"

"Awful." He replied, "My head hurts." He scratched at the cloth wrapped around his head, Peggy quickly slapped his hand. He frowned. "And the bandage is itchy."

"What was it the doctor said again?" he asked after a moment.

"Expect vomit," Peggy reported, "and you may have double vision. You might not think clearly for a bit."

"Beautiful." He sighed.

She sat beside him, leaning against the bed's post, her feet poked at his shoulder playfully. "Do you expect the search party to find him? They've been looking for him all day."

"Yes...." Benedict replied, "I just don't know where he might be." They stared at each other for a moment.

Peggy smoothed her loose blonde hair, "He couldn't have gone far. He's probably still in the city."

Benedict laughed, but quieted when he saw her expression, "I'm not laughing at you, angel, it's just the idea. Washington is probably already in Virginia. If I know him like I think I know him, he wouldn't have stayed in the state."

"So send soldiers out away from New York." Peggy concluded, "Tell the other colonies to stay on their guard?"

"Essentially." Benedict replied, "I only wished I could have sent them out sooner."

"You couldn't help it." She spoke softly, "You were unconscious for a day and a half. You only woke a few hours ago."

"I just feel like we'll never find him. It was so idiotic of me to invite him here!" Benedict snapped.

"It wasn't idiotic, it was sweet. You wanted to make amends, and that's good. You're the type that could hold onto grudges for life. So, I'm proud of you for bringing him here." Peggy patted his leg approvingly. "You'll find him. I know that you will."

"Thank you for the encouragement." Benedict told her, closing his eyes, "I'm getting sleepy…. Am I allowed to sleep?" he asked.

"I think so." Peggy stood to leave. "I'll check on you occasionally."

"Wake me if the soldiers have found him." Benedict called after her.

"Of course!" she called, closing the door.

Benedict hoped that Washington had made it to *Nouvelle Maison* safely. It was more tiring than he had expected, pretending to be innocent of the crime. He hated lying to Peggy, but not to the soldiers, it somehow made him feel like a rebel general again. He smiled and opened his eyes, knowing that the soldiers would never find Washington. Not unless they searched the city.

PEGGY

Peggy closed the door behind her and lingered, hand on the knob. She felt awful for her husband, wanting to magically heal him with just a stroke of her hand. She wondered when the soldiers would find Washington, knowing how quickly he could spread the rebelliousness that her country had so long tried to suppress. She shook herself, eyes wide. She wanted to slap the man for hurting her Benny, but she also found herself wishing that Washington wouldn't ever be found, that he'd be safe. She trembled, knowing that she couldn't ever tell anyone the thought that had entered her mind.

Not even Benedict.

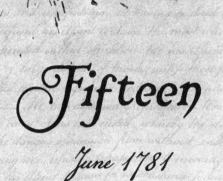

Fifteen

June 1781

NEW YORK CITY, NEW YORK

BENEDICT

Benedict smoothed the wrinkles in his red uniform. It had been weeks since Washington's escape, and he was feeling much better. Physically. Emotionally, he was a wreck. His plan had failed. Somebody had learned that Washington was in New York state. So far, Benedict knew, nobody knew of his involvement in the plot. Alexander had come just the day before, saying that Washington was safe, and expressing his thanks at having his general back. Neither man knew how the news had spread, they just hoped the person wouldn't learn of Washington's exact location.

There were spies in the city. Benedict had known that well, but none of the spies had worked against him before. Sure, whomever it was thought they were doing the governor, the king, and England a favor; but still, Benedict felt betrayed. He knew what Washington had felt was magnified, as Benedict was one of his most trusted generals. Now he began to understand how the man felt.

Benedict, cane in hand, began walking towards the door. He knocked on it gingerly. He checked over both shoulders, happy to see that nobody was following at him. The door opened.

One Hour Earlier

ALEXANDER

Alexander stuck his hands in his pockets. It was a fine day in New York. The sun shone down happily upon the glistening cobblestone streets. The bustle and chatter of the city filled him with excitement. The only downfall was the multitude of British regulars patrolling the streets. One on every street corner, watching every colonist like a hawk would its prey. He avoided their gaze, trying not to be angered by their dominating presence, knowing that no good would come from losing his temper.

It had been a troubling day at work. Shortly after moving into *Nouvelle Maison* he had found a job as a clerk at a mercantile. Today, nearly all of people he dealt with seemed to be personally offended by his very existence. It wasn't an enjoyable occupation, it actually reminded him of his loathsome job in the Caribbean, but it paid the bills. Technically, there weren't any bills for him to pay, but Alexander and Eliza had established from the moment they settled in in the city that they would pay their way. Lafayette, who managed the finances, insisted on paying for food, books, and décor, never accepting any money given to him by the Hamiltons, Thomas, James, Washington, or Aaron (he had recently found himself a job at a law firm.) It was a well-kept secret that all of the group (excluding Adams) slipped their fair share of rent, the food bill, etc., into the marquis's wallet when he wasn't looking. Luckily, Lafayette seemed to own a never-ending supply of money, so he didn't even notice the unwanted payments.

Alexander sat on a bench, watching the people hurry about. It was interesting, watching them. Some of the people glared at the redcoats who walked among them, others smiled at them gratefully. Still, there were others who ignored them entirely, trying to convince themselves that they weren't really there.

He noticed a man sit on the bench across the street. Alexander was about to raise his hand to wave, recognizing the man as Aaron, but his hand fell to his side when he saw another person approach.

It was a redcoat. At first, Alexander feared that Aaron would be arrested, but his fears subsided when the soldier sat beside Aaron. Curiosity filled him as he wondered why the soldier was there. The two leaned forward, lips moving, hushed whispers coming from their mouths, the slight nod of their heads. Alexander regretted that he was out of earshot, that he couldn't hear what they were saying. After a few minutes, Aaron handed the soldier an envelope. Alexander nearly fell out of his seat in stunned silence. The two men parted ways, Aaron heading towards home, the soldier deeper into the city.

What was in that envelope? Alexander's mind raced with impossible scenarios. Could Aaron be a spy? He shook his head.

He didn't trust the man, but he didn't think he was a spy.

Alexander rose to his feet and walked quickly after Aaron, trying to stay close enough to keep track of him, but far enough away so that it wasn't obvious of whom he was following. He trailed him down the street, beside the multitude of shops, keeping his eye on the black hair that was bobbing through the sea of heads. Aaron suddenly began walking more quickly, and Alexander quickened his pace as well, trying to keep up.

"Burr!" he called when the man began to fall out of sight. Aaron continued walking, though Alexander wasn't sure if he was ignoring him or simply hadn't heard him. Alexander walked faster, until he eventually caught up to him. He grabbed Aaron by the arm, causing him to slow. Aaron whirled around, looking frightened, then he realized who it was. The fear left his face and was replaced by relief and surprise.

"Hamilton." Aaron stated, "Hi."

"What was in that envelope?" Alexander cut to the chase; Aaron's eyes widened and he paled. "I know that it's none of my business, but-" A cold stony expression settled on Aaron's face, a harsh look in his eye. Alexander stopped speaking, feeling the mood darken.

Aaron pulled Alexander into a nearby alleyway, where he released his grip. "Wonderful!" Aaron tugged at his hair and moaned, "This is wonderful!"

"What is it?" Alexander asked, leaning against the brick wall, his tri-corner hat slumping over his eyes. Aaron ignored him and began to pace.

"Burr, what has happened?" Alexander asked, looking at him, a hint of impatience and anger in his voice, "Who was that soldier?"

Aaron finally looked at him, like a deer in headlights, frantically thinking of what to say. "That…was a redcoat."

Alexander frowned, annoyed, "I know that. What I want to know is *why* you gave an envelope to a redcoat."

Aaron's face fell, then looked at the ground, "He was blackmailing me…?" He mumbled.

"How?" Alexander exclaimed, "Did he recognize you? Did he say that he'd tell on you if you didn't pay – wait, you don't have much money. At least, nothing worth black-mailing for."

Aaron frowned, nodding, "No… I don't."

"Were you borrowing from Lafayette?" Alexander demanded, his concern shifting from Aaron to the marquis, "That is just unacceptable! He's too kind-hearted to ask for money back-"

"I didn't borrow money from Lafayette!" Aaron insisted, shaking his head adamantly, "I didn't borrow money from anybody."

"Then what did he want?" Alexander inquired.

Aaron opened his mouth, then closed it. He bit his lip, "Um…."

"You don't have any family, money, nothing really." Alexander said, listing the options, ticking them off on his fingers. He paused, realizing the only possibility was the one he dreaded most. He turned to look at Aaron, "Are you a spy?"

"No!" Aaron said quickly, holding up his hands, "Of course not! That's ridiculous!" he chuckled nervously.

Alexander's eyes flickered over him, unbelieving.

Aaron scratched his head, a panicked expression on his face, searching for what to say. He closed his eyes, his breathing slowed. He opened his eyes. His voice lowered into a pleading whisper,

"Please, Alexander, don't tell Washington."

"Don't tell Washington?" Alexander repeated, trying to keep himself quiet, but struggling to do so, "I have to tell Washington! I can't believe it! We broke a traitor out of jail!" He laughed at the irony of the situation, but there was a scowl on his face. He ripped his cap from his head, kicking the air.

"Please," Aaron said quietly, begging, "Please, don't say anything. Please." Alexander grabbed Aaron's arm and began pulling him out of the alley.

"Where are we going?" Aaron asked frantically, worried out of his wits.

"Home. I'm telling everyone that we have a spy in our midst! I assume it was you who said Washington was in New York?" Alexander said coldly.

"It's amazing how fast rumors spread." Aaron mumbled meekly, then pulled himself out of Alexander's grip, "We're not going home." He said defiantly, shaking his head.

"And why not?" Alexander looked back at him, his eyes staring daggers into his new enemy's.

"Because I challenge you... to a – duel!" Aaron's face was full of determination and cockiness, but it quickly paled when he realized what he had said. The color quickly fled back to his cheeks as his confidence returned, but he did look nervous. He smiled briskly once more, the grin hiding the fear in his eyes.

"What!" Alexander exclaimed, then quieted, not wanting to be heard by any curious ears, "One with guns?"

"Is there another?" Aaron asked playfully, "I've never heard of another kind, well with the exception of swords, of course; but it appears that we're both fresh out of those. Do you accept?"

"Who will be the seconds?" Alexander asked, considering the option.

"There will be no seconds. I asked if you accept." Aaron's voice grew tight, his brows furrowed, finally accepting what he had done, "Well? Do you?"

Alexander gulped, nervous about what Aaron had asked, "Do I have a choice?"

"Of course. If you decline, I run away. If you accept, you have a chance at rendering me unable to get away." Aaron explained, "I have my pistol. Do you have yours?"

"No official dueling pistols?" Alexander rubbed the sweat off his forehead with his pocket handkerchief, nodding.

"No. There's no time for that. We have to get this done and over with before you have a chance to tattle."

Alexander nodded, understanding, "Could I say goodbye? To Eliza? I promise I won't tell her. You can stand nearby, hear the whole thing – intervene if you have to."

Aaron debated the proposition in his mind before agreeing, "Yes. But only because I care about her feelings, I know she'd like to have a letter or a speech if she knew she was saying goodbye. If you wanted to say goodbye to anybody else, it would be a no." His voice was lower than usual, letting Alexander know that the man meant business.

Alexander sighed, relieved, "Thank you. I accept your duel. I don't believe that duels are just or a proper way of settling disputes. However, I do not want to throw away my honor or be called a coward. I accept your duel… if you admit that you are, indeed, a spy."

He held out his hand, Aaron shook it in confirmation. "Now, bid her farewell."

ALEXANDER & ELIZA

"Alexander?" Eliza looked at her husband in bewilderment, her hand grasping the front door of their home, "Why didn't you just open the door?"

"Is anybody else here?" he asked, taking her hands into his, looking into her eyes.

She shook her head, confused, "No. Everyone's in town. Why?"

"No reason." He sucked in a deep breath. "Eliza, my Betsey, I want you to know that these past two years with you have been the best in my life. I don't know why I was so fortunate to have you, and I don't suppose I tell you that I love you enough."

"No," Eliza shook her head and placed her hand on his cheek. He encased her hand with the hollow of his own. "No, you're wonderful, you say it enough." Eliza said sweetly.

"I just wanted you to know that." Alexander repeated, "I don't say it as often as I should."

She beamed up at him, her eyes sad and forgiving, "It's not who you are to say things like that. You write the sweet and the flowery. I wouldn't want you to be any different. I love you for you, my dear Hamilton. Don't you know that? These have been the best years of my life as well, being with you and helping you with your passion. Is that what this is all about? You feel like you spend too much time thinking about the new war?"

"No. Yes." Alexander nodded then shook his head, trying not to get off topic, "I do think about the war too much, but that's not why I am here."

"Then what are you here for?" her hand dropped to his shoulder, a serious expression on her face.

"I want to tell you that we'll be together in a better world. I cherish that sweet hope." He squeezed her hand.

"Alexander, you're scaring me." Eliza said, her face pale, "Tell me…. What's happening?"

He shook his head, "I want you to know the you've been the best of wives and best of women. The best woman I've ever known."

"Alexander?" Eliza asked, her eyes watering, puddling beneath her lashes. Alexander could feel tears rolling down his cheeks.

"My Betsey." He replied, wrapping his arms around her. She rested her head on his chest, his head resting on her own.

"Alexander?" she whispered. He sighed and kissed the top of her head.

"Alexander? My Hamilton?" she whispered, hearing the beat of his heart, her tears wetting his shirt.

He kissed her cheek, lingering there for a moment, Eliza crying, holding his hands. "If you pay so much attention to that cheek," she joked, trying to lighten the mood, but it only made her cry more, "the other is bound to get jealous." He smiled shakily, kissing her on her other cheek, and once on her lips for good measure.

He pulled away and held her at arm's length. He studied her, her light brown hair, her dark eyes, the curve of her face, the laugh lines around her eyes. The way her bows glinted in the sunlight. The way the wind moved her dress, rippling it. It looked like the ocean water.

He turned away from her, walking away from the garden and their home, crying silently all the while. Eliza's arms still hung in the air, feeling confused, scared, and loved. She watched until he was too far away to see, a speck in the distance. She still watched.

"Alexander? ...Hamilton? My Hamilton?" she whispered. Crying, she turned away and entered the house.

She collapsed onto the lounge in the study, suddenly feeling so weak. Why was it that she was so frightened? Her shoulders began shaking, and soon her whole body was trembling uncontrollably. Tears spilled down her cheeks and splattered onto her dress. Why was she crying?

...And why did she feel like something awful was about to happen?

ALEXANDER

"That was quite a little speech." Aaron remarked, sitting on a barrel. "Made me teary eyed."

"Please, stop speaking." Alexander replied, turning to look at him, annoyed.

"I'm being honest. No doubt the poor girl's all a nervous wreck about why you were flattering her so." Aaron teased, sliding off his perch.

"It's all true." He admitted, then paused, "Where were you?"

"I didn't suspect you of tattling. Behind a shrub in the garden." Was the reply, "Terribly uncomfortable, but better than the words. The words made me want to gag!"

"I asked you to stop speaking." Alexander dabbed his eyes with his handkerchief, trying not to focus on Eliza. Aaron nodded, understanding. They faced each other awkwardly for a moment, silent.

"I know how you feel." Aaron said softly after a minute, "There was a girl that I knew – loved – actually. Theodosia Prevost. She was married to a British officer, but we were in love. I had to leave her after a while. I was stationed somewhere else. Never had the proper chance to say goodbye. Then I was jailed, and I didn't dare write to her. I didn't want to arouse suspicion, you know, start rumors about her, a married loyalist woman courting a single patriot soldier ten years her junior…. I haven't seen her in years. I still wonder if she'd have me, if still thinks of me…after all that's happened…." Aaron stared off into the distance, a wistful expression on his face, thinking back to happier times. He looked at Alexander, thoughtful, "I thought that you'd like to know that I wasn't a complete monster. I wouldn't ever let what happened to my Theodosia happen to your Eliza, I care about her too much."

Alexander frowned, trying not to grow attached to Aaron's story, but failing, "I've never thought you were a monster…but thank you."

Seconds ticked by, but they seemed like hours. Alexander cleared his throat, "Where would you like to go?" If he phrased it causally, like they were just out for a day of enjoyment, would death feel less certain?

"New Jersey would be preferable." Aaron stated, tearing his thoughts away from his Theodosia, walking in the state's general direction.

"New Jersey?" Alexander echoed in surprise.

Aaron looked back at him, "Yes. Do you object?"

"It's New Jersey!" He rubbed his arm irritably.

"What do you have against New Jersey? It's illegal to duel here in New York." Aaron told him, hands on his hips.

"The only good thing that ever came out of New Jersey was the College of New Jersey." Alexander said.

Aaron glared at him, "*I'm* from New Jersey."

"And look at how you turned out!" he exclaimed, "A traitor to your country and to those who know you!" Aaron, face pink, fists clenched, stared, waiting for Alexander to apologize. The aide looked away, sheepish by his remark, mumbling "...It's also illegal to duel in New Jersey."

"It's more enforced in New York." Aaron reminded him, accepting the unspoken apology.

"Can't we duel in New York?" Alexander asked.

"Why?" Aaron stared at him expectantly.

Alexander looked at him, tired by their bickering, "What's the difference in the matter if we duel in New York or in New Jersey?" he wondered.

Aaron shrugged, "I suppose that there is none, really. I just prefer New Jersey, and it's less likely that we'll get into trouble there."

"And I want New York so we'll be closer to home. That way it isn't so far if, say, one of us shoots the other in the leg." Alexander declared, "or if one of us needs to get help, one can run home and get the others to help with…whatever."

"You have a good point." Aaron changed his direction and began walking down a long dusty road, pointing off into the distance, "There's a big field a few minute's walk from here. We could have our duel there."

"Very well." Alexander followed in silence for a moment before speaking. "Please, tell me why you were a traitor."

"Benedict offered me some money when he first started showing up." Aaron explained, "Back before he became all patriotic again. And so, I became a spy."

"That doesn't seem like the whole story." Alexander said, "I had heard of you in the army, you were a good soldier. It doesn't seem like money was everything to do with it. Was it to impress Theodosia if she ever found out?"

"No!" Aaron snapped, looking away.

Alexander smiled knowingly, and continued, "You were in prison for years, just rotting away like that. If you were his spy, why did he leave you in prison?"

"I'm not 'his spy' as you put it, I'm England's spy." Aaron explained, "And you're right, that's not the whole story. That's the shortened version."

"I see. Care to tell me any more?" Alexander asked hopefully, expecting a refusal.

"No." Aaron said, then pointed up the dirt path, "See that field?"

"Is that it?" Alexander nodded.

"Yes."

There was wheat blowing peacefully in the breeze, the setting sun illuminating the crop like golden grass. A willow's leaves danced gracefully in the center of the field. It was a beautiful place to die.

The two men walked towards the tree, the wheat tickling their legs. Alexander smiled softly, knowing that Eliza would've loved the way the plants performed their windy waltz. He touched the grains gently, fingering the feathery softness of the wheat heads.

"Well?" Aaron leaned against the tree, the willow's leaves brushing against his shoulders, making him look both heroic and villainous.

"Hmm?" Alexander looked up, looked away from his fantastical thoughts, unsure of what his companion meant.

"You're the challenged party. You get to decide where to stand." Aaron reminded him, as though every other person would've known what to do.

"Oh, right." Alexander scanned the field, shielding his face when the sun hit it. "The sun's bright."

"It's like that sometimes." Aaron laughed nervously; he sighed, then spoke in a softer voice. "Have you chosen?"

"Let me think about this." Alexander called to him. The sun, he noted the sun's brightness, knowing that it may be deadly. He turned to look at Aaron, his back to the sun, "I'll stand here."

Aaron nodded, "Let us fire at twenty paces from one another." Aaron walked to Alexander, counting his steps. "It's twenty paces from here to the tree." Aaron explained, "May you back up a few steps so I am not sitting on the tree when we fire?"

Alexander nodded, "Seems fair enough." He turned and walked four paces away, "Is this adequate?"

Aaron counted his way back, then turned to Alexander and

nodded, "Yes, very satisfactory."

"Do we load our weapons now?" inquired Alexander, patting his coat pocket, "We have no seconds to load them for us."

Aaron nodded and pulled his gun from his coat. He began loading his pistol. Alexander watched as Aaron finished and set his pistol on the ground.

Alexander pulled his own gun from his coat and began loading, Aaron watching all the while. He set his gun in the dirt, then stood up. "What shall determine when we fire?"

"A simple 'on three' will do." Aaron replied, "one, two, three, shoot, for instance…. Are you ready?"

Alexander considered the question, "Honestly, no."

"Will you ever be ready?" Aaron dragged out the question, asking it both to himself and his former friend.

"No." his companion replied shakily, wiping the sweat from his brow, "I suppose that I'm ready then." Aaron nodded, gulping down his fear.

The two men slowly bent to the ground to pick up their pistols. Alexander kept a close eye on Aaron while his fingers brushed the dirt, searching for his gun. Upon finding the weapon, he rose, Aaron rising with him. They faced each other, weapons at their sides. They turned, staring across the field at the thin, opposing silhouette.

"Farewell." Alexander said from across the field.

Aaron nodded his approval, blinking back tears, "Farewell."

Alexander straightened his posture, bringing himself to his full height. He knew that he wasn't going to shoot at the man he had come to know, to like; he couldn't bring himself to. It wasn't honorable. He would throw away his shot, he would shoot at the tree above Aaron's head. But Aaron, he knew, though his eyes were laced with regret, wishing that it had come to anything but this, would have no trouble bringing the end to Alexander Hamilton.

He closed his eyes and raised his gun, pointing it in the general direction of Aaron. He pictured in his mind his Eliza, his Betsey. The way she talked, the way she remained calm in a sea of chaos, supporting him all the way through their adventure, though he knew she wanted nothing more than a home and a family of their own. He wondered what would become of her if.... Lafayette wouldn't let anything happen to her, neither, he believed, would James, Washington, or Thomas (if it came to that.) She would go back to her family, remarry probably in a year or – no, he mustn't think like that.

He remembered the way her warm hand felt when it caressed his cheek, how elegant she looked while she was walking down the aisle. Her sweet giggle. The countless pastries and blankets and scarves she had made for him. The look on her face whenever he'd surprise her. He thought of their conversation minutes ago, could he really say goodbye to her?

"One...Two...Three-"

LAFAYETTE, THOMAS, JAMES, WASHINGTON, & ELIZA

"And then off I went!" exclaimed Lafayette, opening the door to

Nouvelle Maison, "To America at the age of nineteen, ready to fight all the nasty Britons!"

Thomas shook his head unbelievingly at his friend's story, "You're going to have to prove that you bought your own ship. The rest I believe but...." He trailed off. Lafayette stared back at him, shocked by the older man's lack of faith.

"No one would take me. It was against the law for French officers to sail to America. Especially me. The law said *mon* name." Lafayette turned back and continued walking through the foyer, "And that, my friends, is how yours truly came to your blessed allied states."

"Allied, almost united." Washington repeated, "I like that." James nodded his approval. The group voiced their agreement at Lafayette's new term, but paused when they heard labored breathing and what seemed like crying. The five turned to find Eliza leaning against the doorway to the study, handkerchief in hand. Her dark eyes, usually so filled with kindness, were brimmed with tears, looking relieved to see them, but also filled with fear.

Lafayette quickly rushed to her side and wrapped his arm around her, "*Madam,* you look horrid!" He guided her back to her chair in the study, which she sat in gratefully. It was true, she did look awful. Her eyes were swollen and pink from crying; her hair was a mess, like she had been clawing at it mercilessly. She was shaking uncontrollably. Her bows, which normally stood so erect, were limp and lifeless.

Thomas sat beside her and offered her his fresh handkerchief, which she blew her nose into, thankful. She sniffled a bit and began to cry silently. Her shoulders quivered erratically. The rest of the men bustled about the study in a flurry, Washington ordering them to get pillows and blankets and hot beverages for their patient.

"What happened?" Thomas asked her once she was through crying and had calmed down enough to speak.

"I-I-I don't know." Eliza mustered, accepting the steaming cup of tea James set in her hands. She brought it closer to her face, trying to warm herself. Lafayette draped a blanket around her shoulders, which she pulled more tightly around herself. "It's hard to explain."

"Could you try?" Adams asked in his most soothing voice, sitting in the sofa before her. James and Lafayette sandwiched him between them. Washington sat beside her, watching her carefully and sympathetically.

Eliza nodded, "It's Alexander, I'm afraid something's terribly wrong." The men leaned forward, curious.

"What is?" James asked.

"That's the thing, I'm not quite sure." Eliza sipped some of the tea, "He came about fifteen minutes ago, acting in the strangest way. He spoke to me like he thought he'd never see me again. Telling me how much he loved me, how he doesn't say it enough, hoping to see me in a better world, things like that. I asked him why he was telling me all of it, but he wouldn't say. I think something's wrong. He's never been like that. He's always been sappy, but mostly only in his writings! He's only been like that a few times in person, but he was- oh!" Eliza began to weep again, Thomas carefully took away the teacup when she began to tremble.

"What do you think's the matter?" Lafayette asked, "What do

272

you think he's up to?"

"I don't know!" Eliza cried, "I just know it's something awful. He must've thought he was to die if he was telling me all those things. Oh, it was so sweet, but it frightened me so. Oh, Alexander! What have you gotten yourself into?" She sniffled and wiped away her tears. Her breathing was unsteady, but slowly returned to normal. She looked around at her companions like it was the first time she had seen them that day. "Where's Aaron?" she asked, sitting up a bit.

"I figure he's off in town." Washington told her, "Why? Why is he important?"

"Oh, nothing." Eliza said softly, sinking back into her chair. She seemed to relax for a second before she shot to the edge of her seat, her eyes as wide as could be, a look of realization upon her face. "That's it!" She stood up and quickly began dusting herself off, a panicked tone in her voice, "I've been so foolish! They've never really gotten along extremely well and I know they don't trust each other, and they both fly their mouths off so easily! They must have...oh dear." Eliza looked at her five companions, all still seated. Her face was grave, paler than porcelain, "I think I know where he is."

"Where is he?" Lafayette asked, getting to his feet.

"With Aaron." Eliza replied, trying to remain calm, though they could all tell that she was frantic.

They all jumped at the quick rapping at the door. Thomas quickly walked to the entry to answer it. The others watched from the study doorway, with the exception of Washington, who shielded himself from view. Thomas looked back at them and shook his head, then turned back to look at the person. It was not Alexander.

"Who are you?" Thomas asked, but quickly stepped aside when the man brushed past him. His bright red coat attracted all of the eyes of the home's occupants, but only Lafayette and Eliza walked forward.

"*Monsieur* Arnold." Lafayette stated, catching the man by his arm. "What brings you here?"

Benedict looked at the Frenchman as though his question was a big inconvenience, "I'm looking for Hamilton. Where is he?" Washington peeked into the entryway, then stepped forward, seeing it to be safe. Thomas closed the door and studied the red-coated man he had heard so much about.

Eliza wrung her hands anxiously. "We don't know," she fretted.

Benedict gripped his cane so tightly that his knuckles turned a pearly white. "Why not?" he asked harshly.

"He's missing." Adams grunted, "And if you wouldn't mind, we'd like to go looking for him."

"Hamilton's missing?" Benedict repeated, his anger turning into concern, "Since when?"

"Twenty minutes ago, give or take." Thomas replied, checking his watch, "Why? What is so important?"

"It isn't really." The governor said, dismissing his thoughts, "Was he taken by the soldiers? I can release him! Did he run off?"

"I think he was challenged to a duel." Eliza admitted, tugging at her hair.

"What!" Lafayette whipped his head around to look at her, "Why didn't you say so?"

"Oh dear." Washington rubbed his temples, as though trying to

274

convince himself that it wasn't true.

"I was about to when *he* showed up." She nodded to Benedict, who appeared flustered.

"Who is the opponent? How do you know he was challenged?" he asked, almost reprimanding her, "You shouldn't go jumping to conclusions."

"It's the only logical explanation." Eliza told him, "He's not one to go running off unless he's ordered to. He wouldn't challenge anybody to a duel, he thinks that they're dishonorable and silly. He'd accept one, though, he hates to be called a coward. He wouldn't act so strangely otherwise. Besides, I know that he wouldn't tell me – or any of us – that he was challenged. We'd all try to talk him out of it. He just came back to say goodbye to me."

"Who is his opponent?" Benedict repeated more urgently, "Do you know?"

"No." Eliza replied, "But I'm fairly certain that it's Aaron."

"Aaron…" Benedict rolled the name over on his tongue, searching through the crevices of his mind, seeing if the name was familiar, "You wouldn't happen to mean Aaron *Burr*?"

The group all looked at him in astonishment, then realized that the two had known each other. And that Aaron was out of jail.

"Yes, Arnold." Washington said, "Why?"

Beads of sweat began rolling down Benedict's neck, "This is serious." He began to rely more than ever on his cane. "We have to find them, now!" he began hobbling to the door as quickly as he could. Eliza marched after him, ready to find her husband.

"What's the matter?" Thomas asked, chasing after them, "Why is Aaron important?"

"Because," Benedict looked back at the stragglers, "Aaron's not a patriot. He's a loyalist spy."

ALEXANDER

"One…. Two…. Three…" Aaron said slowly, "Shoot!"

Alexander closed his eyes when he heard the gun fire. He saw Eliza, perfect little Eliza. She was smiling in the field. He felt sick to his stomach, but also, he felt…fine. Perfectly fine.

Painless.

He opened his eyes and looked at Aaron. He was not standing before the tree as he had just moments ago. Fear flooded through Alexander, he dropped his pistol and quickly ran to the spot where Aaron had been standing.

Aaron wheezed and squirmed, "My gun…it wouldn't fire." Alexander dropped to his feet, scanning his injured companion. "My side…my right side." His abdomen was soaked in a red liquid, a liquid Alexander immediately recognized as blood. More red spots were appearing on Aaron's shirt, causing the man to clench and unclench his fists, his eyes closed tightly, teeth bared.

Alexander quickly began ripping the sleeve off his shirt, surprised at how long it took for it to come free. He found the wound and quickly plugged it with his makeshift bandage. "Are you in much pain?" He felt all the anger and betrayal and hurt towards the man evaporate, now all he needed to keep his friend alive.

"My vision is…. indistinct…. It hurts, but it's bearable…."

Aaron said slowly, "How bad does it look?"

"Try to focus. Look at me." He said, hoping Aaron wouldn't lose consciousness. "I'm no doctor," Alexander admitted, pushing on the wound, "but it looks like the bullet hit one of your organs, probably your liver." He pressed one hand on the cloth, which was soaked with blood, as he tried to rip off his other sleeve. Alexander winced when he succeeded. He switched hands, trying to wriggle the other sleeve onto Aaron's chest. He nearly gagged when saw the amount of blood on his hand.

"Is it any better?" Aaron wheezed.

"Yes!" Alexander lied, pushing his other sleeve against the wound, "I now have double the amount of cloth over the hole."

"That's nice." He said drowsily.

"No! Burr, stay awake!" Alexander snapped, looking between his companion's face and his injury. "I can't have you sleeping. Try to focus on me."

"All right." Aaron whispered, "Talk to me. I don't care what you say. Just talk."

Alexander nodded, "I didn't shoot my pistol, at least not intentionally. I think that it must've been a misfire. Oh, I'm sorry. This was a terrible idea! I just wished I let you go!" His voice tinged with panic when he saw more blood spilling out of Aaron's wound. He realized something. "I can't leave you here. I can't go get help."

"My gun…wouldn't fire." Aaron said, confused, not seeming to hear what Alexander was saying, "Why wouldn't my gun fire?"

"I don't know." Alexander began unbuttoning his waistcoat, but his fingers, drenched in Aaron's blood, refused to grasp the buttons. "How do you feel?"

"Sleepy…. Dizzy…." Aaron replied, "It's hard to stay… focused. I'm cold. I've lost feeling in my legs."

"That's not good." He looked at the man's face, his eyes slowly closing. "Aaron, don't fall asleep on me." Aaron opened his eyes once more, trying to keep them as wide as possible. Alexander slid his arm out of his waistcoat, triumphantly having made it past the buttons. He slipped out his other arm, then quickly began to press his waistcoat to Aaron's abdomen. "You'll be fine. You're going to be just fine." He wasn't sure if he was trying to convince Aaron or himself.

"No…" Aaron told him, "This is a mortal wound, Hamilton."

"No, it's not!" Alexander cried, "You're going to be fine!" *It is a mortal wound. It is a mortal wound.* Alexander knew it was true, but he didn't want to believe it.

"I've never been your biggest fan, Burr; and yes, moments ago I wished that I had never even met you; and yes, I've never trusted you for a second! But, I like you, and I consider you a friend," Alexander said, carefully watching as his waistcoat became blood-soaked. "So, I'm not going to have you die on me. You're not going to die on my watch."

"I don't see how you can determine whether I do or not." Aaron told him, "I can't really feel my wound anymore."

"Oh dear," Alexander winced, worried, "Are you still in pain?"

"No…not really. I can't feel you or the wound." Aaron admitted, "That's not good."

Alexander frowned, "You're not looking too good, either. You're pale."

"I've lost a great quantity of blood." Aaron stated, his voice monotone but irritated, "I don't have enough left to flush my cheeks."

"No, you still have a lot of blood left." Alexander pushed more heavily on Aaron's wound, all of his cloth dark, soaked, and dripping. There was still more blood flowing.

"Don't lie to me. I know it doesn't look good." Aaron snapped, "Tell me, how bad is it really?"

Alexander looked between the wound and Aaron's face. He swallowed bravely, not wishing to admit the truth, "Awful. You've lost more than you should. I don't know if I can – I can make it stop."

Aaron nodded, his words slurring together, "At least I'll die honorably." Alexander felt tears wetting his cheeks. Why was he crying? "That sounds nice, to be honorable, I haven't been these past years…." Aaron said dreamily, "Alexander?"

"Yes?" He responded, pushing on Aaron's side with more determination than ever before.

"If you…you ever see Theodosia…tell her that I still loved her," Aaron's eyes began to close, but he struggled to keep them open, "Tell her that I didn't want to leave." Alexander felt himself nodding, felt himself promising. He cried, knowing that Aaron was truly going to die.

"Don't speak like that. You're still alive. You can tell her yourself." He promised.

"Alexander?" Aaron whispered, gulping down his pain. "Please… tell her."

Alexander cried, "I'll tell her, Aaron, I promise. I'll tell her."

Aaron smiled drowsily, "Alexander?" He nodded, listening.

"Tell everyone what I did. Tell them that they've been good friends, and that I'm sorry." Aaron told him, "Tell them I'm sorry."

COMPANY

"Alexander!" Eliza screamed, running to him, brushing past the golden grass.

He looked up at her in surprise and held up his hand to her, causing her to stop in her tracks. She stood a few feet away from the willow tree, looking at her husband with such relief and worry. Alexander frowned, wishing that he could scoop her into his arms and explain that despite the blood dripping from his hands, he wasn't hurt. His true words were far from reassuring, "No! Don't come any closer!"

"But-"

"No buts!" Alexander shouted, his expression upset and pleading. Eliza stepped back, surprised by his harsh tone. He looked past her and to Lafayette and the others, who had caught up with her. His expression melted away, leaving his face with an almost child-like resemblance, his eyes wide, disappointed, distressed. They were swollen and puffy.

"My gun misfired." He stated, looking to the ground. "My gun misfired and it's all my fault. Please, don't let her look. My gun misfired. Now he's dead. It's all my fault!"

Lafayette slowly walked forward, wanting to comfort his friend,

"*Monsieur* Aaron?" he asked.

Alexander nodded, "He's dead."

Lafayette placed his hand on Alexander's shoulder, who was still sitting by Aaron's side. The Frenchman sat next to his friend, gave him a kiss on the forehead, and looked at the man lying on the ground. Alexander's watery eyes looked to the marquis, who was still trying to find the right words.

Aaron's eyes were closed, and his hands were clasped together over his chest. Alexander was still pressing the fabric against his wound, but the blood flow had stopped substantially. The man's face was pale, and it looked like he was only sleeping. Like he could wake up any moment.

"I'm sorry." Washington looked down at Aaron, "He was a good man. I'm sorry that he's departed."

Eliza began walking towards the group, which was now surrounding the dead man, "I'd like to see." She began moving Benedict to the side, he relented grudgingly.

"No!" Alexander exclaimed, looking back up at her, his previous expression returning, "Please, I don't want you to. It might be too much."

"Then why can everyone else go see him?" Eliza asked, placing her hands on her hips, "I want to see him, too."

"We've seen dead bodies before." Thomas clarified, looking at the girl, "You haven't. It might be too much for a lady."

She snorted, "Oh, *now* I'm a lady. Before you were treating me like everybody else!" Eliza shook her head, "Now if you don't mind, I'd like to see my husband. And also a dead body. I *have* seen dead bodies in my lifetime, so don't go and think I'll faint or lose my wits or anything like that."

"Eliza-" Alexander began.

"We've always treated you like a lady, albeit an exceptionally capable and tolerable one," Thomas explained, "But still a lady. I don't think that you'll really want to see this. Remember, it's not just some random corpse."

"All of the corpses I've ever met I'd known before I attended their funeral." Eliza defended. Thomas frowned, realizing his poor choose of words.

"They were also your siblings that were all alive for less than a week, and a few elderly people that you barely knew." Alexander reminded her, looking at Aaron, then back at her, "This was your friend. Who was shot. There's a big difference. You were a bit sad over the death of a baby. I had an old neighbor that lost a baby. Sure, that was sad, but I was over that by the next week. I cried like a baby when my mother died. I'm still not over that. Then I was in the war, I figured that it wouldn't be too bad. But trust me when I say this, Eliza, Betsey, there's nothing like seeing a person shot, especially one you cared about."

James, sniffling, nodded in agreement.

Eliza frowned, but nodded. "I see your point. I won't look at him. Do tell me what happened though."

"That I will do." Alexander said, "Just, give me a minute." He stared back down at Aaron, "What are we to do? Oh, what are we to do?"

"You mean you already knew he was a spy?" Alexander exclaimed, nearly spilling his tea.

It had been decided that the best course of action would be to drag Aaron into town and leave him in an alleyway. It would be too difficult to explain what had happened to a coroner, and so they left him in town, waiting to be found and buried. Alexander only wished that they could have buried him proper, with a finely carved headstone. Benedict told him that he would issue a law that the soldiers report any unidentified bodies, so once Aaron was found, Benedict would claim him and bury him in Princeton, his hometown.

They were at *Nouvelle Maison* now, crowded in the study. Upon arriving, Alexander had immediately washed and put on a different change of clothes, having decided that he would burn the ones he wore to the duel.

Everybody was seated around the fireplace in the study, listening to Alexander's story.

"Yes." Eliza nodded, leaning her head against her husband's shoulder, rocking him lightly. "Benedict came after you left, wanting to speak to you. We told him we figured that you were with Aaron, and the dots were connected."

"Tell us what happened next." Adams demanded, wanting to see how Aaron had met his demise.

Alexander frowned, "Then I came here to say goodbye to Eliza. Once I was done, I met back with Aaron, who wanted to duel in New Jersey."

"New Jersey!" Lafayette cried, swirling the tea in his cup. He looked at his companion curiously, "Why New Jersey?"

"Dueling is illegal in the colonies," Alexander explained, "but it's not as heavily enforced in New Jersey as it is here in New York. I objected on the location; I figured that it'd be better if we dueled nearby, that way if one of us did end up being shot, the other could run home and get help."

"A nice plan." Thomas remarked sarcastically.

"It would've been if one of us was shot in the leg." Alexander groaned, "I couldn't leave him when he was on his deathbed though. That wouldn't have been honorable."

"And then what happened?" James asked, wiping his nose with a hanky. His voice surprised Adams, who had forgotten his couch companion.

"Aaron told me about this field nearby, and so we started out there. We got there and agreed about our dueling rules." Alexander continued, "Obviously, we had to change some things, as we had no seconds. Then we got into position...." Alexander trailed off, his head now resting on Eliza's, his eyes staring deeply into his tea.

The group looked at each other, each silently telling the others to remain silent.

"My pistol misfired, I never intended to shoot. I thought that it was going to be me in Aaron's place, though I would've been surprised if he had stopped and cared for me." Alexander explained, "Aaron's pistol didn't fire. It took me a moment to register what had happened. When I had fully recovered, I was busy trying to keep Aaron alive. That didn't really work out. When he died...oh...he wanted me to tell you all everything. That he was a spy, that he was sorry for what he had done. He was unconscious for a good half hour before you found us…me. I suspect he was dead for ten minutes by then." Alexander looked into his tea, "He's dead now."

"I didn't know that he was working with you." Benedict spoke after a while. "If I did, I would've told you. I just didn't know."

"There was no way you could've possibly known." Alexander told him comfortingly, "I never told you who was helping me."

"He was my best soldier." Benedict continued as though Alexander had never spoken, "One of them, anyways. A close friend. After I joined the British, he was captured. That day, the one when the three died, Henry, Paine, and Adams, I needed somebody to talk to. Somebody other than Peggy or André. Peggy, she's wonderful, and she can be surprisingly serious and compassionate at times, but I couldn't tell her about how awful I felt. André, he's a good friend, but he's British, he wouldn't understand. A few days before, I had learned of where Aaron was being kept, so I decided to pay him a visit. He was a surprisingly good listener. I told what had happened, and he told me what I needed to hear."

Benedict paused, "It was a fair exchange, he needed companionship, I needed somebody to talk to. Eventually, I think that we changed each other's mindset. I became more and more patriotic, and Aaron? He's always been a reserved man. Not one to get his hands dirty. One day I was feeling pretty awful, saying that I couldn't be a patriot when I was the governor, so I went to visit Aaron. Somehow, by the end of the day, I had paid him to be a spy for England. He would listen to snippets of information through his window, learned a surprising bit of information, too. This soldier was actually a patriot, who was pretending to be loyalists, things like that. I never brought it to anybody. I was just upset that day, I acted rashly."

"Did Burr ever find out?" Washington asked.

Benedict tossed his cane from hand to hand, "I don't know. He never told me. I suppose that he could've found out and was working to buy his freedom. That's why he was in jail for so long. I lengthened his sentence. It was originally six months, but I changed it to a year. Then two, and so on. When he escaped, it frightened me. I never suspected that it was you who helped him escape. I just assumed that Aaron had caught on and escaped on his own. I never thought he had help. I don't know who it was that he was giving information to. I just assume that he was sharing little pieces of information. Telling the soldier that Washington was in New York. I couldn't tell them not to look for him here when they approached me, saying that a spy had seen him. I didn't know it was Aaron. I was just frightened of saying no. I guess that it's my fault that he's dead. I never looked for him, never put him back in jail."

"It's not your fault." Eliza scolded, "It was Aaron's. He was the one that continued spying, and that's what brought his end. It's Aaron's fault." She repeated, this time uncertain.

"It's mine. I'm the one that caught him." Alexander groaned, "I'm the one that held the gun."

"Which misfired. And did you challenge him to that duel?" Eliza asked, poking his chest, "NO. You didn't. It's Aaron's fault, nobody else's. Sure, I'm sorry that he died, but it was his own foolishness that killed him. There's no changing that. Now we best get on with our lives and make do without Aaron Burr." She wiped away her tears, trying to convince both herself and the others.

"I beg to differ." Adams objected, "It *was* Hamilton's fault. He was the one that was holding the gun! How do we even know that the gun misfired?" Alexander's face hardened when he realized what the man implied. Eliza's eyes narrowed.

"All we have his words." Adams continued, rising to his feet, looking around at his companions, "How do we even know that he speaks the truth? He could've been the one that challenged Burr in the first place! For all we know, Hamilton's the spy working for Arnold and they put the blame on an innocent man!"

Alexander and Eliza scampered to their feet.

"That is going too far!" Alexander cried, pointing a finger accusingly at Adams.

"You've known him for months!" Eliza shouted angrily, "Surely by now you know that he would never do such a thing!"

"What reason does Alexander have to be a traitor?" Lafayette was standing now as well, his expression wild, "He's one of the most patriotic men I know! Probably the most, with the exception of *mon* general. If we were back in the army, he'd be training every day, writing like mad! Anything to make your country free!"

"All I'm saying is that you only have his word." Adams said, his hands raised in surrender, "For all we know, he could've been caught by Burr when he was giving information to a lobsterback! Then, unsure of what to do, kidnapped Burr and brought him to a field, where he-"

Alexander grabbed Adams by his shirt, his knuckles white, his eyes blazing. Adams looked at the man, surprise and fear in his expression. Alexander stared at him for a moment before speaking. "I want something to be clear," his tone was low and calm, but everyone knew that Alexander was at his deadliest, "I've never liked you. I suffered through your presence for months because Jemmy wanted us to. If it was up to me, you'd be the one person in this room that would be sent home because he's useless!" Alexander released Adams, who stumbled back onto the sofa. Alexander continued staring down at the man, a reprimanding gleam in his eyes. "I didn't murder him. It was an accident. I just wish I knew what it felt like to be trusted by my own people!"

He stormed out of the study, Eliza and Lafayette scurrying after him. Washington quickly followed, but turned back to look at Adams, a disappointed frown clearly displayed on his face. "Was that really necessary? He was already upset enough as it is. You didn't have to make it worse." He walked off, leaving Adams, James, Thomas, and Benedict in the study, each unsettled by the events.

"He's right, you know." Benedict looked at Adams after a moment of silence, "You didn't have to do that. You don't have any proof, just speculation. Think next time, before you do something even more drastic." Benedict rose to his feet, "I think that it's best if I go, I'll arrange my appointment with Mr. Hamilton later. I give you all my regards, but I suspect that next time we meet, it won't be on friendly terms." He left the room, then the house, slamming the door behind him.

"What does that even mean?" Adams grumbled, sinking into his seat.

"I expect he means that we are no longer united. People will be choosing sides, yours or Hamilton's." Thomas replied, "I don't think that our team will ever be quite the same again. Your accusations built a barrier of distrust. A schism. That's what worries me."

"What do you mean?" Adams asked. Thomas rolled his eyes and stretched out onto the lounge chair. Adams turned to James, expectant.

"It's not my place to say." The little man replied, "For the record, however, I agree with you."

"You really think that I'm right? That Hamilton's the traitor?" Adams seemed to be surprised.

James shook his head, as though the question baffled him, "Of course not. That's ridiculous. Alexander's not a traitor. I just think that he could've handled things differently."

"Jemmy's correct." Thomas said, "There's no way that Hamilton's a loyalist. He's just too much of a firecracker, he doesn't think things through."

"He does think things through," James objected, "He's just impulsive at times. He reminds me of you." he told his friend, "Quite a bit, actually."

"What on earth are you talking about?" Thomas asked, "That's the most ridiculous thing I've ever heard!"

"I can see that." Adams stated, nodding thoughtfully.

"They're so much alike, but also so different." James said, looking at Thomas like he was an interesting attraction at a carnival, then to Adams, "They think so similarly, their personalities are alike as well. They just can't ever seem to agree with each other without being given a good argument by somebody else."

"Can you please stop likening me to Hamilton and speaking about me in third person?" Thomas groaned, "We're all in the same room."

"What should we do now?" James asked, leaning his head against the cushion, "A line's been drawn, and now everyone has to pick sides."

"It's me versus Hamilton." Thomas said, running his fingers through his hair, sighing, "And Hamilton has the advantage."

"What's the advantage?" Adams asked, "But didn't I start this... feud?"

"Hamilton has Eliza, obviously, Lafayette, Washington, and Arnold." Thomas said, ignoring Adams and ticking the numbers on his fingers, "I have you and Adams.... Somehow that seems unfair."

"I know you the best, you're my closest friend." James told him, "Washington and Lafayette are sticking with him either because they agree with him, or they're with him out of loyalty. I suspect both, but it's more likely that Washington simply thinks that Alexander is correct on the matter. Lafayette...it's a coin flip on what he thinks. Benedict just agrees with him.... We can't all agree on the same thing." James rubbed his hands together, "Everybody is just too stubborn! Neither of you will yield, and *everybody* will stick with their leader."

"The peacemakers are on the same side." Thomas pointed out, realizing the problem, "Do you think that Lafayette and Eliza will still be able to calm all of us down and help us look at the big picture?"

"I certainly hope so." James replied, "If they don't, Tom, everything will fall apart."

"I don't understand." Adams said, annoyed by being on the

outskirts of the conversation, "What exactly is happening? Why is the schism a problem?"

James sighed, speaking slowly and clearly, as though he were speaking to a small child, "If we can't get along, the new revolution will never happen. If we can't work together, all of this planning will have been for naught."

LAFAYETTE, ALEXANDER, ELIZA, & WASHINGTON

"I brought some tea." Lafayette set the platter on the end table. "Benedict's left."

Alexander and Eliza were sitting on their bed, both deep in thought. Their faces were still upset, but they were considerably calmer. Washington sat in a chair, also thinking.

"I just can't believe that he'd say such a thing." Alexander said, barely acknowledging Lafayette as he was handed a cup.

"Thank you." Eliza nodded to the Frenchman and sipped her tea. She turned back to her husband, considering what to say, "He's upset at losing Aaron, I'm sure that he didn't mean it the way it sounded." They all knew that it wasn't true.

"This…" Lafayette waved his hand in the air, searching for the right words, yet unable to grasp them, "It will never be the same, will it?"

Washington shook his head, "It won't. I wish that it could've been prevented, but the way you all quarrel…" he shook his head and adjusted his grip on his teacup. "I'm surprised that it didn't happen sooner."

"Me too." Alexander admitted, "It'll be even harder to agree with each other now. Especially with Jefferson."

"You never agree with Thomas," Eliza told him, then amended her statement, "Well, never directly. If Jemmy has an idea, and Thomas supports it, you'd still agree with Jemmy. If Thomas has an idea, you're the last person to ever agree with him. You'll only agree if everybody else has."

"How will we ever start our new country now?" asked Lafayette, "If we can't agree with each other, then how will we start an army, defeat the British, *and* establish a fine country? One that won't fall apart the moment the English leave our land?"

"The same way I kept my army together the first time." Washington said from his corner, "By establishing order."

"How will we do that?" Eliza asked, "We don't even know what we're going to do next, let alone past that! We never thought past releasing you."

Washington's mouth twitched, "People listen to me, Mrs. Hamilton, I'll be able to keep our team from being destroyed. I used to prevent feuds all the time between officers, it shouldn't be too difficult." He lifted the steaming tea to his lips, his eyes shining and smiling, "It's time."

"It's time for what?" Alexander asked.

Washington looked at his three companions, "Why, it's time to start building an army, of course."

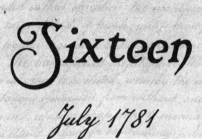

Sixteen

July 1781

NEW YORK CITY, NEW YORK

BENEDICT

Benedict frowned from his balcony. A foursome of redcoats conversed in the street below. He couldn't hear what they were saying, but he knew very well what they were speaking of. Washington.

The British had been after him more than ever, sending the great general himself into house arrest. They patrolled the streets day and night looking for the man, sometimes asking Benedict for orders, sometimes searching on their own. He always sent them in the opposite direction of where Washington really was, but Benedict knew it was only a matter of time before he was caught. Both him, and the general.

"Must you always take the last slice?" Thomas asked curtly, watching as Alexander slathered butter onto the final piece of bread. "I wanted that slice."

"If you wanted it, you should've taken it." Alexander huffed, setting the butter knife aside and taking a big bite of the bread. He made a show of enjoyment, causing Thomas to turn red in the face.

"Must you argue over such things?" Eliza asked coming into the dining room, holding a letter, wiping her forehead with a handkerchief, "That's not the last loaf of bread in the world, you know. There's plenty more where that came from."

"Bread is very important." Thomas grumbled, arms crossed, staring angrily at Alexander, "I eat it every day. I don't like it when I can't have my bread."

"It must be shocking when something doesn't go your way." Alexander spoke tauntingly, "I remember when I was in the army, it was a luxury to have bread like this. You must've never suffered before." He popped the final piece into his mouth, smiling all the while.

"I've suffered plenty." Thomas told him, not caring to elaborate.

Alexander smirked, "If I recall, you *ran away* when the British troops were-."

"Where is the wax!" Eliza cried, holding up her letter. The men looked at her, slightly annoyed by the interruption to their argument. "I can't find the wax for my letter to Angelica."

Alexander nodded, "My desk, second drawer, in the brown wooden box. How are my dear brunettes these days?"

Eliza laughed, "I don't know why you pair us together like that! Her hair's redder than Thomas's! Peg's the other brunette. She's fine though, they both are, and she wants you to write more often."

"I'll write her a letter as soon as I finish eating," Alexander told her, "This is scrumptious, Betsey, is there any more?"

Eliza shook her head and placed her hands on her hips, "One of these days, I'd like to see the amount Lafayette spends on food. I swear!" she threw her hands up in the air, "It's like I'm feeding teenage boys, the way the lot of you eat."

"Is that a yes?" Thomas cried when she left the room. Her response was a sigh. Thomas and Alexander frowned at each other, both blaming the other for her unwanted reply.

Eliza rushed up the staircase and dashed into her and Alexander's room. It was a small room, but larger than the other bedrooms in the house. She sat in the chair in the corner and opened the second drawer in the desk, searching for the wooden box. She smiled when she found it and pressed a smidgen of wax onto the letter, sealing it tightly. She set the letter aside, ready to begin the weekly writing to the rest of her family. She picked up her quill and dipped it into the inkwell, but her hand hung poised above the paper, not wanting to write. She sighed, setting the pen down, and leaned into her chair and threw her hands over her head.

"What's wrong?" Eliza turned around at the sound of the voice. Lafayette's head poked in from the hallway, looking at her pityingly and curiously.

"Oh, please, come in." She smiled tiredly as she pulled at her braid. Lafayette made his way into the room, sitting in her knitting chair. He squeezed a white ball of yarn in his hands, tossing it back and forth before disposing it into its basket.

He looked at her, "What is it?"

"Oh, nothing, I'm just exhausted." She admitted, turning in her seat to look at him. He looked at her, prompting her to say more.

Eliza laughed, shaking her head, "There's just been so much tension in the air." She shuddered, "I feel like all of their squabbles, Alexander and Thomas's, it's going to erupt into something bigger. Something that might destroy our chances at revolution. We've got to get them to stop fighting with each other, I just don't know how. They seem to be fighting more and more every day, and over pointless things like bread and… silverware!"

Lafayette nodded, "I've been feeling the same way, their arguments are about nothing now, just little taunts, like they're trying to see who's alpha. It does have to stop somewhere, if it continues, it will just tear us apart. We have to continue with our rebellion."

"But how?" Eliza asked, "The general said that it was time to start an army, but look at us, it's been a month and we're no closer to an army than when Aaron died. Washington's been locked up in this house for ages, trying to figure out how to move the pawns on the chessboard of war."

"We're all stuck here." Lafayette reminded her, "It's nearly impossible to avoid each other in this tiny house! I think that's what we need, a change of scenery. We have to start working as a team, not fight like opposing armies."

"How are we going to make peace? They're both too stubborn to give in." Eliza wondered.

"They aren't going to make peace." Lafayette said, smiling

cleverly, "We are. We have to give them no choice but to cave. And I know just where to start."

JAMES & LAFAYETTE

"I agree with you," James said, "but we can't work as a team now. There's too much distrust. It may be a risk to be speaking to you. If one of them even catches us speaking, they may get into a heated debate, destroying our ability to cooperate as a whole." He placed his book back on the study's shelf, then turned back to his companion, awaiting his response.

Lafayette frowned, seeing logic in James's statement. He sighed and looked at the whole problem, instead of just a part of it. He needed to find a crack. Just one little thing might be able to solve their predicament. The corners of his mouth turned upwards. He had found it. James watched the Frenchman curiously, seeing the gears at work in his brain.

"What is it, Lafayette?" he asked a bit too eagerly. James cleared his throat and repeated the question, this time pretending to be only mildly intrigued.

"We'll never work as a team again unless somebody extends an olive branch." Lafayette explained, "We both know that Alexander and Thomas will never back down, Adams doesn't seem to care what's going on as long as there is conflict, and *mon* general has just been studying war books day and night, so there's no point in him trying to make peace. That leaves the two of us, along with

Eliza. If we can make peace, then perhaps the others will soon follow."

James turned away from the marquis, considering Lafayette's proposition, he then looked back at him. "What would you like to do? We no longer have a plan to carry out, we have to do something, though. We can't just sit here. It isn't often I feel so useless!"

Lafayette sat in his chair, deep in thought. He looked to James once he stumbled upon a conclusion, "I suggest that we look for potential soldiers. Scan the city for patriots, try to see who's truly patriotic, who are the pretenders, and who are the loyalists."

"A fine idea, it's impossible to accomplish though." James said dryly, "I wish it could succeed."

The Frenchman was confused, "Why can we not do it?"

"We're too memorable," James reminded him, "I'm much shorter than your average person, and I can barely speak to a person I don't know. And your accent...it's hard to understand you entirely at times, Lafayette, especially when you are excited. Which you are... an awful lot."

Lafayette frowned and nodded slowly, "*Oui*, Jemmy, that is a problem. We'll try to work our way around it."

James's eyes grew wide, "Have you listened to nothing?" he snapped, "Why can't Eliza go do it?"

Lafayette frowned, "That would never do. If she goes out looking for patriots, we won't have any decent food."

The little man nodded quickly, understanding the problem. "I suppose we can try, but we mustn't ever leave together. We leave here separately and meet at an agreed upon spot.... Do think Benedict would help us?"

Lafayette shrugged, "*Oui.* He did mention learning some intel from Aaron. I think that he would cooperate fully if he didn't have to watch his image. I might be able to send him a note asking for information, but I doubt that we'd be able to speak face-to-face."

"You're right." James agreed, smiling softly, feeling bold, "When shall we leave?"

"We'll get around to it sooner or later," Lafayette said lazily, "I'd rather get on with it sooner though. Now would be preferable."

"We are once again in agreement." James declared, "I'll go to... the field! Leave after me, but by no later than ten minutes." He began to leave the room, enticed by the prospect of furthering the war efforts.

"Right!" Lafayette waved his hat in the air triumphantly. Wait until Eliza heard about this! She'd be thrilled! The marquis grinned. The revolution was still alive!

"That one, he's most definitely not a patriot." Lafayette whispered under his breath, eyeing the man with curiosity. The Frenchman's gaze was low, eyes shifty, as though he was worried about being spotted. His hat was pulled down to shade his face. He was sitting on a bench in the park, James sitting beside him, observing the different people that were walking by.

"What are your reasons?" James asked routinely, sighing.

The man in question was short, with carefully powdered hair that was tied neatly in a bow. His dress was impeccable, a white and blue suit with laced silk fabric, clothing that stank of wealth.

He held a wooden cane with a rounded gold handle, a cane used for decoration, unlike Benedict's, as the man was clearly fit enough to walk without assistance.

"He reminds me of the aristocrats in *mon* home country." explained Lafayette, "See how he behaves, it's like he thinks he's the king of the world, and everything in it are his playthings."

The man's nose stuck up in the air, a sign of a spoiled and pampered upbringing. He brushed away imaginary grime off of his coat's sleeves, sniffing at the air, like it had a foul odor.

"Why would he wear a coat in the middle of summer?" Lafayette asked, to himself or to James, the little man was unsure.

"Maybe he's sickly." James suggested, intentionally tugging at the cream scarf Eliza had knit for him, "The summer breeze does have a bite to it." He sneezed into his handkerchief, his nose slightly blotchy from being rubbed constantly.

"You don't have to defend him." Lafayette eyed the lace handkerchief James carried, "And I doubt you truly needed to sneeze."

"You're right." James admitted, huffy, "I didn't need to sneeze, but I am making a point. My point is that all of your so-called evidence is just speculation. There's a logical explanation for every bit of proof you find. The coat for instance, my mother used to bundle me up in the summer as well, to keep me warm. I was often sick as a child, and now as an adult. This has been one of my better years. I've only been bedridden once.... The point is that he might get sick easily as well, the coat might help prevent him from catching cold. Another reason he might be wearing the coat is that his form of dress looks silly when he isn't wearing one. I mean, see that waistcoat! It looks ridiculous!" Lafayette frowned at the fashion critic, not seeing how anything he was saying was relevant. James suddenly looked appalled upon realizing that all the time he spent with Thomas did have its consequences.

"Most aristocrats aren't patriots." Lafayette informed him, intent on proving that the man was nothing more than a pedigree loyalist. "I know that. They stick with their king to protect their image."

"We've been here for *hours*! So far, you have no solid patriots, or loyalists for the matter." James told his companion, "Your imagination's taken a turn for the worst. I don't even know why I agreed to this. We've accomplished nothing whatsoever!"

"Mr. Madison? *Monsieur* Lafayette?" a shadow fell over the two men. The duo looked up to find a familiar face blocking the sun's light.

"*Monsieur* Arnold!" Lafayette extended his hand to shake, "We've been hoping to see you."

Benedict waved aside Lafayette's waiting hand, "I don't want to show that we're on a friendly basis. There's eyes watching." He spoke quietly and nodded softly to a group of redcoats inconspicuously gazing at the governor.

"I see." Lafayette nodded appreciatively, then remembered what he had wished to ask the man, "Jemmy and I have been hoping to find patriots to recruit for our new army. You mentioned Aaron telling you the names of some?"

Benedict frowned apologetically, "I'm sorry, Marquis. I don't remember who they were. I never wrote the names down. I figured that I'd never have use of them…. Are you having any luck?"

"Building an army?" Lafayette asked, "*Non*, but I am rather certain that that man-" he pointed to the aristocratic man nearby, "Is not a patriot, but a Torie!"

James groaned loudly.

"I can't speak long." Benedict said urgently, ignoring Lafayette's proclamation, "I need to tell the two of you something." The pair looked at the governor, both curious and anxious about the news.

"I've been hoping to see one of you. I've been needing to tell you this: I won't be able to keep in touch. Not often, at least." Benedict reported, his voice low, barely loud enough for James and Lafayette to hear, "I fear that the British have grown watchful of me. I'm unable to do the things that I once was. Please, don't try to contact me, I need them to see that I'm nothing more than the-governor-that-used-to-be-a-patriot-but-now-is-a-loyalist. I'm sorry, but I fear that I can no longer be of assistance."

Lafayette nodded solemnly, "I understand. I shall alert the others – and may I beg a favor of you?"

"Unlikely, but what is the task?" Benedict inquired, "I doubt I shall be able to fulfill it, as a result of my predicament, but I'll try."

"If you ever do see one of the others again, such as Alexander," Lafayette began, "don't tell him that I was here with James. It might not end well."

"Is this about that fight?" Benedict asked, "That one last month?" James nodded.

"We haven't exactly been getting along or getting anything accomplished." Lafayette told his ally, "Jemmy and I realized that there was no point in fighting, and that we should try to further our cause. If anyone found out, however, we fear that it may be disastrous for our little group. Alexander and Thomas have been quarreling every day, over petty things, I tell you, but we fear that it's just leading up to something bigger. We don't want to give them fuel for an argument that might tear us apart."

Benedict nodded, "That I can do. I'll try to help you if I can, but I doubt that I'll be much help."

"I thank you, *Monsieur*." Lafayette nodded approvingly at the governor. Benedict smiled and nodded back his farewell. When he left, James and Lafayette sat side by side in silence. James turned to look at his companion.

"We've assembled our little army." James stated, "Now we need to bring that army back together. But for now, we need to work on assembling our larger army."

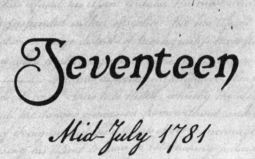

Seventeen

Mid-July 1781

PALACE OF VERSAILLES, FRANCE

ADRIENNE

Adrienne glowered down at her piece of embroidery before frantically unplucking the threads.

"What's the matter?" Dr. Ben Franklin asked, sitting on the lounge chair, watching Patsy play with her dolls. "You worked so hard on those stitches."

"It wasn't good enough." She snapped, glaring at him while untangling the threads from her fingers.

"It wasn't the best embroidery in the world," Ben told her, "but it was better than anything I could do. It was good enough."

Adrienne stood up and walked to the balcony, ignoring Ben. She fingered the silky pink fabric of her gown and stared harshly into the distance.

"It isn't the embroidery, is it?" Ben called to her. She could hear him calling, but it sounded like he was speaking from another world. She forced herself to look back at him.

"*Non*," she admitted, slowly shaking her head, "It's not."

"What is it then?" asked Ben, watching her sympathetically. "Is it Gilbert?"

She nodded, "He's been gone for ages." Adrienne spoke softly, "Seven months. I know that I made the right choice in sending him there, but...." She stared off into the distance, searching for words, "Now, from what he says in his letters, he seems much better; but it seems like he's forgotten all about me. I barely receive word from him, a letter a month at times – and that's not just due to the thousands of miles between us. It frightens me, the letters are so vague, he hardly gives me any details. It worries me, I fear that he's going to get into a bushel of trouble someday, and that he won't be able to get out of it."

Ben didn't speak for a moment, knowing that the marquis had become a delicate topic, "He can take care of himself, Adrienne. He's a grown man. He doesn't need somebody watching over his shoulder."

Adrienne shook her head, "Oh, that's just the thing, Ben! He *does* need somebody watching him. He's so reckless. If there was a sliver of a possibility that he could do something that would further his cause, he'd do it. Oh, Ben! I feel so conflicted!"

She sank into a small cushioned chair, her fingers thumping against the armrest. Ben watched her, confused by her sudden exclamation.

"Why are you conflicted?" he inquired.

Adrienne pressed her cheek against the chair, moaning, "It's selfish and silly and juvenile, I know it is. I want him to be happy, to save his America, to make it free. It's his dream, Ben, and I want him to accomplish it."

"There's nothing remotely juvenile about that." Ben comforted her, "I don't see how that's a problem."

"It's not that. I want him to help build America, I really do…" Adrienne trailed off, her eyes closing. She remained silent for a moment before continuing. "… But I also don't want him to go fight something that's not even his fight. I want him to be here, to be safe, where nothing eventful happens – ever! And we can go for walks and paint together and talk about books and go to the opera and…." Adrienne slowly and suddenly came to a halt. The smile that was there moments ago, when she was listing what she wanted to do with Lafayette, it vanished. A bland, saddened expression replaced it.

"That can never happen…." She sighed, "He's too adventurous to live a quiet life. We'll never be exactly… happy together, *mon* Gilbert and I. I want him here, he wants to go away. He's not content to be an aristocrat whose biggest trouble is deciding which bow matches which coat. He wants to be a dashing young soldier that narrowly saves the day with a jaw-dropping feat of bravery. I just wish that he'd try to take care of himself. I know that it's selfish to want him here, but I just can't help it."

Ben nodded thoughtfully once Adrienne finished. "I don't think that you're being selfish at all."

Adrienne looked at him in surprise, his answer clearly not the one that she had expected.

"It's perfectly natural to want him to be safe. It's also perfectly natural to want to support him." Ben explained, "You're just scared of losing him."

Adrienne smiled softly, "*Oui.* I suppose you're right. I just want him to be safe. I know that he's going to get himself killed one day. I just don't want that day to be soon."

Ben opened his mouth to say something but was interrupted by a knock at the door. He drowsily maneuvered his way to the door, annoyed that somebody had decided to interrupt their conversation.

It was a servant carrying an envelope on a silver platter. "For *Madam* Lafayette." The servant said, bowing slightly. Ben accepted the letter and nodded at the servant, who quickly departed.

"Speak of the devil," Ben muttered, reading the return address while closing the door. He looked up at Adrienne, who was watching him curiously. "It's Gilbert."

Adrienne quickly rushed to Ben's side, snatching the letter from his hand and practically tearing the envelope to shreds. She smiled sadly as she began to read.

"What does he say?" Ben asked after a minute.

Adrienne frowned at him, "He's asking my advice." She handed Ben the letter, a letter filled with the swirling calligraphy that was Lafayette's.

My dearest Adrienne,

I have not written in a long while. I am well, and I hope that you are, too. There's been a fight, here at the New York home. It happened yesterday. Everyone's been choosing sides and within all the chaos, no work has been done to further our cause! Hardly anyone speaks to a person on the opposing side with kindness. I wish that they would forgive each other, but they are too stubborn!!

I write to ask you a question that's been weighing on my mind quite heavily. What can I do to make the colonists patriotic? I've pondered this often as I lie awake thinking while I should be sleeping. I hope to find patriots to recruit as soldiers, but it seems that only myself and my colleagues are the only ones who truly believe in the cause. The civilians have seemed to lost hope. What shall I do? Do you have any ideas?

I've lost a friend this past week. He was a good man, but also a spy. How can I feel bad for a person that spies on me and my friends? Why do I feel bad for him?

Kiss the children on their heads a thousand times for me. Keep some of the kisses for yourself. Love to you all. Tell the good Dr. Franklin I give him my best wishes.

Forever yours,

Gilbert

Ben frowned, "That is a dilemma all right."

Adrienne wrung her hands anxiously, "It is. I don't know what he wants me to say. I'm not American. I don't know how they think." She looked at her friend when inspiration dawned on her, "You're an American, tell me, Ben, what would rekindle your patriotic fervor?"

Ben shook his head, "He's asking *you*, not Dr. Franklin, if he wanted my opinion he would've written to me. He wants *your* opinion. Think about it. What would bring back a way of thinking that you had lost? What would convince you to believe in something that you once did? Word of mouth?"

"*Non*," Adrienne took the letter from his hands, "That's too easily changed. It can easily become garbled and worthless. It's more convincing if it's in…." Her eyes grew large and she quickly ran to a desk, pulling out an inkwell, quill, and a piece of parchment.

"*Mon* dearest Gilbert," she spoke as she wrote, Ben watching from over her shoulder, "Your question confounded me for a moment, but I soon came to a conclusion. I suggest reprinting some old patriotic songs or documents, such as that independence declaration…." She paused and looked at Ben, "What else should I say?"

"I'm not the one writing." He replied.

"True." She said, then dabbed her quill into the inkpot. She touched the quill to the page, ready to continue.

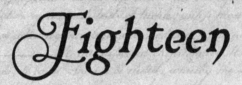

Eighteen

September 1781

NEW YORK CITY, NEW YORK

COMPANY

"And now for *mon* plan of genius!" Lafayette announced, lifting his piece of paper into the air, displaying it for all to see.

They were crowded around the dining room table, Lafayette at the head, and the others all in their usual spots. All eyes were focused on the Frenchman, some showing intrigue, some pretending to be bored, but all were curious.

"You've been speaking for at least a quarter of an hour!" Thomas groaned, "Why didn't you *start* with your plan?"

"What fun is that?" Lafayette asked, grinning from ear to ear, enjoying the attention. He had recently received his reply from Adrienne, and was immensely pleased with her response. He had laid out a plan, one that he hoped would both succeed and bring their team back together.

"Lafayette!" James said pointedly, "I'd like to see your presentation, but please! I'd like to see it before I leave this world!"

"Do get on with it!" Alexander cried, Eliza leaning on his shoulder, both of them trying to stay attentive, but failing.

"General Lafayette!" Washington shouted; the table all turned to him, "Please, my dear Marquis," he said in a quieter voice, "What is your plan?"

"Sorry, *mon* general," Lafayette apologized, looking down at the table shamefully, "I had an idea of how to further the revolution! Technically it was Adrienne's, but I was the one who made it official."

"What is it?" Adams asked, annoyed by the marquis's knack for going off topic.

"We republish the declaration, along with *Monsieur* Paine's *Common Sense*, and some patriotic songs as well." Lafayette said heroically, "I hope that it will ignite the hearts of the colonists, making them soldiers of the rebellion once more!"

The group looked amongst themselves, speaking in hushed tones before looking back to the excited Frenchman.

"How?" Eliza asked, "Those are banned documents! And it's not like we can just go up to the nearest print shop and ask if we can borrow the printing press. Somebody might trace it back to us, then we'll all be tossed in jail."

"Not," Lafayette smiled his daredevil grin, "if we do it properly."

"What are you suggesting?" Alexander asked, liking where this was headed.

"I'll only say more if you two," he looked pointedly at Thomas and Alexander, "promise to not fight anymore."

The two looked across the table at each other, making a silent agreement. Thomas nodded grudgingly, "Tell us more. We can't promise to not fight, but we'll try to behave."

James smiled, "Thank you."

"I was thinking that both *Monsieur* Hamilton and *Monsieur* Madison would agree to write some documents urging the civilians to take up arms against the Britons." Lafayette explained, "Then, once they are finished, *Monsieur* Jefferson and *Monsieur* Adams travel back to Philadelphia to publish the different papers. They spread some about that city and take the others here, where we distribute them here in New York." He clasped his hands together, awaiting his companion's reactions.

"I second the notion!" Adams declared as he slammed his fist on the table.

"I second it as well!" Alexander announced, jumping to his feet.

"It seems plausible," Eliza said, nodding readily, "I hope that it works."

"What do you think, Tom?" James asked, tugging at his sleeve, "I agree. It makes sense."

"It's our best option," Washington reminded him, "You haven't had any decent ideas since I've arrived here, with the exception of the one Gilbert just presented."

Thomas looked at his companions, then at Lafayette, "I admit it, it does make sense. I don't wish to agree, but it appears that I'm outnumbered. I do have one question, however." His tone was calm and collected, masking his annoyance at having to agree with Alexander.

"What is it?" Lafayette wondered, surprised that they had gone this far without an explosive argument.

"Why am *I* the one going to Philadelphia?" Thomas whined.

Lafayette shrugged, "I wasn't sure who to pick at first, but then I remembered that you lived in the city for about a year. You'd know the city best." Thomas nodded, satisfied with his answer. Adams groaned at him, not looking forward to their shared job.

"Shall we begin?" Alexander looked at James, who nodded eagerly. The two men quickly stood and began to leave, headed for the study, ready to lay out the plan for their series of letters.

Eliza frowned and looked at Lafayette, "You do realize that we've lost them for a month or more, do you not?"

Washington chuckled lightly, "She's correct. Hamilton is the best writer I know, Gilbert, but he could write for days without realizing that he needs to rest or even eat. There's been times when I've had to *order* him to sleep. He'll work himself to death."

"As will Jemmy," Thomas agreed, "He's not as drastic, but just as dedicated."

Lafayette frowned, "I didn't know. I just knew that they were good at writing."

Washington glanced off in the direction of the study, "If you want to tell them anything, do it now. They won't be paying attention to anything come tomorrow."

ELIZA

"Here…." Alexander absentmindedly handed Eliza a slip of paper, folded in two, as he dipped his quill into the inkwell, "This is for Jemmy."

She looked at it curiously, "What's this for?" She waited for a moment, then frowned. Alexander was writing furiously, a stack of papers to his left, a few unopened inkwells and unused feather pens to his right. His tri-corner hat was hanging on the end of his chair, his auburn hair hanging loose down his neck, the sleeves of his shirt were rolled up to his elbows. His brow was furrowed in concentration, his expression sharp and focused.

Eliza smiled, hugging him around his shoulders, and watched her husband pen every word that entered his mind. *He's so intelligent*, she thought, *and so dedicated and devoted.* She kissed him on the top of his head before leaving the room, knowing that she wasn't going to receive an answer to her question. He probably had forgotten that she was there. It was just him and his words.

"Is he still amongst the living?" Thomas asked sarcastically as Eliza came down the stairs. He closed his quarter's door behind his back, looking up at her, a teasing expression on his face.

Eliza forced a smile, despite the man's snarky comment, "As to be expected. He's very…." She clasped her hands, her back leaning against the wall. "…obsessive?" she shook her head, "No…focused, concentrated…that sort. He's still alive, but he's practically unresponsive."

Thomas chuckled, "Reminds me of myself when I was writing the declaration. Nothing ever seemed… right…. It's a stressful job, trying to write something to inspire a nation."

"I imagine it is." Eliza commented carefully, looking to the side, expecting a barbed comment directed to her husband, "You did a good job of it, though. I know that anything Alexander writes will be stunning. He has a gift.... I'm sure that Jemmy's work will be lovely as well." She added hastily.

He nodded cordially, "I'm sure they both will be, though I expect Jemmy's work to be far superior." He walked briskly to the study, in search of something to read.

Eliza huffed, stamped her foot, and tapped her hand against her thigh in a desperate attempt to think of a proper response. She failed. How dare he say that to her face! She glared after him, wanting more than ever for Alexander to be finished, simply so she could present his work to Thomas and see the surprised look on his little arrogant face! She frowned, surprised at how bitter she could be.

Childish behavior aside, Eliza turned back to her mission and quietly knocked on the door beside her. "Jemmy?" she called softly, "I have something for you." She heard a grunt coming from inside the room, which she decided she would take as an invitation to enter.

James was hunched over his desk, sitting in a chair bigger than he was, staring at a piece of parchment carefully. He rocked side to side softly, holding a quill in his hand.

"This is for you, Jemmy." Eliza crept up behind him and tapped him on the shoulder. He looked up, surprised by the gesture. He quickly noticed the paper she held out to him and took it from her hands, opening the note.

"Really?" he muttered once he was finished reading it, tossing it onto his desk. He turned his attention to Eliza, looking annoyed.

"He wants to know if there should be a limit on how much he writes."

"Should there be?" Eliza asked, "I hadn't thought of putting a limit on him, but he has been using an awful lot of paper...."

Lafayette poked his head into the room, "*Monsieur* Madison is still here!" the marquis strolled up beside Eliza, placing a hand on James's shoulder, "You've been so quiet that I almost suspected that you'd left."

"I'd never do that." James shrugged the man's hand off and tossed the Frenchman Alexander's note, "What do you make of it?"

"I think the more patriotic spirit the better!" Lafayette exclaimed after reading it, placing the note back in James's hands, "Why didn't he come down here to ask you himself?"

"Who didn't do what?" Adams asked, entering, "Why is everyone in here?"

"Alexander wants to know if we should put a limit to how many essays we write." James informed him.

"Whenever he starts to write he only ever thinks in calligraphy," Washington explained, joining the gathering, "We've been in the same room at times, and I'll be speaking to him when he hands me a note asking how he should respond to a letter from congress."

"It's true." Eliza agreed, "I've never seen him like this before. He's been shut up in our room for two weeks. I've been coaxing him to come to bed. It seems like he writes every second he's awake."

"Why is everyone in my room?" James asked, "Please, I'd like to continue writing. Can't you talk elsewhere?"

They paid him no heed.

"I say that we do put a limit on how much he writes." Announced

Adams, "Remember, I'm the one that has to publish these papers. I don't want to haul five hundred pages to Pennsylvania."

"Then what is his limit?" Lafayette inquired, "He must have written at least a dozen letters by now."

"We could have him stop *now*," Adams suggested, "That way there's less baggage to carry."

"We will look over what he's done," Washington stated. It was not a suggestion, but an order, "Then we'll decide if he should continue writing or not."

"Good plan, *mon* general!" Lafayette declared. Eliza nodded her approval.

"I seem to remember being assigned to write essays as well," James said loudly, "yet I'm the only one who seems to remember this task, or wish to accomplish it."

"Oh, I'm sorry, Jemmy!" Eliza patted him on the shoulder, then began pushing the men to the door, "We forgot. Come, we'll continue discussing this elsewhere."

"Aren't we going to read what Madison's written?" Adams inquired, maneuvering his way out of Eliza's herd of revolutionaries, trying to look over James's shoulder.

"We can do that tomorrow, Mr. Adams." Washington pulled on Adams's arm and began to lead him away, "but now, we let them write – in peace!" Adams grudgingly allowed himself to be pulled out of the room.

James sighed in relief once the door was closed and the group moved on to the study. Now he could continue.

"No!" Alexander snapped at Washington as he began shifting through the stack of papers. "They're not finished yet!"

Washington raised his eyebrow, "Hamilton?" he looked unimpressed by his aide's response.

"I mean, the essays are incomplete, your Excellency, but you may read them." Alexander said slowly and crisply, relenting.

"Thank you, Hamilton." Washington's voice was rich and rewarding, making Alexander feel slightly better. Slightly.

The general looked down at the page and began to read. Adams tried to read the words as well, but was pulled away by Lafayette, who knew that there were few people who were allowed to read his friend's unfinished work. Eliza's eyes glared menacingly at Adams, arms folded across her chest, wondering why he would even attempt to read them.

Washington nodded once he was through scanning them. He handed the stack back to Alexander, who shielded them protectively from view. "Those are fine letters," Washington complimented him, "Are you nearly finished?"

Alexander nodded, "Yes, but I need to go back and rewrite some of them. They aren't perfect. They need to be immaculate. Currently, they're nice essays that need improvement! And I'd like very much to finish these final letters and write them all properly! Please!" He snapped, turning back to his desk, "Thank you." He muttered, nodding respectfully before picking up his pen.

The general turned around and left the room, gesturing with his head for the others to follow him.

"What were you doing?" Thomas asked, book in hand, watching the foursome curiously as they entered the study.

"Seeing how much longer Hamilton will be," Adams replied, "It seems like he'll be at least another week."

Thomas groaned and rubbed his forehead, "I'm ready to start our journey! I have both a copy of my declaration and one of Paine's *Common Sense*. I wish that they'd just hurry it up a bit."

"You should know better than anyone that writing is not to be rushed," reminded Washington, "They're under pressure."

The group stood there for a moment before Thomas slowly nodded, "Yes, I suppose that you're right. It's just our first chance to do something productive-"

"And you're hoping to further our cause as quickly as possible." Lafayette finished, patting Thomas on the shoulder lightly, "You're not the only one who's anxious to get these papers published. Remember, we've been waiting just as long as you."

"Jemmy the longest." Eliza reminded them, "He was the one who planned all of this, remember?"

"*Oui*," Lafayette agreed, nodding, "Now his dream, this team, is reality, and that dream has grown into a dream that's all of ours," he gestured to the circle of colleagues, "it may take a long time to accomplish this dream, this new country, but it will succeed, and England will mourn it's loss and marvel at this new country."

James and Alexander walked into the dining room, carrying stacks of papers. They set the letters on the table with a 'thud', enjoying the moment that the revolutionaries gawked at them.

"*Mon Dieu!*" Lafayette exclaimed, "They *can* leave their rooms!"

Alexander chuckled good-naturedly, his bitterness gone, "We're not complete hermits."

Thomas chewed his bread carefully while watching the two men. Eliza entered the room, carrying a tray holding some slices of buttered bread, and she gasped when she the two newcomers.

"I was just about to bring you some breakfast," she stammered, "Will you be eating here, or up in your rooms?"

Alexander took the platter from her hands and gracefully set it on the table. He turned to her and wrapped his arms around her waist, "We'll be eating here, my Betsey, to celebrate the completion of our writing."

"You're finished!" she exclaimed, thrusting her arms around her husband, "That's wonderful!" Eliza smiled warmly up at him, excited. She looked back at Thomas, who was eating his meal quietly, "That means that you'll be leaving soon, doesn't it?"

"Not immediately," Thomas replied, "We still have to get the wagon in order and supplies to travel that far."

"He's correct," Adams agreed, spooning some oatmeal into his bowl, "But I would like to get on with it sooner than later."

"How many essays did you write?" Washington inquired, looking at the two authors. His tone was cold, a tone Alexander and Lafayette knew as his 'general' voice. It was easy to see that he wanted no more time to be wasted on small talk.

"Um…." Alexander looked down at James, who was chewing his lip. They looked down at their feet, slightly embarrassed by the amount they had written.

"We…uh…wrote," James mumbled, "Eighty."

"What!" Thomas leapt to his feet, dropping his bread to the floor, "but that's impossible!"

"Clearly not," Washington replied, unimpressed by Mr. Jefferson's reaction, "They just did it."

Thomas's brow furrowed and he ran his fingers through his hair, like he was surprised it was still there. He breathed in deeply and closed his eyes before turning to look at James, "You mean to tell me that you wrote eighty essays in a span of a month and a half!"

Alexander shook his head, "Five and a half weeks. And we wrote them in four and half, the other week we spent perfecting our word choices."

Thomas moaned, "How on earth did you do it? It took me seventeen days to write one document! One! How could you possibly write so quickly?"

"We've spent nearly all of our time writing these past few weeks," James shrugged, "You'd be surprised by how much one can accomplish in such a short time."

"How many did *you* write?" inquired Adams, looking at the letters curiously, "We know that you couldn't have written them together."

"I wrote twenty-nine." James replied, "I thought I wrote quite a bit."

Washington nodded slowly, absorbing the information. He looked at Alexander appreciatively, "Hamilton," he said, "you never cease to amaze me."

"You wrote fifty-one!" exclaimed Eliza, "Oh, Alexander, that's incredible!" she kissed him on the cheek, "No wonder you were crankier than usual. I'd never seen you in such a flurry before!"

"Congratulations, *mon amie!*" Lafayette slung his arm around Alexander's neck, then smiled at his shorter companion, "And you too, Jemmy."

The little man's reply was drowned out by Thomas's declaration, "I commend you for your work, Hamilton. But I must admit that I don't know how you did it."

"If it makes you feel any better," Alexander told him, munching on a piece of toast, "I don't either."

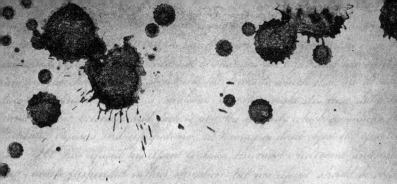

Nineteen

September 1781

PHILADELPHIA, PENNSYLVANIA

THOMAS

"*I* remember this place...." Adams stated as Thomas lit a candle.

"I wouldn't be surprised," he replied, "This was my flat for about a year or so. You came here when you first arrived."

The room was much like they had left it, the only difference being the lack of books and the addition of dust. Thomas's reading nook was still right before the fireplace, the long table just behind that. Before they had left for New York, Thomas turned the key in, but the kindly innkeeper had kept the room waiting, not letting another soul use Thomas's old quarters.

"It's good to be back." He muttered, squatting down beside the table, looking for mouse droppings and dead insects.

"You don't enjoy *Nouvelle Maison*?" Adams asked, setting his bag beside Thomas's chair.

"I do, don't get me wrong, it's the people that's the problem." Thomas looked up at Adams, cheered at finding a lack of unwanted visitors.

"Hamilton, you mean. He's the only one you can't stand." Adams corrected, using a cloth to dust down the table.

"Not entirely," Thomas replied, "Take you for instance, when we first met, you annoyed me. Now I find you tolerable."

"I'm going to pretend that I didn't hear that." Adams said drearily, "Though, for the record, the feeling was and is mutual."

"Jemmy's is a fine companion, my best friend, I could never say anything bad about the man. He's quite a talker once he warms up to you. He's begun to, hasn't he?" Thomas asked.

"If warming up means saying a short paragraph directly to me, then yes, he has."

"And Lafayette, he's enjoyable, but rather excitable and impulsive, a good lad in the heart, though. Eliza's a dear, I don't see how anybody could dislike her, pity she married that idiot." Thomas grumbled, "So, sometimes we don't get along very well. But I like the girl fine."

"I don't like him either, but I certainly wouldn't call him an idiot. Genius? Most certainly. Idiot? Not so much." Adams continued, then paused when a question came to mind, "Have you even given him a chance, or did you decide that you were going to loathe him from the moment you first laid eyes on him?"

"In my defense, I've known him six months longer than you have, at a time where the only people I had for company included a man who could barely speak in public, a woman that threw aside all self-preservation and dashed into a massacre, and a polite, irritating, smart-alack. We were constantly together, always getting on each other's nerves and butting heads. It's a wonder I didn't become mentally ill." Thomas shook his head in wonderment. "So, yes, I would say that I've given him a chance."

"Why do you still remain by our side, if practically all of us annoy you in some way?" Adams inquired.

"I believe in the cause for independence, and I don't think I should abandon the cause simply because I find that others that share my beliefs are people that I wouldn't associate with on an everyday basis." Thomas rose to his feet and sat in his armchair. "I don't think that the general's irritating at all. I think that he's the most inspirational, easiest person to understand of our little group. He's rather blunt, but very intelligent, if you don't cross him, you'll be fine."

"He has a way that makes you want to listen and to obey his every whim," Adams agreed, "But also an aroura of kindness, along with sternness, that's what makes him such a good leader."

"Yes." Thomas said, staring into the depths of the unlit fireplace. "Yes, it is."

THOMAS & ADAMS

Thomas shoved his hands into his pockets gloomily. The pair of redcoats passed him, walking in march-like precision, one bumping into Thomas's shoulder as he walked. Thomas glared after him, muttering under his breath.

"What is it?" Adams asked, looking at his tall comrade.

"I'd quite forgotten how many of those lobsterbacks patrolled these streets. I've grown accustomed to the state of Arnold's New York." Thomas replied, his voice a hushed whisper.

"You must remember that the governor here is a real *Torie*. He's not a Whig." Adams spat the word to the ground, as though it had a bad taste. "He's a redcoat himself, Governor John André. Former major in the British army; he takes his role as governor very seriously."

"I know." Was Thomas's only reply, "I just wish that Benedict was governor of both."

"Well," Adams grumbled, "He's not, and you know that." And he did.

It was a common story, one the redcoats loved to tell, reminding the colonists how rewarding it would be to become a British sympathizer.

In 1777, General Benedict Arnold was one of George Washington's best and most revered commanders, despite having injured himself in battle, rendering him a cripple. While he was recovering, he met a lovely young girl named Peggy Shippen, whom he soon became enamored by. Peggy, a loyalist through and through, slowly changed her new suiter's view of the war, making him more and more of a loyalist than a patriot. A clever, manipulative thing, Peggy introduced Benedict to her former suiter, Major John André, who, at the time, was head of England's spy ring. André, seeing how valuable of an asset Benedict would be, offered him a great sum of money, plus a promising position in the British army, if Benedict would give the British vital information. The three quickly hatched a plot on how Benedict could sneak information to his new allies. It was a simple ploy. Peggy would write letters to her André, which would then be delivered to the major. Unbeknownst by everyone but the three, Benedict would write the real message in invisible ink, between Peggy's words. André would then be able to read Benedict's reports without anyone suspecting.

Soon enough, Peggy and Benedict married, and not long after, Benedict was placed into a tricky scenario. Washington placed Benedict at an important command, a place that was vital the Americans keep control of. Thrilled by his new command, Benedict wrote to André (via Peggy) explaining that he must visit, as Benedict had important information, but wanted to be advised on how he would proceed. André hesitantly accepted the invitation, coming to visit the Arnolds under the guise of Peggy's traveling soldier friend. The two men quickly analyzed Benedict's situation, and André advised that Benedict allow the British to take control of his assigned region, where the army would then kidnap Benedict and bring him to André's headquarters, allowing Benedict to become an official British officer. After planning the attack, André bid his accomplice farewell and returned to his camp.

The plan went exactly as expected. The British took control of Benedict's exceedingly important command and delivered their 'prisoner' into André's waiting arms, Benedict bringing along with him some valuable information he had stolen from Washington's trusting hands. When Washington had discovered Benedict's act of treason, he vowed that he would catch the former patriot if it was the last thing he ever did.

Shortly thereafter, France stopped sending the Continental army supplies, and decided against joining the Americans in battle, despite all of Dr. Benjamin Franklin's pleading. Due to their lack of supplies and funds, the Continental army slowly began to fall apart, losing more battles than they won, until eventually, they won no more.

Washington knew that all was lost, so he tried to guarantee the safety of his men. He dismissed the last of the soldiers, soldiers so loyal that they had continued to fight for their general even though there was no money left to pay them. The soldiers left reluctantly, still believing in their cause. With no more fighting, King George III declared that England had won the war, a war that would come to be known as the 'War of Colonial Rebellion.' British regulars prowled the streets, lying in wait to seize known patriots and anyone acting remotely patriotic. The King sent shiploads of more soldiers to the cities of the colonies – Boston, New York, Philadelphia, all with the purpose to damper rebellious spirit. As a reward for his spying, Benedict Arnold became the governor of New York, where he purchased a lovely home for himself and his wife; but he soon found out that being governor wasn't exactly as he had expected. André became the governor of Pennsylvania, where he strictly made sure that at least one redcoat was posted on every street corner.

Left behind with only his closest and most loyal men, Washington turned his attention on making sure that each of them made it to safety. After helping some of his men hide in Virginia and New Jersey, Washington was accompanied by only one general, Gilbert du Motier (also known as the Marquis de Lafayette,) and his closest aide-de-camp, Alexander Hamilton. Washington made sure that Lafayette was safely aboard a French ship returning home, then began taking into consideration his own safety – mostly because Alexander couldn't stand to see his commander have a complete disregard for his protection. British regulars soon caught the scent of the general and his aide and began chasing them. Washington and Alexander found themselves in New York City, trusting no one but each other. After an unfortunate slip-up, the two soldiers found themselves cornered by a patrol of redcoats – ones who all knew very well who the older soldier was, but not knowing exactly who the bright, surprisingly young one was. Washington, knowing that he could run no longer, fought the redcoats long enough for Alexander to escape, but not long enough to evade captivity himself. The great general was captured and taken into prison, where he was held for nearly two years and six months, and then escaped under the noses of the British soldiers.

Alexander, on his own, then traveled around New York, looking for work and a roof to cover his head, at least until he came to Albany.

"Where are we off to? Not to the Pennsylvania State House, I hope." Adams moaned after a moment, he had no desire to visit the most heavily guarded building in the city. Thomas stared after the redcoats in silence, thinking. "Thomas?"

"Hmm?" Thomas looked down at his companion, "Ah, yes, correct. No, we're not going to Independence Hall, as much as I'd like to. There's a print shop here that I think would be of use to us." He began to walk down the street, the heels of his shoes sounding not unlike the clip-clop of horse hooves.

"Where?" Adams asked, trying to keep up with Thomas's long strides.

"To *The Pennsylvania Gazette*," Thomas replied, his voice less than a whisper, "I only hope that it's still here."

Adams bit his lip and huffed, "I doubt that it's still around. It's the paper belonging to Dr. Benjamin Franklin, of course it's unlikely to be open. I doubt that there's anything remaining of it. It's been years since it was in circulation. Why would you even consider going there?" he demanded.

"Well, do you have a better idea?" snapped Thomas, "I figured that we might as well try all of our resources. Besides, I think that it'd be rather fitting for the papers to be printed by Dr. Franklin's famous newspaper."

"Fitting? Yes, of course it's fitting, but why?" asked Adams, still chasing after Thomas, "Why not try to find some other abandoned print shop?"

"Do you know of another?" Thomas shot back. After seeing the blank look on Adams's face, he answered his own question, "That's my point. There are no other well-known newspapers out there that aren't being dominated by 'Mother England.' Our only chance is the *Gazette*, something that famous back in circulation would surely catch the eyes of the citizens."

"You do recall that we're not actually starting up a new newspaper, correct?" Adams asked, starting to worry, "We'll only publishing a few articles."

"We don't know how long it will take us to print all of these," Thomas told him, "My plan is simple. We print as many as we can in one night, then, later on, an hour before daylight, we bring the work back to our home. After we've printed all of Jemmy's and Hamilton's articles, we'll hide them in newsstands, shops, park benches. You know, inconspicuous spots for a newspaper."

Adams frowned, "That might take months! Months of no sleep!"

Thomas halted and looked back at his companion, "Yes, I suppose it would take months, but at least we have our citizens feeling patriotic. And we wouldn't print every night, just every other, and there are these things called 'naps.'"

"How long do you expect us to be out here? In Torie central!" Adams cried, "I didn't volunteer to spend my time like this! I thought we'd be here for no more than a week!"

Thomas shook his head, "Technically, Adams, you didn't volunteer, Lafayette told you to come. And second, expect to be here through the winter."

Adams gasped, "The winter? Surely it couldn't take that long."

"Don't speak nonsense," Thomas scolded him, "We'll likely be done by mid-December, but we'll wait out the winter to return home. It'd be rather suspicious if we traveled in winter. Who would do such a thing?" he continued walking, nodding politely at the British soldier stationed at the street corner. The soldier nodded respectfully back at him, indicating that Thomas and Adams could cross.

Adams frowned, seeing Thomas's point. Once they had reached the next street, Adams continued his questioning.

"How much longer?" Adams wondered, watching the dirty streets in disgust.

"Really?" Thomas asked, "Such a childish question! Sometimes

I wonder if your sole purpose in life is just to annoy others!... Not far. Have you ever been to the Gazette before?"

Adams shook his head, "Not that I recall."

"Do you at least know how to work a printing press?" Thomas hesitated, knowing what the answer was.

"Not at all." Adams replied, "What of it?"

"Oh dear." Thomas mumbled, *This will be much harder than I anticipated. Anyone would be better than him,* even, Thomas realized, Alexander.

THOMAS

"That was awful!" Thomas threw himself into his old armchair, greatly comforted by its multitude of extra stuffing. Adams followed Thomas into the flat and quietly began to stoke a fire in the hearth. "You'd think, Adams, that there would be at least one printing press that's out of British hands!" Thomas tugged at his hair, causing its white powder to drift onto his shoulders. "Oh, I need something to read!" he moaned. Adams dutifully pulled a book that Thomas had recently placed on one of the room's many bookcases. Thomas grabbed for it bitterly and flipped to the first page. After a moment of quiet reading, he shut the book angrily, unable to focus.

"I can't put that thought out of my mind." Thomas grumbled, "We were so close!"

"Look on the bright side," Adams suggested, feeling a rare spike in his optimism, "At least you know that the *Gazette* still exists."

The information did not raise Thomas's spirits.

After finding the location of *The Pennsylvania Gazette*, Thomas and Adams had happily learned that the shop was in the same condition as it had been when Ben Franklin had left it. Ben, apparently, still owned the shop, and the soldiers in the city respected the man's work as a scientist and helper of the community enough to leave the place unscathed. Unfortunately, the shop was locked. Thomas and Adams had seen the printing press gleaming in the sunlight, but had been unable to reach it.

As a result, Thomas was in a sour mood.

"It's no use if we can't use it!" exclaimed Thomas, wisely setting his book to the side before he had the urge to throw something, "What use is knowledge when it can't be used productively?"

"I suppose that it's no use." Adams replied sadly.

"My point, exactly." Thomas's voice was harsh and mocking. "And all of those other-" he cried out in anguish, "How could it be that the one press that British don't control is locked away? Rendered unusable!"

"You can't have exactly what you want." Adams reminded his companion, "I suggest that we wait a few days, write the others a letter explaining our situation. They might present us with the answer that we need."

Thomas nodded solemnly, his mood lightening, "Yes, Adams, I suppose that is our best option."

"Jefferson!" Adams exclaimed, thrusting the flat's door open,

"Jefferson!"

"What is it?" Thomas asked, looking up from his reading, "What's the matter?"

Adams grinned, "We've got a letter, well, technically it's addressed to you, but it's for both of us." He handed Thomas the letter, which he eagerly began to open. The smile grew on his face as he scanned the page, but quickly deteriorated into a firm frown.

"It's from Hamilton." Thomas huffed, recognizing the penmanship. He began to place the letter on the small table beside him, but his hand was slapped gently by Adams. Thomas looked up in annoyance, "What?"

"It's only written by Hamilton," Adams told him, sitting down in the armchair opposite from Thomas's. "It has information from all of them."

"Fine." Thomas turned his attention back to the letter, "'Jefferson,'" he read aloud, "'We've just received your note. How unfortunate that the doctor's shop has closed! It must have been so aggravating to have been able to see the shop's wonders hidden behind a sheet of glass.'" Thomas turned to Adams, "See! He just wrote to aggravate me!"

"Please, continue," Adams begged.

Thomas sighed, but obliged, "'No fear, however, the rest of us and I are on the case! While you were traveling, the Frenchman received a letter containing a curiosity from his wife. The curiosity was a key, and the letter explained that she had forgotten to send it the time before. The point is that we think that it will be of importance to the two of you, not us. I've enclosed the key in the envelope,'" Thomas stopped reading and held the envelope upside down, shaking lightly, causing the object in question to spill out.

Adams picked up the iron key, looking at it curiously, "Continue reading."

Thomas nodded, "'The commander sends his greetings, and warns you not to do anything too reckless. I, however, speak from experience, and I give you my full permission to do something reckless. It might just save your life. The little man says hello and wishes for you to hurry up, he misses your annoying presence. My wife sends her love and hopes that you haven't been eating anything too awful. You might be wondering why I haven't disclosed any names, let's just say that one can never be too cautious. There may be unwanted eyes watching. Your obedient servant, A. H.'"

Thomas looked up from his reading, "He has the incredible talent for giving me precisely what I want while also mocking me, insulting me, and saying my exact thoughts, only I hear it in his irritating voice." He thrust the letter aside, looking at Adams. A troubled expression covered his face, "That's all it says."

"The redcoats must have started to look through the mail." Adams speculated, "That's the only logical reason Hamilton wouldn't say who's who. Wait, hasn't Lafayette been writing letters to Adrienne? What if the British know of our plans?" Adams gulped, worried by his theory.

Thomas shook his head, "That's not likely. There's no reason for the regulars to search through the mail that's written in another language. Besides, his letters are harmless. He doesn't tell her very much of our happenings, and he's been careful lately. The British have been searching through the mail for ages, it's no surprise that Hamilton writes the way he does. 'The commander' is obviously

General Washington, 'the Frenchman,' Lafayette, 'the little man' is Little Jemmy and it doesn't take a genius to figure out that 'my wife' is-"

"Eliza." Adams finished, "Now that we have that settled, what are we to do?"

"Think." Thomas answered, "Contemplate. Consider. What do we need?"

"To print our papers," Adams replied.

"Excellent," coached Thomas, "Is there anything else that we need while on our mission?"

"No."

"I ask this question, why would Adrienne and Dr. Franklin send us a key, thinking that it would be useful to us?" Thomas wondered, "Why would they forget to send that key in a letter that mentions printing patriotic documents of rebellion?"

"It's the key to the *Gazette*!" Adams concluded, smiling excitedly.

"Precisely!" Thomas clasped his hands together, "Dr. Franklin has given us the key to his printshop, the figurative key to our country, and the literal key to freedom of the press."

"What shall we do now?" asked Adams, excited by the usefulness of the man overseas, "It'll be hours before nightfall. We have nothing productive to do, and that letter makes me want to do more than just wait."

"We *do* have an activity to occupy our time," said Thomas, "We'll go through the papers Hamilton and Jemmy wrote, we haven't done it yet, and it will give us a boost in our spirits."

Adams's hair seemed to move further up his scalp as his eyes widened, daunted by the task, "All of them?"

"All of them." Thomas repeated, "We'll figure out which order we shall publish these letters. One or two of them each edition, along with one patriotic song, a small part of *Common Sense*, and my declaration."

"*Our* declaration," Adams corrected, "It's the declaration of American independence, not the declaration of Jefferson's independence."

"Yes…" Thomas muttered, "We should advertise these essays, give them names."

"Such as what?" asked Adams.

"Let me think…." Thomas rested his head in the palm of his hand, staring into the flickering fire. He, along with Adams, considered a long list of different names, dismissing most, considering many, before finally stumbling upon one that sounded just right.

"*The Revolutionary Papers.*"

THOMAS & ADAMS

Adams shook nervously. The lantern in his hand trembled haphazardly, the candle's flame wavering in and out of existence. His fearful eyes studied the streets, keeping watch for the gleaming scarlet coats of the king's men. The lantern illuminated little of its surrounding area, but Adams feared that it was just enough to alert the soldiers of their presence.

"Hurry!" he hissed, sneaking a glance at his companion.

Thomas grumbled to himself, feeling the door for the lock, "I'd get this done much faster if you'd only shine the light on the doorframe instead of on the cobblestone streets!" Adams moved the light to the door, looking between both its position and the dark misty alleys.

"Must we do this so late at night?" he whined, "It's rather dark!"

"Oh, not at all!" Thomas said sarcastically, having found the lock and was searching for the key in his pocket, "It makes perfect sense to go out and enter a closed printshop of a known patriot to publish rebellious pamphlets in the broad daylight. I wonder why I didn't think of that! Really, Adams? You were the one who organized the Boston tea party, for goodness sakes! Surely you didn't consider dumping those crates overboard in the middle of the day! Sometimes Adams, I wonder why I spent all that time looking for you."

"I do, too." Adams said, his voice slightly higher pitched than usual, "But will you please not dilly-dally! I'd like to get this done as quickly as possible, and this bag is getting heavy! Why aren't you holding anything?" He readjusted his grip on his carpetbag, which was bulging with papers, "These documents are heavier than they look!"

"I'm not holding anything because you grabbed everything as we were leaving," Thomas inserted the key into the lock, smiling as he heard its satisfying *click*, "And because I had the good sense not to offer my help."

"Oh – you!" Adams kicked the door open, not caring any longer if a redcoat heard them, "I'm starting to see why everyone can't stand you!" He bustled through the door, shutting it behind him.

He set the lantern to the floor, along with his bag, then took in his surroundings. The press lay in the center of the room, and a few feet behind that, was a table covered in small lead blocks. Lined up against the east wall was a collection of chests, closed.

"Quickly," Thomas instructed, drawing the curtain, preventing the light from escaping to the street, "we need to get as many done as possible!"

Adams found two other candles, which he quickly lit and set on the table. The light flooded the room, but was undetectable from the street.

Thomas brushed aside some of the blocks and set the papers on the table, ready to begin printing. "Adams, here, I think that you'll be best at this."

"What is it?" Adams asked, looking at the table curiously. Thomas nodded to the multitude of metal blocks, "Each of those is a letter, number, or punctuation," he explained, holding one in his hand. Sure enough, carved onto the small block was an 'L'. "You copy the sentences from these papers onto this, the printing sheet." He gestured to one of the large wooden sheets on the table, "Once you run out of room, let me know, then start onto the next. I'll ready the press."

He walked over the monstrosity of a machine, one so strange looking that it seemed impossible for it to properly print a page, or do anything of that nature. The press, in all of its wooden glory, towered over Thomas imposingly. The wooden bridge-like structure that supported the screw seemed much more like a machine to torture than a machine to spread knowledge. Attached to the bottom of the screw was the block resting place, where

Adams would place the sheet when he was finished. The printing block, once it was full of letters and ink, would fold into position and quickly press itself onto the table, where a piece of parchment would be waiting. Thomas, in charge of pushing the block against the paper, would then hike the block back into the air, then Adams would snatch the printed paper from its resting place and replace it with the next, blank paper. With luck, they would be doing that for most of the night, printing multiple copies of the newspaper, copies waiting to be distributed.

Thomas rolled up his sleeves and gripped the lever that controlled the printing block. Adams placed the sheet onto the block and began to smother the small wooden letters with ink. Satisfied, the man replaced the ink dabber into its holder, then looked expectantly at Thomas, who began explaining the process.

"However did you come to learn these things?" Adams asked as he helped move the block into position. He quickly walked to the nearby table, where there were stacks of unused papers. He returned carrying as much as he could and set them on the floor nearby. He set one beneath the printing block, awaiting both the printed page and the answer to his question.

Thomas pushed up on the lever, pressing the block against the wood. He let it sit there for a second before pulling down, releasing the block. Adams quickly swapped the printed page for a blank paper and presented it to Thomas.

The letters, slightly blotchy, were legible, and Thomas grinned as he read the words printed on the page. "they do write wonderfully." His words hung in the air. Thomas shook himself and began to print the next page, "Back to work, but to answer your question,

I used to come here when I would visit Dr. Franklin. He taught me a few things, and, as you know, I'm interested in everything."

Adams nodded, unsurprised by his companion's answer.

Early December

THOMAS

"We're done." Thomas leaned against the wall.

"Truly?" asked Adams, looking at the piles of papers scattered across the room, "It feels like this is all we're supposed to do anymore."

Thomas rubbed his temples, "Come, help me." He walked to the middle of the room, looking at the papers destined for Philadelphia, and the ones destined for New York, "We must take these back home."

"What for?" Adams wiped his hands on a piece of ink-splattered cloth. "Why not keep it all here?"

"Think a step ahead," Thomas instructed, "The British will assume that we print the latest copy each night, so they will be searching through all of the printshops, but if we never come back here, they have no way of finding us. We'll keep these papers at home, hiding them across the city at night. Once we're done, we'll pack up, bringing us back to New York, along with thousands of copies to spread about the city. It will be easier there."

"There'll be more of us," Adams smiled tiredly, "We'll get more sleep."

"Exactly," Thomas told him, "Now help me get these home before sunup!"

THE COLONISTS

The next night, Thomas and Adams began hiding five-hundred copies of their first edition around the city. Some they hid on park benches, others found themselves in newsstands.

The papers became immensely popular amongst the colonists, nearly every literate citizen had one in their hands. Though there were not many editions, Alexander's and James's essays became the most common piece of literature to copy down. People kept copies of the *Revolutionary*, as it came to be called, in their homes, businesses, and smuggled them into nearby cities. Though there were plenty of other items in the new paper, it was the essays that caught the attention of the people. It became the talk of the city. Men speaking of their favorite essays on hunts with friends; ladies baking pies for their neighbors – an excuse for them to discuss the latest letter. Townsfolk whispered about it under their breath as the redcoats passed; businessmen hid copies of the papers in their stores, giving them to patriots and citizen revolutionaries.

The papers did not become popular amongst the soldiers – or Governor André, for the matter. After the first three letters were hidden, André sent out an order, demanding that the printshop that created such rebellious nonsense be stopped. Just as Thomas predicted, nobody suspected that the papers had all been printed beforehand. All the printshops in Pennsylvania were stormed by soldiers, all searching for evidence of the *Revolutionary*. They never found a scrap of proof of where the newspaper was being printed. All the shops were turned upside down, trashed, and destroyed while looking for the paper, all but one. Nobody looked in the *Gazette*. Maybe it was the fact that it had been closed for years, maybe it was the fact that nobody had been seen in it since before Dr. Franklin left for France. Nobody truly knew why, but for some reason the *Gazette* was completely overlooked. And the *Revolutionary* kept on appearing.

Soon the soldiers began to destroy copies, burning every copy they could find, printed by the *Gazette* or one simply written down by some rebellious colonist. After a month of publication, the redcoats began jailing people who had been reading it. That stopped nothing. Thomas and Adams then began leaving stacks of papers on the front steps of known patriot households. The people then would bring papers to neighbors and shopkeepers, who would continue to spread the word. There was nothing anyone could do. The independent mindset was spreading, and it was spreading fast.

THOMAS

Thomas placed the last of the Philadelphian copies of the *Revolutionary* on the cobblestone street. He stepped back and admired his work. In just a few hours, a shopkeeper would open his door and find these waiting on his steps. From there the man would hide them in his shop, stealthily handing a copy or two to a patriot to deliver home, or he would give a small stack to a man going out of town. From there, that man would give away copies in small towns and villages, where they would be read and copied, and the movement would spread. Thomas leaving some newspapers on a shopkeeper's doorstep started a whirlwind of patriotism.

Adams placed his hand on Thomas's back, "That's it, isn't it?"

"Yes, it is." Thomas smiled and turned away.

"Finally," Adams grumbled, "Now we can go home."

Thomas shook his head, "You forget Adams, that it is winter. We've been lucky so far, there hasn't been many storms preventing us from delivering our essays. We just wait out this weather, and then we go up to New York to deliver more copies."

"It'll be strange to leave this place, I've grown used to it." Adams frowned, "We've been here for so long, and this city is so patriotic...."

"It's not where we are needed," Thomas rounded the block, looking down the street. Despite it being a dark night, he could see the inn in which they were staying, and also his flat's window. "We're needed in New York."

"You there, halt!" Thomas and Adams quickly stopped and looked in the direction of the voice. The source of the voice was a British soldier. The man was marching with his partner, both watching the two civilians with suspicion. They approached the two, both soldiers wearing stony expressions with lack of emotion.

"Good day, sir." Thomas said, nodding to the men, wishing

with all of his might that he was a much shorter, ordinary man who didn't look suspicious and intimidating.

"Good day to you as well." The other soldier's response was polite, but uninterested. "What are you doing out in town this late at night?"

Adams looked up at his friend, panicked, but was relieved to see no signs of fright in Thomas's face when he spoke, "We are on our way home, sir. I am Samuel Johnson, and this is my friend, Adam...Henry."

"Where were you?" asked the first soldier, the one who had stopped the two patriots.

Thomas smiled sheepishly, "I doubt that you'd believe me...."

"Speak up!" the redcoat ordered, "We're searching for that ruffian who prints those ridiculous rebel pamphlets! It's our duty to speak to all citizens that are out past dark, seeing if their stories are believable enough. If I don't find your story trustworthy, we'll have to drag you and your friend off to the jailhouse. So, I recommend you speak up."

"We were in the park." Thomas stammered, "It was a fine day, not too cold, a little warm. A false spring. Anyways, it was a nice day to go to the park. I go there often, you see, to think...The sun was warm and, well, we just happened to take a bit of a nap. We're on our way home now."

"Ah," said the soldier, unbelieving, "And where is your home?"

Thomas turned and pointed to the inn, "See that hotel?" The soldier nodded. "My flat is on the top floor of that building."

"Are you the owner of the establishment?" asked the redcoat, raising his lantern to get a better look at Thomas's face.

Thomas shook his head, "I just own a room. Rent one, actually."

"I've seen you before," the soldier remarked, "I don't remember where we were, but I've seen you before. You nearly frightened the wits out of me."

"Excuse me?" Thomas asked uncertainly, "I don't remember."

"It was my first day," the soldier explained, "and I was all proud of getting my shiny uniform here," he gestured to his coat, "and was being sort of a bother, trying to let everyone know that I was the one in authority. You, you were the smart one, you understood that there wasn't much reason to pay attention to me. I was interfering with your privacy, and I told you to stand up-"

"And I frightened you away," Thomas remembered vaguely, "Yes, I do seem to recall you being a nuisance." He put his fingers to his mouth, realizing he just insulted a person who could very well throw him in prison, "Sorry, I-"

The soldier held up his hand in mock-surrender, "No, it's fine. I deserved it. I wasn't being a proper soldier. I'll be one now, though. You're free to go."

His companion looked at his friend in surprise, "Surely you cannot mean that! His story is hardly plausible!"

"It is, actually." The soldier replied, "I used to see him quite often afterwards, sometimes with a little man. They'd usually be in the park, sometimes talking, sometimes sleeping. I believe him; besides, I don't think that he'd be able to pull off such a stunt. We shouldn't mess around with a person that obviously is not our culprit. Come along, he's probably already delivered dozens more copies of that foul newspaper." The two soldiers turned to walk away, one smiling at Thomas, the other glaring.

346

"What luck." Adams stated, once they were alone, "Let's go home now before we're caught and killed."

"Yes," Thomas replied, beginning to walk back to his building, Adams at his side, "I'm glad that we're done with the *Revolutionary*."

"There's still New York." Adams groaned.

"What I mean is that we no longer have to deal with it here. It will be easier there, not as many soldiers, plus Benedict wouldn't let anything happen to us." Thomas told him, "I'm surprised that this is the first time that we've encountered trouble."

"That is agreed," Adams replied, "but in the meantime, let us help spread this new burst of patriotism."

"That, Adams, is one of the most agreeable things that you've ever told me."

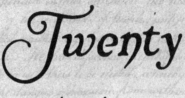

Twenty

March 1782

NEW YORK CITY, NEW YORK

Spring was in the air. The flowers were in bloom, the air smelled fresh and sweet. The sparrows sang songs of cheer as they lighted upon willow trees. It was a fine time to be alive.

The colonists in New York certainly seemed to think so. They were finally emerging from their winter misery, eagerly awaiting the new year that came with new growth. Not only were the colonists shedding their winter solitude, but they were also escaping from the shell that the British had entwined around them. The *Revolutionary* certainly helped with that.

The papers were just as popular in New York City as in Philadelphia, if not more so. Alexander's and James's essays reignited the patriotic fervor of 1780, when the Philadelphian massacre occurred, and also the spirit of 1776. It was the talk of the city, families visiting other families just to read the latest from the unknown authors.

It was just as unpopular amongst the New Yorker soldiers as it had been amongst the Philadelphian redcoats, only they were more puzzled. Why would a person who printed a wide quantity of rebellious papers, whose work was widely read in one city, pack up and print the same papers in another?

Governor Arnold, oddly enough, didn't seem too terribly worried by the *Revolutionary*, despite signs that the colonists grew more and more restless and temperamental every day. Whigs began picking fights with the soldiers, refusing to do what the redcoats ordered, spoke about war in front of loyalists and the King's men, and started hanging Betsey Ross's flag again.

Some people wondered why they were still under British rule.

ELIZA, JAMES, & ALEXANDER

Eliza sipped her lemonade, looking troubled. She was in the study, a discarded book lying in her lap.

James entered the room in search of a good read, but sat beside his friend upon seeing her distressed expression.

"Hi, Jemmy," she smiled sadly, then searched for a topic to begin a conversation, "It was certainly kind of Benedict for letting us use some of those printshops."

"Yes…." He nodded, "I just don't know why he did so. He put himself at so much risk when he did that…. Something's bothering you, Eliza. What is it?"

"The colonists." She relented, her lips puckered, her drink suddenly tasting sour. "They aren't even attempting an organized rebellion. They've reverted back to mob rule! Didn't you hear about that incident at the harbor? It's the Boston Tea Party all over again! They're tarring and feathering innocent people! Loyalists who did nothing wrong! Why can't they see that they're being rash? At least the boycotts have been peaceful…. I've joined the one against tea." She said somewhat proudly, jiggling her glass, the yellow liquid swirling.

"So that's why we've been drinking so much coffee and lemonade lately." James mumbled.

"Why won't they just get into an army and go fight?" Eliza cried, "I know it sounds silly, but can't they get in order?"

Alexander entered the room, curious about the ranting, and turned to his wife, concerned, "Betsey, what is it?"

"Why can't the colonists stop mob rule and just turn into an army!" she exclaimed, sinking into her seat like a deflated cake.

He smirked, chuckling lightly. "It doesn't really work like that, but believe me, I'm ready for an organized rebellion."

"How can we get them in order?" she asked.

"That's what I'm trying to figure out," he said. "The general, Lafayette, and I have been trying to find a way to covertly start up an army, or at least a small militia."

"And?" James hoped.

Alexander frowned, "We haven't really gone past the planning stage."

"Oh," he sighed, leaning more deeply into his seat, "…We have to channel the colonists' energy somehow, otherwise it will just spin out of control."

"That's what we're trying to do," Alexander explained, "I have the basics of the idea, I've been working on it for a week or so-"

"Why didn't you tell me?" Eliza exclaimed, "We haven't done anything eventful in weeks! You could've at least had my brain on the issue! And James's and Thomas's!"

"The thing is, I'm not certain if it's even a good idea. That's why I've been working with Lafayette and Washington, we know how to plan battles and keep an army together, and to differentiate the great ideas from the awful ones." He explained.

She rolled her eyes, "I'm the daughter of a general and a wife of a colonel, I think I've picked up on some things."

"You shouldn't dismiss me and Tom so quickly," James argued, "We could be of use, you know."

Alexander smirked, "I don't mean to offend, Jemmy, but I doubt a former governor who ran away from combat would know squat about our situation; and, tell me if I'm wrong, but I don't think you know any more about fighting than you do about botany."

James frowned, mumbling. He cleared his throat, "Tell me that you haven't consulted Adams, he doesn't know anything about organizing an army, a mob, yes, but not an army!"

He laughed, "Do you honestly think that I'd do that? Excuse me, but-"

"Hamilton!" Washington's voice rang through the halls and into the study, "Where are you?!"

Alexander blushed sheepishly, "I think that-err-I-bye!" he scurried out of the room, leaving James and Eliza to wonder what they could do.

COMPANY

"It's not a bad idea, *mon amie*," Lafayette descended the stairs with Alexander at his side, "I just don't understand why *mon general* doesn't agree."

"Is he being timid? It's not like him to be," the soldier leaned against the wall, running his fingers through his hair, "He usually agrees with all of my ideas. Why is it that to this one he isn't very dedicated?"

"I do not know, Alexander," Lafayette shrugged gloomily, he then smiled and patted his friend on the shoulder, "Chin up though, I will go talk to him and see why he is so hesitant."

"Thanks," Alexander muttered, starting up the stairs again. Lafayette watched as he turned the corner and went into his room. The marquis happily saddled the stair's banister and proceeded to slide down, nearly running into Eliza as she dashed from the dining room to the study.

"*Désolé!*" the Frenchman apologized as he stepped off.

"It's fine, Lafayette," Eliza laughed as she pulled a book from the study's shelf. She quickly ran back to the dining room where James, Thomas, and Adams sat waiting.

"We can't go straight into a mob and turn them into an army," Adams argued, "That will just make them turn on you."

"Don't you think that we've thought of that?" snapped Thomas, "Of course we have! Please, keep up with the conversation."

"Don't be cruel," Eliza scolded, "but you are correct, we are no further along than we were when we started."

"Has Alexander said anything concerning his plan to you?" inquired James.

"Only what you had heard earlier," Eliza said, "He's been avoiding the topic whenever we're together, so it's been slightly awkward."

"Slightly?" Thomas chuckled, unbelieving.

Eliza glared at him, "For your information, *Mr. Jefferson*, we don't always talk about war and rebellion. We talk about my family, our plans for the future, things of that nature, so there is a bit of tension, but we forget about it after we've been speaking for a minute. And I haven't been trying to haggle anything out of him, I respect his privacy."

"We could make flyers," suggested Adams, "advertising the army…nevermind that's an awful idea."

"I just wished that the three of them would ask our opinion," James sighed, "I feel like we're making history… but that we're not part of it at all."

"I'm sure that they'll confide in us eventually," Eliza consoled, "They can't hold up forever."

"The general told me that they've had numerous ideas over the past months, but none of them are good enough! Why can't they at least talk with us, it's not like we'll blow it out of proportion!" Thomas growled.

Eliza opened her book, "They very well might think that, and we very well might. We all act impulsively at times and that may be why they're not telling us. They might be trying to keep the peace. We've been at peace for a while now, maybe they're trying not to disturb that."

"You're a smart woman, Eliza," Thomas remarked, "You may be right."

Eliza beamed, "Thank you!"

"In the meantime, we should make a plan of our own, to present to them if they're having any trouble." James proposed, "Any ideas?"

"My dear Marquis," Washington sat cross-legged in his chair, watching the pacing Frenchman, "Whether or not I agree is not up to you, but to me. I will say, however, that I am intrigued by Hamilton's proposal, and yes, it is the only one that doesn't seem improbable."

Lafayette grumbled and sat in a chair. He made himself comfortable, mumbling all the while, before turning back to Washington, "Please let us go." He whined like a boy asking permission to go the creek.

"You're a grown person," Washington opened a book and began to read, "I can't force you to do anything, or Hamilton for the matter. Actually, I don't have control over anybody, Gilbert; I'm not a general anymore."

"But you're *mon* general," Lafayette shook his head, "You'll be a general soon enough, just let us do this."

"I'm not saying whether or not I'd like it to happen," Washington said curtly, "This conversation is over." With that, he turned his complete attention to his book. Lafayette watched him for a moment before reluctantly leaving the room.

Adams, nodded to him, having watched the exchange from the foyer, "When he was in the Continental Congress, he never said that he wanted to be general; but you could tell after a time that nothing pleased him more."

"Perhaps he's grown too old," Lafayette commented, "he's in his fiftieth year."

Adams grumbled at the man's words, "Aren't you one of the people who know him best? You're his surrogate son, Lafayette! Even I can tell that he's restless."

"Then why does he remain home?" the marquis wondered, his arms folded across his chest.

"He's cautious." Adams assured him, "He's not always the riskiest person. If it's likely for him to lose more soldiers than kill some, he'll avoid battle. He knows that you need him to lead a new army. He's trying to protect himself from harm. Please, Lafayette, don't try to ruin this. You won't be able to convince him to leave."

"Fine," Lafayette said, "But I'm going, and I'm sure that Alexander is coming too. I expect the rest of you will stay here, talk politics, and read?"

"You know us well…" Adams nodded, walking past him and into the study.

Lafayette sighed in disappointment. Sometimes it seemed like he, along with Alexander, were the only persons willing to do something reckless. He touched his stomach after hearing it growl. He walked past the dining room and neared the kitchen, hoping to snag a bit of bread. He frowned when he heard an argument ensuing from the room, rendering him unable to take a piece of bread unnoticed. He leaned against the wall and peeked into the room, expecting to find Thomas and Alexander quarreling over some silly bit of nonsense. His eyes widened, however when he saw the two combatants.

Eliza was leaning against the wall, stirring spoon in hand, a frown on her face. Alexander stood in front of her, waving his hands around, trying to explain. She stared intensely past his shoulder and shook her head.

"No!" she snapped, waving her spoon at him, a bit of batter hanging from its end, "Why on earth would you go do that? You'd kill yourself – and Lafayette and Washington, too." She brushed past him, slapping his outstretched arm aside, and began stirring some sort of batter in her cooking dish, "Did it ever occur to you that I wouldn't like to lose you? I'm not saying that your idea's awful – I think it's wonderful – I'm just saying that I don't want *you* to do it. If some men I'd never seen before came up and told me what you just told me, I'd tell them to go on with it! Go! Build your army! Take over the world for all I care! But that's not the case! My husband, whom I love very much, and some of my closest friends has decided to go off and do this! How can I agree to that?"

"Eliza!" Alexander exclaimed, "Please! It's not just me and Lafayette and Washington that I'd like to go- "

"Oh, wonderful!" She said sarcastically, "I get to lose Thomas, too! This is my lucky day! Now how, if you're still listening to what comes out of my mouth, how are Adams, James, and I supposed to start a rebellion on our own? Ha! We can't!" She focused her attention on her stirring, whipping the batter so hard that pieces flew out of the bowl and into her hair.

"Why would Thomas come?" Alexander spat out the name, then shook his head and put his hand on her shoulder, "I want *you* to come help us."

Eliza stopped stirring. The spoon clanged as it fell against the bowl. She turned to him, pulling bits of batter out her braided hair. "What?" she gasped.

"I'd like you to help me, Washington, and Lafayette start organizing the new Continental army," Alexander explained with a smile, "You've done nothing these past few years but cook and stop arguments-"

"And help break spies out of jail," Eliza cut in, trying not to grin.

"And help break spies out of jail," Alexander added, smiling at her, "and I think that it'd be good for you to help us."

Eliza leaned against the wall again, thinking. She looked at him suspiciously, "You're not just saying this to make me happy, are you?"

He shook his head, "Of course not, if there was a list of names that I could pick from to help me organize an army, I'd still pick you. I pick you because you're the most intelligent, clever, thoughtful woman I know, and there isn't another person I'd rather have on my side. I know that you're useful for more things than making pancakes and people happy, and I'd like your help."

She smiled warmly at him and wrapped him into a hug, "You really mean that?"

"With all of my heart," he told her.

"Why must they be so sappy?" Lafayette whispered to himself, walking into the kitchen, unable to contain himself any longer. "*Mon* general won't come!"

Alexander looked up, "What?"

"Why?" asked Eliza, head resting on her husband's chest.

"I don't know." Lafayette announced, "I do know that he's not coming, and that we should go on without him."

Eliza looked between the two former soldiers, "What's the plan?"

"The plan is simple," Alexander began, breaking away from Eliza's embrace, "We go look for patriots in the surrounding region, explaining that we soon will be forming an American army, intent on driving the British out of America and regaining our freedom. Lafayette and I will scope out the men in the countryside. You become friends with the rest of the womenfolk-"

"Oh, that's why you needed me." Eliza said dryly, "To gossip the ladies up until they say if their husbands and oldest sons are patriots or not."

"Not entirely," Alexander explained, "I find that when a female is present, people seem to trust and like her more than her male companions."

"Once we have a large number of rebels, we bring them to a field," Lafayette continued, "That is where the two of us will teach them about the art of warfare!"

"That's a lovely plan, better than what Thomas, Jemmy, Adams, and I had thought you'd come up with," Eliza sighed, "but I don't see how exactly you're going to accomplish it."

"Simple, my Betsey," Alexander slung his arm around her, "Things like this spread like wildfire. I predict that it won't be long after we start our own little camp that we'll be joined by others across the nation."

"It is our duty!" Lafayette cheered, "You have a fine role, you help us find some of the patriots. You can do that."

Eliza smiled, "Yes, I suppose I can…. When do we leave?"

ALEXANDER, ELIZA, & LAFAYETTE

The horses walked side by side down the road, the gentle clip-clop of hooves like the rhythm of music.

"How long do you think it will take to find the amount of patriots you want?" Eliza asked, readjusting her grip on her horse's reins.

"A month," Lafayette estimated, "Maybe more. Now please, act like a peasant lady."

"Here's the first house," Alexander stated, ignoring the glares being thrown between Eliza and Lafayette.

It was a nice farm, like one from a painting. A respectable white house, one worth being proud of, stood near a field of grass, and nearby was a brown barn of fine proportions. The three turned into the pathway leading to the home, admiring the wildflowers entangling themselves with the property's fence. They reached a post, and Alexander slid off his horse and tied the reins of all three to the pole. He then helped Eliza slide down from her saddle, and they watched as Lafayette leapt to the ground, sending a cloud of dust swirling into their faces.

"Who are you?" called a voice. The three quickly turned around to see a middle-aged woman standing on her home's porch. A basket of laundry was leaning against her hip, a small child clutching her apron. Her hair was kept close to her head, but not the way Eliza usually piled hers. The woman's hair was in a bun, giving her a stern, compassionate, motherly look.

"Hello, ma'am!" Eliza picked up her skirts ever so gently and moved towards the woman. Today, to give her the appearance of a modest housewife, her hair was pulled into a bun similar to the woman's. Her dress was cream, her traveling cloak, white. She seemed every inch a farmer's wife.

"Hello," the woman replied courteously, then remembered her question, "Who are you, though?"

"My name's Elizabeth Lawrence," Eliza introduced herself, curtseying slightly, "I'm new to town, and my husband and I are trying to meet our new neighbors." The woman nodded politely as Alexander and Lafayette came to stand on either side of Eliza. "This is my husband, Johnathan, and this is our boarder, *Monsieur* Motier." The two men bowed slightly to the woman, who tried to hide her smile.

"I have come from France," explained Lafayette, having traded his French uniform for less conspicuous civilian clothing. "I don't speak as much English as I'd like to." He thickened his accent and slowed his speech, making it seem as though he was just learning the language.

"It's nice to meet you all," said the woman, setting her basket on the porch and walking down the steps to get better acquainted with the newcomers. Her young son began to tag along after her, but she sent him into the house. He obediently left, going off to play with his toys while his mother conversed with the strangers.

"Where do you come from?" she asked, straightening the

wrinkles in her grey-blue dress.

"Philadelphia." Alexander replied, "We've only recently arrived. We're living in a small home on the outskirts of the city. How long have you lived here?"

"Oh, roughly fifteen years." She responded, "My husband's lived here since he was a boy. His parents died a little after we married, and they left us the farm."

"What do you grow here?" inquired Eliza, looking around, "I don't see any cotton or tobacco."

"Goodness sakes, girl!" the woman chuckled, "We don't grow anything like that up here. You born in Virginia?"

Eliza nodded slowly, knowing that was where most tobacco and cotton came from.

"Here in New York we grow fruits and vegetables. Here it's mostly cucumbers and cabbage." The woman began walking towards the barn, waving for the others to follow her, "Folks around here say that we grow the best cucumbers there are. We make even greater pickles."

"Pickles!" Lafayette exclaimed, forgetting to thicken his accent, "I love pickles!"

The woman laughed happily, "Come, meet my husband." She banged her fist against the barn door, which was quickly opened by a man wearing a tri-corner hat and a scruffy beard.

"Hello?" he said in surprise, looking at the new faces.

"These are our new neighbors," the woman explained, "Mr. and Mrs. Lawrence, and Mr. Motier."

"Nice to meet you," the man took off his hat and nodded welcomingly at them, "Name's Friedrich Carpenter, this is my wife, Mary."

"Nice to meet you, too," Alexander reached out to shake the man's hand, which he did so happily. "You have a fine farm."

"Thank you," Mr. Carpenter placed his cap back on his head, grinning with pride.

"Friedrich," Lafayette rolled the name on his tongue, "Isn't that a German name?"

Mr. Carpenter laughed, "We're not all English, Frenchie! Sadly, that's a fact that those redcoats decided to ignore."

"You don't like the soldiers?" Alexander asked, peering at the man in interest.

"Don't tell me that you're loyalist!" the man replied, "Otherwise we'll likely never get along."

"I'm a patriot as well," Alexander told him, "All three of us are, it's just a surprise to see someone who admits it so openly."

"Get used to it," Mrs. Carpenter snapped, "It may be different in the city, but out here, there isn't much to keep secret. Nearly all of the people living around here are rebels, many having fought in the war, like Friedrich did."

"You fought in the war?" Eliza asked, slightly intrigued.

"Why, of course. Fought under General Washington himself!" He exclaimed, pulling on his suspenders proudly, "I saw General Lafayette a few times, too," he looked at the marquis closely, who was frowning, slouching, biting his lip, and puffing out his cheeks in an effort not to be recognized, "You look kind of like him, Frenchie, but he always carried himself proper-like. Never slouching. Saw many famous warriors, even Benedict Arnold! The traitor!"

Alexander swallowed his laughter, having forgotten that he was one of the few that knew Benedict was a patriot.

"Is that so?" Eliza asked in feigned wonderment.

And so it went, the trio eventually receiving an invitation to dinner, and the location of patriotic farmers, and the loyalists.

Most of the month they spent searching for patriots, and most welcomes were like that on the Carpenter farm. Some of the men openly admitted to being patriot, while others pretended to be neutral, kicking their Continental army uniform under the table. Not all were rebellious, a great many of the surrounding folks were loyalists, and had no problem telling the trio, but others said nothing about politics whatsoever, their opinion shown by children playing games where the rebels always won, or a framed medal, a polished red coat hanging on a hook. At times, it took a bond to grow before loyalties were revealed, Alexander and Lafayette going fishing with their hopeful recruits and learning the farmers' opinions in confidence; Eliza sewing and knitting with the wives and mothers of the suspects, ladies who often talked too much. By the end of the month, Alexander, Lafayette, and Eliza had quite a list of potential recruits.

"So now we tell them." Eliza stated, riding sidesaddle. She fluffed her coiffured hair and adjusted her brilliant blue bows. Cascading down her horse's side was the shining rippling blue fabric of one of her most favorite gowns, something she hadn't worn in a long while. Her hair upon her head felt almost foreign, having spent so much time keeping it in either a braid or loose down her neck.

Today she was dressed to impress, dressed like the lady she had been brought up to be, and she played her part proudly.

"Yes," Alexander dusted off the shoulders of his blue Continental uniform. It had been years since he had worn it, but he had kept it faithfully for this moment. Unlike when he wore his tri-corner hat and shin length coat, he looked stunning astride his brown horse. His blue officer's hat was perched upon his head at such the right angle; the sun gleamed against the shining golden buttons. The suit complimented him smashingly, making him look regal, even if he had few medals pinned to his coat. It had been so long since he felt important looking, the suit reminding him that he used to be a powerful member of the army.

"I feel bad," Lafayette straightened his shoulders, "Did we truly have to lie to them?" He was in his powdery blue French uniform, his hat sitting on his head elegantly, his wig perfectly situated on his head. Unlike the others, he had worn his uniform quite often while in America, though rarely out in public, so he felt the most comfortable of the three. He stroked the mane of his white horse, "I know that we had to, but still."

"I understand," Alexander replied, looking down the dirt path and into the Carpenter's property from a small hill. "I feel bad as well, just remember that it was for the greater good."

"He'll likely join," Eliza declared, "If he's fought before, he'll surely fight again."

"Ah, my Betsey," Alexander's voice was a near whisper, "You forget that war is a terrible thing. Not a thing one would volunteer for the moment they hear of one."

"Then why are you here?" Eliza laughed.

Alexander's face blanked, but he smiled at her, "Touché."

She regained her composure. "I know it is, I've seen it. I've witnessed battles. We all have. I do believe that we have to fight to free our country, though." Eliza said heroically, "There's no other way."

"And that is why you're such a good patriot's wife. You'd make a horrible loyalist's." Alexander moved his horse close beside hers, reaching over to squeeze her hand, "We make a perfect team."

"I'm beginning to see that you married her for more than her cooking," Lafayette teased. "Perhaps it is also for her stubbornness, brains, and beliefs? She reminds me of a certain friend of mine, one with all of those qualities, but he can't cook well."

Alexander glared at him, "Yes, you're very funny." He looked back down towards the barn and home, "We can't just sit here. We've dawdled too long. If we don't move now, we never will."

He flicked the reins and his horse slowly began his descent down into the property, his companions following.

They were nearing the middle of the property when Mr. Carpenter walked out of the house, looking at the three in awe and fascination. He stared at the three before quickly ducking back inside his home and bringing out his wife, who looked at the horses' and their riders in equal amazement.

After bringing their horses to a stop, Mr. Carpenter approached, watching them curiously. "I know you…." He muttered to himself, studying Alexander's uniform, "You're that Mr. Lawrence, and you're Frenchie." He turned to Lafayette, who smiled at him kindly.

"I regret to inform you," said Alexander formally, sliding off his horse, "That we were not entirely honest with the two of you. We

365

wanted to know if you could be trusted."

"With what?" Mrs. Carpenter asked, staring at Eliza's dress with a dreamy look on her face. Eliza blushed and looked away, unsure of how to respond.

"With being American," Lafayette clarified, speaking normally, "The names that we told you were false. Technically, mine wasn't, but theirs were."

"You're Lafayette." Stated Mr. Carpenter, "I remember your uniform, the way you ride."

"Why, thank you, *Monsieur* Carpenter." Lafayette said, pleased by being recognized, "Your observation skills are not wrong."

"You're truly Lafayette?" Mrs. Carpenter tore her glance from Eliza and shifted her gaze to study Lafayette's polished boots and shining hat.

"Yes." Alexander grumbled, annoyed by all the attention his friend was receiving, "but we're getting ahead of ourselves. We're not new to town, we've been living here for around a year. We're trying to create a new American army, one that will successfully take down the British, delivering our freedom once and for all."

"How big is the army?" asked Mr. Carpenter.

"So far..." Eliza frowned, realizing the size of the army, "two. Maybe three. Probably three. Three."

"We plan to find new recruits, to train them until we have a fine sized army, one that will grow by word of mouth. One person telling another, who will tell another, until we have an army made up of citizens from every colony." Alexander explained, "All led under one great leader."

"Who?" asked Mr. Carpenter.

"We're not revealing his name at the moment." Alexander stated, "We're here to ask you if you'd like to take your Continental uniform out of retirement, to polish that rifle, and fight for your country."

"I will," Mr. Carpenter nodded, "I've been waiting for this for a long time."

"Who are you, then?" Mrs. Carpenter inquired, looking at Alexander, "If Mr. Motier is Lafayette?"

"I," he smiled, "am Alexander Hamilton."

Mr. Carpenter shook his head, "Doesn't ring a bell." Alexander frowned.

"My friend was one of Washington's most trusted officers," Lafayette informed the couple, "wherever there was Washington, there was his closest ally and assistant." A look of appreciation grew upon the farmers' faces.

A small smile appeared on Alexander's own, but it quickly melted away when he spoke, "So, you shall fight for our new country?"

Mr. Carpenter nodded, "With every fiber in my being."

Alexander hoisted himself back onto his horse and began to pull away, leading the horse up the hill. He turned back, "Good."

Twenty-One

April 1782

OUTSKIRTS OF NEW YORK CITY, NEW YORK

ALEXANDER

The dried yellow grass crunched under the horse's hooves. The weeds caressed the shining black boots of the officer. He watched as the men assembled… and sighed in annoyance. There were thirty in all, some boys just becoming men, some men just becoming old. They all watched the officer with determination and hope in their eyes.

Alexander slid off his horse and tied it to a nearby tree. Lafayette jogged over to him, a small smile masking the disappointment in his eyes.

"Is this all we have?" whispered Alexander, glancing towards the men, dreading the answer. The recruits were standing in a circle, socializing, sneaking looks at the two fancily dressed, conversing officers.

"Yes, and some of these men brought friends," Lafayette

mentioned, looking at the group as well, "hopefully those friends will bring friends next time they come."

"*If* they come." Alexander groaned, shaking his head, arms folded across his chest, "There are hardly enough men to outfit a militia."

"It's better than none," the Frenchman encouraged, "Please, try to teach them what you know. I heard rumors that when you first started in the army, your squadron was the most organized in the whole army."

"That's an exaggeration," Alexander's eyes narrowed as he continued watching the men in the wheat field. His eyes darted back to the marquis, and a conspiratorial smile grew on his face, "but it was one of the best." He smiled proudly and focused his attention back to the men, "I'll try to make them somewhat presentable, with luck, they'll be able to fight one battle."

Lafayette frowned, "You shouldn't discourage yourself, *mon amie*. You forget that the American army was once nothing more than just a group of rag-tag men with guns. Then look what happened-"

"We lost." Alexander finished, glaring at the marquis, "Is that supposed to be encouraging?"

Lafayette sighed at his friend's lack of optimism, "We only lost because of Benedict changing sides and my people not coming to help yours. Our army was fine. It just needed more supplies. It needed help."

"Fine!" Alexander began walking away, "I'll try to get them into shape, but you are not – will not – sit on the sidelines while I try to teach them. I'll need some assistance."

"Would I ever do that to you?" Lafayette caught up to Alexander, "You've known me long enough to know that I wouldn't. If you weren't here, I'd teach them myself. You're just better at training. I'm better at shouting orders and leading charges."

"I'm just glad that Eliza's not about to see this." He muttered to himself. Eliza was at home with the others, reading and awaiting news on how the army was. He was not looking forward to his report.

As Alexander grew closer, the men tried to straighten themselves into a line, though their finished attempt seemed to resemble an arch. Alexander rolled his eyes and began to pace in front of them.

"Good morning, men." Alexander said bluntly, "You may address me as Colonel Hamilton, or 'sir'. I will address you all as 'private' until I decide otherwise."

Most of the men nodded, a few mumbled 'yes sir', while others shouted the title with more vigor. Alexander stared at them all until the rest of the trainees matched the vocal capacity of their companions.

"*Good.*" He told them, "Now many of you I have met previously, and many of you I have not. Since this is the first time, I shall be less strict on formalities and allow you to ask questions. However, later on, unless absolutely necessary, do not ask me anything. Now, General Lafayette and I will briefly explain our mission. Then, if there are any questions, you will be permitted to ask them. Any objections?" he scanned the wavy line, pleased with the lack of raised hands. He frowned when he saw a young man at the end of the line, waving his hand lazily. "Yes?"

"Why are you the one leading us, sir, if General Lafayette has a bigger title?" The man asked, looking between Alexander and the marquis. Alexander stared bitterly at the man, but allowed Lafayette to answer.

"Traditionally, it is not proper for the highest-ranking officer to teach new recruits," Lafayette began, "but, since we have so few men, I will be teaching you as well. The reason Colonel Hamilton is leading is because he is the best at training."

"Thank you, General," Alexander said formally, nodding at him gratefully, "Now please explain what our purpose is."

Lafayette stepped forward, smiling at the men, "Good morning, *Monsieurs*. For a long while now, Colonel Hamilton and I, along with our colleagues, have been trying to rekindle the patriotic fire in the colonies. As all of you know, we lost the War of Colonial Rebellion five years ago. Now, my associates would like to start a new war, one that will drive the English out of America and deliver freedom to this new land. Most of you here already know this, there are some of you that have come here after being told of this by a friend or neighbor. To those, I give you *mon* thanks, and please, tell your friends. We'd like to eventually build an army as large as the Continental! Larger even!" Lafayette smiled at the idea, finding it very agreeable.

"I trust that you understand the basics?" Alexander said quickly, not liking Lafayette's sense of familiarity. The men replied with enthusiasm to his question. "Wonderful. Now, how many of you fought in the previous war?"

Nearly all of the men raised their hands, only a few of the youngsters shaking their heads. Many of the men reported who they had fought under, a few having been stationed under

Washington, while most were under Generals Lee, Knox, Schuyler, and Greene. None had been under Lafayette's command before.

"So, all of you know how to fight in combat?" Alexander watched them. Only the youngest boys had not. "Today we will teach you how to fight as one unit, how to pick off British officers, among other things. For most of you, this will be review, but know that you cannot skip this training. There is no such thing as too much practice."

Alexander then proceeded to show the men how to properly fire a volley, disappointed by the wide variety of guns in use: muskets, rifles, even some pistols. After the men could successfully get into position and fire as one a dozen times in a row, Alexander finally allowed Lafayette to convince him that they could move onto a different subject. By then it was late in the afternoon, and Alexander reluctantly dismissed his new soldiers, knowing that some had a long walk back home.

Much to their relief and surprise, the next day, Alexander and Lafayette were met by more smiling faces. Lafayette quickly briefed the newcomers on the previous day's events, giving demonstrations and explanations, before handing them off to Alexander, who was now teaching the men to charge with bayonets.

Each day, new patriots came, some from across the state, some from New Jersey, all eager to fight for their country. Most of the men had fought in the War of Colonial Rebellion and were ready to fight for their country once more. Others were boys not yet sixteen, but just as eager to fight for their freedom.

One day, Lafayette asked some of the men why they were coming faithfully, day after day. Surely they had jobs to attend to.

They did, it turned out, but most were farmers and shopkeepers, who had wives and children just as patriotic as they. The women had been working the farms and managing the shops, the children taking care of the house and meals, just so their fathers and husbands could fight for their land.

Lafayette began to show the men how to take commands, and how to locate their leader in battle. By the time the lessons had a hundred recruits, Alexander started dividing the soldiers into two teams. He then had them perform false battles, him leading one side, and Lafayette the other. Alexander taught the men guerilla warfare, how to properly attack the enemy from high in trees and deep in the woods, a tactic most of the men loved.

Not much to their surprise, the men started to look more and more like soldiers.

WASHINGTON

Washington looked at the men standing in a line, his face portraying no expression. Unlike when Alexander and Lafayette had met them, the recruits were in straight lines, in rows of ten. They stood to attention, watching the famed general with their eyes, their heads facing straight ahead.

The general turned to look at his companions, both of whom were anxiously waiting for the man to either compliment them on their work or scold them for a poor job. It was the first day Washington had come, curious about meeting his new army. The soldiers grew nervous after being told who their new commander was, but were desperate to impress.

"What have you taught them?" Washington demanded, looking at his two officers, both of whom were happy to be the ones worthy of his attention.

"Volley, guerilla warfare, how to fight with bayonets, how to properly care for their weapons, war strategy, and negotiation." Lafayette reported, "They're getting better. We've been performing some mock battles, and they're very good at them."

Washington frowned, "How would you say they are doing?"

"Good," Lafayette stated. Washington turned to Alexander, not fully believing the kindhearted marquis.

"Better than expected." Was Alexander's response. Washington continued staring, so he began to elaborate, "They're not as good as my first regiment, but they had more time to train than these men. They are doing better than I anticipated, but I never had high hopes for them in the first place."

"Are they competent?" Washington asked, growing weary at the flattery his officers were giving their miniature army.

"Decently." Alexander admitted, "We haven't fought any real battles yet, but I expect them to perform... fine."

"Fine." Washington repeated, "just... fine?"

"Some of the soldiers have left here and have started different camps in the state and in New Jersey, Connecticut, and some other colonies." Alexander mentioned, hoping to please the general.

Washington stared at them, trying not to be impressed, but nodded approvingly.

Alexander and Lafayette frowned and looked at each other.

"How about we show you what they've learned?" piped Lafayette.

The general agreed.

LAFAYETTE & WASHINGTON

It was muddy. Very muddy. Mud splashed upon Alexander's boots as he rode through the field, shouting orders to the men. Mud soiled the men's trousers and shirts as they charged, performing a mock battle.

The stench of rain water and dirt flooded Lafayette's senses as he looked nervously at the overcast sky above. "Hamilton!" he called, seeing his friend from across the field. Alexander looked up at him. "Should we go home? The rain just abated!" the Frenchman exclaimed.

Alexander studied the skies, "They've never practiced after it's rained before." He cried happily.

"I, for one, would rather not die of pneumonia before I win the war." Lafayette huffed, "I'm already getting the chills."

"You'll get used to it!" was his reply. Lafayette opened his mouth to say something but frowned when he saw all of Alexander's attention was focused on the battle. He heard the soggy sound of horse hooves against the moist ground, along with a small cough. He looked behind him and gasped in surprise, "*Mon* general!"

It was Washington, dressed in his finest uniform, though it was rain-splattered. The rich blue complimented both his stormy blue eyes and the discouraging rainclouds. He looked every inch like the man he once was, even the stony expression on his face was reminiscent of the olden days, one Lafayette knew to be a sign that the great man was deep in thought. Washington slowed his horse to stop near Lafayette's.

"I didn't know that you were coming today." The marquis stated, smiling, "It's good to see you."

"Why are you still out here?" Washington asked briskly, ignoring him, his tone like an icicle.

"To be honest," Lafayette sighed, his grin vanishing, "I have not one clue."

Washington looked at him quizzically before realizing what the Frenchman said. He nodded, turning back to look at Alexander, who was oblivious to the newcomer. "Doesn't he know that there's to be a bad storm? And that a downpour just ended?"

"Evidently not," Lafayette looked at his commander, "or he doesn't care. He wishes to create the best army he can. You didn't seem too pleased when you met them, so he's been drilling them like a madman ever since."

Washington frowned, "I understand him. If we were at war at the moment, I'd be right by his side, drilling those men just as hard. But now, we are not at war, these men may catch cold and be unable to fight when they need to. He needs to stop. They need to go home." He flicked the reins and rode into the battle, calling to his aide. Lafayette watched on, feeling something wet his hand. He looked up, and felt a droplet run down his nose. It was raining.

Alexander stopped his horse, watching his general ride towards him, a troubled expression on his face. He called for the men to stop fighting, and they parted ways to let Washington ride closer.

"Are you trying to get these men killed?" Washington snapped, the rain wetting his coat, "At the very least you're trying to make them ill!"

His aide frowned, "I'm trying to get them used to fighting in all conditions."

"They *will* get used to fighting in all conditions," the older man said angrily, "Once the war's begun. Look, Hamilton. You need to stop-"

"But sir!" Alexander frowned.

"No buts!" Washington shot back, "You can't overwork these men. We have a small enough army as it is without you sending them off to their deathbeds. You can come back after the storm has subsided. Is that clear?"

Alexander stared daggers at his commander before nodding reluctantly, "Yes, your Excellency," Alexander bowed his head and looked to his men, "You're dismissed. Do not return until the storm has passed." The men looked between him and Washington, then slowly turned around to leave. They spoke quietly as they went, amazed by how quickly their colonel's demeanor could change and how intimidating their general was.

"Really, Hamilton?" Washington pulled his horse away and trotted back to Lafayette, who watched Alexander sympathetically.

"Why were you so harsh?" Lafayette asked, "You said that you'd agree with him if we were at war."

"It seems that you've forgotten something," Washington said softly, turning his horse back to the road, "Hamilton doesn't learn the easy way. You always have to be hard on him." He galloped off, leaving Alexander, Lafayette, and the few remaining soldiers to stand in the rain.

COMPANY

Eliza wiped away the water on their faces with a dry cloth. They were in the study, Alexander and Lafayette both huddled close to the fire, shivering. James wrapped blankets around them, his eyes full of pity for the half-drowned soldiers.

"Why did you stay there so long?" she asked them, "I was worried sick when it started to rain and you hadn't returned."

"They needed more training," grumbled Alexander, pulling the blanket closer around him, smiling gratefully as Thomas handed him a warm cup of coffee.

"And you needed to have your brain thinking logically." Lafayette said, sipping his drink, "*Mon* general was right. You're smart, Alexander, but you just must remember to think at times, think before you act."

"What did he come for?" Alexander asked, ignoring the remark.

"After we were sure it was to rain, Washington decided to go look for you." Eliza sat down between the two men, her touch causing their quivering to decrease dramatically. "I'm proud of him, he has hardly left the house at all. He told me that he was going to see how the army is shaping up, but I expect that he did more than that once he got there. When he came home, he just flew up to his room, muttering about someone being an idiot."

"I assume that was *you*?" Thomas grinned, looking at Alexander.

"*Mon* general was upset because Alexander was training everyone in the rain," Lafayette sneezed, "He said that he didn't want anyone to get sick before the war. He did say, however, that if we were at war, he wouldn't have stopped you."

"Then why did he stop me now?" he grumbled putting his face in his hands.

"Perhaps because he wanted to show you that he was in charge," James suggested, "Another theory is that he didn't want anyone to die of cold. Why try to rid yourself of soldiers before they can fight?"

"I think that you should've continued with your play battle." Adams entered carrying a tray filled with sliced bread. He set the platter down on the coffee table and sat down beside Thomas.

"I suppose that his reasoning is sound," Alexander admitted, grabbing a slice and taking a bite. "I just wish that we could fight sometime soon."

"I expect you will," all eyes turned to the doorway, where the tall man was standing. His tone was calmer than before, but his expression was still blank. Washington's eyes flickered over his companions before he walked deeper into the study and sank into a chair.

"What do you mean?" James asked quietly.

"I mean that war will soon be upon us." He explained, "I doubt that it will be long before the redcoats learn of the camps. I suspect that they will try to disband the little group that you have assembled. The soldiers will be resistant, causing either them or the redcoats to fire, resulting in a scene much like the Boston Massacre or the Philadelphian Massacre." Eliza and Thomas looked at each other, remembering the moment. Washington continued, "Only instead of dispersing, the new army will fight, causing a war. Those other camps that have formed, they will join together to become one army. Then it will be the War of Colonial Rebellion all over again, but hopefully, this time, we'll win."

"But they need more time to train," Alexander whined, "We can't have a war now! We barely have ten thousand soldiers in total."

Washington frowned, "Like it or not, it will begin before the year is through. I don't expect there to be many more months of peace."

The group looked at each other in alarm.

"We only have a few states involved," groaned Lafayette, "How can we defeat an army of fifty-thousand men strong? They have-" he frowned and looked at the ceiling, calculating.

"They have five men for every one of ours," Thomas concluded, groaning, "it's impossible."

"Not entirely." James said, "We just need more men. We can send letters to our allies all over the country. Men like John Hancock and John Jay. We can send letters to people in Virginia, Georgia, Massachusetts. We can build a bigger army."

"That would take ages," Adams pointed out, "Besides, how could we properly inform anyone? The redcoats are going through the mail, and a letter like that one Hamilton sent us while Thomas and I were in Philadelphia… it will hardly make any sense to them."

"We can only hope that the *Revolutionary* spreads further north and further south." Eliza spoke somberly, "We can't reach out to anyone."

"We were able to come together by chance." James nodded,

"I'm surprised that we were all able to find each other, and to stay together. That, in of itself, is a miracle."

"We'll figure it out," Washington encouraged, standing up, "in the meantime, let us try to find ways to hold off on a war. It will come sooner or later." He looked down at all of his companions, "I just hope that it will come later."

He left the room, leaving everyone wondering what to do.

The fire crackled peacefully, a sound that relaxed the revolutionaries. Eliza lay her head on Alexander's shoulder. Lafayette rubbed his hands together, trying to warm them. Thomas stared into his mug, the dark liquid swirling. James gazed into the fire, a troubled look on his face. Adams fingered the fabric of his coat. They all wondered the same thing. *How can you postpone a war that's inevitable?*

Twenty-Two

May 1782

NEW YORK CITY, NEW YORK

THOMAS, JAMES, & ELIZA

Thomas stirred some milk into his coffee and took a sip, then shook his head and added more. "Hello," James entered the kitchen in pursuit of bread. He smiled once he found his treasure in the bread box.

"Hey, Little Jemmy." Thomas replied, sipping his coffee once more, "Of all the boycotts Eliza had to take up, why was it tea?" he grumbled, "Why couldn't she have boycotted coffee?" James smiled slightly at Thomas's displeasure, but his smile quickly disappeared.

"It's late, Tom." James stated, cutting off a slice of bread and placing it on a small dinner plate.

"So?" he asked, reaching to grab another plate, "Cut off a slice for me, will you?"

James cooperated, putting a slice on Thomas's plate. He sighed and looked up at his friend, "I'm worried."

"What for?" Thomas asked, dipping his bread into his coffee and taking a bite, he spit it onto his plate, repulsed.

"They've been gone for longer than usual, and ever since that conversation…." James shuddered, "I've been on edge. I worry that they may be in trouble."

"They're probably just teaching more than usual today." Thomas said comfortingly, "It's nothing. You're just being paranoid."

"What could hold them up for over an hour?" James wondered, "I just hope that it's nothing serious."

Eliza stumbled into the kitchen, holding a handkerchief. She stepped aside James and Thomas, opened a cupboard, and began pulling out different dry ingredients – flour, salt, and yeast. She yanked them from their places with force, her hands shaking. Thomas frowned, seeing that her eyes were red and swollen, her nose runny.

"What is it?" he asked, setting his plate on the island. He looked at her, concerned, touching her arm.

"I'm making bread." She stated, her voice with a strange lilt, like she was trying to convince herself, "Lots of it."

Thomas looked down at James, who was looking up at him, they both turned back to Eliza. She tucked a loose hair behind her ear, one of many that had fallen from the pile on her head. It looked as though she had been smushing her head against a bookcase all day; her bows were askew, wild hairs sticking straight up.

"What's the matter, Eliza?" James asked her. She fetched a bowl from its place and began pouring and measuring the ingredients.

She looked at him, her eyes drowsy, before quickly turning back at her work.

"Nothing." She replied after a moment. She turned away and began to leave the kitchen, "I need water."

James grabbed her hand, pulling her to a stop. Adams strolled by and peeked into the kitchen, curious by the amount of people in the room. "Get water." Thomas whispered to him. Adams nodded slowly, confused, then left.

"You're not well," James tugged her by the arm into the dining room and Thomas pulled up a chair for her. James guided Eliza to the seat, which she sat in dutifully, then alighted on the chair across from her, watching the girl carefully.

She shook her head slowly, "No, I guess I'm not."

"What is it?" Thomas repeated.

Eliza looked up at him, "I'm worried about Alexander…. And Lafayette and Washington." She sighed, "They've been gone for longer than usual. I fear that something must have happened."

James looked at Thomas, slightly smiling at his triumph, "See? It's not just me. There is reason to worry."

Thomas ignored him, sitting in a chair and trying to comfort his friend, "I'm sure that it's nothing, that they're just taking extra time to teach today. They do that sometimes, remember? Are you sure that you're not just uneasy because of the conversation we had a few weeks ago? Everyone has been more nervous lately, it's all right if it's just that."

Eliza shook her head, "They've never been gone this long before. It's usually just a half hour longer, but it's been longer than that. Much longer. It wasn't that conversation. Sure, it left me uneasy, but it's not that. I feel…funny. Like how I felt when Daddy would go off to war and we wouldn't hear from him for a while. All we could do is worry that he was killed. Then we'd get a letter from him, saying that he's alive and well. It feels just like that, except I haven't received my letter yet." She sneezed into her hanky.

James reached across the table and squeezed her hand reassuringly. Thomas patted her on the shoulder, "I'm sure that it won't be long now." But both her and James's concerns had woven its way into his mind.

★ ⭐ ★

Earlier that Day

WASHINGTON, ALEXANDER, & LAFAYETTE

"Today we're going to travel," Washington announced from his horse, riding in front of the line of soldiers, "Most of you are used to traveling, but today it will be different. Today you'll be marching to a specific spot, carrying your weapons and your numerous materials, all while being on the lookout for both British soldiers and potentially dangerous animals such as bears and wolves. Do you all understand?"

"Yes, sir!" The soldiers shouted, saluting and hoisting their rifles onto their shoulders.

"There may not be as many of you as I'd like," Washington announced, "But we'll get on with it." Not many soldiers had arrived that day, only around one hundred and seventy-five. Many were training at different camps, while others were home, sick in bed as a result of Alexander's teaching method.

"Move out!" Washington turned his horse around, and Alexander and Lafayette quickly fell in step beside him. They could hear the thunderous sound of soldiers marching behind them.

"They sound much like the Continental army," Lafayette concluded after listening to their footsteps, "What should we call them?"

"I haven't given that much thought," Alexander admitted, then shrugged, "It has to pay tribute to the former army, somehow."

"The New Continentals." Washington stated, rolling back his shoulders. Alexander and Lafayette grinned at him, surprised by him joining in on their conversation.

"Very good, your Excellency." Alexander nodded, "I like it."

Washington ignored him, instead looking down the dirt trail. He studied the trees and the sounds of the woods, searching for anything unusual. He looked up sharply at the sound of a bird call. He shrugged it off, muttering to himself about being paranoid.

"What is it, *mon* general?" asked Lafayette, "You seem nervous."

"It's nothing," he replied, "Just a little overly suspicious today. I'm not sure why." He trailed off, looking down the road.

They continued riding. The soldiers continued marching. They passed a silver stream, the water hitting the rocks creating a beautiful symphony. Then came the thickly wooded grove, where shadows lurked spookily in nearly every crevice. Past the grove was a wheat field, a place where the sun shined happily, illuminating the grain, giving them a golden glow. Alexander shivered when he saw a lone willow tree, its branches dancing sadly in the breeze, as if mourning the loss of a loved one.

"What's wrong?" Washington asked, alarmed, as Alexander changed his direction, climbing up into the field and riding until he came to the willow. Washington and Lafayette followed him, the soldiers marching after their leaders.

He had dismounted and was sitting on his knees. His head was bowed, and his eyes were closed, almost like he was in prayer.

Washington slid off his horse and walked slowly towards his aide, stopping a few feet away from him. Lafayette stood beside his commander, watching his friend, pity in his dark eyes.

The green leaves caressed Alexander's back as he sat, seeming to sense his distress. The birds sang softly, a slow tune, sweet and low. The wind rushed through the wheat, sounding almost like musical bells or ocean water crashing against the rocks. The sun's rays covered the soldiers, brushing a layer of warmth and hope over the dreary, somber mood.

"It's a beautiful place to die." Alexander stated after a moment.

"This is where…." Lafayette trailed off, remembering. He looked at his old friend, knowing that he must be reliving the moment, feeling the pain all over again.

"Yes." Alexander replied, "He died here."

"He was a good soldier." Washington said respectfully, "And a good friend. You must remember, Alexander, that it was not your fault. I know that you're not over what happened, but you have to understand that-"

"I *promised* that I'd find his Theodosia, tell her that he still loved her. I promised! How can I do that? I promised I would! I don't even know her where she lives!" Alexander cried, "I don't even know where she lives! What *honor* is there in not being able to keep my promises? Every day, I remember that I wasn't able to save him, and every day I remember that I can't fulfil his dying wish. Do you know how horrible that feels?" He buried his head in his hands, sobbing.

Washington and Lafayette looked at each other, stunned by the tenderness from their usually bitter friend. Lafayette stepped forward and knelt down, placing his arms around Alexander and wrapping him into a tight embrace, "No, *mon amie*, I do not know how that feels, but I will tell you this-"

"You there!" Washington, Lafayette, Alexander, and the soldiers all looked towards the source of the noise in alarm. It came from the left, out of the mouth of a man wearing a scarlet red coat. Alexander and Lafayette slowly rose to their feet, all thoughts of Aaron Burr having left their minds.

It was a band of redcoats, all bearing arms, all staring at the small army menacingly. They were approaching the small collection of colonists, cold expressions on their faces. Washington, Lafayette, and Alexander walked forward to meet a man standing in front, who seemed to be their leader.

"Good day," said the British officer, a captain of some sort.

"Good day," Washington said politely.

"What is this?" the officer asked, sneering at the men, "and why are they all here?" he eyed Washington's and Alexander's uniforms in confusion and disgust, and looked at Lafayette's with distaste in his expression, "and what are..." you waved his hand at their attire, "those?"

"This is a group of men." Alexander replied smartly, "and these are uniforms. And we are here because…we want to be. Is there a law against that?"

The redcoat frowned, his fellow soldiers mimicking his expression. "No." he admitted, "But all colonists should answer to the king's men when they ask a question. And king's men like complete answers, not smart little boys who make fun," The man paused, pointedly looking at Alexander with distaste. Alexander's face flushed, fists clenched, and he opened his mouth to argue when Lafayette grabbed his hand, giving him a tight squeeze, "… and king's men can keep prisoners for…undetermined amounts of time, so I would listen to the king's men…. Would you like to answer my questions again?"

Alexander pretended to consider the question for a moment before replying, "No, I don't think I'd like to."

The officer looked at Washington and Lafayette, "What about you? Would you like to answer?"

Washington shook his head, "Why would I tell you that? I'd tell that only to an officer whose rank matches my own."

"Not particularly," Lafayette replied, a rare bland expression painted on the canvas of his face.

The officer looked flummoxed. "Then I'll have to detain you for resisting an officer in the king's army."

"I don't have a king," Washington readjusted his hat, "And how can you arrest a person who isn't a member of your nation?"

The redcoat frowned. "I know where I've seen your uniform! It was when I was in the army, and when I was fighting against those *peasants* in the War of Colonial Rebellion." The officer stepped back and glowered down at the New Continentals. He raised his voice, making it possible for all of the soldiers, both colonial and British, to hear him. "Please drop your weapons and you will not be harmed." He called. The redcoats began pulling their muskets from their shoulders.

"Stand your ground." Washington called back to his men, his hand curling around the hilt of his sword. Lafayette and Alexander echoed his order, each realizing that the only weapons they had on hand were their swords. The three leaders began walking briskly to the back of their line, knowing that they'd be the Britons' first targets.

The men stared back at the redcoats, not budging, waiting to see how the Englishman would react.

The officer gulped, "Drop your weapons?" he repeated, his voice pinched and nervous.

The New Continentals did not oblige.

"You've been warned!" the officer yelled, retreating behind a tree, "Men, open fire!" The British dropped to their knees and began a volley. The crack of bullets leaving the barrels entered their ears, the foul smell of smoke filling the air. A grey cloud appeared in front of the British muskets. Alexander could see the officer telling something to one of his men, then seeing the soldier run off, looking for more redcoats in case things got out of hand.

He could hear Washington call for his men to volley. The New Continentals did so, dropping to the ground and readying their rifles, just as they had rehearsed. Lafayette winced as he saw one of his men fall to the ground. A cloud of smoke filled the American line, the sign of the men firing. Two lobsterbacks fell, dead.

Shouts back and forth from officers to soldiers. The crack of gunfire. The foul smell of smoke. Red stains on uniforms. The crunch of bodies falling against the wheat and dead grass.

"Alexander!" Lafayette called, "Look!" He pointed with his sword, Alexander turned his gaze to where he was pointing. Another team of redcoats was running towards the fighting, ready with new bullets and powder.

Alexander's eyes widened, but he turned and shouted to the marquis, "Go!"

Lafayette's face hardened and he pushed up his hat. He ducked behind the American lines, shouting uplifting words and orders to his men. "*Attaque!*" was one of the few words Alexander could hear over the gunfire.

He ran to Washington, whom he could see faintly between the bursts of smoke. The commander finished tying the reins of the frightened horses to the willow. He ran back towards the battle, but stood a safe distance away. He pulled the spyglass from his pocket and began watching the fighting. Alexander grabbed his arm urgently, "General!"

Washington looked down, "Hamilton!"

"What should we do?" Alexander asked him.

"There's nothing to do." Washington replied, "We have no useful weapons. We can only hope that this ends soon, without too many casualties. The only way we'll ever fight is if one side runs out of bullets and are forced to use bayonets, then we could use our swords. I only pray that it will not come to that."

Alexander frowned, "I only wish that I could-"

"I know," Washington replied, "You've always wanted to fight.

It's not your fault that you're such a good secretary, Colonel. I just can't risk losing you."

"Sirs!" Mr. Carpenter looked over his shoulder to Alexander and Washington, "What should we do? We can't fire our weapons! We've run out of bullets!"

Washington frowned, annoyed that the man would even ask the question, "Then use your bayonets!" he roared, unsheathing his sword. Mr. Carpenter nodded and quickly started to fix his bayonet to the end of his musket, his fellow soldiers did the same. For a brief moment, there was no smoke, no gunfire, just the sound of men on both sides attaching bayonets to their guns.

The New Continentals finished first, and, with a fearsome Indian-like holler, charged at the British, bayonets at the ready. Lafayette cheered as he ran towards the enemy, sword drawn, ready for battle. He lunged forward, leading the charge, the rest of the New Continentals patriotically running after their leader. Alexander unsheathed his own sword and, before Washington could stop him, began chasing after his allies, eagerly awaiting the fight. The general hung back, gasping when he saw yet another clan of redcoats running towards his men. He looked back at the men, some of them falling, others pulling their bayonets out of dead redcoats. He saw Lafayette grinning wildly as he dodged a slice an Englishman took at him. He saw Alexander swat aside an oncoming gun, the look on the redcoat's face when he realized he was at the young officer's mercy.

"Retreat!" Washington swung himself onto his horse, "Retreat!" he called again, releasing the reins from the tree. Alexander and Lafayette looked at their general, surprised by his order, then looked back at their enemy. They gasped when they saw the added number of redcoats and began shouting at their companions to flee. The New Continentals reluctantly turned around and began to run, Alexander and Lafayette amongst the last of the stragglers. The two officers turned tail and fled, rushing past their horses, trying to keep up with their general and away from the British.

The redcoats chased after the soldiers, some stopping to fire at their opponents, others trying to stab at the running men. The New Continentals continued to run until there was no longer any soldiers chasing them. They eventually slowed to a halt, gasping for breath and leaning against trees. After a moment they began to laugh and cheer, proud of their first battle.

As the New Continentals were cheering, Alexander and Lafayette walked somberly towards their general, concerned looks on their faces.

"It's happened," Alexander stated, "The war's begun, hasn't it?"

Lafayette frowned, "*Mon* general, what do you wish us to do?"

Washington looked down at his two loyal companions, "Have hope."

COMPANY

"Alexander!" Eliza threw her arms around him and kissed him, "You're alive!"

He smiled happily at her, cupping his hand around her cheek and nodded. Thomas shook Lafayette's hand and nodded respectfully at Washington.

"What happened?" James asked, looking at the men, his hair in a flurry, "Was there a battle?" The group began walking towards the dining room, where they all sat down in their respective seats.

"Say something," Adams begged, annoyed by the silence.

"We decided to take a walk today," Lafayette stated, "and we walked for a ways."

"We came to the field where I shot Aaron," Alexander said slowly, "we sat there in silence for a while. Then a group of redcoats approached."

"Their leader asked us some questions," Washington continued, "We didn't reply to them to his satisfaction, so he ordered his men to fire upon us. They did, and I called for the men to fire back. It was a battle, and more British kept coming."

"Eventually our men ran out of bullets," Alexander explained, "so we fixed our bayonets to our muskets and began to charge at them. Lafayette and I didn't have any guns, only our swords-"

"Which we brandished dashingly!" the Frenchman interjected.

"Then more redcoats came and we retreated," Alexander remembered, running his fingers through his hair, "then they chased after us for a time. Eventually we arrived back at the field in which we practice. The men went home, and we rushed back here."

Everyone looked at each other in silence. Each thinking the same thing.

AUTHOR'S NOTE

Throughout the book I have sprinkled the words of some of my characters, most notably Alexander. While reading his letters, I found many phrases that I fell in love with, most of them were directed towards his wife. (What can I say? I'm fascinated by Alexander and Eliza's romance!) Other quotes are what Alexander – and also Washington – allegedly said, which I found fitting. Lastly, many of the nicknames in this book were entirely real, while others are of my own imagining.

When they were engaged, Alexander feared that Eliza wouldn't want to give up her finery and live within their means. This resulted in a letter in which he, in a teasing manner, asked his "pretty damsel" if she would be willing to give up a coach for a wagon, to wear home-spun instead of brocade. It was in this letter that he wondered if she would "soberly relish the pleasure of a poor man's wife?" He continued wondering, saying that, if not, she should correct the mistake "before we begin to act the tragedy of the unhappy couple." Before reciting their vows, I have Alexander ask if she would "soberly relish the pleasure of being a poor man's wife." Eliza's response is entirely my own. None of Eliza's letters to her husband have survived, so her comments on her future husband's letter are unknown.

In 1804, Alexander was challenged to a duel by Aaron, though, unlike in my book, it was Alexander who perished. While going through his things, Eliza found a letter addressed to her, one written mere days before he died. It was his farewell to her. In it, he told her that they would meet "in a better world," and that "I shall cherish that sweet hope." He ended the letter to Eliza: "Adieu, best of wives and best of women. Embrace all my darling children for me." Upon reading the letter, I grew extremely attached to Alexander and felt the need to pay tribute. Thus, the scene where Alexander says good-bye to Eliza before the fatal encounter with Aaron. In it, Alexander mentions meeting her in a better world and that he "shall cherish that sweet hope." Of course, Alexander had to tell Eliza that she was "the best of wives and best of women." I couldn't exclude that line.

In the fictional duel, Aaron says, "My vision is…indistinct," and "this is a mortal wound." Both of the phrases actually belonged to Alexander. After being shot above his right leg, Alexander told the nearby physician, (there were seconds and a doctor present – standard duel procedure,) "This is a mortal wound, doctor," before fainting. Later, after regaining consciousness, he remarked, "My vision is… indistinct." Alexander was paralyzed from the waist down before dying the next day.

In my book, during the battle, Mr. Carpenter told Washington that the soldiers couldn't fire their muskets, and Washington tells him to use his bayonet. This (alleged) exchange took place at the Battle of Trenton in 1776, after Washington's famous crossing of the Delaware River (which is in… for some reason… New Jersey.) The weather was extremely cold, and it was snowy. Apparently, as the temperature dropped, their muskets and rifles began to fail. A soldier asked the great commander, "What should we do? We can't fire our muskets!" Washington replied, "Then use your bayonets!"

While writing, I paid particular attention to what everyone called each other. Although Peggy likely didn't call her husband, "Benny," the other nicknames were – or likely – real. Alexander's special name for Eliza was Betsey, and he would often refer to her as "My Betsey" in his letters. Likewise, Eliza had her own name for him, "My dear Hamilton." The eldest Schuyler sister, Angelica, was called "Ann" by Eliza, and it only seemed natural for Alexander to call her that as well. The three were very – some would say unusually – close. Alexander would teasingly refer to Eliza and Angelica as "my dear brunettes," which is slightly confusing; according to a portrait believed to be of Angelica, she was a redhead. James was called "Little Jemmy," by his friends, or just plain "Jemmy." Later on in his career, however, James's enemies used his nickname to mock his height, though he continued to be called Jemmy. James might have called Thomas "Tom," but I'm not sure, it just seemed natural to have James give Thomas a nickname, given their closeness. Angelica and Eliza's youngest sister wasn't called Peg, but Peggy. I thought it would be too confusing to have two Peggy-s, though Peg likely called Eliza "'Liza." The Schuyler sisters' mother known as Kitty, but Little Phil was Philip. Little Phil was actually the nickname of Alexander and Eliza's youngest, as he was named after their firstborn who died shortly before the next Philip was born. Benjamin Franklin was referred to as Ben, and also Dr. Franklin, though peculiarly, he didn't have a degree. Benedict likely didn't use generic terms of endearment for Peggy, he probably did have a pet name for her, but I liked the idea of him calling her whatever came to mind.

Usually, in the author's note of historical fiction books, the author informs the reader what is real and what is not. I am not going to do that. There's too much to say! I've referenced different battles, people (essentially all of my characters are real, excluding Mr. and Mrs. Carpenter, the jailer and guard, herald, the various soldiers, and the mob,) and have tipped my hat to many different documents and events. *The Revolutionary Papers*, for example, is a reference to *The Federalist Papers*, which Alexander wrote 51 of, and James 29. I've included many small facts, which, if one knows enough about the characters, will be able to spot. This author's note would take forever to read if I mentioned everything from whether or not Alexander and Eliza had conjoined wedding rings (silver, with their names were engraved onto them. Eliza wore hers, and later Alexander's, until they day she died,) or if Thomas really had a Nicoló Amati violin (he did.) If you're interested, it's up to you to learn about the Arnold-André spy ring, the battle of Brandywine, and what happened to Lafayette when he came back to France (great story.)

I also recommend researching Eliza. What I haven't mentioned deserves mentioning. While you're at it, you should also look into Alexander, Thomas, James, Lafayette, Washington, Aaron, John and Sam Adams, Angelica, Philip, Peg, Peggy, Benedict, Adrienne, Ben, Thomas Paine, Patrick Henry, Theodosia, and André. No, seriously, you should.

ABOUT THE AUTHOR

Eliza Starkey has always been fascinated by history. Her love for the American Revolution and the founding fathers (and mothers) only began blossoming into a great love after reading a book on Alexander Hamilton. One year later, this book debuted. Like many fourteen-year-olds, Eliza's hobbies include reading, writing, playing the piano, listening to music, and watching musicals. Unlike other fourteen-year-olds, Eliza tries to find out as much as she can about the founders. She also enjoys rereading multiple decades worth of *Peanuts* comics, playing board games, eating chicken, and answering the questions on *Jeopardy!*

Made in the USA
Las Vegas, NV
27 January 2021

16611826R30236